A MASQUERADE

Pilar led Heath into the kitchen, where Stevie awaited him. Stevie was as nervous as a cat. Just being in the same room with the gambler unnerved her.

At first she refused to look at him. When she did, the first word that came to mind was *beautiful.* But how could a man so masculine, so physically overpowering, be beautiful? If Preacher Black could be believed, Lucky Diamond was a violent man—a man who ate innocents like her for breakfast.

Heath smiled down at Stevie. She just stood there, resembling a wide-eyed, frozen goddess. He reached for the small hand fisted at her side. He pulled it forward, pumped it up and down as one would work a reluctant well handle.

He couldn't bring himself to release her immediately and cradled her hand in both his own. She curled her fingers, making their contact more intimate. Heath was mesmerized, his eyes riveted to the small hand.

How could he have failed to notice her Comanche heritage at their first meeting? Her Indian features framed by her platinum hair made her quite possibly the most beautiful woman he had ever seen. When he smoothed her fist and kissed her palm lightly, he was gratified by her sharp intake of breath.

Straightening, he released her. He produced a bowie knife and presented it to her with mocking gallantry. "I believe this is yours."

"I was amazed at how well you handled yourself yesterday when you sidestepped my knife." Her cheeks flamed. "And, Mr. Diamond, I'm truly glad you did."

"A read that keeps your heart thundering with pleasure . . . Teresa Howard gets better with every book!"

—Janelle Taylor

TERESA HOWARD

VELVET THUNDER

ZEBRA BOOKS
KENSINGTON PUBLISHING CORP.

ZEBRA BOOKS are published by

Kensington Publishing Corp.
475 Park Avenue South
New York, NY 10016

First Printing: March, 1994

Printed in the United States of America

This book is dedicated to my son, Heath,
with a wealth of love and gratitude for
allowing me to borrow the name I saddled him with nine-
teen years ago.

And to my sister-in-law, Stephanie,
whose lovely name and free spirit were my
inspiration for Stevie.

And as always, with love and respect
to my husband, Dr. George Howard.

ACKNOWLEDGMENT

Second to her family, perhaps the most important person in an author's life is her editor. These talented men and women take the words that have sprung from our souls and dot the i's, cross the t's, polish the prose, point out the holes, and sprinkle the end product with fairy dust.

I have been fortunate to work with three exceptional editors, kind women who have exceptional talent. They are Ann La-Farge, Debra Roth Kane, and Monica Harris. It is not possible for me to say how much I admire these women, how much I appreciate everything they have done in my behalf. All I know to say is thank you. Never have two words seemed so inadequate.

Prologue

New Mexico Territory

The flickering glow of lanterns cast eerie shapes about the walls of the cavern. A veritable rainbow of colors: sparkling blues, gilt yellows, and vibrant crimsons reflected off tiny crystals embedded in the flowstone. Shadows danced to the rhythmic picking and hammering of the two workmen, to the constant dripping sound of water throughout the cave, to the pounding heartbeat of the well-dressed gentleman perched on a stone slab—unsmiling—watching the laborers at their task.

When the workmen finished, they turned in tandem to the seated man. "All done, boss. Just like you ordered," the oldest worker reported. "Only an expert'll know they're fake." His lips spread in the smile of a man satisfied with a job well done. His partner had the same pleased, trusting smile stamped upon his craggy features.

The seated man rose, brushed dirt from his trousers, and strode across the room. After examining the work in minute detail, he nodded dispassionately. Then without blinking, he whipped out his Smith & Wesson .44, leveled the deadly weapon, and shot the unsuspecting miners through the heart. While they were yet warm, the expressions of shock and betrayal frozen on their faces for eternity, he dumped their bloody corpses into a nearby pit.

Adjusting his black cloth eye patch, he exited the cave.

One

The mid-morning sun beat down upon the plains, burning away the cool of the day.

Lulled into a trancelike state by the gentle sway of his mount, the clouds scudding across the azure sky, and the haunting call of an eagle in flight, U.S. Marshal Heath Turner gave his mount, Warrior, a brown steel dust, free rein to follow the dusty trail west.

He surveyed his surroundings with an appreciative eye. To his left a band of wild horses thundered across the plains. A single lusty stallion stood majestically on a bare peak, silhouetted against the sky. Heath's lips spread in a purely masculine smile when the virile animal, wild with freedom, whistled, reared on his hind legs, then darted toward his harem.

The grasslands he'd just passed had given way to vast stretches of bunchgrass and mesquite. A dust devil, tossed by the breeze, moved lazily across his path. A road runner darted before his mount, kicking sand into the air, seeming never to tire.

Heath couldn't say the same about himself; he was exhausted, thoroughly and totally exhausted. He had been in the saddle so long, he feared the chunk of leather had become a permanent part of his anatomy. His immediate destination was a sleepy little town called Adobe Wells and he couldn't get there soon enough to suit him. All he wanted was a soft bed, a hot meal, a cool drink, and after a bit of rest, maybe a warm, willing woman.

Squinting, he looked at the ball of fire that masqueraded as the sun in these parts. The heat rising from the ground wavered like drunken ghosts dancing the minuet. Dizzying, he remained upright through sheer strength of will.

Suddenly, a rifle shot split the morning air, kicking up dust in front of his horse. The powerful steed danced in alarm. The second shot sent Heath's hat flying off his head.

"What the hell?" he growled, sawing back on his reins, bringing the powerful animal under control.

In a dead run, he dipped to retrieve his favorite Stetson—some things were worth risking one's life for—and placed it firmly on his head. Heading to the east side of the mesa, he made for cover. Just as he galloped behind a large boulder, another shot rang out.

The unexpected attack sent stamina flowing through him like hot lava, warming him from roots to soles, energizing his tired body, heightening his awareness. Though he didn't know the nature of his assignment in Adobe Wells, he'd bet a month's pay the ambush was connected with it.

"Usually they wait till I get to town before shootin' at me," he groused, dismounting in a blur. He pulled his Winchester from its saddle scabbard and cautiously peered around the rock, scanning the cliffs for any sign of the sniper. The shot had come from the ragged precipice that jutted out from the mesa. As far as he could see, there was nothing amiss in that quarter.

Squatting on his haunches, he filled his lungs with warm arid air and tipped his hat back with a tanned finger. He replayed the last few minutes in his mind. The second and third misses were excusable since his horse had been in a dead run, but not the first. His slow, ambling gait had made him a sitting duck.

"Maybe he's just a piss-poor shot," Heath suggested to Warrior. "Or maybe it was a warning."

Apparently, his mount didn't have an opinion on the matter. All Heath heard, other than the sound of his own voice, was the wind singing off the face of the cliffs.

When another shot rang out, slamming into the rock just

above Heath's head, the impact of the bullet sent fragments of stone and dirt flying into his face. "You're starting to get on my nerves," he hissed to his unseen assailant, returning fire blindly.

There was no response to his gunfire as he scrambled back out of sight. The sun burned down upon him and sweat trickled between his shoulder blades. He shifted uncomfortably.

A great shadow fell over him as Warrior nudged his shoulder. "Thanks for the shade," Heath muttered, absently stroking the animal, considering his options. He could wait the sniper out and then slip past him in the night. Or he could backtrack and travel southwest to Adobe Wells. The circuitous route would make the trip much longer, however.

He chewed a dry piece of grass, deep in thought. "Whatcha think boy?"

The huge animal snorted on cue.

"I agree." Rising in one fluid motion, Heath stowed his yellow boy in the saddle boot, checked the ammunition in his Navy Colt, retrieved a rope from around the pommel, and tied it to his belt with a rawhide piggin string.

Soundlessly, he began climbing the east side of the rock shelf. He lost his footing halfway to the top, dislodging loose gravel from the sheer face of the cliff. Grabbing a toehold, he gasped for breath.

"Damn!" A blind deaf-mute would be alerted by that. Apparently, he was more fatigued than he thought, and it was likely to get him killed. Pressing his cheek into the rock, he expected to feel the sting of hot lead piercing his hide. It never came. After a nerve-settling respite, he continued his ascent, more slowly, carefully.

Easing over the top, he padded on silent feet to the southern rim of the plateau. All was quiet below; peace embraced him on all sides. If he didn't know better, he would think he had imagined the ambush. But the breeze, ruffling his hair through the bullet hole in his John B., proved that someone was out there, someone who posed a grievous threat.

"Where are you, you bastard?" he asked quietly. Exasperated, he jerked his hat off and ran his fingers through long ebony hair.

At first he saw nothing. Then he shifted his gaze and caught glimpse of a slight movement. The toe of a scuffed boot protruded from behind a rock about twenty feet down the abutment.

"Pay dirt." There was a whisper of triumph in his voice. He watched as gingerly, the sniper stepped into clear view. "Well, I'll be damned."

To Heath's surprise, his assailant was a girl, dressed from head to toe in black leather. A small Stetson perched atop her head cast her face in shadow, but he could tell that she was young, painfully young.

"And skinny as a fence post," he muttered. The rifle in the crook of her arm was bigger than she.

Standing stock-still, sucking on the end of a waist-length platinum braid, she looked like nothing so much as a precocious child. "A child?" Not hardly! Children don't take potshots at perfect strangers, no matter how precocious they are. He narrowed his eyes, glaring at his nemesis.

A hazy warning quickened Stevie's gut. She felt as if she were being watched. Tamping down the niggling sense of fear, she cast about for sign of the gunslinger.

If she didn't find him and scare him off, she might well end up like Jeff. Unshed tears caused her nose to tingle. But she gained control of the pain and grief of losing her brother. Pure cussedness stiffened her spine.

With Jeff gone, Pa needed her to be strong. She was all he had. Now was no time to go missish on him.

Thinking of her pa, she spat the silken strands out of her mouth and instinctively wiped her tongue on her shirtsleeve. Pa said ladies don't suck their hair, or bite their fingernails, or dress like boys, or curse like waddies.

Well, who said she wanted to be a lady anyhow? Defiantly, she lifted the end of her braid and clamped it firmly between her front teeth.

A tight coil of apprehension unwound in her chest. She still couldn't shake the feeling that someone was watching her.

Where was that gunslinger? she wondered again. The man couldn't just disappear into the air, could he?

Heath watched the girl step closer to the ledge and scan the horizon, obviously searching for him. He smiled a predator's smile. An introduction was in order, he decided. Fashioning a Blocker loop, he tossed the rope over the rim. It fell with a muted hiss and circled her narrow shoulders, effectively penning her arms to her sides. "Gotcha!"

Stevie shrieked and dropped her head back, squinting against the sun. Her rifle fell to the rocks below with an echoing clatter. Desperately, she tried to wrest her revolver from its holster, all the while struggling to escape bondage.

Heath chuckled at her display of outrage, hoping the willful chit didn't shoot her foot off. Enraged, she spoke the language he recognized as Comanche. He understood the foreign tongue with the rolling R's well enough to wonder if some of the vile threats she made against his poor naked body were physically possible. Some of them sounded quite intriguing though.

"Hold still, kid," he shouted down to her.

His chivalrous intent was to restrain the girl before she did herself grievous harm. Muscles bulged, straining the seams of his cotton shirt as he began pulling her to the upper ledge of the cliff.

Wiggling like a fish on a hook, she hung in midair, spitting another string of curses, even worse than the first. "Damn, filthy, lowdown, stinkin', bast—"

"Be still before I drop you," he interrupted. "And stop using that filthy language, dammit!"

When he pulled her over the rim, she flew into him, clawing like a panther, hissing like a snake. One fact was incontrovertible; the kid knew how to fight. What she lacked in physical strength she made up for in passion. Bemused, Heath slipped her revolver from its holster, tucked it in his belt behind his back, and held his arms in front of his face, allowing her to attack him like a setting hen flogging a curious rooster.

"You ass! Cur dog. Bastard!" she slurred him, and questioned his legitimacy again, stomping his booted foot for emphasis.

His Hessians cushioned her slight weight, but frankly, he was tired of her abuse. He subdued her by wrapping his arms around her waist. "Behave yourself."

"Let me go!" she shrieked, digging in her heels as he

dragged her away from the rim of the mesa, creating a wavy trail of dust in her wake. "How dare you rope me and haul me up here like a sack of potatoes? You . . . you stinkin' pile of horse shit."

"And how dare you shoot at me, you pint-sized brat?" he growled against her ear. "Call me peculiar, but I take exception when people try to kill me."

Stevie didn't hear his sophisticated northern drawl for the blood roaring in her ears. She had never been held so familiarly before; she found the gunslinger's nearness strangely unsettling. Sensing there was more to fear from him than a bullet, she stopped struggling. "Turn me loose!" she ground out, unable to hide the desperation in her voice.

"You promise to behave yourself?" Heath waited for an answer. Receiving none, he squeezed her around the waist in silent warning, then cautiously released his hold.

She turned to face him, slowly easing away.

His eyes widened at his first clear view of her. She was beautiful; doe eyes, black as midnight, tilted exotically. Skin, dusky bronze, like melted caramel or ripe apricots. High cheekbones, cradling a thick fringe of sooty lashes. Hair, the delicate hue of moonlight on water, so pale as to be almost colorless, so silky as to beg a man's touch. Breasts full and firm, rising and falling with each labored breath. Wasplike waist, flaring into gently rounded hips. Legs, though short and slender, nicely rounded.

But it was the animation of her character that held him spellbound. The female glaring at him possessed an ethereal face, a curvaceous body, and the temperament of a grizzly with a sore behind. In all, an intriguing combination! He grinned and shook his head, totally absorbed with the enchanting hellion. "Well, beautiful, you want to tell me why you tried to kill me?"

"If I was tryin' to kill you, mister, you'd be deader'n vomited maggots!"

"Now, that's a lovely image. Tell me, princess, where did you go to finishing school?"

Obstinately mute, she knew full well he was making fun of her. Raising finely arched eyebrows, her gaze moved over him with a sweep of her lashes. Trying for a look of total disdain, she failed miserably. He was quite possibly the most handsome man she had ever seen; tall as a church steeple, muscled as a Thoroughbred, glossy black hair, and deep blue eyes—the color and luminosity of blueberries covered by the morning dew.

She didn't possess the vocabulary to describe his overwhelming physical presence, let alone the raw sensuality emanating from him.

Damn shame she'd probably have to kill him!

"You stroke my ego with your scrutiny, little one. Dare I hope that you like what you see?"

"Go to hell!" she spat out.

Chuckling, he took a step toward her.

"Stop!" She warded him off like an evil spirit. "Don't you dare move one inch closer!"

He regarded her with an amused gaze, but halted.

She drew a deep breath, collecting herself. "Now, I wasn't trying to kill you," she repeated. "Just warn you that workin' for Judge Jack ain't too healthy. It'll only get you shot . . . or worse." With her chin held high, she looked down her nose at him. A difficult task considering that he was a foot taller than she. "So you've been warned. And, mister, only one warning to a customer." Her threatening expression grew blank. "Now, give me back my gun and I'll go," she finished authoritatively.

Blessing her with one of his heart-stopping smiles—to no avail—he removed the cartridges from the weapon and handed it to her with a flourish.

Enraged that he had confiscated her ammunition, she raised the weapon above her head and lunged at him, connecting solidly with his shoulder.

"Damn you! You little termagant," he grunted, drawing her flush against his solid length, chest to chest, belly to belly, thigh to thigh. Circling her ankle with his foot, he jerked back and swept her off her feet. Literally. They both hit the ground with a resounding thud.

Disappearing underneath him, she spat and sputtered, fighting to fill her lungs. "Get off me, you overgrown sex maniac!"

After the choking dust settled, he gave her a look that would have sent the hardiest cowpoke scrambling for safety. Unmoved, she tried to buck him off, twisting and jerking, slamming her lower body against his.

"Look, lady—and I use the term loosely—if you know what's good for you, you'll hold still!"

He wondered if she felt his growing desire pressing against her leg. More to the point, if she was worldly enough to know what it was, to understand what it meant.

When fear darkened her eyes, he cursed silently, fighting to tamp down his burgeoning desire. Obviously, it had been far too long since he'd had a woman. But the sprite gazing up at him as if he had two heads was not the kind of woman he needed. Although she was dressed provocatively in snug black leather pants and a tight fringed vest, he knew she was a lady, at least an innocent. He could almost smell her virginal fear.

Losing himself in eyes as black as midnight, he sought to remind himself that he was a sophisticated northern gentleman, and as such he didn't take advantage of virgins. No matter how damned adorable they were.

Unconsciously, he shifted against her, increasing her unease, spurring her into action.

"You rutting boar," she accused him, feigning bravado. "Get the hell off of me."

The scent of her, the feel of her, called forth something primitive, untamed, passionate in Heath; her breath, brushing warm against his face, was the final blow. Dipping his head, he ground his lips against her own and silenced her with a kiss.

She gasped, enticing him to slip his tongue between her lips. As he deepened the kiss, all thoughts of propriety and ladies burned up in the heat of desire. He wanted more; he wanted all of her. Shifting to his side, he slid his hand down her back, cupping the firmest little fanny he'd ever had the pleasure to fondle.

She ceased her struggle as he continued his tender assault, skimming his hands over her writhing form. One hand found its way to the silken braid that rested on her breasts. Grazing the sensitive flesh with the backs of his fingers, he untied the scrap of rawhide that imprisoned her hair and sifted his fingers through the cool silver strands, spreading her hair like a gossamer cape about her shoulders.

When she made a helpless noise in her throat, he gentled. His tongue made long, lazy forays into her mouth. Pleasing him, she returned his kiss shyly. She tasted of lemonade, sunshine, and willingness.

But when he insinuated a knee between her thighs, she came to herself. Acting on pure instinct, she clamped her perfect white teeth down on his tongue.

His runaway passion flickered, dimmed, and died in the space of a heartbeat. "Owww." He rolled off her and touched his throbbing tongue with the tip of his finger. A single drop of blood glistened in the sunlight. He held it close to her face. "See what you did."

She was unmoved. Every inch of her rigid body shouted defiance. "You deserve worse, you depraved son of a bitch."

"Why you little—" he began, reaching for her.

She surged to her feet and scampered to the edge of the cliff. After scrubbing her tingling lips with the back of her hand, she spat his kiss into the dust. "If you ever touch me again, I'll blow so many holes in you, you won't hold water."

"You'll find I don't scare easily." His tone was smug, for in her potent gaze, he read a combination of anger and desire. He suspected that he had just given the girl her first kiss and that she hadn't found it as objectionable as she pretended. Arrogantly, he winked at her, knowing that it would enrage her further. But why he wanted to provoke her, he couldn't say.

Surprisingly, her expression relaxed. Offering him half a smile, she slipped her hands behind her neck, as if to rebraid her hair.

Her shirt, pulled tight across firm young breasts, caused him to suck in a sharp breath. He imagined shaping those breasts in the palms of his hands. Pleasantly distracted, he failed to see her withdraw the bowie knife hidden in the scabbard under her collar.

With a flip of her wrist she sent the deadly weapon sailing toward him.

"What?" he yelled, barely sidestepping the knife. Clearly astounded, he wondered what kind of a hellcat he had stumbled upon.

She was horrified to have missed the mark, not to mention seeing such rage on his face. "Oh, shit!"

Scrabbling over the rim, she slipped and slid down the cliff. With a safe distance between them, she stopped at the base of the cliff, shaded her eyes with an unsteady hand, and peered up at him. He stood on the upper ledge, silhouetted by the blazing sun, looking larger than life. She was momentarily mesmerized.

Their gazes met and held. Something indefinable, as old as time itself, passed between them. Bending slightly, he touched the brim of his hat in mock salute.

"Arrogant ass," she muttered without heat. Fleet as a deer, she whirled about and ran west.

Heath watched her retreat. She disappeared behind an outcropping of rocks. Still, he watched. After what seemed an eternity, the sound of horses' hooves echoed through the valley. She burst into view, riding a palomino. His heart thundered in his chest. Woman and horse, wild with freedom, their silver-blond manes streaming in the wind, galloped across the plains as if the devil himself were nipping at their heels. Not only was she riding astride, but without a saddle.

A faint smile sculpted Heath's lips. "Until later, little hellion."

A tall man dressed in unrelieved black, lurking across the valley atop Mustang Mesa, lowered his army field glasses. He had witnessed the confrontation with interest.

Climbing down from his high perch, he headed toward Sandy Johns's spread. His orders were to kill the rancher. If he timed it right, the man who had just kissed Miss Johns senseless would be blamed for her father's murder.

Two

"I don't think the little lady likes you."

Heath pivoted and drew his gun, crouching low. Straightening, he exhaled with relief and leathered his weapon. "Damn it, Jay! You want to get yourself shot? You know better than to sneak up on me like that!"

U.S. Marshal Jay Hampton regarded his partner wryly. "You were expecting me, weren't you?" he asked rhetorically. "Besides, since when could anybody sneak up on you?"

"Well, I was a little distracted."

"So I noticed. That was some distraction!" Jay whistled his appreciation, clearly unaffected by Heath's surly disposition. Being cursed at, shot at, and practically stabbed to death by a delicious demon in breeches could wear on a man's patience, he allowed.

Still, he was somewhat alarmed at Heath's obvious exhaustion, physical and emotional. Ever since the two had served as special aides to Abraham Lincoln during the American Civil War, they had been closer than brothers. Now working for the Justice Dcpartment—riding together, chasing outlaws across the country, and saving each other's hides time and again, their bond was even stronger. They often communicated without words. Jay knew the exact instant his irritation waned.

Releasing the last of his tension with a sigh, Heath sauntered over to Jay. "Good to see you, partner."

"And you." Jay shook Heath's hand firmly. Smiling, he

raised a questioning brow. "By the way, who was that sweet little confection you were attempting to gobble up?"

Characteristically, Heath muttered something unintelligible and slapped his hat against a rock-hard thigh. "Damned if I know! I was riding along, enjoying the scenery, and next thing I know somebody's taking shots at me. When I tried to subdue her, she threw a knife at my head."

Leaning against the boulder at his back, Jay crossed his feet at the ankles, plucked two cheroots from his vest pocket, and offered Heath a smoke. "Looks to me like she was aiming at something a sight more vital than your head."

Heath halted in the act of lighting his cigar; his brow furrowed. Had the girl really been aiming at his privates? Considering the scandalous way he had treated her, pawing her and kissing her as if she were little more than a trollop for hire, he wouldn't blame her.

But surely not! Decent women didn't try to geld strangers, even west of the Pecos. But he wouldn't put anything past her. A twisted sort of fascination teased his mind. Very twisted, he acknowledged.

"You would be wise to steer clear of her, partner," Jay broke into his thoughts. "Even if she doesn't kill you in your sleep, she'll be nothing but trouble."

"Tell me something I don't know."

Hoping Heath could handle the itty-bitty female, he pushed away from the boulder, looking every inch a serious lawman. "Just don't say I didn't warn you"

Heath nodded.

"Oh, well, we're not here to talk about our love lives. Or lack thereof. And I'm your partner, not your priest."

Heath voiced agreement. Taking Jay's cue, he ground his half-smoked cigar beneath the toe of his boot and turned to business. "Well, partner, why have we been summoned to Adobe Wells?"

"Not we. You," Jay corrected him. "After I fill you in on your assignment, I return to Indian Territory."

Heath merely nodded. He didn't want the team to be split up, but it never occurred to him to question orders. "Why have *I* been summoned to Adobe Wells?"

"Apparently half the outlaws in New Mexico have swarmed there. You're to mingle with them; pass yourself off as Lucky Diamond again, and see what you can learn." Jay smiled conspiratorially "Captain said to tell you he's enlarged your reputation a bit."

Heath grimaced. "What have I done this time?"

Jay placed his hand over his heart. "Sent Barnes Elder to that great poker game in the sky."

Heath whistled softly. "I'm getting good! If I didn't know it was all fabrication, I'd be impressed myself. Barnes Elder, huh?"

"Yeah, poor ol' Barnes never even cleared leather," Jay said of the fictitious gunman. "Seems he was dealing aces off the bottom of the deck. Being a professional gambler, you couldn't allow that."

"Certainly not."

Jay sobered. "You know this means every downy-faced sodbuster with the price of a bullet will be gunning for you. And you won't get much help from the local law. The sheriff's a green kid who's afraid of his own shadow, and the territory judge is a fancy dresser with a questionable character. Name's Elias Colt Jack. Has an eye patch and sometimes goes by the moniker One-eyed Jack. He's trying to take over the whole valley, but we don't know why. The only thing we know for certain about him is that he's not a judge."

"Let's see now . . ." Heath began dryly, counting off on his fingers. "I'm going up against virtually every shootist in the territory—every novice who wants to make his reputation by drawing on the man who killed Barnes Elder—without my partner at my back. All in a town where the law consists of a wet-behind-the-ears sheriff and a greedy judge who's not really a judge. Do you have any more good news?"

Jay threw Heath an impudent grin. "If you add the doll who practically castrated you, I'd say that about covers it."

"The lengths we go to t' serve our country," Heath deadpanned.

Jay chuckled. "Yep. Makes you wonder about our intelligence, doesn't it?"

Heath raised an ebony brow, agreeing. "What's your assignment, as if I didn't know."

Jay's smile disappeared. "I've got to find Rachel and put that bitch away again. For good this time. I don't know how long it'll take me, but as soon as I square things, I'll be back."

For the past two years, Jay—and Heath, when he wasn't on other assignments—had been chasing a cold-hearted murderer named Rachel Jackson, who had broken out of the Arkansas Territorial Prison, killing two guards in the process.

Rumor had it that Rachel was in Santa Fe. While Heath spent time in New York, visiting his ill father, Jay visited New Mexico's territorial capital. But the report hadn't panned out; Rachel was nowhere to be found. So Jay had received orders from their captain to alert Heath to the problems in Adobe Wells, then head back to the Nations after Rachel.

"How's your dad?" Jay asked quietly.

"Rad and Chap"—he referred to his doctor twin brothers—"say he's stable for now. He's still having pains in his chest though, and they're keeping him in bed."

"Knowing the general, that can't be easy."

Despite the worry about his father, Heath returned Jay's smile. "No, I imagine not. That's why both Rad and Chap closed their practice in Richmond indefinitely. They're staying for the duration." He looked out over the valley, his deep, husky voice betraying a sense of guilt, "I should be there too."

"I know how you feel, Heath. But the general wouldn't want you to sit by his side. It would make him feel as if you were waiting for him to die. And if I know the old man, he'll pull through."

Heath drew a deep, cleansing breath. "Dear Lord, I hope you're right."

"I am." Jay cleared his throat, knowing it was time they were both on the trail. "Guess I'd best be movin' on. I'll be back this way soon as I finish up in the Nations."

Heath nodded. The two returned to their horses, parting company with reluctance.

"Watch your back, partner. You hear?" Jay drawled.

"I will." Heath watched as Jay mounted and rode away. "You do the same," he called to Jay's retreating form.

With a backward wave, Jay disappeared from sight.

High atop Warrior, Heath kicked his horse into a gallop and headed toward Adobe Wells.

Hopefully, there was still time to reach town before nightfall.

Three

Stevie Johns hopped off Whiskeypeat and settled him in the barn before making her way to the sprawling ranch house.

A low growl greeted her from the shaded porch. She halted on the bottom step and raised her gaze. Two yellow eyes peered at her for a scant second, then the furry body of a wolf flew through the air, hitting her in the chest, tumbling her backward, flattening her on the ground.

Before she could raise her arms to shield herself, the animal's huge, cavernous mouth opened. Time suspended as the wolf's head grew larger, moving closer and closer to her face.

Stevie shrieked when Sweetums's broad, wet tongue snaked out and bathed her from cheek to cheek. Laughing and rolling on the ground, she fought playfully with her pet.

It occurred to her that this was the second wolf attack she had endured today. "Give me a four-legged wolf any day," she muttered, surging to her feet, pushing the door open, and following Sweetums into the front hall.

"Who's there?"

" 'S'me, Pa," she answered, slightly out of breath.

Sandy Johns entered the foyer, staring at his daughter in the doorway, her figure limned by the glow of late afternoon sunshine. For a moment she might have been her mother, identical slight frame, same regal profile.

Then she bent to pet Sweetums and the fringe on her vest swayed, breaking the spell. With small, gloved hands, she brushed the worst of the dust from her pants. Straightening, she placed her rifle by the door, then glanced at her father's scowling face.

"Don't even start!"

Sandy held up his hands in a defensive gesture. "Did I say a word?"

She jerked her black kid gloves off and shook them in her father's direction. "You don't have to. Your face says it all."

He shrugged noncommittally. "It's just a shame for a youngun as pretty as you to go around dressed like a man. You're a woman, Stevie. It's time you started behaving like one. Time you settled down and took a husband."

"I'm not a woman. Not to the people in town. I'm a savage."

"Here now!" He closed the distance between them. "You know I don't allow talk like that in this house. As for being a savage, you're only half Comanche. But it wouldn't matter if you were full blood. You're a beautiful young woman, and if you dressed like a female and gave the men in town half a chance, you'd have more men buzzin' around here than you could shake a stick at."

Stevie had heard it all before. She was in no mood to hear it again. "Don't we have enough problems without you harping on what I wear? And who wants to attract men who think the only good Indian is a dead Indian? Not me, I can tell you! Besides, it's not like I just started dressing this way, Pa. I haven't worn girls' clothes since I was ten years old. And I don't intend to start wearing them anytime soon. So do us both a favor and let it lay."

The last time Stevie had worn a dress was to her mother's funeral. Delicate, beautiful Swan had died giving birth to a stillborn baby boy ten years ago. She could have been saved, but the town doctor refused to tend an Indian.

The memory of her mother's last few hours caused her throat to burn. Watching Swan suffer an agonizing, senseless death, holding her hand as the life's blood ebbed from her body, made an irrevocable impression on Stevie. In one fell swoop it robbed her of her childhood and her desire to be female.

So now, at twenty, on the threshold of womanhood, she dressed like a man, hoping to make herself invisible to the

opposite sex. It had worked until her body started changing
Unconsciously, she crossed her arms over her chest, hiding he
budding breasts. Unbidden, she remembered the gunslick
hands on her. Her cheeks flamed. Feet planted, she forced her
self to drop her arms at her sides.

"And I don't want a husband," she emphasized in case he
daddy hadn't been listening the first time. With short, jerk
movements, she tucked her gloves in the pocket of her breeche
and dropped her gaze to the tip of one scuffed boot.

Sandy touched her cheek. "But, honey, I'll not always b
around to protect you."

"Don't say that."

"It's true."

"Well, I'll just have to take care of myself, 'cause I'm no
gonna get married. Ever." She paused, then blinked her eyes
fighting tears. Her voice was soft, unsure when she continued
"Who would have me, Pa? What white man would want a half
breed for the mother of his children?" Shaking her head wryly
she finished, "And I just can't see marrying a Comanche. With
my sharp tongue, he'd scalp me on our honeymoon. And a
much as it hurts to admit, I have to agree with the townspeople
Most Indians are savages. The men anyway."

Stevie had been a tender child of four when she overheard
her first account of a Comanche raid. The tale was so horrible
bloody, and vicious that she had never gotten over it. Women
raped, their babies' brains bashed out, men murdered and
scalped, their tongues cut out. She'd had nightmares for week
afterward; still did at times. She shuddered involuntarily.

Her mother had tried to explain why the People attacked the
White Eyes. But the concept of a dying nation protecting it
ancestral home had been far too sophisticated for Stevie to
comprehend.

So she carried the shame of her Indian blood in her heart
Plagued with insecurity, she was a lonely girl in a woman'
body, a woman without a people, a woman who felt she didn'
belong to anyone—except her pa and little Winter. That would
have to be enough.

Flashing her father a disarming grin to cover her emotion

she continued. "Fact is, men are a pack of trouble. You're proof of that."

Sandy smiled sadly. He knew what was going through his daughter's mind. "Sometimes, Stephanie Kay, I think I should've sent you east to live with my sister, where you could learn how to be a proper lady."

Stevie paled. "You couldn't do that to me and you know it. You needed around the ranch. And now that Jeff's gone—"

The look of pain in her father's eyes halted her in mid-sentence. Like Stevie, Sandy was still grieving. It was evident in every line etched in his weather-beaten face.

Jeff had been missing for two months. His horse had returned to the ranch, blood staining the expertly tooled saddle his pa had given him for his twenty-first birthday. Adobe Wells's sheriff had searched halfheartedly before giving Jeff up for dead. Sandy said the lawman had abandoned the search because he was stupid and cowardly—not much more than a kid himself. Stevie thought it was because Jeff was part Comanche.

She was certain that the man who killed Jeff was in the judge's employ. Silently, she had vowed to discover the truth about her brother and avenge his death, if it took her the rest of her life. She just had to find a way around her pa and his propensity to smother her with fatherly concern.

She averted her gaze, knowing it wouldn't do for Sandy to see the fire of vengeance burning in her eyes. He'd lock her in her room for sure, or worse, send her east to live with her oh-so-proper aunt.

Purposefully, she approached the window, pushing aside the fluttering curtains. A glossy blue bird perched on the cottonwood, warbling an airy tune. Stevie stared at it with unseeing eyes.

"Who else would take care of things around here if you managed to marry me off or send me to live with Aunt Avesta? Now that all the hands are gone."

Sandy crossed the room, placing his hands on Stevie's shoulder. "Don't worry, kitten. I won't send you away." Sandy didn't want Stevie to leave the Rocking J any more than she wanted to go. But he feared for her safety. Damn Elias Colt Jack to hell!

Looking out the window over his daughter's shoulder, Sandy conquered impotent rage and allowed himself a moment's reflection, remembering what life was like when he, Jeff, and Stevie worked side by side, reigning like kindly lords over the little kingdom his ancestors had carved out of the wilderness, when the ranch was alive with the sounds of men, horses, and cattle.

He sighed heavily. Would it ever be that way again? Not if Judge Jack had his way, a still, small voice answered. The judge's determination to own the Rocking J knew no bounds. At first he had tried to buy the place, but when Sandy refused to sell, the real trouble began. Stock disappeared; wells were poisoned, outbuildings burned to the ground.

The theft and vandalism had taken a financial toll. Except for a small nest egg in the bank that Sandy had put aside as Stevie's dowry, he was as broke as the Ten Commandments.

Dowries were fanciful, he knew, but he was determined that Stevie have one. For once in her life, she was going to be like those hoity-toity debutantes his sister was always writing about, the ones who took something into their marriages besides the clothes on their back. Short of starvation, he wouldn't touch that money.

But starvation wasn't their greatest threat; being cast out of their home was. When it appeared things couldn't get any worse, the judge sent the sheriff out with an injunction informing Sandy that he didn't hold clear title to his ranch.

Enraged, he tore the paper into shreds and tossed it in the sheriff's face. They were given three months to vacate the premises, and now their time had come to an end.

Stevie watched her father out of the corner of her eye. She ached at the hopelessness she saw on his face. Leaning back against his chest, her heart mirrored his anguish.

Her own sense of hopelessness angered her. But no matter how brave she appeared to the rest of the world, there were times when she feared she was little more than a scared child. A child who not only needed her pa, but her mother—the gentle creature who had been taken from her before she could teach Stevie how to live in a world divided by prejudice, a world torn apart by the likes of Judge Elias Colt Jack.

"Have you given any more thought to taking a room at Pilar's?" Sandy spoke softly, broaching another sensitive subject.

Stevie whirled about. "And leave you here? No sir!"

With trembling hands she unfastened her gun belt, signaling the end of the discussion. She passed the weapon to Sandy.

He placed it on the rack inside the door, then retrieved her rifle. He sniffed the barrel. "Stephanie Kay, this long gun has been fired."

Stevie refused to meet Sandy's probing gaze. Thinking of the handsome gunman, his devastating kiss, and the feel of being held in his strong arms, her heart accelerated and her mouth grew dry. "I stumbled across a snake."

Her father didn't believe a word of it. "Stevie?" He invited her to try again.

She pecked him on the cheek, put the rifle away, then headed for the kitchen. "I'd love to stand around and jaw with you, Pa, but I've gotta fix supper."

"Halt!"

Stevie paused in mid-stride, surprise sculpting her lovely face. "Yes, sir?"

Sandy had sounded so dictatorial. It was a tone he rarely used with Stevie since she usually had him wrapped comfortably around her little finger. He grinned at the shock on her face. "Whenever you offer to cook, I get nervous."

She relaxed. "Pepper's gout is giving him trouble."

Sandy snorted; Stevie's excuse didn't hold water. They both knew that Pepper had complained of gout since God was a child. Gout, or a myriad of other ailments, not surprising since the old codger was born back when the earth was still cooling. "What are you trying to hide?" he probed.

"Nothing. I'm hungry and I don't feel like listening to Pepper grumble. And I sure don't feel like eating your cooking." She tried to look affronted, with a measure of innocence thrown in. "He managed to fix son-of-a-bitch stew. All I gotta do is cook the sourdoughs."

Sandy shrugged. "Okay. Far be it from me to stem your domestic urges. They come so rarely."

She narrowed her eyes, warning him that he was treading on dangerous ground again.

"Don't frown, kitten. It'll wrinkle that beautiful face."

"You're hopeless." The love she felt for him was evident in her soft reproof.

"I'm taking a ride out to the cave." Sandy buckled on his gun. "I won't be long."

Stevie's smile disappeared. She rushed to the door, grabbing her father by the arm. "Wait. I'll come with you."

"You've gotta fix supper, remember?" he teased good-naturedly. Stevie started to argue, but her father was having none of it. He stroked her cheek, the tip of his callused finger rasping against the satiny texture of her skin. "I'll be right back, hon. You're such a worrywart."

"I come by it honest."

"Daddies are entitled to worry." He patted her hand where it lay on his arm, then pushed through the screen door. "Try not to burn the biscuits," he called over his shoulder.

Stevie leaned a slender shoulder against the doorjamb and watched her father until he topped the brow of the hill and disappeared from sight. She turned back toward the kitchen, smiling faintly. "Try not to burn the biscuits, my fanny."

She had taken no more than two steps, when she heard a gun shot ring out. The second blast was drowned out by her scream.

As he rode toward Adobe Wells, Heath allowed his thoughts to wander idly. Now that the stimulating hellion was absent, fatigue claimed him again, stronger than before. Frankly, he'd found the girl exhausting in a pleasant way.

In his mind's eye he pictured the land before him with buffalo freely roaming the plains, much as they had before the great shaggy beasts had been slaughtered by profiteers for the gold their coats would bring on the northeastern market. But tragically, the buffalo wasn't the only species in danger of extinction in the American West. Indians were killed for sport in this untamed land, just like the animals upon which they depended for their existence.

The thought of shooting human beings for no reason at all save the accident of their birth made Heath's blood run cold. He tightened his grip on the reins and stiffened in the saddle, lifting his eyes toward the horizon.

The haunting beauty of the Plains Indians' ancestral home soothed him. He could almost feel their spirit surrounding him; he was humbled by the sensation.

When the Justice Department had approached Jay and him about being special agents to see that justice was dispensed in the West, they assured them there would be equal justice for all, Indian and white. That was the only reason the twosome had accepted the job.

But the assurance was a lie. Despite the intervention of men like Jay's brother-in-law, Chase Tarleton, the Comanches had been rounded up and herded onto a reservation in Oklahoma. Just like Chase's Cherokee family had been herded up and marched from Georgia to the wilds of Oklahoma Territory, along the infamous Trail of Tears.

Heath had an appreciation of the Indian that went beyond lip service. He truly ached for their dismal plight. But optimistic by nature, he pushed the painful thoughts aside and considered the black-eyed beauty with hair the color of a palomino, the brazen angel he'd met on Mustang Mesa.

Granted, she was beautiful. She gave rise to feelings that weren't totally physical in nature, however. He was inexplicably drawn to her.

And there was something familiar about her, as if he had known her before. During their few moments together—despite the combative nature of the encounter—he hadn't felt as if they were meeting for the first time. It was more like they were becoming reacquainted, worse, that he had been searching for her all his life. It was almost enough to make a skeptical man believe in fate. Almost.

He felt unaccountably restless, inordinately lonely, ever since he'd visited his family in New York. His two brothers, Chap and Rad, were happily married. Their older sister, Emily, was widowed. His youngest sister, Ann, remained unwed, though at last account she was engaged. So that left him as the only Turner progeny who had never experienced true love, the only sibling who had never pledged himself exclusively to another.

He would never admit it aloud, but there were times lately when he wanted someone special to love so badly, his gut ached. Not just someone to share his body with, but someone to entrust with his heart, his hopes, his dreams, his future.

A man could easily find physical release. All he had to do was locate the nearest honkytonk, drop a few coins, and lie between the plump thighs of the woman of his choice. But these biological encounters—as he and Jay labeled them—often left him more frustrated than satisfied.

But the angel of Mustang Mesa's shy, inexperienced response to his kiss held more satisfaction than a promised night of debauchery with the highest paid whore the Wild West had to offer.

As the vision of her face grew more vivid, his strange yearning for her expanded. Just as quickly it vanished, snatched by a gun shot splitting the heavy afternoon air. The shot came from beyond the next rise. Heath kicked his horse into a gallop as another shot rang out.

His heart pounded against his ribs. Surely his feisty shootist was not firing at another unwary passerby. Worse yet, was someone firing at her?

He palmed his gun and thundered over the hill. Relief and dread filled him in equal measures when he saw that the victim was not the girl but a tired-looking old man, lying unconscious beside a mesquite bush, all alone, his head cradled in a spreading pool of his own blood.

Heath cast a quick glance around. The man's assailant was nowhere in sight. He pulled rein and slid out of the saddle before Warrior had fully stopped. Still holding his gun, he approached the injured man.

Stevie shrieked as she topped the rise, "Get away from him, you rotten bastard." Falling down at her father's side, she pulled his head into her lap. He was unnaturally pale, frighteningly still.

"Oh, Pa," she cried softly, holding him, rocking him. There

was so much blood. She wondered if anyone could lose so much blood and live.

"Why?" She raised stricken eyes to Heath. "Why did you have to shoot him? Why couldn't you just leave us alone? Why can't you all just leave us alone?"

The strain of the past several months and the thought of losing her pa overwhelmed her. She buried her face in Sandy's hair and clutched him protectively to her chest. If she lost him, she and Winter, her child, would have no one left, no one at all.

Heath cursed beneath his breath, disturbed by the girl's distress. She looked so helpless, kneeling at his feet. Somehow he knew that moments of weakness were few and far between for this girl. He hated seeing her beaten, subdued. Idiot that he was, he would rather have her taking shots at him.

"Pia, mother." A shrill voice drew Heath's attention. Riding up to them, his face taut with fear, an Indian child slid from a painted pony. "Grandfather Sandy, he is dead?" Winter asked in Comanche.

"No," Heath answered for Stevie. "But if we don't get him to a doctor, he soon will be."

In her distress, Stevie failed to notice that Heath understood Comanche. She raised tear-filled eyes to him. "Are you sure he's not dead?"

He nodded. "Just stunned."

Stevie closed her eyes, whispering a prayer of thanksgiving to her father's Christian God and to the Great Spirit of the Comanches. She tilted her chin up and wiped her eyes on her shirtsleeve.

Heath chose to ignore the accusation in their moist depths. "Do you have a wagon?" he asked quietly.

"Yes, sir," Winter offered.

Heath took the six-year-old child's measure. He looked quite capable, and he could certainly ride a horse well. "Good. Go get it, son." As an afterthought he added, "Is there someone to help you with the harness?"

"Pepper will help," Winter said, looking to Stevie for instruction. When she gave him leave, he jumped on his horse and made for the ranch.

Hesitantly, Heath knelt on the grass, reaching forward to check Sandy's head wound. Stevie scooted backward, attempting to pull her father away from Heath.

"Let me check him, dammit," Heath ordered, perturbed by her mistrust. Fighting for composure, he balled his fists and rested them on bent thighs. "I just want to make sure the bleeding has stopped."

"You touch him and I'll kill you," she snarled. "He would rather die than accept help from one of Judge Jack's henchmen. Especially the sidewinder who shot him!"

A muscle in Heath's jaw twitched, evincing the tenuous hold he had on his rising temper. "You blind fool! I'm not Judge Jack's henchman. And I sure as hell am no murderer. So get that notion out of your demented head. I'm a simple gambler who has had the misfortune of running into you twice in one day. Now, if you want your pa to live, you'll let me help you. When the kid gets back, I'll put the old man in the wagon, and you can take him into town. Beyond that, you can go to blazes as far as I'm concerned."

Carefully, she laid her father out on the soft stand of grass and rose to her feet.

Heath never took his eyes off her, a thread of tension running the length of him. Years of living by his wits made him wary of her. He wasn't particularly surprised when she whipped a benign-looking snub-nosed derringer from inside her vest pocket. "I guess this means you don't want my help," he surmised.

In answer, she cocked the small but very lethal gun. "If my pa dies, I'll hunt you down and put a bullet through your black heart." Stevie had never killed a man, but there was always a first time. "I might do it anyway. Just for the pleasure."

She was deadly serious, and Heath was wise enough to realize it. Standing, slowly so as not to startle her, he dropped his gaze to the injured man at his feet. The head wound was superficial, just a crease, and the bleeding had stopped.

Satisfied that he could do no more, he doffed his Stetson and sketched a chivalrous bow. "It's been an experience meeting you, my lady. Not particularly pleasant, but an experience nonetheless." His voice was frosty as Christmas morn. "I leave you to see after your own."

And he did, without noticing the gaping hole in Sandy Johns's chest.

Four

An hour before sundown Heath rode into town. With thoughts of his job occupying his attention, he had put the day's unpleasantness out of his mind.

Thick red dust rose with every clop of his horse's hooves. Heath raised his neckerchief over his nose to filter the dust, and scanned the streets, instinctively noting the avenues of escape and the areas suitable for ambush—the places a yellow-bellied brigand bent on shooting an unsuspecting marshal could hide.

Adobe Wells was a typical western town. The buildings were one and two story flat-top adobes with portals. Two streets, one running north-south, the other east-west, intersected at the center of town, forming a dirt plaza. On either side of the plaza were adobe-framed wells. A few trees, mostly cottonwood, offered the mingling inhabitants little shade from the late afternoon sun.

Not surprising, there were three saloons in town. In addition, there were two hotels, a jail, a general store, a respectable looking eatery, a livery stable, a hardware, and a few other nondescript establishments, along with five or six private residences.

On the north side of town a number of miners' shacks had been haphazardly constructed from makeshift materials. The temporary city looked like a sea of cast-off lumber and tin, swarming with sooty, bearded lifesize ants. Men wearing overalls or heavy trousers held up by suspenders busied themselves with evening chores. Some of them were tending to stock animals, mostly burros; others were busy cooking the night's fare over open fires. The distinctive smell of onions and fried beans caused Heath's nostrils to twitch, his stomach to rumble.

He had not expected to see miners in Adobe Wells. No precious metals or minerals of any sort had ever been found in this area. There was, of course, gold in California, silver in Nevada, and copper in Arizona. But as far as he knew, this area was good for grazing cattle and little else.

Except producing beautiful angels with positively diabolical dispositions. Smiling at the memory, he removed his neckerchief and stopped at a stately home on the edge of town. A wooden sign reading MANCHEZ'S BOARDINGHOUSE swayed and creaked in the afternoon breeze. Sliding from the saddle, he secured Warrior's reins to the white picket fence circling the front yard, shouldered his saddlebags, and pushed through the gate.

A burst of energy infused him now that his long trip had come to an end. Taking the front steps two at a time, he rapped gently on the frosted pane of the front door.

An attractive Mexican woman in her mid-forties opened the door and invited Heath inside out of the summer sun. Her clean, crisp, lemon-yellow calico gown was in striking contrast to her soft, dusky complexion. Masses of shiny black hair were imprisoned in a demure bun at the back of her head. Her apron, starched stiff, was as white as the first snow in winter. Her smile was open, friendly.

"Buenos tardes, Señor."

"Señorita." Heath greeted her with the instinctive charm that never failed to give the fairer sex a moment of rapid heart palpitation.

It had its usual effect. *"Señora* Pilar Manchez," she said, wishing that she were ten years younger.

His face hinted at disappointment before he bowed over her hand. "A tragic loss, *Señora.* I wonder, are all beautiful women married?"

Pilar's cheeks flamed at the offhand flattery despite her years of maturity. "Surely not. I myself am a widow." She paused respectfully. Clearing her throat, she continued. "Now, how may I help you?"

"I need a room for an undetermined length of time."

"I have one available on the second floor. A large cottonwood tree shades it in the daytime, *Señor.* I think you will find it comfortable."

After being shrieked at for most of the afternoon, Heath found Pilar's gentle spirit, lilting accent, and serene smile soothing. *"Gracias."*

A man in his line of work had to be wary of strangers, but he had a feeling it would be difficult to remain aloof around the woman regarding him with open friendliness. He liked her instantly. She reminded him of Rad's wife, Ginny. Calm, gentle, tranquil.

He followed Pilar to a room that was typically western in decor except for a tap over a zinc basin. Indoor running water was unusual for this part of the country, and Heath was suitably impressed. He complimented Pilar on her home.

"Gracias, Señor . . ."

"Diamond. Lucky Diamond. Please call me Lucky." He watched his hostess warily, hoping she wouldn't ask him to leave. Most respectable women shied away from professional gamblers. And with a name like Lucky Diamond, there could be no doubt in Pilar's mind of his profession.

Not one to be predictable, Pilar caught Heath off guard. "You plan to try your hand at gambling in our town, Lucky?" She might have been discussing the weather for all the emotion in her voice.

More than surprised, Heath was relieved. He was far too tired to go room-hunting today. And he did like Pilar. "Yes. But first I would sell my soul for some good home cooking and a hot bath."

Pilar laughed. "It will be my pleasure to pamper you. Much as your own mother would."

"If only all the ladies in this area were as gracious as you . . ."

"You have found our ladies otherwise?" she expressed her surprise.

"Only one." Leaning against the bedpost, he tried to hide

his apparent interest. "I was waylaid by a young girl about seven miles east of town. She took several shots at me from the cliffs in front of Mustang Mesa."

Pilar clutched her throat. "Oh, dear. Stevie!"

"Stevie? No. I don't think so. I didn't catch her name, but this very definitely was a girl. I got close enough to determine that delightful fact."

"Yes. Our Stevie is very much a girl. No matter how hard she tries to be the son her father needs. But you mustn't hold her"—she paused, searching for the right words—"unorthodox behavior against her, Lucky. She's understandably upset. It was recently declared that her father doesn't hold clear title to his ranch and Sandy and Stevie are to be evicted any day. She probably thought you were one of Judge Jack's hired guns, sent to throw them into the streets."

Almost as an afterthought, she mused, "I'm surprised that you got by her so easily."

Heath grinned. "Who said it was easy?"

Pilar assessed Heath, taking in his long, muscled six-foot-four-inch frame, the rakish twinkle in his eye, his shiny black hair, and engaging grin. She couldn't imagine him having trouble with any woman. "The sentiment of most men regarding Stevie," Pilar said cryptically.

Heath felt a twinge in his gut that was too damn close to jealousy for his peace of mind. To his knowledge, he had never suffered from the petty emotion. Jealousy was for the ranks of the insecure. And he possessed more than his share of confidence; some uncharitably called it arrogance. But things had always come easy for him—money, friends, women, success. Who wouldn't be confident?

"Miss Pilar, Cook needs you in the kitchen," a small Mexican girl interrupted, staring shyly at the gringo.

"Please tell her I'll be right down, Maria." Pilar turned to Heath. "You'll want to have your bath before supper. My guests use the shed out back. I'll have Will Eagle fill the tub. Supper will be served in the dining room in an hour."

"Thank you, *Señora* Manchez."

After stabling his horse, Heath made his way to the shed behind the hotel. Will Eagle was an Indian of about sixty winters. His long braided hair was the color of newly fallen snow. He was dressed in faded jeans that bagged at the seat and a well-worn buckskin shirt that hung from his gaunt frame. Despite his shabby clothing, he had an exalted bearing.

Perched smartly atop his head was a black top hat. It looked as if it had been squashed repeatedly over the years. Now it stood only half as tall as it originally did.

To the casual observer, the headgear appeared ready for the garbage heap. But to Will Eagle it was more precious than a bank vault filled with gold. It had been presented to him by the white captive, Cynthia Ann Parker, and her Comanche husband, Wanderer. He wore it with all the defiance of the renegade bands of Comanche, who rejected the forced removal of the People to government reservations.

Heath introduced himself to the stoic old man, extending his hand. For a long, tense moment, he met Will's eye respectfully, something most white men neglected to do.

Will was pleased. He shook Heath's hand, pointed him toward the tub, and, without uttering a word, left him to his bath.

Feeling that he had passed muster, Heath shed his dusty clothes and, sinking into the tub, gave an audible sigh of appreciation. He soaked until his sun-bronzed skin began to wrinkle like a prune.

Still, he was reluctant to rise. The tepid water and frothy suds made his sore, aching body feel as if it had died and gone to heaven. On the trail he was afforded few opportunities to pamper himself. And even though he could rough it with the toughest hombre, his blue-blooded ancestry reared its head from time to time. This was such a time.

Finally, the water turned cold. Leaving the tub, he dressed quickly and headed back to the house, eager for Pilar's home cooking. The kitchen exuded the tempting scents of beefsteak, potatoes, and peas, freshly baked bread, and boiling coffee, drawing him like a siren's song.

While Heath made his way to Pilar's table, Stevie kept vigil at her father's bedside.

Dr. Ian Sullivan fought diligently to save his friend's life.

"The shot to the head just stunned him, I'm thinking, Stevie darlin'," Sully said in his lilting Irish brogue as he worked. "It's the hole in his chest that could send your da to his reward. As much as it hurts to hear it, lass, you have to be prepared for the worst." He ignored her quick intake of breath and continued. "Saints preserve us, but I've seen wounds like this kill younger, healthier men."

Stevie jerked her chin, looking stubborn as Jenny, her pa's most obstinate mule. Blinking rapidly, she refused to cry at Sully's dire warning. She had to be strong for Winter, the frightened child cradled in her embrace.

She caressed the locket nestled between her breasts as if it were a talisman. The shell pink cameo held a lock of her mother's blue-black hair. And it was Stevie's most prized possession. It had always brought her luck before. Today would be no different. Her father would live. She told the doctor as much in a tone that brooked no disagreement.

"I pray God you're right, Stevie darlin'. I truly do." Sullivan straightened beside the bed, washed his hands in the sanguine water, dried them on a scrap of muslin, then unrolled and buttoned his shirtsleeves. "I've patched him up the best I can. He's in God's hands now."

"Pa will get well," she vowed again. "And I will get even."

Her face hardened with such hatred that Sully crossed himself. "Here now," he sputtered. "What are you about?" He blinked like an owl, then narrowed his blue-gray eyes in patent disapproval. "Explain yourself."

But there was no need to explain herself to Sully, and Stevie knew it. He could see clear through to her soul, if she still had one. The judge had stolen everything else; why not her very soul?

"Do you know who did this to your da, lass?" he asked anyway.

Dropping her gaze, she remained stubbornly silent.

Sully lifted her head until they were eye to eye. "I insist that you march right down that street and tell Marshal Reno who you suspect. This is men's work, Stevie darlin'. Not that of a girl like yourself. Ted'll see to the matter. That's what we pay him for."

Stevie rolled her eyes and pulled her chin out of Sully's grasp like a turtle drawing into its shell. "Ted Reno would pee in his pants if I asked him to go after the man who shot Pa, and you know it."

Sully couldn't dispute that. Everyone knew that Sheriff Reno was yellow as a daffodil with the backbone of a jellyfish. Undoubtedly that was why Judge Jack had appointed him.

Granted, Reno was all they had for now. But Sully had written the territorial marshal, requesting help in dealing with Judge Jack and the stranglehold he had over Adobe Wells and its law-abiding citizens. Just yesterday he had received a letter saying help was on its way. An unnamed lawman would be working undercover. For security, no one, not even Sully, would know his identity.

The man could come disguised as Queen Victoria for all he cared, Sully declared silently. Just so long as he came, and soon. It would be all he could do to keep Stevie from getting herself shot while Sandy was laid up.

"You're going to give me gray hair, lass," he muttered, settling in the chair at Sandy's bedside, prepared for a long vigil that could well end with his best friend's death.

A short time later Stevie lay Winter, her child of the heart, on a mat in front of the cold fireplace and began to pace. While the boy slept peacefully, she boiled like a kettle of water over an open fire. Her emotions awakened, swirled, rolled, as if she would burst forth and overflow, scalding everything in her path.

Sully didn't care to be in that path. "Why don't you run over and get Pilar? We should've called her before now," he suggested.

When she turned her darkened gaze on him, Sully sucked in his breath. He had never seen such pain.

"I don't want to leave him, Sully. He might—" she broke off, her lips trembling.

Sully folded her in his embrace. For all her bravado, this courageous young woman was afraid. "Everything will be all right, Stevie darlin'," he whispered into her hair. "I promise.

It'll take more than a couple of slugs of lead to stop a man like Sandy Johns."

Ignoring the fact that Sully's reassurance was contrary to his earlier warning, she held it close to her heart.

Five

Sporting clean clothes, Heath looked quite the gentleman. He was dressed in a dark, expensive frock coat and a charcoal-gray waistcoat over an open-collared linen shirt. The sapphire silk scarf tied around his neck matched his blue eyes to perfection. The overall effect was sedate and sophisticated, as intended.

The western contribution to his ensemble consisted of his hat and weapon. The hat—which he removed at the table—was a flat-crowned black Stetson with a wide brim, its shiny band made from beaten silver. His Navy Colt, a constant companion, rested in a side holster tied to his muscled thigh.

He absolutely refused to dress in the bright clothing of a professional gambler. There was only so much he would do for his country. And that didn't include wearing bright yellow waistcoats or crimson silk cravats, as gamesters were wont to do.

Nodding to the other guests at the table, he took the chair beside Pilar. Studying him with an appreciative eye, she decided that he looked like a dangerous dude with whom the fainthearted shouldn't tangle.

"Well, what're you waitin' on?" the old codger across from Heath barked at Pilar.

Not offended, Pilar smiled and passed the first dish.

Heath glanced at the disgruntled man and his petite wife. She smiled; her husband scowled. The old couple spoke exclusively to each other throughout the meal. The fact that they failed to address him didn't disturb Heath. He was too busy enjoying the first decent food he'd had since he couldn't remember when.

And of course, Pilar's other boarders demanded his attention. In addition to the old couple, she had assembled an off assortment of nesters; Miss Smelter, Adobe Wells's old maid schoolteacher, Joe Waters, a drummer who was just passing through, and Penelope and Gwendolyn Dough, two short spinster sisters who were twins. The twins personified their name—white, fluffy, doughy, as wide as they were tall. Premature at birth, neither had weighed over three pounds. Their mother had lovingly christened them Itsy and Bitsy, they told Heath.

When Heath smiled and complimented their nicknames, they both tittered like girls fresh out of the schoolroom, a disconcerting fact since they were on the shady side of forty. But they were sweet ladies and he charmed them instinctively.

Miss Smelter was a horse face of a different color, however. She found life very distasteful, quite miserable actually, and she wanted everyone to suffer along with her.

Unfazed by Miss Smelter's dour personality, the drummer seated to her right smiled continuously, even when he ate. He brought to Heath's mind a jackass eating briars as he informed him that he sold notions. Not ideas, he teased, notions. Everyone—except Miss Smelter and the old codger—chuckled politely at the tradesman's standard joke.

Looking over the rim of his coffee cup, Heath allowed his gaze to wander idly around the table. He wondered if Jay would believe his description of these people. Mentally, he shook his head. Not in this lifetime.

When everyone was finished eating, Pilar removed the plates and announced that there would be gooseberry pie and fresh cream for dessert. The Dough sisters could hardly contain their excitement.

Abruptly, the old man turned to Heath. His eyes narrowed, his lips slightly tense, he stated flatly, "Name's Robert Pridgen." He jerked his head toward the diminutive lady at his side. "My wife, Nellie."

Heath nodded respectfully. "Ma'am."

Pridgen's mouth took on an unpleasant twist. "What the hell are you doing in Adobe Wells?"

Heath choked on his coffee. The scalding liquid slid down the wrong way, bringing tears to his eyes as he tried valiantly to meet Mr. Pridgen's inquisitive, no-nonsense glare. He was too startled to reply immediately.

The twins gasped their horror at Mr. Pridgen's swearing. Embarrassed, they left the table, casting a last longing glance at the gooseberry pie. Miss Smelter sniffed her disapproval and quit the room as well. Chuckling, the drummer just melted away.

"Pardon me, sir?" Heath wheezed finally.

"Are you deaf, boy? I asked what the hell you're doing in Adobe Wells?"

Heath regained his equanimity, quelling the urge to smile. He had not been called *boy* since he turned fourteen years old and topped six feet.

He considered asking the man if he was kin to Stevie Johns, but thought better of it. His tone deferential, he replied, "I'm just passing through, sir."

"Few people come here these days unless they want to see Judge Jack." Pridgen's accusation was apparent.

"Now, Dad, leave the young man be," Nellie scolded.

"A man has a right to question strangers if he's a mind to." Pridgen's voice was gruff, but his parchmentlike face grew soft when he looked at his beloved wife.

Astonished, Heath decided that he liked the crotchety old gentleman. He saw something in Pridgen's eyes that he admired; a sense of pride in his home. Obviously Judge Jack was threatening the citizens of Adobe Wells and this old bird didn't intend to take it lying down.

"Please call me Lucky, Mr. Pridgen." He paused, a look of sincerity sculpting his features. "And I assure you I haven't come to see Judge Jack."

Pridgen took the gambler's measure. Persuaded by what he found, he nodded tersely.

Heath realized he had passed muster . . . again. "I am curious about Judge Jack though. He must be rather"—he searched for a word that wouldn't inflame Pridgen—"influential."

Pridgen snorted, biting back a curse. "*Influential* isn't the word I'd use. *Ruthless* would fit his pistol. Since the first day he came here, a year ago, that bastard, pardon, Pilar, Mother, has wielded absolute authority over Adobe Wells and the surrounding territory like he was Jesus H. Christ."

"With all due respect, why did you elect him as judge?" asked Heath.

"We didn't," Pridgen responded heatedly. "Colonel Banes from over at Fort Bascomb brought him to us. Before you could spit, he had installed the crook as judge over the entire area." He gestured expansively, barely missing his coffee cup in his exuberance. Puffed up like a toad, he was fair to bursting with righteous indignation.

"But he carried no written credentials from Washington, or from anywhere else. Said he didn't need 'em. And since the son of a—the judge was backed up by a hoard of hardcases, we had no choice but to accept him." Pridgen looked away, embarrassed. "We've just tucked our tails and given him a free hand. Adobe Wells is a town under siege. And there's not one damn thing we can do about it."

"The Johns resisted him." There was a hint of pride in Pilar's voice.

Mrs. Pridgen wrung her hands. "And considering what happened to Jeff, Stevie and Sandy are just courtin' disaster."

Heath took a sip of coffee. Sandy was obviously Stevie's father, the old man who had been shot. He hoped his wound was as superficial as it appeared; Sandy Johns would be needed to fight another day.

But who was Jeff? Stevie's husband? Heath remembered the Indian child who called Stevie "mother." Was the beautiful hoyden a wife and mother? He just had to ask, "Who is Jeff?"

"Stevie's brother. He disappeared a couple of months ago," Pilar explained. "Didn't I mention him earlier?"

"Judge Jack had him killed!" Pridgen interrupted with a divine pronouncement.

Ever the voice of caution, Mrs. Pridgen patted her husband's arm. "Now, Dad, we don't know that for sure."

Heath stared down at the table, deep in thought. He was

inclined to agree with Pridgen; Judge Jack was undoubtedly to blame for Jeff Johns's death.

And it appeared that he *had* taken this town hostage. But why? What did Adobe Wells have that the judge could want? Badly enough to kill for?

Well, that's what he was being paid to find out.

"Stevie's hot after Jeff's killer, but so far all she's done is rile the judge." Pilar penetrated Heath's thoughts.

"And shoot at strangers coming to town." He leaned forward in his chair, resting his elbows on the table, unaccountably angry. "It's just a matter of time before the little fool'll get herself killed! Can't anybody in this town control her?"

"Nobody can make Stevie do anything she doesn't want to."

Heath narrowed his eyes. He could have sworn that Pridgen had just offered him a challenge.

Averting his eyes, Pridgen unfolded his gnarled frame, picked up his cane, and limped from the room. "If I was twenty years younger, I'd show Jack—that no good son of a—" His muttering faded away.

Excusing himself, Heath strolled outside onto the veranda for a smoke. He was so tired, his nerves throbbed, yet he was energized in a strange way as well. It was probably the challenge of the new job.

The sun dipped slowly below the western horizon like the last few notes of a lover's concerto, casting hazy fingers of reddish purple to grip the darkened sky. A cool night breeze blew over his sun-bronzed face, infusing Heath with a false sense of peace. A cloud of blue smoke, tranquil as the atmosphere around him, hovered about his head.

Raucous noise from the saloons wafted to him, pianos, punctuated by the soft tinkle of female laughter and the rumble of rowdy men relaxing after a day's work. It was a familiar sound to Heath, one that drew him like a magnet. Tossing his cigar away, he stepped off the porch into the dark night.

He never even saw his assailant coming.

Six

Claws bared, Stevie launched herself at Heath's back.

"What the hell?" he yelled, hitting the ground, Stevie spread the length of him.

Gasping, he wrapped his arms around the writhing, growling termagant and rolled her onto her back. He held her tight against his chest, fighting to fill his starving lungs with air. Somehow, his sense of humor was intact. "If you wanted to finish what we started on the mesa, sweetheart, all you had to do was ask."

Enraged, she drew her arm to the side and slugged him.

"Damn you," he grunted. "Stop it. I don't want to hurt you."

"But I'm going to kill you, you son of a bitch."

"What is your problem, lady?"

She arched her back sharply in an attempt to dislodge him, slamming her lower body against his. The sensation was painful and pleasurable for them both.

"Oh, God." His voice was low and husky, evincing his burgeoning desire.

Feeling his male hardness against her belly and her responding hunger rise in a heated rush, her eyes widened. She grew inert beneath him, becoming still as a corpse. "Get off me!" she yelled, her voice thick.

Instinctively, he pressed his hips to hers, striving to ease the ache rapidly uncoiling in his groin. Her body, hot and stimulating, burned his yearning flesh through their clothes. He pressed hard against her belly. A moan of passion escaping his lips, he caressed her with his eyes.

Lord, she was exquisite; moon dust brushed her face, perfectly sculpted nose, slightly curved jaw, high, regal cheekbones, and dusky skin so smooth and soft that it might have been fashioned into shell-thin porcelain from melted caramel. Her tip-tilted black eyes were shaded by half-lowered lids. Mesmerizing. She was beauty personified, her head cushioned in a halo of platinum hair.

But it was her lips that held his gaze. Full, sensual lips, slightly parted, just begging to be kissed. Drawn like a moth to a flame, he bent his head. To his delight, she met him halfway. He kissed her lightly, then lifted his face until his mouth hovered just above hers. "I want you, precious," he breathed, exciting them both with his confession.

Groaning, he smothered her with his kiss. It was moist, easy, practiced, his lips soft and sensitive. Then he *really* kissed her. She opened her mouth with a small whimper. His tongue moved inside with strong, impelling strokes, caressing the inner walls of her mouth, familiarizing himself with the honeyed sweetness of her dark, velvet recesses.

The sweet throbbing of his lips made her shift closer to him. She clung to him, wanting the kiss to go on forever.

Time and space lost all relevance. Neither Heath nor Stevie was cognizant of anything outside the circle of their arms. They were a mass of raging passion. He slipped a muscled thigh between her legs and pressed against her warm flesh.

They were not driven by passion alone. It was as if they communicated on a spiritual plane, in a way that denied all reason, defied all logic. With the same mind they knew if they didn't become one physically, they would never be whole.

Suddenly, Stevie drew back, her startled gaze fixed, like a deer before it bolted. Acknowledging that she wanted this stranger frightened her as nothing else ever had. More than the danger Judge Jack posed, more than the prospect of losing her home. But not more than the threat of losing her father.

At the sudden thought of her father, she tensed. How could she lie beneath the man who shot Pa, her sensible self berated.

"Precious?"

She was uncertain whether he spoke or communicated the word from his mind to her own.

"Stevie?" Pilar's shocked voice stole the last vestiges of Stevie's smoldering passion. "Mr. Diamond, what do you think you're doing to that girl?"

Unfortunately, nothing, Heath complained silently. Levering himself up, he pulled Stevie to her feet. He bent at the waist and brushed grass off his immaculate trousers. It took great effort to hide his profound reaction to the events of the past few moments.

Pilar stood looking down at them, hands fisted, resting on her hips. "I demand an explanation," she continued imperiously.

It occurred to Heath that her outrage didn't quite ring true. He distinctly heard a note of pleased amusement in her thick accent.

"I assure you, *Señora* Manchez . . ." he began.

Having momentarily regained her composure, Stevie wheeled toward Heath. He turned toward her at the abrupt movement. Catching him by surprise, she swung her slender arm and slapped his face soundly.

"Stevie," Pilar gasped. "Why on earth did you do that?"

Ignoring Pilar, Stevie regarded Heath as if he were an insect under a piece of glass. "If I had my gun, I'd shoot him."

Heath rubbed his cheek, a bemused expression on his handsome face. Damn her beautiful hide. She had wanted him as much as he wanted her. That's probably what made her so mad, he decided. That, and unfulfilled desire.

"You sure shootin' me's what you want to do, darlin'?" He raked her with a suggestive glare and spoke so that she alone could hear him. "It felt like you had somethin' a site more pleasurable in mind a minute ago."

"Of course I want to shoot you," she began sweetly. "But first I'd like to stab you and peel your worthless hide, inch by torturous inch. Then I'll shoot you. Just before I hang you."

Heath chuckled.

By then, the Pridgens had joined Pilar, followed by the Dough twins and the disapproving Miss Smelter.

Stevie threw the spectators a heated glare collectively. Providing half of Adobe Wells with a night's entertainment was not her idea of fun.

Heath had no such qualms as he stepped closer to Stevie. "I thought you liked me?"

The twins almost fainted.

Stevie balled her hands into fists at her sides. "Like you? I loathe you. You tried to kill my pa."

Pilar sailed off the porch.

"What's this about Sandy?" Pridgen asked before Pilar could get the words out.

"This snake shot him," Stevie announced, pointing at Heath. "In the head and chest."

At that, all hell broke loose. Pilar begged Stevie for more information. Where is Sandy? How is he? Heath loudly proclaimed his innocence. He had shot no one. Stevie accused him of everything short of assassinating President Lincoln. Smelter shouted that she had known the stranger was no good from the first. The twins argued that Heath was being judged unfairly.

It took a thunderous blast to gain their attention. Standing in the front yard, Pridgen held a smoking gun. "That the peashooter he used to shoot Sandy?" He pointed to Heath's Colt.

Gasping for breath, she jerked a nod.

"Well, young fella, maybe you best give me that hog leg." He leveled his gun on Heath to add weight to his demand.

Cautiously, Heath made his way over to Pridgen, never taking his eyes off the gun that was trained on him, and handed his weapon over, pearl handle first.

Pridgen sniffed the barrel, then relaxed. "This gun ain't been fired recently, Stevie. I think you owe the dude an apology."

The Doughs beamed.

Miss Smelter threw them a glare.

Stevie jerked her chin stubbornly. She was not yet ready to admit a mistake.

"It's not necessary," Heath said quietly. "I'm sorry about your father, Miss Johns." He was upset with himself for not checking Sandy more closely. For failing to notice the man's second wound might have cost him his life. "I didn't know he'd been shot in the chest. I wouldn't have left you alone with him if I'd known."

His words were so sincere, so reassuring that Stevie felt small for her earlier accusations. Still, her only response was a slight nod.

Pilar, her eyes bright with tears, put a comforting arm around Stevie's shoulders. "Is he at Sully's?"

"Yes."

"Nellie, will you ask Cook to get Stevie something to eat while I check on Sandy?" Pilar tried valiantly to keep her voice steady. She patted Stevie's cheek in a motherly gesture. "Why don't you freshen up, then rest some after you eat, hon? You'll want to stay in town to be close to your father. We can share my room." Worry for Sandy sculpting her face, she turned away.

Miss Smelter pointed rudely at Stevie. "She's staying here?"

Heath felt Stevie stiffen at his side. He had never slapped a woman before, but his hands itched to wipe the supercilious smirk off Miss Smelter's pockmarked face. Absently, he wondered what there was about Stevie that the spinster objected to.

Stevie's cheeks flamed. She knew that the schoolteacher looked down on her because she was Indian. Well, she didn't care what the old bitch thought, never had. But she hated to be ridiculed in front of the gambler.

"Do you have a problem with that?" Pilar asked her boarder.

"She's an Indian," Miss Smelter hissed as if that incontrovertible fact should end the discussion.

Stevie winced as Heath stared at her intently. He was surprised to learn that she was Indian, but she read his reaction to Smelter's revelation differently.

"So?" Pilar broke through the tension cloaking the assemblage.

"Indians shouldn't reside with decent people."

"Miss Smelter, that's not very Christian of you," Bitsy intoned.

"Not very Christian of you at all," Itsy agreed.

If Heath hadn't been so enraged with the woman standing at their side, he would have kissed the portly sisters. He agreed with them wholeheartedly.

Miss Smelter drew herself up in a huff. "I will not remain in a home that houses savages."

"Good," retorted Pilar. "That'll leave plenty of room for

Stevie and her son. I suggest you leave immediately, Miss Smelter. And do not bother to return."

"I'll do just that." When she looked like she would say something further, Heath's glare sent her packing. Stevie's gaze was trained on the hazy outline of the mountains in the distance, so she missed the exchange between Heath and Miss Smelter.

"Honey, I'm sorry."

Stevie waved away Pilar's apology. She was used to the kind of treatment she had just received. Still, she wondered if it would always hurt. "I'll walk back to Sully's with you." She hoped her voice didn't sound as husky to the others as it did to her.

"Miss Johns, I'd like to have a word with you first. Then I'll escort you over to the doc's when you're ready." Heath's request was extremely respectful.

More respectful than she deserved, after all she had done and said to him since they met, Stevie allowed. The least she could do was hear him out. "Very well."

Her pa would be fine with Pilar. If Sandy woke up, it's likely that he would want to see Pilar anyway. Sandy Johns was a healthy man whose needs Pilar met on a regular basis. Even though Stevie pretended ignorance, she knew that the two were in love; more to the point, her father's two nights a week in town were spent in Pilar's bed. She wondered what the high-and-mighty Gertrude Smelter would think of that.

Smiling, she preceded Heath into the house.

Seven

"Damn flighty female!"

Heath had been cooling his heels in Pilar's parlor for an hour now, waiting for Miss Johns to finish freshening up and spare him a moment of her time. Surely a woman who dressed like a man could finish her toilette in less than an hour.

He waited another thirty minutes. Still, she failed to appear. He had expended all the curses he knew in English long ago. He was well into the long list of French oaths his year abroad had taught him.

Actually, when he analyzed it, he didn't know why her failure to show irritated him so. He only wanted to tell her that he was sorry about her father and that he thought Miss Smelter was an idiot. If things went well, he had planned to caution her about taking the law into her own hands.

But apparently she didn't want to hear anything he had to say. She probably would've shot him for his well-meaning advice at any cost. Shoving his hands through his hair, he cursed some more. He'd waited long enough for a hellion who was obviously not coming down.

Turning on his heel sharply, he made for the front door. He almost ran over Mrs. Pridgen.

"You goin' out, Mr. Diamond?" she asked, jumping back out of his way.

He clenched his jaw. "Yes, ma'am. Thought I would take a short walk before turning in."

"Would you mind taking this to Stevie?" She handed a boy's lightweight jacket to him. "She left in such a hurry she forgot it."

A muscle twitched in Heath's jaw though his expression remained perfectly pleasant. "I wasn't aware that Stevie had left the house. If you'll tell me where I can find her, I'll be glad to see that she gets it."

She'll get it! A piece of my mind, she'll get. How dare she just walk out and leave him waiting! Heath was entirely unused to being treated so shabbily by a woman. Actually no one—if you didn't count Rebels—had ever treated him with as little regard as that feisty, exasperating, irritating, infuriating tomboy.

Mrs. Pridgen was concerned at the high color in Heath's face. "Dear me. Are you unwell, Mr. Diamond?"

"I'm quite all right. Thank you for your concern, ma'am." Heath bowed chivalrously, placed his hat firmly on his head, grasped Stevie's coat in his white-knuckled fist, and after receiving directions to Dr. Sullivan's home, left the house. With every stride, his anger grew. Until he was in a rage.

Knowing it would be unwise to confront Stevie in his present frame of mind, he decided to have a drink first. If nothing else, the respite would allow his blood pressure to return to normal and his irritation with the blond Indian beauty to subside.

He preferred a nest of cold-blooded killers over an irascible woman any day. But he wasn't in town to deal with a woman—irascible or no. He was in Adobe Wells on government business.

Pushing through the batwings of the Silver Dollar Saloon, he became the efficient U.S. marshal he had been since the war. Tonight wouldn't be a complete waste if he could learn more about the infamous Judge Jack.

The Silver Dollar Saloon was in full swing. In addition to a bar and gambling tables in front, the back half of the establishment contained a dance hall where painted ladies displayed for a hungry clientele more than their good dispositions.

He spotted an empty table in the rear of the long, narrow room and made his way to it. Years of self-preservation had taught him to cover his back. He sat down, facing the door.

"What will you have, *Señor?*" the Mexican barkeep shouted

over the continual hum of voices, the rattle of dice, the swishing of cards, and the scraping of chairs.

"Whiskey." Heath's voice barely carried over the din.

The barkeep filled a shot glass and brought it to him. Heath tossed it off in a single gulp, savoring the burning liquid as it slid down his throat. It warmed him from the inside out. He tossed a gold piece on the table. "Now bring me a bottle of the good stuff." He would need more than Tabasco-flavored rotgut to restore his customary good humor.

"Sí, Señor."

Heath nursed his second drink slowly, studying every man in the room while appearing to lounge lazily in his chair. Some of his irritation oozed away, though he was still mentally alert.

He lowered his lids halfway, withdrawing a deck of cards from his frock coat pocket. With deft fingers he fanned them absently, restacked them, then fanned them again, with the sure, smooth movements of a professional gambler.

Suddenly, the batwings swung open with a bang, magically quieting the saloon. A distinguished middle-aged gentleman with blond hair flowing from under his black bowler entered the saloon, a sense of authority blatantly tangible in his stride. He was accompanied by two gunslicks and a Mexican bandito wearing artillery low on their hips.

Heath would bet half his father's fortune that he was looking at Judge Jack and his gun-slinging entourage. Jack was a big man with what some would call a handsome face. A pirate's patch covered his left eye, lending him an ominous air. He was dressed in a stark black suit, smartly accessorized by a gold chain running from one vest pocket to the other. A slight bulge suggested that the chain was attached to a watch fob, or a snub-nosed derringer.

The judge and his men ordered drinks at the bar, oblivious of Heath's presence. They drank and conversed in soft tones.

Heath was unable to make out their words. But he watched them closely, cataloguing their moves, demeanor, and weapons.

Knowing one's enemy was important to a lawman if he wanted to stay alive. This tried and true philosophy had saved him before, even when squaring off against men who were faster, more ruthless, but, thankfully, not as cautious and prepared as he.

One of the judge's men noticed Heath, the smallest, meanest-looking of the gunslicks. He finished his drink and slammed his glass down on the bar with more force than necessary. Drawing himself up in a transparent show of self-importance, he headed Heath's way. His hands were soft and white, undoubtedly unused to the labor of a workingman. Crow's-feet ringing his close-set, beady eyes falsely bespoke character. In keeping with the rest of him, his lips were thin, cruel.

Every haughty move he made was an obvious attempt to compensate for his small stature. Heath knew only too well that his kind could be deadly. He had often said that a calico could be more vicious than a mountain lion, if only to prove his prowess.

Miss Johns was living, breathing, spitting, hissing proof of that. Dismissing the thought, he braced himself for the upcoming confrontation. Preoccupation with desirable women had been the downfall of more than one western male. Heath enjoyed staying alive too much to fall into that trap.

"I'm Henry Sims and I represent Judge Elias Colt Jack," the gunman announced smugly when he reached Heath's table.

"How nice for you." Heath nodded cordially. His words were mockingly insincere.

The answer brought a scowl to Sims's face. "You wanta tell me what brought you to Adobe Wells?"

Heath almost said "My horse," but he didn't think Sims would appreciate his cowboy humor. "Not particularly." His tone was silky and deceptively friendly.

Sims was taken aback. He had hoped to get a rise out of the fancily dressed newcomer. "Judge Jack don't take kindly to strangers comin' to town without checkin' with him first. So either tell me what your business is. Or move on. Now!"

The judge walked up to Heath's table and stood with Sims, arms akimbo, feet firmly planted. His remaining companions took their places on either side of him, like large, disreputable bookends. One was a corpulent man with unkempt black hair. The other was a squatty Mexican wearing a large embroidered sombrero. Twin bandoleers crisscrossed over his chest. His mendacious grin was topped by the largest and ugliest mustache Heath had ever seen. It was a foot long if it was an inch.

"Most folks stand up in Judge Jack's company," Sims spat out.

Heath took another sip of his drink, his charming smile still firmly in place. "Guess I'm not most folks."

Sims's face mottled with fury. He moved his hand closer to his gun. "Get up, damn you, or I'll blow a hole in you big enough to drive a train through."

Without taking his eyes off Judge Jack, Heath retorted in a not-unpleasant whisper, "You're welcome to try, friend. You won't be the first." Slowly, almost lazily, Heath rose to his feet, slanting his eyes at the brigand. "And I promise that you won't be the last."

The hair rose on the back of Sims's neck. He threw Judge Jack an imploring look, a look that shouted, "Get me out of this."

The judge nodded almost imperceptibly. His smile didn't reach his cold, fathomless eyes. "I don't think there's any need for violence, gentlemen." He dismissed his entourage and turned back to Heath. "If I may have a word with you?"

"Certainly." Heath dropped into his seat again and pushed an empty chair out from the table with the toe of his boot.

In the time it took Jack to take his seat, Heath decided that he would have to investigate this lawless band from outside. A more disreputable hoard of cutthroats he had never seen. He could never infiltrate a gang that consisted of scum like Sims and company. He would stand out like a sore thumb; he was, after all, human. He wasn't so certain about them.

Ignorant of Heath's unflattering assessment, Judge Jack sat down. "I appreciate the opportunity to speak with you . . ." he began.

He had noticed the look of steel in Heath's eyes when he had faced Sims down. He could use a man like that. All he needed to learn was his price. Everyone had a price was Jack's unspoken philosophy.

Heath shocked Judge Jack by speaking first. "Were you or any of your men out at Sandy Johns's spread today?"

Judge Jack stiffened straight as a ramrod. His gaze sought

Heath's. He wondered if the gambler was as tough as he acted, or if he was just tired of living.

He would not have the opportunity to question him on the matter, however. And Heath would never learn the answer to the taunting question he presented to the judge. For Stevie Johns chose that moment to burst through the batwings, a curse on her lips, the fires of hell burning in her eyes. This time, at least, she wasn't after Heath.

"I've been looking for you, you no good, lying son of a bitch," she snarled at Judge Jack, crossing the saloon floor like a whirling dervish.

"What the hell?" Judge Jack bellowed, jumping up, overturning his chair.

"I'll kill her myself," Heath muttered beneath his breath, keeping track of the judge's entourage as they rushed to their boss's side. "If they don't do it for me."

"Miss Johns." Having regained his composure, Judge Jack bowed elegantly. "What brings you to my saloon this time of night?"

Heath groaned. Attacking the judge was one thing, doing it in his own den was something else altogether. One was foolhardy, the other suicide. The girl had no more sense than a bessy bug rolling ten pounds of dung up a hill.

The scene that followed was like something out of a Wild West show—vicious outlaws squaring off against a virginal young girl protecting hearth and home. Naturally, Heath painted himself in the picture as the invincible hero.

But the threatening look in the naive heroine's eyes didn't fit the picture. When she swung her gaze to the sign over the bar reading INDIANS NOT ALLOWED, her expression grew absolutely vicious. She raised her gun, centering Judge Jack in her sights.

Her hand was steady, her nerves rock solid. It would be so easy to pull the trigger, to kill the murderous snake responsible for the ambush on her pa. She wanted to so damn much, she could taste it.

When the judge went unnaturally pale, Heath silently applauded Stevie's courage in the face of overwhelming odds. He hoped to hell she would be satisfied with scaring the man and leave it at that.

Just then another of the judge's men circled around behind Stevie with his gun in hand. Heath went as pale as the judge. He had to neutralize the situation—now.

Gambler that he was, he decided to bluff their way out. "Well, sugar, if you wanted me, all you had to do was send for me." He skirted Judge Jack and his men, hurrying to Stevie's side, wrapping his arms around her securely.

"Let go of me." She squirmed against him.

He cut her off with a passionate kiss, the likes of which had every red-blooded male in the saloon hooting and clapping. She writhed in his embrace, struggling to get her knee in position to do him mortal damage. "Oh, no, you don't," he growled against her lips.

Stilling her legs by cradling them with his thighs, he renewed his assault. He kissed her breathless. When they came up for air, she was no longer in possession of her thoughts, nor was she in possession of her gun. It was tucked in the waistband of Heath's trousers, reminiscent of their confrontation at Mustang Mesa.

She was momentarily stunned by his passionate ministrations, then a hot flow of color flooded her face. "You bastard"—she hissed—"I knew you were in cahoots with him. Give me back my gun."

Heath pushed her face into his neck, trying unsuccessfully to muffle her threats. "Whatrya gonna do?" He shrugged at their audience, looking quite put upon. "Women. Can't live with 'em and can't live without 'em."

"I'm going to blow both of you to hell," she vowed against his bare neck.

When she bit him dangerously close to his jugular vein, Heath decided it was time to get her out of there. Women had bitten him in moments of passion, but this was ridiculous, he mused wryly, hefting her up on his shoulder, one arm across her hips, one over her thrashing legs. "Good night, Judge. I'm certain we'll meet again." He sketched an awkward bow, almost dropping Stevie in the process. A wide hand to her derriere, he pushed her back into place.

The jacket he was supposed to be bringing to her forgotten on the back of his chair, he made his way across the saloon. The hard-drinking patrons' bawdy suggestions of how he could tame his lovely bundle blended with Stevie's shrieks of outrage. Most of the suggestions were quite risqué. In fact, Heath thought some of them bore further exploration, but he was fairly certain Stevie wasn't interested at the moment.

She beat his back with her fists. His muscles were considerably harder than her delicate fists. "Oww," she cried, rubbing her stinging hands.

"Well, behave yourself and you won't get hurt," he spoke as if to a child.

He carried her all the way to Pilar's, but he didn't enter the house. Instead, he took her to the shed he had used earlier as a bathhouse. Kicking the door open with a booted foot, he entered the dim interior.

"Let me down, you, you—" She was so angry, she couldn't think of anything bad enough to call him.

"You want down?"

She failed to recognize the cold rage in his deceptively soft words. "Yes, you stinkin' pile of horse manure. I want down!"

"All right, I'll put you down." He elbowed the door shut behind them, crossed over to the table, and lit a short taper. The tub he had used earlier was still filled with cold water, the surface clouded with a gray layer of soap scum.

"What are you doing?" Bracing her flat palms on the middle of his back, she tried to rise up and peer around his yard-wide shoulders, with no success. "I said put me down!"

"Delighted." With a quick flip of his forearms he tossed her into the water, then jumped out of the way lest a surging wave splash over his freshly polished boots.

She went underwater with a whoosh and shot out like a cannon. Knee deep in his bathwater, she exhausted her supply of English oaths and Comanche threats. The People didn't curse, but as Heath knew all too well, Stevie did.

Advancing on her, he wrapped his hands around her upper arms and shook her like a dog would a rabbit. "You little fool!"

He glared down at her and tried valiantly to ignore the soaking white shirt adhered to her bare breasts. It was a losing proposition. He stared shamefully, expecting steam to rise off her chest from the heat of his gaze. The spitfire wasn't wearing anything under her blouse. Never in his misspent youth had he known a lady who didn't wear underwear. But then, he had never known a lady like the one before him—the one who had almost gotten them both murdered, he reminded himself.

With a strength of will he hadn't known he possessed, he lifted his gaze to her snapping eyes. "Are you trying to get yourself killed? 'Cause if you are, I'll give you your gun back and you can shoot yourself now. I'll watch." He released her as if her arms were firebrands. "It should be interesting," he raved, pacing in front of her, careful not to look at the seductive picture she presented. "I've never seen a suicide before. Really. I think it might be quite an experience." He jerked her gun from his waistband and thrust it into her hands. "Go ahead. Put the barrel to your head and pull the trigger. Blow your brains out."

She regarded him as if he had taken leave of his senses. "I wouldn't do that."

"Why not? It would be no more foolhardy than taking Judge Jack on. You'd be dead either way. At least if you committed suicide, there would be no doubt who was to blame. I mean, it would be one killing in town you wouldn't blame me for. 'Course you wouldn't be around to blame anybody. Would you?"

"Why do you care what I do?"

Heath ceased his pacing. He stood there, tall and enraged, his sapphire eyes dark as thunderclouds. Rancor sharpened his voice. "Because, Miss Johns, you very nearly got both of us killed in there."

"I didn't ask for your help. And I was doing just fine without you."

"If you believe that, you're even dumber than I think you are."

She flinched as if she had received a physical blow, feeling suddenly embarrassed in the face of his repudiation.

Her wounded look took him off guard. He had to get away from this girl. In less than twenty-four hours she had him turned inside out, wanting to bay at the moon, whip her firm little fanny, then kiss her senseless.

He spoke in a low voice, taut with control. "You're right about one thing, Miss Johns. Your affairs are none of my concern." He looked at her intensely, then turned on his heel and strode out the door.

"Well, what the hell got into him?" she wondered.

Eight

Both challenged and aggravated by his encounter with Stevie, Heath headed for the nearest saloon, the Golden Nugget. He slipped into a chair beside the window, in clear view of the street outside.

His brows drawn together in an angry scowl, he watched for the irritating Miss Johns. Shortly after he was served his second drink, he saw her pass down the street—dryer and more subdued, yet even more beautiful than when he'd last seen her. She made her way to Dr. Sullivan's house. Though he was loath to admit it, that was what he had been waiting for.

He marveled that this tomboyish child-woman who wanted his gizzard for supper had the uncanny ability to captivate his interest when he should be thinking of nothing but his job. If he hoped to remain among the living and retain his unblemished reputation as a lawman, he had better get hold of himself, he scolded vehemently, tossing off a shot of whiskey.

Try as he might, he couldn't dismiss her from his mind, nor could he extinguish the fire she set in his loins, not with all the whiskey in Adobe Wells.

He was truly bewildered by his fascination with her and even more so by her resistance to him. He and all the Turner men had a way with women. Everyone said so, he thought defensively.

Chap's wife, Kinsey—the infamous Rebel spy known as the Vixen in Gray during the war—said it was in their genes. They passed their unprecedented success with women from generation to generation. She said it was their cross to bear, much to their chosen ladies' delight.

So why didn't Stevie Johns recognize this incontrovertible fact of nature and behave like other women? Why wasn't she as attracted to him as he was to her? Perhaps it was her resistance to him that had him obsessed. A wry, bemused glint appeared in his eye. Heath Turner, obsessed with a woman? He was usually the object of obsession, not the one obsessed. Of course, Stevie was not an average woman.

She brought out the worst in him. Given a chance, she might bring out the best.

One fact was certain—nothing he said or did around her was true to his nature. Groaning silently, he recalled dumping her into a tub of icy water. Harrington Heath Turner—a sophisticated northern gentleman, a charming man-about-town who had never even raised his voice to a member of the fairer sex let alone thrown one across his shoulder like a sack of feed and carried her out of a saloon—had behaved like a beast. Still, one didn't usually encounter gently reared ladies in saloons, he weakly justified his heinous actions.

Rising out of his chair like an explosive, he uttered, "To hell with it."

A flash of silver outside the window caught his eye. The prickling sense of impending danger raised short hairs on the back of his neck. Growing unnaturally calm, his breathing slow and shallow, his heartbeat swift but steady, he approached the barkeep. "Is there a back way out of here?"

"Sí, Señor." He pointed to Heath's left with a damp towel. "Through the storeroom in the back."

"Thanks." Flipping the barkeep a four-bit piece, Heath made his way through the storeroom, stepping into the night. The barren alley smelled of dirt and decay. Twinkling stars illumined the velvet sky overhead as he stood silent, still, allowing his eyes to adjust to the relative darkness.

Approaching the side of the building he saw a man standing in the shadows, watching the front entrance of the saloon. His long-blade knife was poised to do some unsuspecting soul mortal harm. Heath recognized him as one of Judge Jack's men, the brigand who had tried to sneak up on Stevie.

Quietly, Heath moved up behind him and locked an arm around his neck, effectively cutting off his air supply. The man put up a fierce struggle, but he was no match for Heath's strength. When he lost consciousness, Heath pulled him deeper into the alley, tied him securely with a length of rawhide, and gagged him with the silk scarf he wore around his neck.

Moving on silent feet, he checked the other side of the building and found another man crouching in the shadows. Heath leaned slightly away from the wall. Glancing across the street, he saw Judge Jack perched on a bench in front of the Silver Dollar, surrounded by his hoard of cutthroats. He had a front-row seat to witness Heath's ambush.

"Sorry to disappoint you, old man," Heath uttered.

He returned to the saloon through the back door. Retrieving the bottle from his table, he pushed through the batwings and turned right, heading in the direction of Dr. Sullivan's office. When he approached the edge of the building, the man waiting in the shadows jumped out, swinging his knife in an arc toward Heath's throat.

Before the knife found its mark, Heath smashed the bottle against the side of his assailant's head. The shattering glass reduced the man's face to a bloody pulp. He sank to the boardwalk, lying unconscious in a pool of his own blood.

Looking pointedly in the judge's direction, Heath saw that Jack was now standing. Sims and the Mexican were shaking their fists. They were content, however, to remain where they were, safe at the judge's side.

Heath's eyes sought the judge's. In a battle of will, Judge Jack was the first to look away. Heath suppressed the urge to preen.

Tonight, at least, he had won the battle. But the war had just begun, a war that would be waged in the little kingdom Judge Jack had erected for himself. Undoubtedly, there would be bloodshed, perhaps even Heath's.

Oh, well, that's what the United States government paid him for.

Tipping his hat to Judge Jack and his men, he turned his

back on them, inordinately vulnerable, blatantly unafraid. This simple act of bravado impressed and intimidated them as little else could. Bold as brass, he sauntered down the street. Adding insult to injury, he threw back his head and whistled an airy tune.

His feet seemed to have a mind of their own as they followed the invisible path Stevie had taken through town. He didn't question his motives for following her. In fact, he concentrated on the stars overhead so he wouldn't think of her at all.

Goose bumps covered Stevie's skin like snow dusting the open plains. She had the distinct feeling that she was being watched.

"Is it too cool in here?" Sully asked.

"Feels fine to me," Pilar murmured from her chair beside Sandy's bed.

"Guess it's just me." Stevie chafed her skin to warm herself. She must have caught a chill when that horrible man threw her in the tub. Which was just one more reason for her to hate him. So, if she hated him so much, why did she keep wondering where he was? More to the point, why did she keep wondering what he was doing and with whom he was doing it?

As if it mattered to her . . .

Pilar noted the strained look on Stevie's lovely visage. "Stevie, you're done in. If you don't get some rest, you'll make yourself sick. Why don't you run back to the house and get a few hours sleep? Sully and I will be here with Sandy. We'll call you if there's any change."

Stevie shook her head no. Still feeling odd, she stared out the window quietly.

Pilar used her most effective argument to get Stevie to do what was best for her. "Don't you think Winter would sleep better at my place?"

Stevie glanced at the sleeping child. Sighing, she nodded. Pilar was right; Winter would rest better snugly tucked in bed at the boardinghouse. And she needed to let Sweetums in the house for the night. "You promise you'll come for me if there's any change?"

"Promise," Pilar said.

Gently, Stevie lifted Winter into her arms. At the door she whispered, "I won't be long."

"Take your time, lass," said Sully.

After checking his horse at the livery, Heath made his way back to the boardinghouse. Pridgen was sitting at the portal, a bottle of whiskey resting on a small table next to his chair.

"Heard you disabled two of Judge Jack's men outside the Golden Nugget."

Heath never ceased to be amazed at how fast news traveled in small western towns. "Guess you could say that."

"Was it that bastard Sims?"

"I didn't have time for a formal introduction, but no, it wasn't Sims." Heath sat down beside Pridgen. He leaned his chair back on two legs and propped his feet on the railing of the portal. "Sims, a fat guy, and a Mexican watched the show with Judge Jack from across the street."

"Damn cowards!" The old man poured two fingers of whiskey into a glass and pushed it toward Heath. "The fat man is Bear Jacobson. He got his name by killing a bear when he was just a boy. Looks like he would move with the speed of thick molasses in January. But don't let his appearance fool you; he's fast as lightning. The Mexican is Carlos Garcia, one of the most ruthless gunslingers I've ever known. He always has that damn grin on his face." Pridgen shivered involuntarily. "Turns my blood cold."

Heath cast him a quizzical glance. The old codger sounded almost civil. Where was the irate citizen who had challenged him at the dinner table? he wondered.

Pridgen had obviously drunk a great deal of whiskey and was in a talkative mood. Any other time Heath would have seized the opportunity, interrogated him carefully, compiling information that might help him with his case. But he was so damn weary. Silently, he declared that he was off duty for the remainder of the night.

He removed his hat and leaned his head against the wall. Every muscle in his body relaxed, Heath's mind wandered. Pridgen's soft chatter lulled him into a state of half wakefulness.

"I've taught school in this wilderness for twenty years," Pridgen said. "Tried to make my mark in this godforsaken country, to do something worthwhile. Taught homesteaders, ranchers, and Indians side by side. I'm retired now, too old to do any more. Nellie, bless her heart, and I want to live our remaining years in peace and quiet. We thought Adobe Wells was the place for that." Pridgen sighed heavily, sloshing himself another drink.

A bullfrog croaked down by the creek. A host of crickets and tree toads began a discordant chorus. An owl hooted from a clump of cottonwoods, perhaps expecting a call in return. The old codger and the young lawman listened to the night creatures together, in companionable silence.

With words slightly slurred from emotion and drink, Pridgen's voice was as warm and smooth as the whiskey sliding down his throat. "Since Judge Jack has taken over, he's turned this town upside down. He brought in those rough miners. They're digging up everything for twenty miles. God only knows what they're looking for. They have little regard for human life, and the gunmen who trail around after the judge have no regard for it at all. Damn if a body knows what to expect next." He said this last softly, as if to himself.

Heath placed all four legs of his chair on the floor. Bending over, he rested his forearms on his thighs. "I'm curious about the miners." He slanted his head toward Pridgen. The abrupt movement and drinking more than he should caused his head to spin. He saw two Pridgens; he addressed the one on the right. "I didn't know there was anything in this area worth digging for."

"Isn't."

"So what are they doing here?"

Pridgen hesitated briefly, then erupted like a Fourth of July pyrotechnic display. Grabbing his cane, he waved it around in a wild gesture, barely missing Heath's head. "That's it!" He shook the deadly scrap of wood in Heath's face. "That's why he took over Sandy's place. So's he could get to his caves."

Pridgen looked at Heath as if he should stand and salute his brilliant deduction. "Don't you see? There's something valuable in Sandy's caves, and Judge Jack knows it. That's probably why he came to Adobe Wells in the first place. It was Sandy's place he wanted all along. But Sandy wouldn't sell. The only way for Judge Jack to get the Rocking J was to run Sandy off—or kill him."

It occurred to Heath that this was unusually clear reasoning for a man as well into his cups as Pridgen. But then, what did he know? He was half drunk himself.

As if to celebrate, Pridgen poured another round of whiskey. Heath groaned, just what they needed.

As drunks were wont to do, Pridgen changed the subject abruptly. "So you were gonna talk Stevie outta shootin' the judge." Pridgen laughed until he lost his breath, choked, and coughed. "She's a hellcat, that one. Whooee!"

His amusement disappeared like the sunlight at dusk. "But what's one girl in the face of so many? And a Comanche at that?" He jerked his head toward Heath, pinning him with a bleary glare. "Not that bein' Indian makes one whit of difference to me."

He was silent for so long, Heath thought he had fallen asleep—or more likely, passed out.

In the darkness, Pridgen's eyes took on a wistful look. He peered off in the distance, not seeing the black outline of the mountains, but the distant past. "Swan, that was Stevie's ma. She was a pretty little thing when Sandy found her out on the range. Half starved, more dead than alive. Never did know why she was by herself, why her own kind deserted her. Frankly, I never asked. Sandy loved her so much, nothing else mattered. And he said she was the best damn wife a man ever had."

His gaze hardened. "But some of the townsfolk didn't see it that way. They wouldn't accept her, God-fearin' souls that they were. They all but tortured that gentle soul. Just like that hard-hearted Miss Smelter did to Stevie tonight."

"I'd like to slap that woman's ugly face." Heath's sentiment was decidedly ungentlemanly. But he was racked with righteous indignation on Stevie's behalf, and just drunk enough to want to take on the whole world for the fair damsel in question.

It was a good thing Stevie wasn't around. He would make a fool of himself good and proper otherwise. Hopefully, by tomorrow he would be sober and out of the notion of fighting her battles for her.

It was also fortuitous that he didn't know Stevie was standing just inside the front door, listening to every word he and Pridgen were saying.

"Lord knows, they never were fair to Jeff," Pridgen droned on. "They don't give a tinker's damn that he might be dead at the judge's hand."

The oath Pridgen hissed shocked Heath. Stevie was suitably impressed.

"If she's not stopped, Stevie'll take it on herself to find the killer. And I'm afraid they'll kill her just like they killed her brother."

If they killed her brother, Heath added silently. "She sure knows how to use a gun."

This drew a pleased smile from the eavesdropping girl.

"And I don't think I ever saw a woman, or a man, better with a knife."

She was fairly beaming now.

"But she doesn't stand a chance in hell against hired gun-slingers," Heath declared, trying to focus on Pridgen's fuzzy image. "Why doesn't your sheriff handle these gunmen?"

Stevie suppressed a derisive snort.

"Reno's a good kid, but he's too young and inexperienced to handle a man like Judge Jack. He keeps a room here at Pilar's. But he spends most of his time fishing and drinking. He's scared shitless of Sims and Garcia." Those were Pridgen's last words before he slumped back in his chair in a drunken stupor.

"Damn!" Heath rose. After several near misses, he hefted his unlikely drinking buddy and threw him over his shoulder.

When Stevie heard his movements, she deserted her position and scampered up the stairs.

Below, Heath berated himself. This town and its inhabitants had unsettled him. If he didn't watch himself, he would break his cardinal rule: Never become personally involved while working on a case.

He couldn't afford to care about the people in Adobe Wells; he wouldn't be very effective if he did.

But he feared it might already be too late. Thoughts of the pint-sized hellion who heated his blood more than all the courtesans of Paris teased his mind. His traitorous body responded predictably. Surprised at the strength of his urge, he leaned his forehead against the wall beside the front door. Pridgen rode his shoulder, snoring loudly.

A cool night breeze soughed through the leaves of the trees. Somewhere deep in the forest a coyote gave a mournful howl. Puddles of liquid silver dotted Pilar's green velvet lawn. Soothed by the blanket of nature, Heath straightened and pushed through the door.

Heath left Pridgen sleeping comfortably on the sofa in the parlor. Climbing stairs that seemed never to end, he put one leaded foot in front of the other. He couldn't remember the last time he'd been this weary. Just two more stair steps, down the hall, through the door, and he could fall into bed. He wouldn't even bother to remove his clothes. He didn't have the strength or the presence of mind.

When he stepped onto the landing, the sight before his eyes sobered him. Lying in the middle of the dimly lit hall, just outside his room, was the most vicious-looking wolf he had ever seen. Its yellow eyes shot threatening beams in Heath's direction. In a blur, he palmed his gun and cocked the weapon. The wolf growled low, threatening.

Stevie opened the door to her room. She took in the scene with a sweeping glance.

Heath was crouched low, gun raised. "Get back."

For what seemed an eternity to him, Stevie stood silent. If he didn't know better, he would think she was trying to suppress a smile. Maybe she laughed when she was frightened. He had known people who did.

"Just step back slowly and close your door, hon," he whispered. "I won't let him hurt you."

"Sweetums."

Stevie's affectionate tone startled Heath. "What?"

Smiling, she stepped back, allowed the wolf to cross the threshold into her room, and closed the door in Heath's face.

He straightened and leathered his gun. For a moment he had thought she meant the endearing term for him. Instead, she was speaking to a wild beast.

"Why am I not surprised?"

Nine

The next morning Heath awoke later than usual.

During his first few moments of half wakefulness, he marveled that he awakened at all. His alcohol-swollen brain was bursting. His head felt as if he had cradled it on jagged rocks all night.

Certain he could feel his hair growing, he struggled to a sit. Nausea rolled over him in thirty-foot waves. He drew deep breaths into his lungs until the room stopped spinning, then gingerly, he slipped out of bed. He dressed in a gray haze, holding on to the chifforobe to remain upright.

As he descended the stairs slowly, he cursed his overindulgence. If he lived through this hangover, he would never touch a drop of whiskey again. Each torturous step he took meted out his just punishment.

He sincerely hoped the wolf wasn't about this morning. And he didn't think he could face the tittering Doughs either, sweet as they were. When he reached the kitchen, he found Pilar standing at the sink, elbow deep in the breakfast dishes. "Morning," he croaked.

"Buenos días, Señor Diamond." She turned, wiping her hands on her apron. *"Madre Dios!* Your eyes are red. They look terrible."

"You should see them from this side," he groaned, sounding as though he had been guzzling gravel.

He took a seat across from a middle-aged gentleman. As far

as he remembered, the man wasn't one of Pilar's regulars. But the disapproving way he was regarding Heath's bloodshot eyes didn't sit well. If he had been able to summon the energy, he would have glared in the man's direction. As it was, he shot him a bleary grimace.

"You'll feel better after you eat." Pilar patted Heath's shoulder as she placed a dish of tortillas and beans before him.

Swallowing, he pushed the plate away. "Just coffee. My stomach's a little chancy this morning."

Pilar nodded understanding. The man glaring at Heath cleared his throat forcefully. Pilar spoke softly, mindful of Heath's headache. "Where are my manners? *Señor* Diamond, this is the Reverend Jenkins Black. Pastor of the community church."

Heath raised his gaze to the reverend. Black was a tall man with a bulbous red nose and a face creased with deep wrinkles. He wore a coal-black suit and tie, blinding white shirt, and god-awful yellow waistcoat—the same color as Sweetums's eyes. His graying hair, slicked back with macassar oil, hung long, dripping onto his collar. Heath disliked and distrusted the man on sight.

"*Señora* Pilar tells me you're a gambler."

Heath nodded.

The reverend didn't bother to hide his disapproval. He screwed his face up as if he smelled something vile. "Will you be here on the Sabbath, Mr. Diamond? I have a very strong sermon against the evils of gambling."

Heath made no comment. He pressed his temples between his thumb and middle finger. Just what he needed, a Bible thumper. And he thought yesterday was bad. . . .

Black was insulted by Heath's refusal to answer a direct question. He went on the offensive. "I was just informing *Señora* Pilar about your violent activity outside the Silver Dollar last night."

Heath contemplated the steam rising off his coffee, paying the pious old bird no mind.

"And the fact that you have somewhat of a reputation. You did, I believe, kill Barnes Elder." Black paused for Heath's reaction to his accusation.

Still, Heath remained silent.

Pilar flashed Heath an apologetic look. He smiled slightly.

Stevie Johns stood just out of sight, listening to Reverend Black's harangue with mounting interest. It occurred to her that she was turning into a regular snoop. Oh, well, half-breed spinsters get their pleasures how they may. She shrugged the uncomfortable thought away, listening more closely.

"Violence is not the answer to all of life's difficulties, young man. Sometimes we feel we should take the law into our own hands and strike back against men like Judge Jack. But we must remember, vengeance belongeth to the Lord."

Black crossed his arms over his chest.

As he sipped his coffee, Heath imagined tucking a lily into Black's folded arms, knocking him on his tail, dumping him into a coffin. . . .

The reverend's face grew mottled at Heath's lack of verbal response. He spoke through clenched teeth. "Years ago, when my wife was taken from me, God rest her soul, I felt an urge to punish the men who killed her. Through prayer and fasting I humbled myself before God and was able to forgive my adversaries. Someday the Lord will punish them for what they did. But that will be His doing, not mine."

Heath rose and sauntered over to the stove, pouring himself a refill.

Pilar threw a glance in his direction, then bounced it back to the preacher. In the doorway Stevie bit back a chuckle.

The reverend puffed up with righteous indignation. As if a string from the ceiling were attached to the top of his head, he rose straight up, anger emanating from his rigid body. He pointed an accusing finger at Heath. "You, young man, are a violent, hungover reprobate!"

Slowly, Heath turned. His face carefully blank, his body deceptively relaxed, he responded in a low voice, "You, Reverend Black, are right."

Preacher Black gasped, then with as much dignity as he could muster, the irate clergyman quit the room.

Heath and Pilar's chuckles followed him out the door.

* * *

"Where is he?"

Pilar grabbed her throat. "Stevie, you scared me out of ten years of my life."

Leaning against the pie safe in Pilar's dining room, Stevie looked like she had spent a month on the trail. Her braids were half unraveled, her plaid shirt wrinkled as a dog's tail, her wide, intelligent eyes were dulled, evincing her lack of sleep and worry for her father's health. Winter clutched her shirttail in a brown fist, Sweetums stood licking the child's dusty, bare feet.

"Well?"

"Well what?"

"Where is he?"

"Who?"

"The dude."

"If you mean *Señor* Diamond, he's up in his room."

"Sleepin' it off," she muttered. Dropping her gaze to her son, her tone gentled. "Winter, would you take Sweetums outside to play?"

The child nodded and ran from the room. The wolf nipped at his heels.

Stevie pivoted and headed purposefully toward the staircase.

Pilar raced behind her, catching her by the elbow on the second step from the bottom. "What are you up to?"

"I'm gonna hire me a gunman."

It took Pilar a moment to catch on to what Stevie intended, another moment for the shock to subside. "*Señor* Diamond?"

"Do you know any other gunslicks in town? Who aren't on the judge's payroll, that is?"

"He isn't a gunman. And you couldn't hire him if he were. Sandy would lock you in the corn crib for even suggesting such an irresponsible, not to mention illegal thing as hiring a man to commit murder for you."

"Well, Pa isn't exactly in a position to argue with me," Stevie said dryly. "And we both know that Judge Jack put him in that condition."

Pilar raised an imperious brow. "Are you sure, Stevie? Yesterday you accused *Señor* Diamond of shooting Sandy."

Stevie winced. She had been wrong about the gambler, she allowed. But she wasn't wrong about Judge Jack.

When she said as much to Pilar, the older woman pulled her into the parlor. Seating her on the brushed velvet settee fronting the fireplace, she tried to reason with Stevie. "It would be all right to ask *Señor* Diamond to look into your problems. But not to do murder."

"It wouldn't be murder."

"I won't debate that with you."

Sighing heavily, Stevie conceded. "All right. You think he'll check around if I ask him?" She fingered the locket around her neck. "I don't think he likes me very much."

It always amazed Pilar how naive Stevie was, how unaware she was of her effect on men. She simply had no idea how lovely she was. Once when Pilar had tried to point this out to her, she said that most white men wanted only her body, that they thought she was just another Indian slut.

Pilar knew nothing could be further from the truth. There were many men in Adobe Wells—young, handsome, up-and-coming ranchers—who would have been proud to call Stevie their wife. But Stevie wouldn't believe it. She had a blind spot where white men were concerned. And the tragedy of it all was that it might well rob her of any future happiness.

A surge of motherly love washed over Pilar. She reached over and gently wiped a smudge of dirt off Stevie's cheek. Cradling her chin, she said softy, "I think if you comb your hair and wash your face, you can persuade him." She smiled, mischief twinkling in eyes as dark and lovely as Stevie's. "If you put on a dress, you could probably convince him to do just about anything."

"Not you too?" Stevie scoffed. "I don't even own a dress, as you well know." She paused, frowning. "S'pose I could wash my face though."

"Well, don't get carried away." Pilar teased, patting Stevie's cheek. "We wouldn't want him to think you're running after him."

Ten

Stevie decided to have money in hand, just in case Pilar was wrong and Lucky Diamond's gun was for hire.

The sun was high overhead as she pushed through the door to the Adobe Wells Bank, where her pa kept his rapidly dwindling bank account. Having helped Sandy with his bookkeeping, she knew they had five hundred thirty-two dollars and seventy-three cents in their account. Five hundred, her father insisted, was for her dowry. The remaining thirty-two dollars and seventy-three cents was earmarked for running the Rocking J.

If Stevie had a nickel for every time she told Sandy she wouldn't need a dowry, they would own the Adobe Wells Bank. But her pa was as stubborn as his daughter. No matter what she said to the contrary or how many times she said it—he insisted the five hundred dollars belonged to her.

Well, today she would avail herself of it. Lifting her head high, she strode past the gawking patrons, stepped up to a teller's cage, slapped her short black gloves against her palm to gain the fastidious banker's attention, and informed him that she wished to withdraw five hundred dollars from her father's account.

"I'm sorry, Miss Johns. But I must have your father's authorization to release such a large sum."

"Somebody bushwhacked my pa yesterday. And he ain't in much shape to be authorizin' nothin'. I'm the head of the Rocking J now. And I need five hundred dollars." She took a small step backward, placing her hand on the gun riding her slim hips for emphasis.

The teller gulped, reddened, but held his ground. "I'm sorry, Miss Johns. But I cannot release the funds."

A peg-legged rowdy leaning in the corner had been watching the transaction with interest. He hobbled up to the cage, palmed his gun, shoved it against the teller's left nostril, and growled, "Give the little lady her money."

"Whatever you say," was the banker's nasal reply. With trembling hands he counted out five hundred dollars. Instead of handing the money to Stevie, however, he thrust it at her unlikely knight in dusty buckskins.

Leathering his gun, he accepted the funds on Stevie's behalf, presented it to her with a flourish, and bowed at the waist.

"Thanks, mister," Stevie murmured. She squared her slender shoulders and addressed the teller again. "Please deduct that amount from my father's account."

"Yes, Miss Johns."

The sound of a booted foot, alternating with the dull thud of a wooden peg, faded away. Stevie stuffed her money into a beaded bag and rushed outside. But Peg-Leg Smith had disappeared.

Pilar led Heath into the kitchen, where Stevie awaited him. Even though the weight of the money in her reticule was reassuring, Stevie was as nervous as a cat. Just being in the same room with the gambler unnerved her.

At first she refused to look at him. When she did, she wished that she hadn't. The word that came to mind was *beautiful.* But how could a man so masculine, so physically overpowering, be beautiful? If Preacher Black could be believed, Lucky Diamond was a violent man—a man who ate innocents like her for breakfast.

"*Señor* Diamond . . ." Pilar began. "You remember *Señorita* Stephanie Johns." She widened her eyes in mock innocence.

Heath smiled down at Stevie. She just stood there, looking up at him, resembling a wide-eyed, frozen goddess. He reached for the small bare hand fisted at her side. He pulled it forward, pumped it up and down as one would work a reluctant well handle.

He couldn't bring himself to release her immediately. He cradled her hand in both his own. Dropping his gaze, he noticed that her delicate skin was as golden brown as his own. But hers was satiny smooth, not callused like his.

She curled her fingers, making their contact more intimate. He was mesmerized, his eyes riveted to the small hand he held.

She was inherently dark, due to her Indian ancestry. How could he have failed to detect her Comanche heritage at their first meeting? Easily. She was so lovely, she befuddled a man's mind. Her distinctly Indian features softened by her platinum hair made her quite possibly the most beautiful woman he had ever seen.

He wondered then if she craved a pale alabaster complexion like other women of his acquaintance. It would be a sacrilege if she did. The striking contrast of her caramel-colored flesh with that gorgeous hair of hers—as light and shiny as the silk of ripe corn—was breathtaking. It did things to a man's insides that didn't bear revealing, things that were physically hard to hide.

His expression didn't betray his lusty thoughts as he mentally shook himself and bowed formally over her outstretched hand, acting the perfect gentleman. When he smoothed her fist and kissed her palm lightly, he was gratified by her sharp intake of breath.

Straightening, he released her. He produced a bowie knife and presented it to her with mocking gallantry. "I believe this is yours." He elevated a single ebony brow.

Stevie tried not to groan. She had forgotten about the knife. If she wanted this man's help, she had to get control of the womanly urges his nearness provoked to have the presence of mind to succeed.

She would also have to forget that he had dumped her into a tub of cold water. Actually, she didn't blame him for that. She had accused him of murder. And that only after she had taken three shots at him and thrown a knife at a very valuable area on his person. If she wanted his help, she had some fence-mending to do, a powerful lot of fence-mending.

"I want to apologize for the reception I gave you yesterday at Mustang Mesa. I thought you were one of Judge Jack's gunmen."

He looked deep into her eyes and saw nothing but sincerity. She looked so incredibly innocent. But her pale hair was hanging loose, streaming down her back in seductive disarray. Incongruous with the sensuous image she presented, her face glowed as if she had scrubbed it for hours, giving her the clean, wholesome look of a child fresh from her Saturday night bath. He felt an uncomfortable—actually unprecedented—stirring around the region of his heart. It scared the hell out of him. His manner grew distant. "And I apologize for my ungentlemanly behavior . . . in the saloon and later."

Stevie cast a quick look in Pilar's direction. She didn't want the woman who was like a mother to her to know that she had gone after the judge in his own saloon. And for reasons she couldn't name, she didn't want her to know that Lucky had dumped her into a tub of water, like an overflowing basket of last week's dirty laundry.

"Let's put the past in the past." She tried for a sincere smile. "Since there was no harm done to either of us."

"Certainly. It's forgotten." He placed his hand beneath her elbow and led her over to the kitchen table.

A frission of heat skittered up her arm from his touch. A bit unsteady, Stevie allowed Heath to seat her. She clutched the old reticule that contained five hundred dollars in her lap.

Pilar poured coffee and joined Stevie and Heath at the table. Both women faced Heath, who sat silently across from them. Surreptitiously, Pilar nudged Stevie in the ribs.

When Stevie raised her head and looked him full in the face, the thought that at the ripe old age of twenty she was ready to become a woman crossed her mind. And Lucky Diamond, the handsome devil, could be the man to make her a woman. Silence reined in the kitchen. In Stevie's mind, two words rang out. *His woman.*

"*Señora* Manchez said you wished to speak with me," he prodded, uncomfortable at the look she was giving him.

She spoke in a rush, trying to hide her intense feelings. "Yes. I wanted to apologize for running out on you last night. I know

I said I would meet you in the parlor, but I was worried about my pa. Eager to get back to Sully's, I forgot. It really wasn't intentional. I mean I wasn't trying to hurt your feelings or anything."

Heath raised his hands. "Whoa." He chuckled indulgently, deciding she was a poor liar, but cute when she was flustered. "Apology accepted."

Silence reigned again. Still uncomfortable, Stevie grasped the first thought that came to mind. "I was amazed at how well you handled yourself yesterday when you sidestepped my knife." Her cheeks flamed. "And I'm truly glad you did."

He looked skeptical.

"Honest, Mr. Diamond. I didn't really want to hurt you. I just lose my temper sometimes. And I do things that I regret later." She shrugged, uncertain why she was being so candid with him.

Heath quelled the urge to grin at her formal tone. After rolling around on the ground with him last night, the least she could do was call him by his first name. "Please call me Lucky."

"If you'll call me Stevie," she felt obligated to say.

"I'd prefer Steph." He smiled broadly. "I can't imagine calling such a pretty lady by a boy's name."

Pilar watched as Stevie and Lucky engaged in small talk. To say that Lucky turned on the charm would be incorrect. He didn't have to turn it on; he was charm incarnate. Yet, she noticed, he held a part of himself aloof.

Even at half power he was overwhelming, if Stevie's unease was any indication. Pilar sympathized with the girl; to withstand a man like Lucky would be slightly more difficult than keeping the tide from coming in.

"I overheard Preacher Black mention that you bested two of the judge's men. And that you killed Barnes Elder," Stevie blurted out, gaining Pilar's attention.

He shrugged dismissively. "I wouldn't make too much of idle gossip."

She smiled genuinely for the first time since he'd entered the room. "I bet Judge Jack's mad as hell. What I don't understand is how you got away with it." She wrinkled her brow, truly perplexed. "If anybody else had done it, he'd have been given a necktie party by now."

Heath laughed. "Maybe Judge Jack realizes that I pose no threat to him. After all, I'm known for minding my own business. I've learned that a person lives longer that way."

Stevie stiffened. "You're welcome to your own opinion." Her tone said the opposite. "But Judge Jack and his gunslingers shot my pa, they likely killed my brother, and have driven us off our ranch. He's nothing but a penny-ante crook, and I intend to stop him." She paused, fortifying herself for what came next. "Pilar thinks that I could maybe use some help."

Heath bit back a chuckle at the hesitancy in Stevie's voice. It was abundantly clear that she was unused to asking anybody for anything. His admiration for her grew several degrees. He had never known a lady like her.

Most of the women he knew had no aversion whatsoever to wheedling what they wanted out of a man. It was what women did, and they did it well. He didn't think less of them for it. In a pragmatic way, he considered them quite clever. They were the weaker sex—physically—so they used their God-given assets to their best advantage, naturally. And that meant unleashing their sex appeal, manipulating the stronger sex into slaying their dragons for them.

Apparently, Miss Stephanie Johns wanted to slay her own dragons. Unfortunately, the heinous creatures threatening her world were too many, too powerful, and much too vicious for an untried innocent such as herself.

He knew that she wouldn't appreciate hearing that, however. So instead, always the chivalrous gentleman—unless he was tossing a beautiful hellion on her pretty little rear into a tub of water—he decided to make it easy on her. "Perhaps I could be of assistance." It didn't occur to either of them that his offer of help was at odds with his just-expressed philosophy that he usually minded his own business.

Her relief was visible. "Pa and I would appreciate it." And she hadn't even had to offer him money. Things were definitely looking up.

The softness of her voice when she referred to her father struck a nostalgic chord in Heath. He glanced through the window over the sink. The deep green plains stretched out until they were blocked from view by a thick stand of trees. Summer grass, blown by the lonely wind, rippled freely across the prairie. Beyond his sight, way beyond, flowed the mighty Mississippi River. And beyond that, his home, his family, his father . . . who needed him.

The memory of his father's illness made him all the more eager to solve Adobe Wells's—and Stevie Johns's—problems so he could head east. "I'll do what I can. I'll go see the marshal right away." He started to rise.

She halted him with a hand to his forearm.

"Marshal Reno's a coward." Stevie's words weren't meant to be unkind, rather a statement of fact. "He's afraid of the judge's hired guns. He has to get drunk just to walk down the streets of his own town. Besides, he's disappeared. Nobody's seen him in days."

Heath dropped down into his seat. Pridgen had said something about Reno, but Heath had been under the influence, so it hadn't registered. Had the judge run the local law off? If so, the situation in Adobe Wells was more serious than he had first thought. He would have to find the gutless marshal and give him a stern talking-to. Deserting his town in a time of crisis, indeed!

"Then I'll see Colonel Banes. I understand he's the one who installed Jack as judge. Surely he has the power to remove him. If the judge is as bad as you say, Colonel Banes should be made aware of it."

This set Stevie off. Rising, she vented her spleen at him with the force of a thirty-pounder cannon. "Are you doubting my word?"

"Of course not. I apologize if I offended you," he said, trying to placate her. "I suppose I have a lot on my mind. I assure you I will be very discreet when I question the local authorities." Actually, he didn't plan to talk with Banes. He just thought that was what Pilar and Stevie would expect him to do. Unless he missed his guess, Banes was up to his elbows in Judge Jack's nefarious scheme.

"You don't need to question the marshal and you don't need to talk to Banes," Stevie interrupted his thoughts. "They won't help us. It's just you and me. We have to investigate it on our own. Got it?"

Heath was characteristically silent.

Pilar recognized a man who was unused to being dictated to by a woman or anyone else. "Perhaps she's right, *Señor* Diamond," she soothed him. "The fewer people who know about this, the better. We wouldn't want anyone else getting hurt."

"Which is why Miss Johns will have to leave this to me."

Stevie jumped up, stamped her foot. "It's my family, my home, and my town the judge is threatening." She punctuated each undeniable fact by thumping her chest with the flat of her hand. "If you think I'm going to sit idly by, then you're more simple-minded than most men of your profession." She drew herself up, looking like an irate virgin at a cut-rate brothel.

Heath smiled coolly. So the self-righteous spitfire was looking down her pert little nose at him because he was a gambler. Well, hell would freeze before he would defend himself about anything.

"I don't need your help. Nor will I accept it."

"Then you're fired."

He did the worst thing he could given Stevie's volatile nature; he laughed at her. "How can you fire a person whose never been hired?" he reasoned.

Stevie was beyond reasoning. She couldn't bear for people to laugh at her. They'd been doing that her whole life. Hurt, enraged, and not wanting to make a bigger fool of herself than she already had, she ran from the room.

"Damn." Heath grimaced. "I don't think I handled that very well."

Pilar shook her head, dismissing his concern. "Don't worry. Stevie'll get over it. If you hadn't been young and handsome, and she hadn't been so worried about Sandy, she wouldn't have reacted so . . . explosively."

Heath suspected that explosively was the only way Miss Johns knew to react. She probably could have persuaded him to take her on as a partner if she had exercised a bit more patience. He was glad that patience wasn't one of her virtues, for chastity wasn't one of his. And if he was around her for any length of time, particularly alone, neither of them would remain celibate. It was undeniably for the best that she had run out on him, even though he hated that she had left in a fit of pique.

And that he was even more intrigued with her now than before.

That evening, Heath was as frustrated as a mama cow without teats. Try as he might, he was unable to get the inhabitants of Adobe Wells to open up about Judge Jack. He had walked the streets that day, questioning everyone on two feet, but all to no avail. It was as if a cloak of fear had been thrown over the town.

His first day in Adobe Wells, the exploits of Judge Jack was all he heard. Now the townspeople had developed a remarkable case of lockjaw. Hoping that after a few drinks, over a hand of cards, someone would be more forthcoming, he headed toward the Golden Nugget.

The fire Stevie Johns had lit in his loins was still smoldering. But he renewed his vow to steer clear of her and the temptation she presented, no matter how damn hard it was. He groaned silently at the mental double entendre.

Perhaps an accommodating long-legged woman would be on duty at the Golden Nugget. Surprised that he couldn't manufacture more enthusiasm at the prospect of a heated toss in the hay with a hurdy-gurdy girl, he pushed through the swinging doors of the saloon.

He squinted at the heavy cloud of smoke, weaving his way through a sea of revelers. He dropped into a chair at the rear table, much as he had the night before. Instinctively cautious, he slid his chair flush against the wall.

"What will you have, *Señor?*" the same Mexican barkeep shouted over the familiar deafening roar.

"Whiskey," Heath called. His hangover was forgotten, as was his vow to avoid intoxicating spirits for the rest of his life.

The barkeep filled a shot glass and placed it before him. Heath nodded absently, his gaze wandering idly about the room.

"Shall I bring two glasses?" one barkeep asked.

Heath raised his brow in question.

"My friend Blue will keep you company."

Almost without conscious thought, Heath responded, "By all means."

How many times had he acted out this scene? Too many to count, but he had never done it with less enthusiasm. And he refused to believe that Stevie Johns was the reason. He had done little more than kiss the girl. How could she have captivated him so?

In a short while the barkeep served him a bottle of Scotch. He grinned when he placed a second glass on the table. "Blue will be here in a few minutes. You will like her."

"Gracias."

Heath filled his glass, took a long drink, and sat back to wait. As he waited for one woman, his thoughts were of another. In his mind he replayed every encounter he'd had with Stevie Johns. He couldn't help but marvel that she had very neatly tied him into knots since the first moment they met.

Usually, he was a very logical person. He approached a problem, analyzed it, then responded appropriately. Stevie had blown that mode of operation to hell. Instead, he approached her, was mesmerized, and acted like an irresponsible, horny idiot.

But there was one overriding truth in this situation that he couldn't ignore or alter. Stevie Johns was the kind of lady—though rough around the edges—men married, not the kind men bedded for recreation. She wasn't for him.

What he needed, if and when he decided to marry, was a woman with a background similar to his. His mother would undoubtedly find him a New York socialite with an impeccable bloodline. She would be petite, blond, pale, soft-spoken, and terribly, terribly polite.

Once he decided to give up marshaling, or gallivanting in the godforsaken wilderness, as his mother characterized his present career choice, he would join his father's shipping business and his proper wife would be an excellent hostess to his wealthy business contacts. They would live in a mansion on Thirty-fourth Street, have two well-mannered, pale blond, fair-skinned children—a boy and a girl. And they would all be incredibly content.

He tried to ignore the fact that it sounded absolutely ghastly to him. Worse than ghastly, it sounded boring.

Visions of half a dozen dark-skinned, platinum blond hellions bouncing on his knee teased his mind. And their beautiful mother driving him to distraction teased his body.

No! He and Stevie Johns were not right for each other, not to mention that they were virtual strangers. And despite his hell-raising days in the Wild West, he and Stevie were from two different worlds. Because of the hardships he suffered in the war, he had been unable to step back into his life of wealth and ease. Consequently, he decided to become a U.S. marshal . . . for a time. But that time was coming to an end. He wasn't meant to live his life with a girl like Stevie. No matter how much he wanted her.

He would never be able to make her happy. She needed to settle down with a nice, dependable rancher, raise a few kids, and grow old watching her grandchildren play in the yard . . . tormenting the chickens. He chuckled at his fanciful description of Stevie's future, then groaned when he painted himself into the picture as her rancher husband.

That would never happen. What *would* happen if he didn't maintain control of the situation is that she would give him her innocence, have a passionate affair with him, then eat his dust as he rode out of town.

His gut ached at the thought.

Pilar and Sully didn't see Stevie standing in the doorway to the medical office. She had come to tell them her pa was conscious and hungry as a bear. The secretive way they were speaking made her reluctant to interrupt. Once again she found herself eavesdropping.

"Pepper said they came right after Stevie and Sandy left the ranch"—Sully continued quietly—"Judge Jack and a group of miners. He set them to work in that cave Stevie and Jeff were always playing in."

"Stevie's hiding place?"

Sully nodded.

"What could they be looking for?" This was from Pilar.

"Damned if I know. But they're sure looking for something."

"What about Pepper?"

"He's hiding out at the old line shack."

Soundlessly, Stevie slipped out the front door. She went in search of Winter. He was sitting on the porch at Pilar's, rubbing Sweetums's coat, both under the watchful eyes of Itsy and Bitsy. Stevie expressed her thanks to the tittering twins, then set off with Winter in search of Lucky Diamond. It took a while for them to discover his whereabouts. When they did, she handed the child a note.

"Take this to him. *Namasi-kohtoo,* quick, quick." She raised her eyes to the noose dangling ominously in the center of town. "And be careful."

Eleven

The soiled dove crossed the room, her movements practiced, seductive, fluid.

She looked anything but soiled. Heath guessed her age to be about twenty-five, but he couldn't be sure. The heavy cosmetics painted on her face disguised her age. He suspected they hid her beauty as well. It was almost as if she wore a mask, concealing her true self.

The mental image of Stevie, her face scrubbed until it shone, teased his mind. He pushed it aside with a well-trained sense of will and ran his appreciative gaze over the woman before him.

Blue was a voluptuous woman, dressed in bright crimson. Her form-fitting satin dress barely reached her knees, showing shapely legs encased in black net stockings. Heath smiled; he had a weakness for black net stockings.

He tore his gaze away from her legs and raised it to her waist-length hair. Framing her bare shoulders, the glistening curls were even darker than her stockings. She returned his smile, managing to look respectable.

"Good evening."

"Ma'am." Heath rose to his feet, pulling Blue's chair out. "Won't you sit down and have a drink with me?"

Heath thought he detected a note of sadness in her pale blue eyes. But as she settled her short skirts about her, she lowered her lashes, effectively hiding her gaze. Shrugging away the thought, he filled their glasses with amber liquid. His hand shook slightly, sloshing the whiskey as he handed Blue her drink.

She thanked him, her words lost to the ever-increasing din in the saloon. Raising the tumbler to her mouth, she allowed the whiskey to touch her lips but drank none. Finally, she leaned forward and introduced herself. "They call me Blue."

Heath bent close to her ear. "I'm Lucky Diamond." He felt the warmth of her bare neck against his cheek. The clean smell of lavender filling his nostrils caused his deprived body to react instinctively. His heart, however, wasn't in it.

"Do you plan to stay long in Adobe Wells, Lucky?"

"Now that I've met you, I might." He smiled, his inherent charm practically oozing from his pores. It was no chore for Heath to seduce a woman. In fact, it would take a conscious effort to do otherwise.

Blue was suitably charmed. The handsome gambler was looking at her if she were a real person. It had been a while since anyone had looked at her like that. Most men were pigs. They didn't want conversation, just a poke. They didn't care about the women they used, not as people, just hunks of meat for their pleasure. Lucky Diamond seemed different. He was nice, neat, handsome—and clean, like Jeff.

Sadness clouded her gaze again. This time Heath recognized the expression for what it was. The girl was grieving, as if she had lost a loved one.

The thought that saloon girls had loved ones was rather novel. To his shame, he realized he had never thought much about these women after he had finished with them. They were businesswomen, and he was a paying customer. It was as simple as that. He never spent all night with them, just did his business and left.

Though he treated them well, he never really thought about their lives outside the bordellos in which they plied their trade. Most, he suspected, had no life outside the honkytonks.

Blue was different, he was convinced. She was unlike any soiled dove he'd ever encountered.

He shouldn't have been surprised. Thus far, none of the women in Adobe Wells had been what he expected. Pilar wasn't; she seemed protective of Stevie, yet approved her risky plan to investigate Judge Jack. God knows Stevie wasn't what one would expect of an innocent. And Blue—a woman who went to bed with men for a living—appeared quite the lady.

Leaning back in his chair, he studied her, intrigued. He found himself hoping that she just drank with the customers . . . then went to bed alone. He hated to think of her putting up with men groping at her night after night.

But he knew better. The barkeep had known what he was looking for and had provided Blue to meet his needs.

Heath smiled at Blue gently. He wasn't particularly surprised to discover that he didn't want to take her to bed. The prospect of spending a few quiet moments talking with this kind woman appealed to him much more than the idea of getting naked and sweaty with her.

Though he was loath to admit it, in less than twenty-four hours Stevie Johns had taken away his desire for other women. But he couldn't have Stevie, he reminded himself for the umpteenth time. She was young, a lady, and he would be moving on soon.

"Where are you from?" Blue interrupted his musings.

"Back east," he answered vaguely. "But I've been around. How about you?"

"Santa Fe."

Heath refilled his glass and relaxed. As soon as he decided not to bed Blue, some of the tension left his body. After more companionable talk with her, he slipped a white lace handkerchief from his shirt pocket. True, it wasn't pearls and diamonds, but it was the gesture that counted. Women liked gifts. Blue's glowing eyes assured him she was no different.

He had purchased the gift several days earlier for an occasion such as this. A fellow marshal, Winn Marable, and a number of other lawmen had been with him at the time. Winn had almost laughed Heath out of town. But Heath had bought the delicate item anyway—after threatening to bust Winn's jaw if he didn't stop his guffawing. In the end—after Heath reminded Winn that women weren't exactly panting for a glimpse of his smile—Winn had also bought a handkerchief.

The store owner, taking in the group of lonely lawmen who

lined up to purchase the lacy things clutched in their callused hands, claimed he would have to start ordering the fripperies by the case. Two dozen guns were drawn, cocked, and the clerk completed the transactions in silence.

The handkerchief lay on the table in front of Blue, her eyes riveted to it. Heath's hand rested on the stark white material.

"It's very beautiful." Reverently, she fingered the delicate lace. Their hands touched and Heath jerked back as if he'd been shocked.

He was embarrassed at his action. "Take it."

Blue smiled and held the gift to her cheek. "Why?"

"Why what?" Heath pretended not to notice the sheen in Blue's eyes.

"Why are you giving me this?"

"A beautiful gift for a beautiful lady." His eyes scanned the room. He didn't mind charming his lovely companion, but he didn't want to be overheard sounding like a fancy dude. After all, the man who killed Barnes Elder had a tough image to live up to. "Surely a lovely lady like yourself receives gifts all the time."

When her tears overflowed her eyes and spilled down her cheeks, he covered her hand with his own.

"I'm sorry," she whispered, bowing her head.

Heath bent his head until they were eye to eye, then blessed her with the platonic smile that always charmed his sisters out of the mulligrubs. "I've been told I'm a good listener."

"You came here for a good time. And I—" she couldn't finish.

Most men were uncomfortable with crying women, but not Heath. He found them a special challenge. He had discovered that good-natured teasing and a dose of genuine affection could cure most anything. He captured a glistening tear on the tip of his finger. "Guess it's a good thing I gave you a handkerchief, huh?"

She blessed him with a watery smile, drying her face with his precious gift. When she had regained a measure of her composure, Heath again invited her to confide her troubles in him. She remained silent.

"It has to be a man. My sister, Ann, says that the only thing that can make a woman cry is gaining weight and unfaithful men." He leered at her comically. "Since your body is dang near perfect, it has to be a man. What did the scoundrel do?"

Never in her twenty-one years had Blue confided in a customer. She had told Jeff her darkest secrets, her brightest dreams, but then, she never considered Jeff a customer.

Actually she had a hard time thinking of the man smiling at her with such kindness as a customer either. Lucky Diamond was the sort of man a woman could call a friend. In a town like Adobe Wells a woman needed all the friends she could get. Blue didn't have any friends now that Jeff was dead.

"It is a man. I loved him. But he's gone." She shrugged slightly, only the sadness clouding her eyes showing how very much she missed him.

"Well, he must be a fool to run out on you—" Heath began.

Blue's chin jerked defensively. "Jeff didn't run out on me," she said heatedly. She covered her mouth with her hand; she hadn't meant to say his name.

Heath sat straighter in his seat. "That wouldn't be Jeff Johns, would it?"

Blue's eyes met Heath's. She didn't know whether to trust him or not. Something in his sapphire gaze decided the matter for her. She nodded, yes. "Did you know Jeff?"

"I didn't have the honor. But I know his sister." And I'd like to know her a lot better, he added silently.

A sudden hush fell over the saloon. Heath glanced up to see Judge Jack standing in the doorway. He paused, then entered the saloon, followed by his gunslinging entourage. They trailed after him like a gaggle of geese.

Fear darkened Blue's eyes. "It's Judge Jack. I have to go."

Heath's glance bounced from the frightened woman at his side to the man crossing the floor. He took both of Blue's hands in his own.

"Please stay." He squeezed gently. "I have no business with Judge Jack. I want to talk with you about Jeff."

"I can't." Her voice quivered; her hands trembled in his.

Heath studied the judge closely. What was there about Elias Colt Jack that scared people so? Although he was a big fellow, he didn't look particularly threatening. Actually, at first glance he looked quite the gentleman. Of course, that black pirate's patch was somewhat ominous. And the hawkish look in his other eye made him seem menacing.

But his disreputable entourage was far worse. Now standing at the bar, they surrounded him. Fatty and the Mexican had been joined by a tall man who covered the judge's back. The newcomer was an albino. Glaring into the mirror over the bar, his pale eyes conveyed threatening messages to the men in the room.

Just then a slight Indian boy entered the saloon.

"What do you want?" the barkeep barked at the child.

"I have a message . . ." the child began.

Before he could finish his statement, Jacobson grabbed his arm and snarled into his face, "You filthy Comanche, your kind ain't welcome here."

The boy looked up, terrified. The man addressing him was not just big, but enormous. Bear Jacobson looked like a pod of whales all by himself.

Heath could well imagine how frightened the boy must have been, confronted by a monster like Jacobson. The child was so incredibly overmatched.

Bear backhanded the youth across the face. Blood leaked through the small, dark fingers covering his mouth and nose, but the child never made a sound.

Heath growled low in his throat, so low, only Blue heard him. He felt sick as he watched the injured boy run from the Golden Nugget.

It was the child he'd seen on the Johns spread. The lad who called Stevie "Mother." Heath was glad Stevie Johns hadn't witnessed the incident firsthand. She would have drawn on Jacobson, understandably so. But even if she had killed him, one of the judge's remaining goons would have put a bullet through her.

Just as they would shoot Heath now if he blew the man to hell, as he wanted to do more than anything on earth. He would have to wait till later to deal with the man. And deal with him he would.

Blue's gasp of pain drew his attention. He was still holding her hand. The rage he felt at the scene had caused him to squeeze too tightly.

He released her instantly. "I'm sorry."

"That's all right." Paling, she appeared unsure of him now.

Heath cursed soundlessly. This night was not turning out as he'd planned. Those bastards at the bar were to blame. He glared at them, catching the albino's eye in the mirror.

Walking toward Heath, his pink eyes resembled ghostly specters ringed by thin circles of blood. A wide-brimmed hat topped his snowy hair. He was a deadly wraith and his first words were for Blue. "Get upstairs, where you belong." He barely spared her a glance.

"She's with me." Heath gently took her hand again.

"Personally, I don't give a damn what the whore does." The wraith glared at Blue then. "But Jacobson might not like it. He hasn't seen you yet. You want me to call him over?"

Neither Heath nor Blue answered the wraith's threat.

The wraith turned on Heath. "What the hell are you doing in town, mister?"

"Didn't I play this scene last night?" Heath muttered to himself. Aloud, he cursed, "I swear and declare. This has to be the most inhospitable town it's ever been my misfortune to stumble into. Ever since I rode in, somebody's been shooting at me or asking me to leave."

He surged to his feet and shot toward the ceiling in one fluid motion. The room quieted; every eye turned his way. "I have an announcement to make. In case any of the rest of you are interested, my name is Lucky Diamond. I came to Adobe Wells to play a few hands of cards, sleep a coupl'a nights in a real bed, and get some hot food in my stomach." He winked down at Blue. "This lovely lady has consented to be my good luck charm. If any of you are interested in losing some money to us, we are at your disposal." With that, he bowed chivalrously and dropped back down into his seat. "Now, run on back to your boss, you plug-ugly phantom," he spat out.

The wraith's hand inched toward his gun.

"Draw, please," Heath taunted.

"Whitey." A steel-hard voice halted the aggressive movement.

Heath smiled, his cool blue eyes frigid as a glacier. "Damn! He's got you trained better than a lapdog," he exclaimed softly. The look in Whitey's eyes told him he had just made a deadly enemy. What the hell? One more didn't matter.

The judge, ringed by Sims, Carlos Garcia, and Bear Jacobson, stood at the bar. They occupied their usual positions, with their feet firmly planted; Bear on the right of the judge—glaring at Blue—Garcia on the left, just like last night. It was almost as if they had those particular spots reserved. Heath wondered if Jack slept sandwiched between those two thick slices of garbage.

Slowly, Jack ran his fingers across one end of his mustache, then the other. Heath supposed that his deliberate movements were designed to intimidate. One would think after last night he would be reluctant to challenge Heath so soon, but some men never learned.

Tension thrummed in the air. With a jerk of his head the judge summoned Whitey. Before leaving the saloon with his entourage in tow, Jack shot Bear Jacobson a glance.

Bear remained behind, glaring at Blue through the deep folds of flesh surrounding his eyes. He approached Heath's table, never taking his hostile gaze from the frightened woman.

"Hadn't you better run along, Jacobson?" Heath derided Bear.

"She's mine," Bear hissed.

Heath winked at Blue. "Now, that's a revolting thought, isn't it, sugar?"

Heath appeared relaxed, good-natured, almost cordial. In truth, he found Jacobson nauseating. He could hear every breath the slob drew. It was a liquid sound, squeezing upward through mounds of flesh. His ponderous gut hung over his belt, completely covering the buckle. He bore a remarkable resemblance to a hippopotamus Heath had seen at a circus in Europe, though Jacobson wasn't as clean or sweet-smelling as the animal.

But most of all Heath didn't like what he saw in the man's eyes as he stared at Blue. And he didn't like the fact that the girl was trembling with fear. "Do you mean to accept my invitation, Mr. Jacobson?"

"I'll play." Bear dropped heavily into a groaning chair and pulled a wad of bills from his vest pocket.

"Oh, we're not playing for money, my fat friend." Heath's deadly soft words halted the brigand's progress.

"What're we playin' for?"

"Blue."

Twelve

"Name your game. Poker, whist, or brag?" Heath asked.

"Huh?"

Heath bit back a grin. "What game do you fancy? Poker, whist, or brag?" Bear didn't strike Heath as an intellectual giant. He suspected the man would be taxing his brain to get through a good hand of blackjack. But he couldn't resist taunting him.

Jacobson regarded Heath with a blank stare. "Poker," he grunted finally.

"Very good." Lucky, the gentleman gambler, nodded his head politely. "Five-card stud."

Expertly, Heath shuffled the deck of cards that were a constant companion of Lucky Diamond's. He handled them as if they were an extension of his fingers, moving smoothly, faster than the eye could see.

It would be easy for a man with Heath's talent to cheat at cards, but he didn't. He was so good, he didn't have to. The man sitting across from him was another matter; he would need watching. Men like Bear would sell their own mothers for a profit. If men like Jacobson had mothers . . .

The game and the challenge were over almost as soon as they began. Heath drew four aces, Bear, a pair of threes.

"I'll deal with you later," Bear leaned across the table and growled at Blue.

Lucky surged to his feet. He grabbed Jacobson's shirt, cutting off his breath. "If you so much as harm one hair on Blue's head, I'll make you wish you hadn't."

Frightened, Bear nodded. When Heath shoved him back in his chair, he lugged his tonnage to his feet and lumbered across the room. Pridgen was wrong: Jacobson wasn't fast. But Heath suspected that he was ruthless.

Without saying a word, Blue and Heath followed Bear to the door. Heath expected to find him preparing an ambush reminiscent of the night before. Instead, Jacobson entered the saloon across the way, without a backward glance.

Two things happened next . . . simultaneously. Blue threw her arms around Heath's neck and planted a grateful kiss on his mouth. While his back was turned, Stevie Johns surged through the door, the note she had sent him earlier—stained with Winter's blood—clutched in her hand.

Her sharp gasp drew both Heath and Blue's attention. The look on Stevie's face was one of pure outrage. Reckoning it was due to jealousy, Heath grinned infuriatingly.

"My dear Miss Johns." He bowed chivalrously, unmindful that his arm was still around Blue's crimson-encased waist. "I'm honored that you would seek me out two nights in a row."

Stevie wanted to slap the supercilious smirk off Heath's face, but she'd be danged if she'd allow him to make a fool of her again. Somehow, she managed to keep her voice steady. "You rotten, no good." She gritted her teeth. "You're nothing but a . . . a man!"

He released Blue and stepped closer to Stevie. "I'm glad you noticed."

Blue smiled when she noticed the pink glow on Stevie's cheeks at Lucky's nearness. She had seen Jeff's sister only at a distance until then. Stevie was as pretty as Jeff said she was. And as feisty, if the venomous look she was giving Lucky was an indication.

In the dark of night, when Blue lay alone in her bed upstairs after the hoards of rutting, filthy, profane men left the saloon, and she had scrubbed as much of the shame from her body as she could, she dreamed of being a decent woman, of having a best friend like Stevie Johns. It was a dream that would never come true now that Jeff was dead.

"Answer me one question if you will." Stevie's tone was caustic enough to strip paint from the barn wall. "Were you cavorting with that woman while my son was being beaten up?" She shook the bloodstained note in front of his face.

Blue didn't take offense. She recognized a smitten woman when she saw one. If she had found Jeff kissing another woman, she would have said far worse.

The question of how someone as young as Stevie could have a child Winter's age, especially without benefit of a husband, flickered through his mind. It was immediately burnt away in the face of righteous indignation on Blue's behalf. "You leave Blue out of this. She hasn't done anything to you." He glanced at the note and grew even angrier. "So, you're the fool who sent that child in here."

Stevie was more than embarrassed; she was ashamed of herself. He was right on both accounts. Blue had never done anything to her. And she never should have sent Winter into the saloon. She had been a fool . . . about many things.

"I apologize, miss," Stevie said sincerely to Blue, then left as quickly as she'd come.

"Well, don't just stand there like a simpleton. Go after her," Blue ordered Heath with more life than she'd shown in a long time.

Heath kissed her cheek. "Sounds like good advice to me. You sure you'll be all right?"

"I hardly think Bear Jacobson will bother me tonight after the warning you gave him." More than a little hero-worship lit her eyes.

Heath was oblivious of it. All he could think of was Stevie. "Okay. I'll check on you in the morning." With a smile as big as the state of Texas on his face, he hurried from the saloon.

He almost tripped over Stevie where she sat on Pilar's stoop in the darkness, her hands fisted together, pressed between her updrawn knees.

"Sorry, I didn't see you."

She remained silent.

"Mind if I sit?"

She scooted over to make room for his large frame. The note she had sent to the saloon fluttered to the ground.

Heath retrieved the missive. "May I?"

"It's for you."

He was intrigued. "Me?" Striking a match on his boot heel, he held it up to the paper and read: "Mr. Diamond, I'm going out to the ranch tomorrow to look around. You can tag along if you want. Stevie Johns."

Heath hid a smile. Short and sweet, just like the woman who'd written it. He had certainly received more eloquent pleas for help. But it was exactly what he would expect from a woman like the one beside him—the one who was trying to act as if she couldn't care less about his reaction to her note. He carefully folded the paper and placed it into his waistcoat pocket. "Why the change of heart?"

"I've learned that some of the judge's men have moved out to our land and are digging around in my hiding place."

"Your hiding place?"

Stevie had not meant to refer to the cave in that way. Not wanting to explain the significance of her terminology, she hurried on. "I'm good with a gun, Mr. Diamond, but I'm no match for a dozen or more hired guns."

He blessed her with a devastating smile. "It's always important to recognize your limitations."

"This may be a joke to you."

"I'm sorry . . ." he began.

"But my home and family are being threatened. Frankly, I have a hard time laughing about that. Now, are you going to ride with me or not? If not, I have to try to find someone else. Considering the stranglehold the judge has on this town and the fact that I'm part Indian, that might be a bit difficult."

Not to mention that you're a woman, Heath added silently. He heard the bitterness in her voice and regretted that one so lovely and so young had so much to be bitter about. Pushing aside the sympathy it evoked—which he was sure she didn't want—he tapped her nose lightly. "When you put it so graciously, sugar, how could I refuse?"

Her heart was banging against her ribs long after he excused himself and took the warmth of the night inside with him.

Thirteen

Heath tried his dead-level best not to gape. Truly, he did. But the sight that greeted him the next morning as he opened his bedroom door all but took his breath away.

Bending at the waist, talking to Winter and Sweetums, Stevie's backside was framed by Heath's open door. It was a vision to behold. She had exchanged her black leather outfit for one that was white. Apparently, she had bleached buckskin until the fabric was soft and snowy as cotton, then fashioned trousers and a vest that hugged her body like a lover's caress. Every curve was gently outlined, on display for every randy cowhand north of the Rio Grande.

This last thought caused Heath no little distress. When he spoke to her, his voice showed his annoyance. "I hope you don't plan to take that damn pet of yours along."

Stevie jerked up and wheeled toward the angry lawman. As usual, she reacted to his nearness in a painful-pleasurable way. Her inability to control her reaction set fire to her temper as well. "Sweetums is not a pet. She's a friend." Instinctively, she dropped her hand and ruffled her friend's fur. With a sickly-sweet smile, she purred, "But don't worry, I won't let her hurt you."

Heath winced. Throwing his words back into his face was not the best way to get on his good side. Any more than looking like she needed to be tossed on her pretty little backside and loved long and hard, all day and into the night. "I might've known you'd name a man-eating wolf Sweetums."

"Men aren't fit to eat."

Not even wanting to pursue the intriguing possibilities, he threw her a falsely disinterested look. "I'll meet you out front soon as I've had my coffee. I have an errand to run before we leave town. We can take care of it on the way out." With that, he presented her his back and sauntered down the hall.

Stevie had a strong urge to stick her tongue out at his retreating figure. She wondered what the mysterious errand was, then pushed the thought aside. She bent to Winter's level. "Pilar will take care of you until I get back . . ." she began in Comanche, sifting her fingers through his shoulder-length black hair.

When he squared his frail shoulders and jerked his chin, looking like a Comanche brave whose honor had been insulted, Stevie changed her tack. "She needs your help. With all the bad men in town, and me gone and Pa shot, she needs a brave man in her house. Will you and Sweetums take care of her while I'm gone?"

Winter jerked a nod, looking much older than his six years. His lower lip trembled before he could still it. Men didn't cry, he reminded himself, Indian men or white men, and neither would he. But his heart would hurt awful bad until his mother returned to him.

Stevie would suffer likewise. She had found Winter behind the Silver Dollar Saloon when he was less than two hours old. The woman who birthed him was a soiled dove who had expelled him from her body, then thrown him out like the contents of a slop jar. The whore was a full-blood Comanche. Stevie learned that the woman died less than a year later, shot in a barroom brawl. Stevie had been the only mother Winter had known, he, she decided, the only child she would ever have.

Like most mothers, it hurt unbearably to leave her child, if only for a few hours. But Stevie knew it would be longer than a few hours before she and Winter were reunited. She had a sixth sense, always feeling impending doom. She knew that she and Lucky would not return to Adobe Wells for some time.

Stevie lay a trembling hand alongside her son's jaw and

smiled with love. Slowly, her fingers mapped his face, lightly skimming the telltale bruises inflicted by Bear Jacobson. Her heart ached at the thought. She would see that the man paid one day; he would die. For now she pushed the rage and hatred aside, allowing love and tenderness to fill her. "My fingers want to see your face so I can remember you while I'm gone."

While she would never have a husband or children of her own, God had blessed her with Winter. He eased the ache, filled the emptiness. And she loved him for it with all her heart.

"I love you, Mother," he whispered.

"And I love you, my precious child." She kissed his cheek gently, then told him one more time how much she loved him. Rising unsteadily, she smiled and whispered, *"Toquet,* it is well."

Eyes shining, he nodded bravely. *"Toquet."*

"What's the errand?" Stevie asked as she and Heath rode away from Pilar's.

"I have to see Blue."

Stevie stiffened in the saddle. "You can say good-bye to your whore without my presence!"

Heath reined in, throwing her a bemused glance. "If I didn't know better, Steph, I'd swear you were jealous of Blue."

"Not hardly! And don't call me Steph. It's Stevie. Or better yet, call me Miss Johns."

Heath threw his head back and laughed. She was striving so hard to look intimidating and disapproving. Instead, she looked adorable. Kind of like the furry calico he had given his sister, Ann, for her seventh birthday. Perhaps with a little coaxing Miss Johns could be as affectionate as the feline had become.

He stared at her just for the joy of taking in her beauty. The breeze blew lightly, fluttering the fringe on her vest. Movement over her right shoulder caught his eye. His brow furrowed. A hangman's noose dangled from the tree, swaying in the breeze.

"What kind of town leaves a noose hanging from a tree?" he asked rhetorically. Giving no prior thought to his actions, he closed the distance and cut the rope down with one swish of his knife. He looked up in time to see two men dash into the stagecoach office on the other side of the plaza as if they expected the world to come to an end within the next three seconds.

When he returned to her side, Stevie commented, "That was a mistake."

He regarded her with surprise. Her face was as devoid of emotion as her voice.

"Why?"

"Judge Jack said it was to be left there."

"Maybe it's time Judge Jack learned he can't have everything his way." There was something about Stevie's carefully controlled demeanor that struck Heath as odd. He had seen her infuriated, passionate, even amused, but never like this. "There's more to this than you're saying."

She shrugged dismissively. "Last week Judge Jack hung an Indian who was accused of stealing his prized stallion. After the hanging, Jacobson rode into town, leading the horse behind him. He had taken the animal over to Fort Bascomb for a special kind of shoe job." When she grasped her locket, Heath noticed the fine tremor in her hand. "Lame Wolf hadn't touched the horse. When the judge learned that he had hung an innocent man, he just shrugged his shoulders and said, 'Tough. The stinking redskin should have stayed out of town.' "

Heath's voice was low and intense. "What did you say the Indian's name was?"

"Lame Wolf." Her voice was husky, sounding almost reverent.

Heath felt as if someone had hit him in the chest with a sledgehammer. Lame Wolf was a famed hero among the plains Indians. He had heard of his daring exploits while in Red Feather's camp. The Comanche were gifted storytellers, and Lame Wolf's brave deeds provided them a wealth of material. For a man who was a living legend, a source of great pride to his people, to have been executed so callously was almost more than Heath could bear. Trying to regain a measure of control, he stared at the noose in his hand.

"Don't take it so hard, Lucky." She paused. "He was just a breed."

Heath jerked his head toward her. Had he not seen the pain

in her eyes, he would have taken her to task for her remark. "Let's go, hon."

She rode quietly at his side, thinking that the noose looked quite like a teardrop.

Heath slid from his saddle and tossed the reins over the hitching post in front of the Silver Dollar Saloon. Reaching up, he circled Stevie's waist with his hands. "You're coming with me."

She pushed against his shoulders. "No. I'll wait here." She did not want to see Heath kiss Blue again. Just as she did not want to speculate on why the mere thought caused her heart to hurt.

For reasons Heath couldn't name, it was important that Stevie understand about Blue, that his interest was not romantic but humanitarian. "Come on." Tightening his grip, he pulled her off her horse.

"Let me go." Her objections died when their bodies made contact.

Slowly, he slid her down the length of him. If she'd had any doubt about which woman stirred his blood, the physical contact with his lower body cleared it up nicely. She dropped her gaze to a conspicuous area of his person. "Do you need two women to take care of that?" Her taunt was made through tightly clenched teeth. It was apparent that Heath wasn't the only one fighting to tamp down the raging tide of desire.

Chuckling softly, he tapped her nose affectionately, much as he had the night before. "You and Blue would constitute one and a half women, little bit. But then, I've always said the best presents come in small packages." He took her hand and pulled her toward the saloon.

When they entered the dim interior, Heath's nostrils twitched at the smell of oiled sawdust. The room was empty except for the Mexican woman who swirled her broom, picking up a residue of tobacco juice and other waste from the floor. Heath asked her to point out Blue's room. Stevie was pleased that he had to ask.

"It's the second one on the right. Up those stairs."

Stevie tried to pull free of Heath's grasp. "I'll wait for you down here."

"Oh, no, you won't. I'm far too much a gentleman to leave a lady alone in a saloon."

"If you were a gentleman, you wouldn't have dragged me into this den of iniquity in the first place."

"You may have a point there." Despite his words, he escorted her up the stairs. Winking down into her face, he knocked on Blue's door.

Muffled noises came from inside. Blue cracked the door, but when she saw Heath and Stevie, she slammed it in their faces. "Please go away."

Heath was enraged at what he'd seen. "Blue, open this damn door before I knock it down."

Stevie hit his arm. "Would you hush your bellowing? You're scaring her."

Heath paid her no heed. He was too busy berating himself. Last night he had been so enraptured with Stevie that he failed to protect Blue. He had put her in danger, then deserted her. Some lawman he was! "Blue, do you hear me? Open this door."

"Lucky, please, just go away."

Reading Heath's intent, Stevie shouted, "Move back, Blue!"

Heath kicked the door in, breaking the latch.

"My God," Stevie breathed at her first good look at Blue. She acted instinctively, moving to Blue's side and taking her hands in her own. "Are you all right?"

Blue's face was unrecognizable. It was a mass of black and purple bruises, her nose obviously broken, her lower lip cut, her left eye swollen completely shut.

Heath uttered an oath that surprised both women, it was so vile. "Who did this to you?" he gritted through clenched teeth.

"No one. I fell down the stairs last night."

Stevie wrapped her arms around Blue's shoulders and held her. "Tell him the truth."

Blue broke into sobs at Stevie's act of kindness. She cried into her shoulder until she was too weak to cry anymore.

Stevie smoothed Blue's blood-matted hair, soothing her as if she were an injured child. "You might as well tell him . . ." she began gently. "He's such a pain in the ass, he won't leave until you do." This elicited a small smile from Blue and an imperiously raised brow from Heath.

"What the hell are you doing in here?" a harsh voice sounded from the doorway.

Heath turned to see Bear Jacobson standing in the doorway. His eyes were ablaze with hate and alcohol. His unkempt black hair hung down onto an oil-slicked brow. He held a wicked-looking knife in one wide hand. Blue cowered at the sight of him, leaving no doubt who had beaten her.

"You son of a bitch," Heath growled, rushing Bear.

Bear swung the knife wildly back and forth.

With the speed of a striking diamondback rattler, Heath ducked the blade and sank his doubled fist into the folds beneath Bear's chin. Jacobson collapsed on the floor like a fallen oak, clutching his neck.

Heath stood over him, hands fisted at his sides. "Get up, you gutless slob."

Coughing and sputtering, Bear got to his feet. Heath jerked his fist back and buried it in Bear's face, crashing him through the door. The railing splintered. Bear rolled like a giant ball of butter down the stairs. When he reached the saloon below, his body spread out like a fattening hog, wallowing in the mud.

Heath turned to Blue and noticed that she looked more frightened than before.

"Please leave. Both of you." Her voice trembled; her eyes teared. "When Judge Jack finds out you've been here, he'll kill us all."

Heath and Stevie spoke in unison.

"Let him try!" exclaimed Stevie.

"The hell he will!" Heath shouted.

"Please, I beg you. Leave before Bear comes back with a gun. Please!"

She turned imploring eyes on Stevie. All the pain she was suffering would be slight compared to the guilt she would experience if Jeff's sister were hurt because of her.

Stevie glared at Heath. "Are you going to go after him, or shall I?" she asked him indignantly.

Heath looked from Blue's pitiful face to Stevie's determined glare. He touched both women gently, his hand lingering on Stevie's hair a moment longer. "You stay with Blue."

He disappeared through the door and sprinted down the stairs. Jacobson was trying to get up on his feet. When Heath reached him, he grabbed him by the hair and yanked him up, slamming him against the wall. The fat man's eyes widened with terror.

Heath relieved Bear of his knife and pressed the point of it into the corner of Bear's left eye. A small trickle of blood colored his cheek; he whimpered like a child.

"Listen, you bastard. I'm going to leave this miserable town for now. But when I come back—and I will come back—I'll cut both your eyes out if you've touched Blue. You tell Judge Jack the same goes for him too."

Heath released Bear. Jacobson slid to the floor, lying in a pile of sawdust and sweat, vowing never to touch Blue again.

Heath looked back up the stairs. Blue and Stevie stood at the top. Blue's face showed a myriad of emotions: fright, gratitude, affection.

Stevie's lovely visage was inscrutable, as always. She was smiling down at him slightly, though she shrugged her slender shoulders as if she had expected him to do no less. They were lost in each other's gaze for a moment. Shaking free of Heath's spell, Stevie turned to Blue. "Get your things together. You're coming with me," she said in a no-nonsense fashion. She knew nothing of the prostitute, but to a woman like Stevie, who identified with the wounded creatures of the world, Blue was a woman down on her luck. That was all she needed to know.

Blue was astonished. "What? Where?"

Heath joined them on the landing. "What've you got in mind?"

"I'm taking Blue to Pilar's. She can help take care of Winter. And heal at the same time." She smiled at Blue. "But let the boy think he's taking care of you."

"I appreciate it . . ." Blue began uncertainly. "But I'm a . . . what I mean to say is that Miss Pilar wouldn't want a . . ." She trailed off helplessly.

"You're a friend. Just as Pilar is a friend. She'll welcome you." And in Stevie's mind the matter was settled.

Jeff had teased Stevie all her life about taking in strays. Crippled birds, motherless calves, stray dogs, half-dead wolves, even abandoned Indian boys, the list went on. She had no way of knowing how much he would appreciate her kindness toward Blue.

Leaning a muscled shoulder against the wall, Heath threw both women a smile that accelerated their heart rates accordingly. "You might as well save your breath, honey"—he addressed Blue but winked at Stevie—"there's no use arguing with her when she gets that mulish look in her eyes."

Shocking, embarrassing . . . and thrilling Stevie, he pushed away from the wall and dropped a kiss on her lips. "I'll wait downstairs, sugar."

Fourteen

Santa Fe

Judge Jack and Colonel Banes entered the Territorial Bank of New Mexico.

A teller, Ebenezer Ribbons, greeted them cheerfully. "Welcome, gentlemen, what can I do for you this morning?"

Judge Jack spoke first. "I'm Elias Colt Jack, district judge of Adobe Wells, and this is my associate, Colonel Willard Banes, the commanding officer of Fort Bascomb. I represent a prospective mining group from Adobe Wells. Colonel Banes has been kind enough to accompany me for security reasons. I have a bag of valuables that I would like to deposit in your vault."

Jack was holding a medium-size leather valise close to his right side. Banes stood next to the bag, ostensibly guarding it.

Smiling broadly, Ribbons responded, "Gentlemen, we appreciate your trust in our bank. May I ask what your valuables consist of?"

Jack looked questioningly at Banes.

"I have advised Judge Jack not to disclose the contents of his bag for security reasons." Banes sounded very official.

"I see." The teller eyed the bag suspiciously. "If you will take a seat, I'll get our president, Mr. Clark."

Jack nodded.

On the far side of the bank lobby a brilliantly clothed woman was seated on a blue-striped settee, acting as if she were reading a newspaper. The chandelier overhead shot flickers of light onto her bright red hair. She was just past the flower of her youth, a bit on the corpulent side, but in a provocative way. Purposefully, she turned her back to the two men.

Shortly, Mr. Ribbons returned with a distinguished-looking gentleman who appeared to be in his early fifties. Ribbons made the introductions, emphasizing the titles of the customers.

Clark smiled broadly at Jack and Banes, impressed with their titles and appearance. "Mr. Ribbons tells me that you have some valuables to place in our vault."

"And a sizable deposit. I believe I failed to mention that to Mr. Ribbons."

"Won't you come into my office, where we'll be more comfortable?" Clark's elegant office was furnished with a gleaming mahogany desk strewn with official-looking papers. He motioned for his guests to be seated in two leather-upholstered chairs fronting the desk, while he assumed his position of power behind it.

The men engaged in small talk, touching on the lovely weather and territorial politics. The preliminaries over, Mr. Clark turned to business. "What, may I ask, do your valuables consist of?" he queried, eyeing the leather bag resting on Jack's lap.

"As I told Mr. Ribbons . . ." Banes began. "I have advised the judge not to disclose that information . . . for security reasons. You understand."

"Certainly." Clark was magnanimous. "I understand that you represent a prospective mining group." The inflection of his voice clearly invited Judge Jack to reveal more about their business.

"Correct," was all Jack said.

This piqued the bank official's interest as intended. "And the size of your deposit?"

"Twenty-five thousand on this visit. I expect to have a larger sum next time."

Clark's eyes grew round when he heard the amount of money to be placed in his bank. His interest in the valuables waned. The bag could be full of nitroglycerine for all he cared. All that mattered was the money. "The security system in our bank is one of the best anywhere. I assure you that your money will be safe."

Judge Jack opened the leather bag and took out a handful of bills, all of large denomination. He counted them out on the desk, handling them negligently as only the wealthy can do.

"Twenty-five thousand," the judge finished. "And my valuables will remain in the bag, which, as you can see, locks." The judge locked the bag and placed the key in his waistcoat pocket. "Now, if you don't mind," he continued, "I would like to place it in the vault myself."

Clark jumped to his feet. "Certainly, certainly. Ribbons"—he shouted through the open door to the clerk—"write out receipts for twenty-five thousand dollars cash and for"—he hesitated, eyeing the bag—"one valise filled with valuables." He chuckled at the vague description.

It was clear that he considered the acquisition of this new client a banking coup. After the soft-sided valise had been placed in the vault and the receipts had been delivered to Jack, Clark accompanied his guests through the bank to the front door. Just as they were preparing to leave, he held the door closed momentarily and blocked their departure with his body.

"Gentlemen, the annual ball honoring the 1850 formation of the territory of New Mexico is tonight. Our territorial governor and other dignitaries will be in attendance. I would be honored to have you as my guests. The ball begins at eight o'clock in the town hall."

Jack and Banes looked at each other questioningly. Finally, Jack nodded graciously. "We would be delighted. Until tonight, at eight."

At precisely nine o'clock that evening Judge Jack and Colonel Banes entered the ball. Jack was dressed in evening wear, a black suit of superfine with a winter-white silk cravat and waistcoat. He carried a gold-topped cane in his gloved hand. Colonel Banes sparkled in his military dress uniform. Their late arrival created somewhat of a stir, as was their intention.

Clark hurried over to greet his esteemed guests. He introduced them to the welcoming board: John Carrington, owner of the White Castle Hotel, Leonard Albert, chairman of the Cattleman's Association, and Judson Smyth, secretary to the territorial governor.

"Judge Jack"—Smyth threw his head back and adopted an official tone—"I would like to present the governor of the Territory of New Mexico, His Excellency, Mr. Ned Casson."

Jack listened for the sound of trumpets as Smyth stepped aside, revealing the governor. Casson had a strong-boned face with a hard, sardonic quality to it. He was the ultimate politician, outgoing, warm, and friendly, while at the same time calculating, fake, and slightly arrogant.

As if he were giving his inaugural address, the governor explained the significance of the ball to the Territory of New Mexico, giving minute details of its history. He then shared his vision of the glorious future of the territory, predicting that Congress would soon grant them statehood.

Jack and Banes listened attentively, nodding occasionally to show agreement or surprise. Finally, Casson moved in for the kill. "The future of our territory depends upon men like you. I've been told that you've struck it big in the mine fields. May I ask what you've found? Gold? Silver?"

Colonel Banes looked at Judge Jack and then back to the governor, stalling for time. He cleared his throat and feigned gravity. "You understand our desire for secrecy."

The governor assured him vigorously, barely able to contain his excitement.

Judge Jack stepped closer and spoke softly. "The group I represent has discovered what appears to be one of the biggest diamond strikes in the world."

Casson's eyes snapped with delight and burned with greed. "Does the bag you deposited with Mr. Clark today contain samples?"

"It does," Jack conceded. "But I would remind you that we don't want word of our strike to get out until we have verified the gems through an independent expert and have had time to form a corporation for their extraction and disposal. I'm sure you understand."

"Absolutely," the governor fawned. "I assure you that nothing you reveal to me or to Mr. Clark will go beyond us." He paused. "I would like to see your samples, however."

Jack appeared to consider the matter gravely. When sweat popped out on the governor's brow, he hid a smile. "Very well. If it is convenient, we will meet you gentlemen at the bank in the morning, say about ten o'clock."

Governor Casson beamed. "Very good!" He bid Jack and Banes good-bye reluctantly and moved to the other guests.

The colonel turned to Judge Jack. "You sly devil. With your cunning you should be in the Washington diplomatic corps."

"That's a thought, my friend. But I understand the pay isn't so good."

Jack and Banes chuckled together. A moment later Judson Smyth approached them with a brightly clothed woman slinking along at his side.

Judson might be in his mid-thirties, but he looked older. He was a short, rather nondescript person, slightly balding, with an unattractive paunch, the kind of person whose age is difficult to determine.

"Judge Jack, Colonel Banes, may I present my wife, Rachel Smyth."

Jack and Banes bowed over Rachel's hand. Jack decided she was attractive in a showy sort of way.

With long eyelashes fluttering, she enthusiastically greeted the judge, not sparing Banes so much as a glance. Her bois de rose ball gown was cut very low, revealing the high swells of her blue-veined breasts. Masses of red curls were elaborately arranged in a chignon, complete with feathers and a miniature bouquet of dog roses. The feathers looked like a bird in flight each time she flirtatiously tossed her head.

Everything about her seemed calculated to get a rise out of a man. In Judge Jack's case, she succeeded. A slight flicker of recognition crossed his mind, but he was unable to place her.

"You're a judge?" she questioned Jack with her heavy Southern drawl. I didn't know we had such handsome judges out west."

She stared overlong at Judge Jack's eye patch. When he glared back, she appeared distressed. "Oh, you must forgive my rudeness, staring like that. It's just that your patch adds a hint of mystery. Did you lose your eye fighting during the war?" she asked brazenly.

Jack nodded. "At the Battle of Atlanta." It was a brazen lie. He had never served in the army. Actually, he had lost his eye in a scrape with the law. But the war-hero scenario was much more beneficial, particularly with women.

Rachel affected an exaggerated pout. "You poor thing."

"You mustn't distress yourself on my account, Mrs. Smyth. One becomes accustomed after a while." He waved her concern away. "I even find it amusing when my friends call me One-Eyed Jack."

Rachel laid her hand on Judge Jack's arm. "Just so, you're a hero. In fact, you're obviously a man of great accomplishment. I understand you've made a big strike in the mine fields."

Sputtering and coughing, Judson interrupted his wife before she could say more. "My wife speaks a little bluntly at times, Judge." His face flamed with embarrassment. "I hope you will forgive her."

"I think your wife is charming, Smyth."

"How sweet you are," Rachel oozed, then cast her husband a fulminating glare.

"We should mingle, my dear." He grabbed her arm, showing more spunk than Judge Jack would have thought him capable of.

"Very well." Rachel jerked her arm out of his grasp. "I'll save you a dance, Judge. Later." Her eyes promised more than a dance.

"It will be my pleasure."

Smyth led his wife away, talking to her in low tones.

"I believe the lady's being scolded." Banes chuckled. "She's a brazen hussy, I'll have to say."

Judge Jack's response to Banes's observation was not a smile, but a leer.

During the course of the evening Jack and Banes were questioned time and again about their strike. They always dismissed the issue out of hand.

Satisfied that they had aroused the curiosity of Santa Fe's

wealthiest citizens, Jack decided it was time for him to collect on Rachel Smyth's verbal promise of a dance . . . and her non-verbal promise of much more. He ambled over to her. "Mrs. Smyth, may I have this dance?"

"I'd be delighted."

He took her into his arms and led her lightly over the floor. As they floated to the tune of a Viennese waltz, he maneuvered her into an alcove that was blocked from the ballroom proper by a series of overgrown palms.

They continued to sway to the music. Rachel pressed her lips against Jack's throat, breathing shallowly, flicking her tongue out, causing goose flesh to rise on his neck. "My husband's work takes him away from home. A healthy woman gets lonely." She moved against him seductively.

Jack's passion was kindled by Rachel's forwardness. The desire flashing in her eyes made her invitation unmistakable. "It's a shame for such a beautiful woman to be lonely," he played along. "When do you think your next lonely moment might occur?"

A gleam of triumph shone in Rachel's fiery eyes. "Right after the ball. Seems there's an emergency. My husband has to go to Albuquerque on government business tonight. He'll be leaving in a few minutes."

"Rachel honey," Justin's voice called from the other side of the palms as if on cue.

"I live on San Francisco Street just three blocks from here. You can't miss it; it's the big white house on the left," she whispered before disappearing around the foliage.

Jack and Banes made their way to the hotel. The judge paused at the entrance to the open bar. "How about a drink?"

Banes yawned hugely behind his hand. "Believe I'll turn in."

"Okay. You go ahead. I'll have a nightcap. See you in the morning."

Fifteen

Jack approached the Smyth home, cutting through the darkness swiftly, like a hot knife through butter. A candle burned in the window, lighting his way up the walk. He smiled in anticipation and rapped his knuckles against the carved oak door.

Rachel opened the door immediately, dressed in a transparent nightgown of scarlet lace. The room behind her was dimly lit by red tapers. The faint glow of candlelight failed to reveal her more obvious physical imperfections. With her flaming hair hovering around her torso like a silken cape, she was a sight to accelerate any man's heart.

Any man save the blond lawman watching the twosome intently from across the street. He knew Rachel for the hard-hearted, lying, murdering trollop that she was. And if it was the last thing he ever did, he would see her punished for the heinous crimes she had committed.

"I thought you would never get here," Rachel said flatly, drawing the judge into the room and slamming the door, hiding them from the jewel-green eyes that burned in the shadows.

The seductive mood was shattered. All coquetry was gone from Rachel's voice. She took Jack by the hand and led him to her bedroom. A bottle of wine rested on a small table beside a flickering candle. Two wineglasses had already been filled. "Sit," she ordered.

Jack sat down, somewhat bemused.

She perched on an embroidered chair and stared soberly into his eyes. "Tell me, Judge, do you miss Chicago?"

A flash of surprise crossed Jack's face before he hid his alarm. "I'm sure I don't know what you mean, Mrs. Smyth. I've never been to Chicago."

She smiled like a hound on the scent of a hare. "Indeed? Does the name Josh Elam mean anything to you? You remember, the president of the First State Bank of Chicago?"

Jack's color rose in the dim light. "Go on."

"It's not very flattering that you don't remember me."

Jack searched his memory for a woman who resembled Rachel. The vision of a raven-haired teller came to mind.

"Ah, you do remember. That's better." She smiled, the air of seduction evident in her expression and demeanor once again. "I must compliment you. Your scheme was the finest piece of double-dealing chicanery I had ever seen. As I recall, you walked away with one hundred thousand dollars."

"You have a good memory, my dear. With admirers like you, I regret leaving Chicago."

"Oh, I don't think so. If you had stayed around, Josh Elam would have lynched you." She made a show of reaching for her glass of wine, taking a sip, and staring wide-eyed at Jack over the rim. "When I saw you in the bank this morning, I knew you were involved in another scam. And that masquerade you put on tonight, acting coy about your big strike . . . how shameful." Her expression said something else altogether. "Those fools hanging around the governor haven't the sense God promised a cross-eyed mule. Else they would have seen right through you."

"But they didn't see through me." His expression was mildly menacing. "And they won't unless you tell them."

"Oh, I won't tell them," she whispered huskily. "I want in on the deal."

"Why should I let you in?"

"I could send you to jail for the rest of your life"—she paused, a hard glint entering her eye—"you wouldn't like jail. I've been there. It's not a nice place at all."

"You, in jail?"

She waved his question away. "It's not a subject I care to

discuss. That's in the past. I'd rather discuss the future. Our future. I have much to offer you. I'm in a position to know the governor's thoughts on nearly every subject, practically before he even thinks them. Since he obviously fits into your plan, not having to second-guess his next move could be invaluable." She raised her perfectly arched brows fractionally.

"I'm still listening."

"I'm also quite adept at using my feminine charms as a means of persuasion." She smiled and fluttered her dark eyelashes provocatively.

This time Jack was unmoved by Rachel's flirtations. "What do you want out of all this?"

"A share of the take. And I want out of here. When you leave, I want you to take me with you. Unless I miss my guess, when you pull this off, you'll have to go far, far away. I want to go with you." Where Jay Hampton can never find me, she added silently.

"And what about your husband? What if he presents a problem?"

"Then we'll just have to kill the son of a bitch, won't we?"

Jack studied her for a moment, considering her proposal. She was correct; prior information regarding the governor's thinking could prove invaluable. Her feminine charms might also come in handy somewhere down the line. Furthermore, since she already knew who he was, he either had to take her in or kill her. At the moment he didn't want to kill her. It might raise suspicions. And her body was tempting. "You're in."

He summarized his actions thus far, as the seduction commenced. As he spoke, he reached across the table and took her hand. First, he explained, he had gotten himself appointed district judge of Adobe Wells through the efforts of Willard Banes. This enabled him to raise capital through taxes and fines. Second, he had either bribed or intimidated the mayor and town council until they allowed him to take over Sandy Johns's land, which was the ideal setting for his diamond mine, far enough out of town to provide privacy, close enough to be readily accessible. He left out the part about having Jeff Johns shot. That act had discouraged opposition from anyone else. If only his men had checked to be sure the breed was dead . . .

"Where did the diamonds come from?" She sighed as his fingers inched up her arm, brushing the outside of her breast in passing.

"Through an acquaintance of mine in South Africa I bought uncut diamonds to entice even the most conservative capitalist." He placed his fingers on Rachel's cheek, slowly tracing her porcelainlike skin down her neck. "I've hired miners to give the project an air of legitimacy. Two of them had served time in prison for salting mines. The promise of a generous reward persuaded them to try it again. The diamonds are embedded in the walls and ceiling of a hidden chamber. It'll take an expert to discover the fraud."

He rose and walked around to her side of the table. Standing, she placed his hands on her breasts, then slid them down over her lace gown to rest on the swell of her hips. His breathing quickened.

"Go on," she whispered.

"I plan to convince Clark and Governor Casson that the mine is genuine. Using their influence, I'll sell my interest to the highest bidder, then clear out of town before the scam is uncovered. By the time mining engineers are hired and production has begun, I'll be long gone."

Rachel placed her lips on his. Her tongue moved lightly across his mouth. "*We'll* be long gone."

He nodded. "Undoubtedly, the governor will send an expert to inspect the mine. If I refuse, Casson'll shy away from the deal. But if I have advance warning, I'll be able to ensure that the expert agrees with our story."

"And what of Colonel Banes and the two miners who salted the cave? What's their cut?" Rachel's voice was husky, sensual.

"The two miners have already been taken care of. I'm the only one who knows where the diamonds are," he continued. "As for Banes, I haven't decided on his fate yet. Right now he's useful. Whether he survives or not remains to be seen."

Rachel smiled appreciatively at the judge when he finished his tale. "Judge Jack," she said softly, brushing her hips against his, "you're a brilliant con. But do you have what it takes to help this lonely lady get through a dreary night without her husband?"

"Let me know in the morning," Jack growled hungrily. With a sweep of his arm he cleared the table of bottle and glasses. Broken crystal lay about them, crimson wine soaked into the expensive rug under their feet.

"Down on your back," he ordered harshly.

Rachel obeyed, jerking her gown up to her waist.

With her obvious charms bare and spread for him, Jack ripped his trousers open. Buttons joined the shattered remains on the rug as he fell upon her. Vigorously, he entered her in one long thrust. He pounded into her like a stallion covering a mare and wrapped his hands around her pale neck.

Her eyes grew wide as he tightened his hold. At first fear, then uncontrollable passion, darkened her gaze. He cut off her breath, causing the sensations below her waist to sharpen, grow more intense. Vigorously, she bucked against him. Just as she was about to lose consciousness from lack of air, violent completion seized them both.

Shouting his fulfillment, he collapsed on top of her, releasing his hold.

"That was the best," she rasped, rubbing the bruises that were forming on her neck.

"We're just getting started."

The look in his eye as he led her to the bed made Rachel shiver. She wondered if she had finally met a man more evil than she.

Surely not.

When Judge Jack and Colonel Banes reached the bank the following morning, there was mass confusion outside the stone building. The street and sidewalk were filled with reporters from various newspapers and magazines throughout the country. Elbowing their way through the crowd, Jack and Banes saw Governor Casson, Mr. Clark, and three expensively dressed gentlemen waiting for them.

Clark hurried their way. "Please let these men through," he shouted over the din of voices.

The reporters' shouts merged into one voice.

"Where's the strike?"

"Can we see the diamonds?"

"Why is the governor here?"

Mr. Clark raised his hands for silence. Jack and Banes slipped past him into the bank. "We will inform you of the results of our meeting when we are finished." With that, Clark joined the others.

"I apologize for the crowd . . ." Governor Casson began lamely. "I have no idea how word of your strike spread so fast. I sincerely hope you don't think that I or any of my staff had anything to do with this." To the governor's relief, Jack appeared unperturbed by the mob.

"No. Of course not. It's hard to keep something like this bottled up," Judge Jack said, gazing at the three strangers standing behind Governor Casson.

Casson cleared his throat. "I have taken the liberty of inviting these gentlemen to the meeting. Wilhelm Reins from the Territorial Office of Mines"—he pointed to the tallest of the three—"Sterling Travis from the Albuquerque Territorial State Bank"—the fattest—"and Ronald Albano"—the happiest—"who owns and runs a jewelry store here in Santa Fe. I hope you have no objection."

Jack managed to look mildly put upon. In reality, he was amazed at how fast the governor had worked, and quite pleased.

The party of seven withdrew into Clark's office. Jack's leather bag lay on the desk, awaiting inspection. An armed guard, standing beside the desk, was dismissed as soon as they entered the room.

Soberly, Jack retrieved the key from his vest pocket, unlocked the bag, and poured its contents out on the desk. There was an audible gasp from all but Jack and Banes.

The diamond experts went to work immediately, inspecting each stone carefully with their convex lenses. Mr. Reins was the first to lay his glass aside. "Governor." He beamed with excitement, his close-set eyes flashing. "There is no question in my mind; these stones are genuine uncut diamonds."

The other two laid aside their tools as well.

"I concur with Mr. Reins's evaluation," Mr. Travis said solemnly.

"Same here," Mr. Albano added.

Governor Casson thanked the experts for their assessments and summarily dismissed them. "Well now, gentlemen . . ." he began. "What is your next move?"

"First, we'll have our own expert examine the stones. I have contacted Elanzo Welch from San Francisco. He, of course, is one of the foremost geologists in the country. If he agrees with the assessment of Reins, Travis, and Albano, we will then form a corporation and begin production in earnest."

The men sat in silence for a few minutes.

"I've had some experience in mining ventures. And I'm aware that they take a great deal of initial capital outlay." The governor paused for emphasis. "Would you be interested in investors?"

Jack pretended to consider the governor's proposition seriously. He ran his fingers slowly along each side of his mustache. It seemed as if time were suspended. He noticed with alacrity that Clark and Casson were barely breathing. "Without committing myself at this point, I would be interested in hearing your proposal." He appeared to choose his words carefully as he continued. "I assume there will be others besides yourself—"

"Certainly," the governor hastened to assure him.

"Very good. While I wait for Mr. Welch's report, you can pursue the matter from your end. If you wish."

Shortly thereafter, Jack and Banes were led out a back door in order to escape the clamoring reporters. They congratulated each other on their success and left respectively for Adobe Wells and Fort Bascomb.

Sixteen

It was almost high noon before Heath and Stevie settled Blue in at Pilar's boardinghouse and left town.

Just as Stevie predicted, Pilar had welcomed Blue into her home. In fact, Pilar seemed almost relieved that the young woman had left the saloon and was now under her protection.

As for Winter, Stevie had taken him aside and asked him to care for Blue while she was gone. One look at Blue's face had brought a sheen to the Indian child's eyes. When asked to help the poor, abused woman, he squared his frail shoulders and vowed to keep her safe.

Heath and Stevie left their odd assortment of friends shortly thereafter. Passing the temporary city erected by the miners, they rode side by side, slowly so as not to attract undue suspicion.

"That was a good thing you did," Heath said, breaking the silence.

"Which thing?"

Heath caught her gaze, her eyes stygian black, his, sapphire blue. "What you did for Blue."

Stevie was uncomfortable with his praise. She was even more uncomfortable with her growing desire to please this man—this white man. She shrugged, breaking eye contact. "It was nothing."

Their conversation died a natural death and they galloped along at a relaxed pace in silence. It was mid-afternoon when they reached the grotto area. The cave was situated in the side of an outcropping of rock that rose a hundred feet straight up from the floor of the plateau. Tall sentinel pines guarded the base of the outcropping, forming a natural shield for the entrance to the cave.

Stevie stretched in her saddle. "We should approach it from over there"—she pointed west—"away from the main road."

Heath nodded. "Lead the way."

Riding in a wide circle, she led him to within two hundred yards of the cave. They tethered their horses to a tree and slipped stealthily down to survey the grotto's entrance. Lying on their bellies, they observed dozens of miners passing in and out of the cave like ants streaming to a picnic.

"I never dreamed there would be so many of them," Stevie said with wonder.

"Most of them will leave as soon as the sun goes down. We can't do anything until then." He laid his head down, close beside her hip. Startled, she scooted over. He pushed his John B. over his face, hiding a satisfied grin. "I'm beat. Wake me at sundown."

She balled her fist and hit him square in the belly.

Muffling a yelp, he jackknifed into a sitting position, rubbing his washboard abdomen. "What was that for?"

Mindful to keep her voice low, she hissed, "I didn't bring you along to watch you sleep, pal. Surely there's something productive you can do while we wait. Search the area. Do surveillance. Something."

He raised a taunting brow. "The only thing we need to search is that cave. And we can't get in without being seen. Not till after dark. But feel free to survey the miners to your heart's content. Just don't let 'em see you. Now, if you have no further objections, I'm going to get some shut-eye." He plopped back into position, then added as an afterthought, "And don't ever hit me again. I might not know it's you having a tantrum and shoot first and ask questions later."

She cursed the male gender in general and him specifically. But she kept her hands to herself.

Heath covered his face again, ignoring her petulant mutterings. "I have a feeling we won't get much sleep tonight." His words were muffled beneath his hat. "And frankly, knowing that there was a wolf across the hall from me, I didn't get much last night."

Stevie snorted. "I can't believe you were afraid of Sweetums. Are you sure you're as tough as they say you are?"

Now Heath snorted. Who wouldn't be uneasy around that yellow-eyed devil? To his profound relief, Stevie had left her wolf at Pilar's, to sound the alarm in case of an intruder, she said.

Actually, she figured one wolf was all she'd need on this adventure. On second thought, glancing down at Heath's body, powerful and compelling even in relaxation, she feared she still had one wolf too many. And much to her dismay, she didn't want to keep her hands to herself.

"Don't forget to wake me." He turned on his side, stretching lazily, muscles rippling with the effort.

"As valuable as you've been so far, I wouldn't think of making a move without you." Her feigned sarcasm was thick enough to cut with a knife.

Heath glanced back over his shoulder and winked. "You just haven't had the opportunity to see what I'm really good at, sugar."

Her cheeks burned and her mouth grew dry. "I'm not sure I want to."

He swept her with a suggestive look. "You're not sure? Let me know when you decide."

Stevie was innocent . . . technically . . . but there was no doubt in her mind that he referred to the pleasures of the flesh. And she could well imagine that Lucky Diamond was quite good in that area. "Don't hold your breath." Her trembling lips said one thing, her woman's heart quite the opposite.

Two of Judge Jack's men sat by the fire that blazed against the side of the wall just inside the opening of the cave. Whiling away their time, one was whittling a block of wood. A pile of shavings and sawdust covered his dusty boots. Grimacing, the other was drinking coffee as thick as mud and bitter as quinine. His eyes were glazed and fixed, staring blindly into the glowing embers of the fire. He was more asleep than awake.

"I thought I told you to wake me up," Heath whispered against Stevie's ear, clamping a hand over her mouth to muffle the scream he knew was coming. Slowly, he removed his hand.

"Don't sneak up on me like that! I might not know it's you and shoot first and ask questions later." She threw his words back at him, a bit unnerved by his nearness.

Actually, she had just awakened herself. She had curled up next to him and slept the afternoon away. Warmed and unsettled by the proximity of his body, she had moved to the edge of the clearing, needing to put as much space between them as possible.

"Very funny." Brow furrowed, he peered at the guards.

"How are we going to get past them?"

"We'll have to wait until one of them comes out."

"What if they stay in there till morning?"

He glanced back at her, grinning. "Sooner or later that fellow drinking coffee will need to take a walk."

She blushed at his implication that the guard would have to answer the call of nature. Stevie was sadly lacking in the area of propriety, but even she knew men didn't speak of such things to ladies. It was a good thing she had a dark complexion. Otherwise she would be red-faced around Lucky all the time, given his suggestive comments and unsettling effect on her. The handsome rake could give the term *redskin* a whole new meaning.

As if to prove Heath's prediction true, the tallest and ugliest of the guards left the warmth of the fire to answer the call of nature, unbuttoning his trousers as he walked into the woods.

Heath moved on silent feet, crossing the area between them and the guard before Stevie even knew he was gone. With a low thump he rendered the man unconscious with the butt of his revolver. He dragged him back to a wide-eyed Stevie and tied his hands and feet with a piece of rope. They waited silently for another twenty minutes.

"Hey, Frank," the other guard called in a low voice. When he received no answer, he took a step into the clearing. "Frank!" Again silence. Retrieving his long gun, he stepped back into the inner recesses of the cave, out of sight.

"Damn. Guess it was too much to hope that he would come

out to see what had happened to his friend." Speaking as if to himself, Heath continued. "I'll have to wait for the fire to die down before I can go in."

Stevie and Heath waited in tense anticipation, both aware of the dangers they faced. An hour later only a few embers smoldered in the opening of the cave, providing scant illumination.

Heath turned to Stevie. "You stay here until you hear an owl hoot. Then come on in. If you don't hear it in fifteen minutes, get the hell out of here."

"I'm coming with you."

He grasped her shoulder. "No."

"You can't dictate to me!" She struggled against his grip.

His voice was soft, his hold firm. "Use your head. If I get captured, I'll need you to rescue me. If we go in together, he might get us both."

She narrowed her eyes at the disarming grin that was more or less a constant part of his handsome face. "Thought you said for me to get the hell out of here."

Standing, he dropped a light kiss on her brow. "Only if you're sure I'm dead."

She took his hand. "Don't say that. Even teasing."

He bent slightly, breathing his words against her cheek. "Ah, Miss Johns, it almost sounds like you care."

She jerked back. "Of course I care. I'd have to ride all the way back to town for help if you got killed. And I'm scared of the dark." She paused for effect. "Besides, I might not find anybody else dumb enough to go up against the judge with me."

"You may be right," he deadpanned. "Never let it be said that you're not all heart." Smiling, he chucked her under the chin, checked his weapons, settled his hat on his head, then made to leave.

She touched his arm. Looking intently through the darkness, she saw golden flecks of starlight dancing in his eyes. She also saw an emotion that disturbed her. No man had ever looked at her like that. "Be careful," she cautioned, speaking to both Heath and herself.

His answer was a light kiss on her lips. "See you in a minute, sugar."

He crawled on his belly toward the cave. Keeping to the far side of the opening, away from the smoldering fire, he edged inside.

At first, he heard nothing; then a shuddering sigh betrayed the miner's position. A dying ember glowed brightly for an instant, just long enough to reflect the guard's eyes. He was squatting down on his haunches not more than ten feet from Heath, wholly unaware of Heath's presence.

Heath gathered his legs under his body and lunged like a mountain lion. He slammed the guard back against the rock floor, knocking the breath from his lungs. A fluid shift and he circled the guard's neck with a steel-hard arm. The man fought, kicked, gasped, then stilled. Heath placed two fingers alongside the miner's neck. A slow but steady beat pulsed against his fingers.

Rising, Heath stepped to the aperture and mimicked the hooting of an owl. Almost immediately, Stevie stood before him.

"I see you don't take orders very well," he observed wryly.

She shook her head, not at all repentant. "I never have been good at that. Pa was always commentin' on it."

"I bet."

"Besides, I'm your boss. Remember?"

Smiling indulgently, he took her by the hand and pulled her into the cave. He struck a match, revealing several oil lanterns lined up on one side of the entrance. He lit two of them and handed one to Stevie.

The lamps gave off an eerie glow in the dark cavern as Heath secured the felled guard's hands and feet and dragged him away from the entrance. When he halted abruptly and Stevie ran into him, he recognized her unease. "You okay?"

"Let's just get this over with and get out of here." It struck her as odd that she could find her hiding place so threatening. As a child, whenever she was frightened, hurt, or when the children in town would spit on her and ridicule her for her Indian ancestry, she would crawl into her mama's lap for comfort and security. Swan always comforted her, stroking her hair, telling her that the circle of her arms was Stevie's hiding place. There, no one could hurt her, she was completely safe.

After her mama died, when she was hurt or frightened, she would run to this cave, her hiding place, where no one could find her or hurt her. But now Judge Jack had defiled it. Tears stung the backs of her eyes. What did a person do when they lost the one place on earth they felt secure?

As if he sensed her need, Heath circled her shoulders with his arm and drew her to his side. He smiled when she leaned against him. They were standing in a large cavern that stretched as far as the eye could see. It was starkly beautiful. Formations of stalactites, stalagmites, anthracites, helictites, gypsum flowers, and needlelike crystal aragonites, created by the dripping of calcareous water over thousands of years, picked up the glow of the lanterns. Millions of tiny particles reflected the light in brilliant colors of red, blue, and yellow.

The chamber looked like a cathedral from the Middle Ages. A narrow set of rails over which the mining cars ran wound its way into a rift leading off from the main room.

"You okay?" Heath asked again when her trembling stilled.

She nodded, embarrassed to meet his eye. She stepped out of his embrace. Her gaze fell on a shiny object lying between her feet. "What's this?"

The small crystalline rock sparkled in her dusky palm. Heath cupped her delicate hand in his own and rotated it from side to side, allowing the colored light to play in the center of the stone. His warm hand cradling hers and the cool surface of the rock against her palm were so at odds that Stevie was momentarily amazed.

"I don't know. Ever see anything like it in here before?"

She shook her head, not trusting her voice.

"Well, hang on to it. We'll get it analyzed when we get back to town." He jerked his head. "Let's see what else we can find."

She tucked the rock into her pants pocket. They followed the rails down the rift for some four hundred feet, then came to a small compartment, which ended in a cul-de-sac. There was evidence of ongoing excavation all around them. This was clearly where the miners had been doing their work, though the area was so cramped, not more than ten men could safely swing their picks at one time.

"I'll check the right wall. You take the left," Heath said.

They set about their task, picking specks of rocks and tiny crystals out of the walls and keeping a sharp lookout for minute veins of silver or gold. When they met in the middle of the back wall some thirty minutes later, they piled their meager gleanings on the floor between them. Nothing resembled the rock in Stevie's pocket.

She was the first to speak. "Doesn't look like much to me."

Heath agreed, pitching a handful of pebbles and fragments out onto the flowstone floor. "There's got to be something we're overlooking."

"Maybe the strike is in another cavern and this area is a decoy," Stevie suggested.

"Maybe. But the cave is so huge, it would take us forever to find it." He rose, pulling her up with him. "Better get started."

Just then Stevie tightened her grip on his hand. "We've got to get out of here." Her voice held such urgency that Heath stopped in mid-stride.

"What's wrong?"

She had a premonition of danger. But how could she explain her gift to Heath without giving him the impression that she was some kind of Comanche medicine woman who told the future by rattling eagles' claws and throwing buffalo bones? She couldn't. "We've got to go. Now," was all she said.

He saw the apprehension on her face. "I'm right behind you." They retraced their steps through the tunnel to within sight of the cathedral room. Just as they reached the end of the corridor, they saw lighted lanterns in the entranceway. The harsh voice of an angry man rang throughout the cavern.

"You damn fools!" It was Henry Sims berating the men Heath had disabled.

Extinguishing the lanterns, Heath pulled Stevie back into the corridor from which they had just emerged. He wrapped her in his arms and held her close.

"Get in there and flush him out. He's not to leave here alive. When Judge Jack returns from Santa Fe, we'll all lose our jobs if he thinks security has been breached."

"Our jobs ain't all we'll lose," one of the men muttered.

Heavily armed with rifles and six-guns, they started for the shaft, where Heath and Stevie were hiding.

"We're between Scylla and Charybdis," Heath observed quietly.

Stevie leaned back to look up in his face. "Who?"

"Never mind." He pushed her braid behind her shoulder. "It's a long story. And we don't have much time."

Seventeen

Heath had only moments to plan his next move.

"Bring your lantern, sugar." He darted out of the shaft, sprinting down into the lower area of the cathedral room, stumbling over rocks and rises in the floor as he went.

Stevie ran at his side.

"There they go," one of the guards shouted.

Heath pulled Stevie around in front of him and shielded her with his body. A fusillade of shots rang out as the brigands fired indiscriminately at the fleeing couple.

"Feel free to empty your gun into their carcasses," Heath shouted.

They aimed their six-shooters in the general direction of their assailants and fired on the run. They heard one of the guards scream out in pain, then all was silent behind them.

Heath and Stevie slid to a halt behind a solid pillar that was covered with flowstone. One large shadow, they slipped out of sight. Their breathing was loud and harsh in the stillness as they reloaded their weapons in preparation for another assault.

"Could you see who it was?" Sims yelled from the aperture of the cave.

"No, boss. But there are two of 'em."

"Well, get down there and flush 'em out."

"Not me. It's pitch black down there. They got Red. I'm not hankerin' to catch any lead."

"All right. Come out of there," Sims said begrudgingly.

"They're not going anywhere. This is the only exit. And we'll be waiting for them."

Heath and Stevie heard the guards stumbling. Red moaned as they dragged him along. Soon the cave opening darkened as they all moved outside, taking the last of the light with them.

Stevie and Heath were left in total darkness.

"Alone at last," Heath teased to lessen the gravity of the situation.

Stevie moved closer to him. "Any suggestions of what we do now?"

He placed a reassuring arm around her shoulders. "Don't worry; there has to be another way out."

"Not that I know of."

"Where's your faith, Miss Johns?"

"I left it outside with the horses."

He chuckled. "Bring your lantern and hang on to me."

With mincing steps they made their way to the inner recesses of the cave. The floor sloped downward for fifty feet, then rose gently. They soon reached a point that was above the level of the cave's aperture. Heath climbed up the slight rise, then pulled Stevie up behind him.

"I don't think they can see us here. I'll light one of the lanterns."

Stevie sighed relief. Despite her earlier teasing, the darkness had been closing in on her; she felt as if she could hardly breathe. When the lamp burst into flame, she drew a deep, cleansing breath.

Heath studied their surroundings closely. They were in a large, cavernous room. The back wall of the chamber was honeycombed with leads going off in all directions. It was a life-size maze and Heath felt like a very confused rat. However, he was careful to hide his confusion.

He took a rock and scraped the form of an arrow on the wall, pointing in the direction of the aperture. If they were unsuccessful in finding another exit, they would eventually have to return to the cathedral room and confront Sims and company; it would be nice to know at the end of which tunnel danger lurked.

"Let's go, sugar." Moving briskly down the corridor for several hundred feet, they emerged into another large room. Two more channels led off into further recesses of the grotto. Selecting one, Heath again marked it with an arrow before they continued. They wound around a bewildering labyrinth for an hour, then stopped to rest.

"This is a big cave." Heath verbalized the obvious after taking several hard breaths. "Surely there's another way out."

"I don't guess we'd have much success shooting it out with Sims and his men?" Stevie wasn't sure whether she wanted Heath to say yes or no. If he said yes, she would have to actually try to kill those men.

Heath shook his head grimly. "I'm afraid not. Our revolvers would be no match for their heavy firepower."

After the discouraged couple had rested for a while, Heath cupped Stevie's jaw in his hand. "Ready to push on, boss?"

Stevie smiled genuinely. "You don't have to call me boss. After getting shot at together . . ." she trailed off.

"Can I call you Steph?"

She grinned, shaking her head, no. Frankly, their moment of silliness was calming her nerves. And the caressing way he said Steph was extremely distracting . . . pleasantly so.

"I can't make myself call you Stevie." He ran his eyes over her dusty form. "You just don't look like a boy to me. So what do I call you?"

"Well . . ."

"What?" Heath was intrigued by the seductive glint in her eye.

"Sugar is kinda nice."

Heath chuckled low, sexy. "No, sugar is sweet," he whispered against her lips. He kissed her then. Not passionately as she would have expected, but sweetly, almost lovingly. "Just like you." He raised his head and looked down into her ebony gaze; he swore she had stars in her eyes.

His intense perusal made her self-conscious. "Reckon we better go?"

All he did was nod. Taking her hand in his, sliding his fingers warmly between hers, he led her down a damp corridor. When they came to a crawl space, Heath groaned. "This is going to be a tight squeeze for me. I'll go first and see if its negotiable."

Lying on his back, he slid into the crawl space. His chest lodged between the floor and the ceiling, panic advanced like the incoming tide. But years of facing danger with a cool head had prepared him for times such as this.

Exhaling, he collapsed his chest. Inch by tortuous inch he pushed with his heels and hands and scooted through the narrow space.

He emerged on the other side, the ceiling at normal height. He bent over, resting his stinging palms on his knees. His brow dotted with perspiration as he drew deep gulps of air into his lungs. "Okay, sugar, come on through. Slow and easy."

Stevie pushed her way through the crawl space. She made the passage with ease. "How on earth did you get through there?"

Heath chuckled. "It was a tight squeeze."

They moved on. A short distance beyond the crawl space the corridor sloped downward, leading to a lower level of the cavern. The floor was damp. As they continued, the water level rose to their ankles, then their knees. "Here," Heath said, taking Stevie's lamp.

The soft swish of water as they moved steadily forward was the only sound to break the stillness. Panic advanced on Stevie every inch the water rose. Eventually, she was submerged to her shoulders.

Heath stopped suddenly. "We're going to have to swim through that passageway." When Stevie didn't remark, he turned back toward her. "Please tell me you know how to swim."

"I do" was all she said.

"I imagine this sump is short." His words didn't appear to relieve her. "What's wrong, sugar?"

Stevie remained mute, unwilling to admit that she had an unnatural fear of water. Not long after her mother died, two boys from town had found her alone by the lake that watered their herd. They had ridiculed her for her Indian ancestry. When they finished taunting her and pushing her about, they held her head underwater. Jeff rode up on his pony and fired his long gun in the air, running them off. But she had been terrified of water ever since. She refused to meet Heath's eye. "Can't we backtrack and find another way?"

He regarded the characteristically fearless girl. She was pale and biting her lower lip. His heart was strangely warmed. "Sure, honey," he said. "We'll try another way."

After retracing their steps some fifty feet, a draft overhead ruffled Heath's hair. He was elated. Holding his lantern high, he illumined a corkscrew chimney. It led straight up into the darkness.

"Think you can climb this chimney? It has to lead into an upper gallery." He pointed upward. "At least up there we'll be closer to the outside surface."

She smiled into his face. "And farther away from the water."

He lowered his lid, blessing her with a sexy wink that brought color to her face. "Thought you might see it that way."

He jumped up into the vertical shaft and wedged himself with his hands and arms against opposite walls until he could work his feet up. Bracing himself with his feet on one wall and his back on another, he inched his way up a short space.

"Hand me the lanterns," he called down to Stevie. He bent down, grasping the wire loops in one hand. Pressing his back and feet on opposite walls, he extended his other hand to Stevie.

She jumped as high as she could, missing his fingers by a fraction of an inch. On the second try she got a good hold. She was amazed at the strength in his arm as he lifted her effortlessly. Taking his lead, she wedged her feet and back against opposite walls. She followed him up the chimney until they reached the top some thirty feet above.

Heath was lying on the floor, panting, when Stevie topped the rim. She was breathing hard too, but not as hard as Heath. "I didn't know you were so old and out of shape," she teased, collapsing on the floor.

He rolled over to where she lay and wrapped his arms around her. Growling into her neck, he said, "I'll show you who's old." He pulled her under him and kissed her. His hands mapped each delightful curve as his tongue made love to her mouth. His breathing came in short, rapid pants.

Supposing he was beside himself with raging desire, she grew excited. Her hands wandered over him, up his muscular chest, over his broad shoulders, down his sculpted torso. His right side felt sticky, warm. The rest of his shirt was wet, but it felt cool to the touch.

She pressed the warm, wet area. When he groaned, she knew it wasn't from passion.

She pulled her hand back; it was stained with Heath's blood. He had taken a bullet during the gunfight but had said nothing about it. Her reaction to his injury was odd; she hit his shoulder with her fist.

"Ouch! All you had to do was say no."

"You idiot. You're bleeding. Why didn't you tell me you were hurt?"

"It's only a scratch. We don't have time to worry about it. We've got to find a way out of here before the lanterns run out of oil."

Just then, as if on cue, the first lantern began to flicker.

"We don't have time to treat your gunshot wound, but we have time to roll around on the floor like hounds in heat?"

"Well, some things are more important than survival." His tone was light, teasing, but his face betrayed him. It was pale and drawn from pain and loss of blood.

Then Heath disappeared before Stevie's eyes as the light went out. Fumbling in the inky blackness, he located the second lantern and struck a match to it. The globe shined brightly.

In the pool of light she gently pushed him back to the floor and opened his shirt.

"Now, that's more like it," he quipped.

"Oh, hush! Don't you ever think about anything but sex?"

He pretended to consider the matter seriously. "I don't think so. No! When you're near, I know I don't."

She uncovered the dark bullet wound in his side and gasped. It was worse than she had thought; there was no departure wound. "Give me your bandanna," she ordered. After saturating it with water from a small trickle that ran down one wall, she cleaned the wound as best she could, applying steady pressure in order to stop the bleeding. She moved slowly, stalling, giving Heath time to rest, for she was certain he would insist they move on as soon as she finished.

"The bullet's got to come out." She was quite proud of herself; her voice didn't break.

Struggling to his feet, he held the bandanna close against his side. "Not now."

Slowly, she rose. They stood facing each other. She held him captive with her gaze, pushed a lock of hair over his brow, and regarded him with concern. Finally, she whispered, "You're the boss."

"I thought you were the boss."

"No. I have a rule. Anyone shot trying to help me automatically becomes the boss."

"Well, this little mosquito bite might be worth it, then," he teased, leaning heavily against her. "Come on, sugar. We don't have much oil left. If we don't find an exit soon, this bullet will be the least of our worries."

They had covered a short distance when they came to a large chamber. A strange organic substance was thick on the floor. Heath held the lantern high.

Stevie gasped at the sight of thousands of bats hanging from the ceiling. Like any other woman with a brain in her head, she was terrified of bats. "They look like flying rats."

"It's a bat roost. That mess on the floor is guano, bat dung. The bats won't bother us if we don't bother them. But the guano is highly flammable and explosive. We'll have to be careful with the lantern."

Great, Stevie thought. Flying rats are harmless, but bat crap will kill you. Looking up, she shivered instinctively. Give her the bat crap any day. . . .

She cringed as they crossed the cavern, her boots sticking to the floor with every step she took. "This is awful!"

Heath chuckled indulgently.

They both gave a sigh of relief when they entered another corridor, but their problems weren't over. The passageway sloped downward again, leading inexorably to the same level they had been before they had ascended the chimney.

Suddenly Stevie's worst fears were realized; the corridor led down into another sump. "Great! We escape bats and run into a watery grave," she muttered.

She pulled Heath over to the wall. He leaned against it wearily, weakened by his loss of blood. He closed his eyes as she tended his wound again, futilely trying to stop the bleeding. "We'll have to backtrack and find another way," she said.

He shook his head. "We can't do that, sugar. I think we're close to an opening in the cave. A draft was blowing in the chimney; the wind had to come from somewhere. And those bats back there . . . they have to have a way out."

She hated admitting her weakness, but there was no help for it. "I'm terrified of water. The chances of my swimming through the sump and coming out alive on the other side are not very good. If I don't drown first, I'll die of heart seizure."

Heath remained silent. He recognized what a painful admission that was for Stevie to make. As he weighed their options, the lantern began to flicker. He shook the lantern to get the oil flowing again, but it was no use. In spite of his efforts, the lamp went out. They were left in total darkness.

The two greatest fears of Stevie's life were confronting her. Darkness and water. She clutched the front of Heath's shirt in her fists, clinging to him like a lifeline.

He wrapped his arms around her and held her close, hoping to share his courage and strength with her. "There's no way we can backtrack now," he whispered into her hair. "Our only hope is to swim to the other side of the sump."

For a moment the cave was silent as a tomb. They both realized that if they didn't move on, that's exactly what it would be—their tomb.

"Lead the way. I'll follow."

Heath squeezed her one more time, then pushed off the wall. He grasped her hand firmly and pulled her down into the sump. When the water reached chin level, the ceiling was only one inch above his head.

Stevie had to hold on to his shoulders and kick her feet in order to keep her head above water. Her feet cleared the floor by a good fifteen inches. Her heart pounded so loudly, she could barely hear as Heath spoke to her.

"It's time, sugar. I'll go first. As soon as I'm gone, take a deep breath and follow me." In the darkness he cradled her chin in his palm. "You can do it, angel." He kissed her gently. "I'll see you on the other side." He still didn't go.

"Well, what're you waitin' for?" She tried to laugh, but it sounded more like a sob.

Heath plunged into the murky depths and swam, nearly expending his waning strength. Twice he tried to emerge, only to feel solid rock above his head. Just when he thought his lungs would burst from lack of oxygen, his head broke water. He surged into an air-filled cavern. Gasping for breath, he waited for Stevie. He prayed as he had never prayed before. The seconds seemed like hours.

He waited and waited.

She didn't come.

Eighteen

Frantic, he dove back underwater and found her floundering a few feet away. He had never been so relieved in his life. Grabbing her by the arm, he pulled her through the corridor up into the air-filled cavern.

She gasped for air, then coughed and sputtered to rid her lungs of water. Wrapping her arms around Heath's neck, she hung on for dear life. He crooned words of reassurance, praise, affection.

For a moment he closed his eyes and pressed his cheek against her sodden hair. When he opened his eyes and dropped his head back on his shoulders, thanking God silently that she was safe, he saw that they were in an underground pool. The ceiling was shaped like an arch. Early morning sunlight streamed through a small window that God and time had carved in the dome

"Thank you," Stevie whispered against his cheek.

He smiled down at her face. The adoration he saw in her eyes made him feel ten feet tall. He seemed to soar in the heavens. The warm, wet stream of blood staining the water brought him back to earth.

He had to find a way out of there. His gaze sweeping the enclosure, he noticed a window some twenty-five feet above the pool. "Don't move," he instructed Stevie.

Swimming over to one side, he looked for footholds, vines,

anything that might help them reach the top. He squinted. Surely he was seeing things.

Treading water, Stevie watched him closely. "Is that a rope?"

"Looks like."

A rope ladder dangled from the window to within a few inches of the surface of the water. Obviously someone had used the cave before, perhaps to cool off on a hot summer day. Silently blessing them, he tested the rope that might well save their lives. He wrapped his hands around it, lifted his feet off the floor, and bounced twice. It would hold his weight. "Come on, sugar. Let's get out of here."

"You don't have to ask me twice."

Once they reached the outside, Heath lay on a blanket of pine needles, totally exhausted from the climb. Stevie dropped onto her knees at his side. She flattened her palm on his forehead, then caressed his pale, drawn face. "You're burning up."

He tried for a sexy smile. "Mmmm-hmmm."

She opened his shirt. Taking his wet bandanna, she cleaned the wound and pressed the cloth tightly against him in a vain attempt to halt the renewed bleeding. Finished, she surveyed the surrounding territory. They were high up on a ridge.

"See anything familiar?" His voice was inordinately weak.

Purposefully, Stevie tamped down a feeling of panic. He would be all right if she kept her head and acted responsibly. "We're about three or four miles from where we left the horses." She pointed in the direction of the cave. "If we can reach them, I have some jerky, biscuits, and coffee in my saddlebags."

"I've got a flask of whiskey in mine."

She smiled. "I mighta known."

Helping him stand, she took him by the hand and started over to the side of the ridge. They had taken no more than two steps, when he collapsed.

"I'm sorry, sugar," he muttered, coming up on his knees. "I'll be fine after I rest a few minutes." He was bleeding freely now. His eyes were closed, his breathing labored.

"Of course you will."

Her whisper, sounding more like an order, elicited a soft smile from him.

She pulled his head into her lap. His smile widened. "This is just so you'll be more comfortable. Don't get any fresh ideas."

"Your warning comes a coupla days too late." He chuckled with the last of his strength before he fell unconscious.

Stevie ran trembling fingers through his damp hair. Guilt threatened to overwhelm her. She had coaxed him into helping her, and now it looked as if he might die because of her taste for revenge. Even if he didn't bleed to death before the day was through, he couldn't return to Adobe Wells. Neither of them could, not until he was well. He would need all his strength and quickness to fight off the men who would now be after their blood, thanks to her desire for vengeance.

Well, sitting around berating herself wasn't helping anyone. She would go after the horses, and when she returned, she would take care of him. He would get well and together they would go after the judge. If Lucky didn't make it, God forbid, she would go after the judge by herself. They had suffered too much to give up now. God help him when she found him. Dropping her gaze to Lucky, she realized she had even more reason to kill Judge Jack now than before.

Determination sculpting her visage, she made Lucky as comfortable as possible, then started off at a brisk pace in search of the horses. The way through the forest was familiar, but hard going. It was rough, dense country covered heavily with pine, spruce, piñon, cedar, aspen, and a thick crop of undergrowth.

Limbs tore at her hair, cut her cheek, and ripped the shoulder out of her buckskin shirt. She was so concerned about the wounded man she had left behind, she paid her discomfort no mind, nor did she notice the figure blocking her path.

"Howdy."

She jumped and drew her gun. "Pepper!" she shouted at their ranch cook. "Dammit. You nearly scared me to death." She leathered the weapon.

"Reckon if I'da been one of the judge's men, that's just what you'd be. Daid."

She blushed at the set-down, well deserved though it was.

"Where you headed in sech a all-fired hurry?"

"Back to the cave. Did you know the judge has men working there?"

"Yep. And they ain't the first."

"What?"

"Some fancy man, couldn't see who he was—mighta been the judge, mighta not—went in there t'other day with two old sods. He come out alone." Without giving Stevie a chance to question him further, he narrowed his eyes. "Who was that young feller you was sneakin around with?"

Stevie wasn't surprised that Pepper knew that she and Lucky had been at the cave; he knew everything that happened at the Rocking J. "His name's Lucky Diamond. He's gonna help me with the judge."

"Where is he?"

"He got shot. He's back a ways."

"Won't be much help iffn he's shot," Pepper stated flatly.

"I know. I'm takin' him up into the Sangre de Cristoes till he heals. Will you see that Pa gets word? Ask Pilar to take care of Winter till I get back. And tell her to do all she can to make Blue at home."

"Another stray of yourn?"

"She's a saloon girl. Bear Jacobson beat her up. She's a friend."

Pepper laughed so hard, he almost swallowed the tobacco pocketed in his cheek. "Bet that high-and-mighty Miss Smelter near 'bout busted her gusset when you brung a dove to Pilar's."

Stevie's voice was low, flat. "Miss Smelter doesn't live at Pilar's anymore. Look, Pepper, I've gotta go. Lucky's gonna bleed to death if I don't get back to him."

"You sure it's safe goin' off with that dude all on your lonesome?"

She avoided looking directly at him. Actually, she had thought of little else but having Lucky *all on her lonesome* since the first moment they met. Her hands trembled at the prospect even now.

When she stuffed them in her pockets to hide the tremor, her fingers brushed against the rock she found earlier. Instead of answering Pepper's leading question, she said, "We found this in the cave. Think you could get it over to Fort Union?

See if they can analyze it. It might shed some light on what the judge is up to."

He snorted. "'Course I can. What you think I am? A tuckered-out old man?"

Stevie hid her smile. "Never." She started to leave.

"You be careful with that dude, now. Ya hear?"

She turned back and kissed his bristled cheek. "Don't worry. If he tries anything I don't like, I'll just shoot him again."

With a backward wave she ran off toward the cave.

"That ain't what I'm a-worryin' 'bout. I'm sceered he might try doin' somethin' you'll like."

Stevie found the horses where they had tethered them the night before. They nickered a greeting, sounding as if they were scolding her for being gone so long.

She untied her mount, then approached Lucky's stallion carefully. The powerful animal smelled his master's blood on her clothes. He reared up on his hind legs, eyes wide, ears held back.

"Whoa, boy," she coaxed. "Don't have time for you to be finicky now. We've gotta get back." Like most males, he responded to a woman's soft words and gentle caress.

The ride back to Heath was rather quick, the whole trip—including her conversation with Pepper—took less than two hours. To her relief and utter amazement, Heath was conscious when she returned.

Rummaging through his saddlebags, she found the flask. It was made of sterling silver, ornately decorated, the letters *HHT* engraved in the center of a ring of ivy. She rubbed her thumb over the initials, wondering what Lucky's name really was.

Noticing Stevie's look of suspicion, Heath accepted the flask. "Won it in a poker game."

She tried for a disapproving glare. "Take a stiff drink. You're going to need it when I fish that bullet out."

"I'm certainly looking forward to that."

She admired his ability to tease in view of his condition. He was tough, much tougher than a mere gambler. Ransacking her own saddlebags, she withdrew the needle and thread she always carried.

Heath ran his eyes over Stevie. "What happened to you?"

Not understanding his alarm, she looked at him blankly. "What do you mean?"

He picked leaves and twigs from her hair. She turned her face toward him. Touching her cheek gently, he withdrew bloody fingers. "You're hurt."

On cue, the cut began to sting. "It's nothing."

He dropped his gaze to her torn shirt. "What the hell?" He tried to rise.

Pushing him down, she followed his gaze. Her cheeks flamed when she noticed the large expanse of skin showing, the shadow of cleavage that seemed to mesmerize Heath. Shrugging, she quipped, "Alter I finish sewing you up, I'll take a needle to that. But first, I'll make use of this." Opening her palm, she revealed her bowie knife.

All thoughts of her disheveled state fled his mind. He grimaced. "I hope you're as good with that thing as I first thought."

"Guess you'll just have to wait and see. Take another drink of whiskey and lie still. This is going to hurt like the devil."

"You don't say." Heath did as he was ordered. Lying deathly still, staring up into the sky, he took control of his mind, purposefully shutting out everything but the fluffy white clouds drifting by.

In his mind's eye he saw a rambunctious boy hunting with his father in the New York countryside surrounding their summer home. They were stalking a deer on the edge of a clearing. The man raised his rifle and took aim. The boy placed his hand on his father's arm.

"Let me do it, Father."

The tall man lowered his weapon and nodded. The lad took his gun and crept stealthily along the edge of the clearing while his father watched intently. When he raised his weapon and fired, the bullet entered the deer's heart. It was dead before it hit the ground. The father walked up to his son's side, praising him for his marksmanship.

Somewhere outside of himself, Heath heard Stevie whisper a Comanche prayer, then felt the knife sink into his flesh. He twitched involuntarily as the sharp pain struck him. He didn't make a sound, just paled a bit.

The scene changed. It was night. The boy and his father sat around a campfire, eating roasted venison. The lad listened intently as his father told him stories of fighting for his country. Fighting Mexicans. Fighting Indians. Such daring deeds.

The man was Heath's father, affectionately called the general. And Heath was the impressionable young lad, thrilled at the time spent with his father . . . just the two of them. Those times, so precious and rare, made him the man he is today. They gave him the desire to be a father, a desire that was growing stronger with each passing year.

Heath wondered if he would sit around a campfire with his own son one day, telling stories of fighting for his country. Fighting Rebels. Fighting gunslingers, men like Sims and Jacobson and Carlos Garcia. One day, would his son think his deeds daring? He hoped so.

And what would the boy look like? The picture of his son that burst into his mind captivated and touched him in the region of his heart. He smiled at the dark-skinned lad who looked up at him with adoring black eyes. He pictured himself brushing back a lock of platinum hair from the boy's dusky forehead. His heart ached with love and loneliness.

When Stevie spoke, drawing Heath back to the present, it was with newly acquired awe and respect. "It's over. You didn't make a sound." Just like an Indian, she thought proudly. She wasn't certain if she was proud of the Indian Nation's stoic legacy or of Lucky's bravery. Both, she decided.

Heath looked up into her admiring gaze, into black orbs very like the eyes of his imaginary son. "Must have been the whiskey," he said huskily before he lost consciousness again.

Nineteen

Heath awoke the next day shortly before noon.

The air vibrated to the light tune of winged choralers. The sky above was so blue, so vibrant that it hurt his eyes. Limned by the azure palette, Stevie held a wisp of golden hair in the corner of her mouth, chewing on it like a wayward child, just as she had the first time he saw her. Worry etched her brow. Lavender half moons rode beneath her fathomless eyes.

"You look terrible."

She spat the braid out of her mouth, frowning, obviously insulted. "Why, Mr. Diamond, you do know how to turn a girl's head."

He grabbed her wrist with more strength than she would have expected. "Did you stay awake all night?"

Embarrassed, she cleared her throat. "No, of course not."

"Come on, hon, you can tell me. Bet you couldn't sleep a wink for worrying about me."

She rolled her eyes heavenward. "Deliver me from conceited men! I was awake all night, but not worrying about your worthless hide." The concern in her eyes softened her words. "I went back to the ranch for provisions."

He paled visibly, not from pain. "Are you crazy? You could have been killed." His world faded in and out of focus when he tried to rise.

She eased him back down, ignoring his rebuke. "Don't you dare get up. You're weak. What you need is some of my delicious jerky broth." She grimaced comically. "Men come from miles around to sample my world-famous beef broth."

Heath was distracted, as was her intention. He regarded the liquid she poured into a tin cup as if it were lethal.

She chuckled at his doubtful look. "At least it'll help you regain your strength."

"If you say so."

Hiding a smile, she spoon-fed him.

"Sweetheart, this sh—This broth tastes terrible, but I could get used to your tender loving care."

"Take my advice. Don't." Still, she continued feeding him.

"Steph . . ." he began, and halted at the narrowing of her eyes. Apparently, she really didn't want to be called by a girl's name. Strange. The expression in her eyes was a mixture of defiance, challenge, and pain. "Sugar"—he corrected himself—"thank you for what you did."

She waved his gratitude away. "I didn't do anything."

"You saved my life."

"Nah. It was just a little scratch." Their eyes met and held. Finally, Stevie looked away. "You'll see. You'll be good as new in a few days."

He enfolded her hand and lifted it to his mouth, kissing each fingertip. "As much as I'd love to lie here and let you pamper me for three or four days"—he said between kisses—"we can't spare the time. They'll guess that we found another way out of the cave and come looking for us."

"That may be so, but we're not going anywhere until tomorrow. At least. Now, finish your soup."

"Tomorrow, then. No later." Obediently, he drank the remainder of the broth. "I feel better already." He grinned up into her face. "Wanna feel?" He raised his eyebrows.

She tried for a derisive snort . . . and failed. It sounded suspiciously like a chuckle. "I was right yesterday. You don't ever think of anything else!"

"Else than what?"

His words were a light caress sliding across her heated skin. Whether his voice was made soft and husky from pain, gratitude, or desire she wasn't sure. She probably shouldn't pursue that risky question.

"Lean down." His eyes glowed with purpose, leaving no doubt what he was after. "And let me thank you properly."

She shook her head warily.

"I just want to hold you a minute," he said honestly.

She tried to hide her surprise . . . and her pleasure. "But you're hurt."

"A little bullet wound can't slow me down. Not when I'm this close to a beautiful woman." He tried to raise his hand to her cheek. The lazy appendage refused to obey his command. In fact, his whole body felt as if it were weighted down by the Rocky Mountains.

Stevie smiled and batted her lashes. "No, but all that laudanum I put in your broth can. It could fell a bull."

As if to prove her words, Heath's lids fluttered briefly, then slid down over his sapphire eyes.

Stevie released the breath she had been holding.

Early the next morning Heath awakened with a start. When he stood and stretched, he was sore, a little light-headed from his medication, but greatly improved. Stevie lay wrapped in a blanket close to where he had slept. He shook her gently by the shoulder. "Hon, wake up."

She yawned and stretched like a lazy feline. "What is it?"

"A noise at the foot of the ridge. We may have to ride quick."

She jerked awake instantly, jumped up, and began packing their saddlebags as Heath moved silently down the ridge. When he reached the edge, he saw just what he expected, Judge Jack's men cutting for sign on the plateau below. There were seven of them, led by an Indian scout. "Damn! Two Paws."

He returned to camp as quietly as he'd come. "It's Jack's men. They haven't picked up our trail yet, but it won't be long. Two Paws is leading them."

Stevie had heard of the Mescalero Apache who was known for his uncanny ability to track anyone, anywhere. He was also known for his absolute ruthlessness. "That's all we need," she muttered, helping Heath break camp.

They doused the smoldering embers from the fire and strewed

leaves and branches around, hoping to obliterate the campsite. Undoubtedly, Two Paws would spot it anyway.

"Ready?"

Stevie jerked a nod. "Are you sure you can ride?"

He gave her one of his heart-stopping grins. "Thanks to you, I'm fit as a fiddle."

"I'll bet." When he mounted, she was glad to see that he showed little sign of pain.

With the soft jingle of harness and the muted thud of horses' hooves against the sun-baked earth, they headed up into the mountains. They burst through the underbrush, plunging into a fast-running stream. Some three hundred yards upstream they came to a rocky bench that led off into a hollow.

"Follow in my tracks as closely as you can," he called softly over his shoulder.

They walked their horses slowly down the bench. Then in single file they backed their mounts to the stream where, reentering, they continued upward. As they climbed the mountain they repeated this procedure six times. Finally they left the stream and continued the ascent through thick underbrush.

"Do you think that'll shake Jack's men?"

"No. At least not for long. Two Paws'll figure it out."

"You choose the darnedest times to be honest. A reassuring lie would be appreciated from time to time."

He smiled and kicked his horse in a gallop. They rode hard and fast, trying to put as much distance as possible between themselves and the men who were tracking them. They worked their way carefully from one slope to the next.

The majestic peaks of the Sangre de Cristoes were covered with snow above the timberline. The bright ball of fire overhead and the exertion of hard riding warmed Stevie. She didn't need her coat, but noticed that Heath donned his. She hoped he wasn't having chills. There was no time to question him as they pushed ahead.

If their circumstances had not been so dire, it would have been a beautiful trip. The scenery was breathtaking. Their only companions were the teeming wildlife that watched their passage with wary interest. Deer and elk, standing as proud sentinels, regarded them stoically. A host of smaller animals—squirrels, fox, raccoon, pika, and endless species of birds—scattered, squeaked, and chattered as they passed through their domain.

Periodically, Heath rested the horses. Stevie checked his wound each time. It was no longer bleeding, but there was an angry red ring surrounding it; as she feared, his skin was hot to the touch. She kept her concern to herself. The men chasing them posed a greater threat at the moment than Heath's physical condition. Still, they would have to make camp soon. Neither of them could go on much longer in this high altitude.

When the sun passed behind the mountain, they pulled up for the night in a naturally formed hideaway. Vegetation was sparse, but their mounts grazed contentedly on occasional bunches of crabgrass.

Heath was freezing. Shivering, he started a small fire for coffee, confident that the distance between them and their pursuers was too great for Two Paws to see the smoke.

Stevie watched him from across the camp. He hunched down in his coat as if he were chilled to the bone. Cross-legged, he sat as close to the dancing flames as possible. As she feared, his eyes were glazed over with fever. Panic was a growing thing in her heart. She couldn't let him die; she just couldn't.

She squatted at his side. "Are you bleeding again?"

"Don't think so."

When he opened his coat, she ran her hand inside. He trembled, whether from chill or her touch neither knew.

"It's dry." However, the heat around the wound had intensified since the last time she checked. He shivered again, this time more violently. She closed his coat quickly, trying to preserve the warmth of his body. She buttoned his duster from top to bottom, then pulled the leather collar up around his chin. Without a word she retrieved the blankets from her saddle and made a pallet for him to lie on. "Roll over here." She wrapped the remaining blanket around his shoulders. "Better?" she asked softly.

"Mmmm."

Apparently, his temperature had not reached a dangerous level yet, for his shivering grew less. Stevie was greatly relieved. She was shocked at the depth of her concern for this man who was little more than a stranger. Was it the danger they faced together that drew them so close, so fast? she wondered.

Chancing a glance at his pale face, her heart lurched. He had lost a great deal of blood; he was sure to be thirsty. She retrieved her canteen, lifted his head gently, and placed the rim against his lips. After he drank his fill and murmured his appreciation, she moistened a handkerchief and mopped his face and brow, hoping to lower his temperature.

Finally, he fell into an unnatural slumber. Stevie tucked the blanket more tightly around him, then settled back to watch over him as he slept. Sometime after sunset he tossed the blanket aside. He awakened, his temperature down.

"Feeling better?" a soft voice came from his side.

"Much." He started to rise. "I'm going to kill a deer for our supper."

"At night? In your condition?"

"Be back soon." He retrieved his weapon and planted a hard kiss on her lips, stunning her. Before she could pull free of the spell and physically restrain him, he left camp.

Shortly, the sound of his gun reverberated through the mountains and canyons. Two Paws probably heard it, Heath thought. But he desperately needed something substantial to eat if he hoped to regain his strength.

He and Stevie were on the run. He was all that stood between the woman who had saved his life and scum like Two Paws and Sims. Now was not the time for him to turn into an invalid.

Smiling, he retrieved the deer that lay unmoving on the rock floor and made his way back to camp. He dropped the deer at her feet, looking like a caveman providing meat for his mate.

Unmoved by his offering, she scolded him for his foolishness. "You get over there and lie down before you fall down."

Chuckling softly, he obeyed. Frankly, he wasn't as strong as he had thought. He dropped down on the pallet. Lids half-closed, he watched her.

Not counting the noxious broth she had forced down his throat, apparently Stevie was an experienced cook. She cleaned a portion of the deer and prepared a roast as if she were accustomed to cleaning game and cooking over an open campfire every day of her life. She appeared domestic, in a rustic way.

He couldn't help but mentally compare her to the women he courted on his rare trips to New York. Remembering the O'Hara triplets in particular, he smiled wryly. They were sweet girls. Wealthy, well-bred, not so educated that they would make troublesome wives, well versed on the ins and outs of high society. And they were extremely easy on the eyes: willowy, fair, blond, and blue-eyed. Rad and Chap had dated them during the war. The Turner twins had taken all three of the beauties to Lincoln's second inauguration.

After his big brothers met Kinsey and Ginny—the women they eventually married—Heath had sort of inherited the triplets. He escorted them one at a time, however. Didn't matter which one, most of the time he wasn't even sure which sister was clinging helplessly to his arm. He just called the one he was with at the time "honey." That was fairly safe. And they blushed and batted their lashes prettily when he said it.

Of course, he always acted the consummate gentleman with them. They were ladies, after all. He hadn't been particularly tempted to do otherwise. There were two kinds of women: those you bedded and enjoyed and those you respected and married. It was the code proper gentlemen were supposed to live by, the code Heath had cut his teeth on.

But Stevie called that code into question. Brow furrowed, he stared at her more closely. He had never respected a woman more than he respected her. Nor had he ever wanted a woman more.

Before he met her he'd never found it difficult to be a gentleman—and all that that implies—around ladies. He took his pleasure with whores. Ladies, he charmed and escorted to whatever fashionable function they desired. And he always . . . always brought them home as chaste as the day they were born.

The hell of it was that he didn't care. He was lusty, sure. But he had never met a virgin that he couldn't live without. He liked his bed partners experienced. And he didn't want entanglements once the passion cooled.

The fiery beauty leaning over the cook fire had changed all that. And the hell of it was that he didn't mind.

Noticing his intense look, Stevie grew nervous. She began upbraiding him, telling him how foolish he was to run off into the woods as he had, informing him that she would shoot him herself if he moved so much as an inch from his place by the fire.

"Yes, ma'am." He snuggled down into the blanket, a broad smile on his face. There was nothing nicer than a beautiful woman clucking about, worried about your health, a woman you wanted physically and emotionally, no matter the consequences. It was almost worth getting shot. The enticing smell of fresh coffee and roast deer filling his nostrils, coupled with his waning strength, lulled him into a restful sleep.

Stevie shook Heath's shoulder gently. "Lucky. Wake up."

He opened his eyes and saw the face of an angel, her platinum halo limned by the smoldering fire at her back. "Have I died and gone to heaven?"

She raised her brow skeptically. "I'm not convinced heaven's where you'd go." An affectionate smile lit her face. "Are you hungry?"

He came to a sitting position. "Ravenous."

"Then you're not in heaven. I'm sure men aren't hungry in heaven," she teased, wondering at his strained smile.

He was in somewhat of a dilemma. His most urgent sensation at the moment was not hunger for food nor even for her beautiful body. It was the discomfort caused by a full bladder.

How did one tell a beautiful woman that he needed to relieve himself in the bushes before he sat down to supper? Campside etiquette was not a subject taught at the expensive boarding school Heath and his brothers had attended. Nor did the curriculum at West Point include a course on the matter.

Pity he didn't have his copy of Arthur Freeling's, *The Gentleman's Pocket-Book of Etiquette* close at hand. Surely such problems were covered therein. Ah, well, one improvised. "You'll excuse me for a moment?"

"Excuse you?"

"I need to take a short walk."

Understanding his meaning, her face pinkened.

Heath rose, the blankets pooling at his feet. He swayed slightly from weakness.

Stevie steadied him with a hand to his chest. "Would you like me to go with you?"

Heath touched her flaming cheek with the tip of his finger. "I think I can handle things myself." He thought he heard her mutter, "Pity."

Surely not.

When he returned to camp, Stevie was standing stock-still, facing the far end of the clearing. Five mounted Indians wearing war paint stared back at her from the shadows.

Heath's heart skipped a beat. His rifle was lying on the ground beside the fire, out of reach. He started to place himself between Stevie and the warriors. She waved him away.

For a long while Stevie and the Indians stared at one another. The braves made no attempt to raise their weapons. Stevie made no effort to retreat.

Just when Heath was sure he would yell his frustration, the warrior out front threw a lean, muscled thigh over his horse, slid to the ground, and walked briskly into camp. Stevie relaxed visibly. She met him halfway across the clearing.

Heath tensed, first in apprehension, then, when Stevie and the Indian embraced, in jealousy. How dare the half-naked warrior hold Stevie so familiarly?

The twosome spoke in quiet tones. Heath was unable to decipher their soft Comanche words. The affection in their eyes as they gazed upon each other was enough to incite his temper. Through the years many had called him an Indian lover, but at the moment there was one Indian he could do without. And it wasn't Stevie.

"It's been a long time since I've seen my sun-haired cousin," Black Coyote observed. As a young girl, Stevie had visited her mother's people. Black Coyote and Jeff had been nearly inseparable. But as the Johns children grew older, they lived in the white world exclusively.

"A while." Stevie nodded, wondering at the familiar feeling of guilt that she had somehow abandoned a people who had at one time abandoned her mother. Shrugging away the uncomfortable thought she pointed to his war paint. "Why the medicine, cousin?"

"Comacheros stole our horses."

An Indian band's survival depended upon its remuda. With that one avaricious act, the thieves had virtually sentenced every man, woman, and child in Black Coyote's village to death. "I'm sorry."

Black Coyote looked her full in the face. "Save your pity for the Comancheros. When we find the thieving dogs, they will pay."

She nodded tersely. *"Toquet,* it is well." She didn't want to know what grisly torture awaited the thieves, no matter how well deserved their punishment. "You must be hungry."

After a moment's hesitation Black Coyote nodded.

"You and your brothers are welcome to share my fire and my food. But you are not to hurt my man. He has done nothing to you. He has been shot and is not well. I will protect him." She told herself she referred to Heath as her man simply to protect him from the Indians. Liar!

Black Coyote met Heath's sapphire glare. He knew a jealous man when he saw one. Indian or white, men were the same when it came to their women.

The Indian turned back to Stevie and smiled knowingly. He caught the unguarded expression on her face. It was clear to him that his half-white cousin was as smitten as the man she protected. She looked like a she-bear protecting her cub. "We will not harm your man. But can you promise Black Coyote that your man will not hurt us?"

She cast a glance in Heath's direction, pleased to see that he didn't like her talking with her handsome cousin. Could he possibly be jealous? She turned back to Black Coyote and stood on tiptoe, placing a kiss on his cheek. Out the corner of her eye she saw Heath's jaw tense. "You're on your own." She chuckled softly.

The action was so intimate, the sound so provocative that Heath was ready to commit murder.

"I think your man does not want to share *Yo-oh-hobt Pa-pi,* Yellow Hair, with Black Coyote."

"You're probably right. White men are funny that way," she deadpanned.

She felt a slight sense of unease when she heard her Comanche name pronounced after so many years. It gave rise to feelings too complex to deal with at the moment. Pointing toward the meat, she told Black Coyote's warriors they were welcome to eat.

They descended upon the venison as if they were starved. Their protruding ribs and gaunt frames caused Stevie's heart to ache. At one time Black Coyote had been as big as Heath. Now Heath outweighed him by at least thirty pounds. Obviously, times were harder for the Comanche renegades than she realized.

Glad that the Indians were eating their fill, she took a plate to Heath, noticing how closely he watched the men.

They were renegade Indians on the warpath, Heath knew. But somehow they didn't look very savage eating the meal Stevie had cooked, teasing her as if she were their kid sister.

But what surprised him most was Stevie's wariness around them. She smiled at their good-natured jests. Yet somehow her smile seemed strained.

Was she embarrassed? Heath wondered. Was she ashamed of her relation to them? He sincerely hoped she didn't think he was so small as to think less of her for her Indian ancestry.

Perhaps she looked down on herself because of it? He had known half-breeds who tried to hide their ancestry. But he couldn't imagine Stevie hiding anything. She was the most straightforward, unassuming woman he had ever known. It was one of her many traits he found so appealing. Yet he remembered the poignant way she told of Lame Wolf's hanging. He sensed that Stevie's feelings about her ancestry were quite complicated.

"Do you have far to travel, cousin?"

Heath's head jerked up when Stevie called Black Coyote cousin. He was uncomfortable admitting how relieved he was that she was related to the man she seemed to care about so much.

"Far."

It pained Stevie to see Black Coyote and his men reduced to riding bony nags. Comanches were the greatest horsemen in the world. This indisputable fact was a source of pride for the Nation, particularly these renegades in New Mexico Territory who resisted being confined to the white man's reservation.

Their wealth was measured by the number and quality of their mounts. The worthless horseflesh cropping at the edge of camp was more than inconvenient for Black Coyote and his men; it was humiliating. No one should be humiliated, she affirmed silently, remembering all the times she had felt the sting of shame. "I know where there's a good string of horses not far from here. There's a group of white men camped on the south slope. They're trailing us."

Black Coyote pulled himself up, pride evident in his posture. "We will steal their horses and make them walk home."

Heath had been totally silent up to this point. Stevie and the Indians assumed he didn't know what they were saying and was unable to join in the conversation. He surprised them when he spoke Comanche. "They have rifles; you and your men have only bows and arrows to fight with."

Black Coyote took exception. He turned an indignant gaze on his cousin's man. "We are not afraid of their fire sticks."

Heath retrieved his Winchester where it lay by the fire. After searching through his saddlebags, he found two boxes of cartridges. He handed the rifle and shells to Black Coyote.

Black Coyote barely managed to mask his surprise.

Stevie failed altogether. She pulled Heath aside. "What do you think you're doing?"

He peered down at her from his superior height. "I'm giving your cousin a fighting chance."

"But the whites and the Comanches are enemies. He'll kill those white men with your gun." She lowered her voice, but the pain was evident in its husky tone. "And any others he comes across."

"I doubt he'll kill anyone who doesn't need killing," he said for her ears only.

Black Coyote watched the exchange, then slowly rose to his feet. "Why do you give this to your enemy?"

"You're not my enemy," Heath stated flatly.

Wiping his greasy hands on his naked thighs, he lay Heath's gift aside, then presented him a bow and arrow.

Heath accepted Black Coyote's gift graciously.

"Do you know what to do with that?" Stevie asked, her disapproval of his actions still evident in her tone.

Heath cast her a bemused glance. He and Black Coyote exchanged meaningful looks. "I think I can figure it out."

Black Coyote's intense gaze clung to Heath and Stevie for a moment. Appearing satisfied, he motioned to the others. Rifle in hand, he led his men out into the forest.

They disappeared as quickly and as quietly as they had appeared.

Twenty

Stevie sat silently by the fire.

She didn't really know why she had reacted so negatively when Heath gave Black Coyote the rifle. Fact is, if the men who had stolen the Indians' horses were standing in front of her, or the men tracking them were within sight, she would shoot them herself. So why did it bother her that Heath provided Black Coyote the means to do so?

She sighed heavily. As always, she found her feelings regarding her mother's people confusing.

Heath joined her on the blanket. "Well?"

"Well what?"

"Are you going to tell me what that was all about?"

She turned away from him, resting her chin on her updrawn knees. "What was what all about?"

Grasping her shoulders, he turned her toward him. "You know what I'm talking about. The way you behaved around Black Coyote and his friends. If I've ever seen an ambivalent attitude . . ." he trailed off.

She jerked out of his grasp. "I can't dispute that since I don't know what ambivalent means. Remember, I'm just a dumb Indian."

Purposefully, he responded to her in Comanche. "That last remark was beneath you."

She shrugged as if she wasn't particularly interested in his opinion. "Why didn't you tell me you could speak Comanche?"

"'Cause you didn't ask. Now, are you going to answer my original question?"

"I forgot what it was."

"Somehow I don't think you forget much of anything," he scoffed. "What I want to know is why you acted as if you were ashamed of your cousin. And seemed to love him at the same time."

"I'm not ashamed of Black Coyote." She appeared truly horrified at the notion. Being ashamed of the violent acts committed by Comanches was one thing. Being ashamed of her family was quite another. It occurred to Stevie that the line separating the two was uncomfortably thin. "I do love him. He's one of the few men in this world who has been good to me."

"So what was wrong with you?" he asked quietly. "You were as tight as a bow string. It was almost as if there were two of you, one who wanted to welcome Black Coyote and one who wanted to run from him."

Self-disgust made her queasy. It was bad enough to wrestle with her own conflicting emotions, quite another to hear them verbalized. Feelings of inferiority, of not belonging, of loneliness, isolation, they were all part of being from two different worlds. Who wouldn't be—what did he call it—ambivalent?

"I'm not ashamed of him, or any of them," she said finally, gazing at him in the dim firelight. "Actually, I haven't seen them since I was little." Silver beams of moonlight glinted off her stygian-dark eyes. "But I love my mother's people. What's left of them." At that, her voice broke. "What they represent . . . the things they're forced to do . . ." She trailed off, realizing how vague she sounded. "It's hard to explain."

His heart was strangely warmed at the anguish in her eyes. He touched her cheek lightly. "I've been told I'm a good listener."

She was surprised to realize how much she wanted to open up to someone, needed to share her burden. "I'm half Indian."

"And?"

"And it's hard not having a people to belong to." She gestured vaguely, searching her mind and heart for the words to explain. "When you're half white and half Indian, you're not a whole anything. You don't belong to white society, if for no other reason than you're not welcome. And I can't really blame them." This last was muttered to herself. "And you're not really an Indian. Not if you can't condone the things they do. And no matter how much they love you, they can't understand why you disapprove of their . . . their hunger for revenge."

"You don't approve of the Comanche protecting their ancestral lands?"

"It's what they do to protect it that I can't bear."

"They do what they have to."

"You just don't know what they're capable of." She shivered involuntarily, looking over Heath's shoulder in the distance, as if she were thinking back in time. "When I was four years old I overheard Sully telling Pa about an Indian raid. The things my people"—her voice softened—"did to those settlers were inhuman." A wealth of pain could be found in the depths of her eyes. She lowered her lids.

Heath wrapped his arms around her. He caressed her shoulders gently. Such small, fragile shoulders to carry such an enormous burden of guilt. Misplaced guilt, granted, but guilt nonetheless.

The Comanches were being systematically destroyed, their way of life annihilated, their culture decimated. And why? Greed, prejudice, and hatred. Stevie and thousands more like her would be innocent casualties.

He wished he knew how to help them, how to help the woman he held in his arms. But he was ill equipped to deal with her problems; their lives had been so different. He, who had known nothing but a life of wealth and acceptance, could do little more than comfort her.

True, during the war, during his incarceration at Libby Prison, he had been mistreated and despised for being a Yankee. But that wasn't the same as enduring a lifetime of racial prejudice.

Taking her hand, he rubbed her dusky palm and listened to the fire crackling and the steady rhythm of her breathing. "Your skin's so soft," he marveled.

"And dark."

Her bitterness disturbed him. "It's beautiful. You shouldn't be ashamed of it."

"I shouldn't?" She jerked her hand back, suddenly angry. "I suppose I should be glad that I'm half Comanche. Never mind that because of my Indian ancestry I will never have a life like other girls. I'll never have babies of my own." She blinked back tears. "I'll never have a husband of my own or a home. I'm twenty years old and this is as good as my life's gonna be."

Heath was taken aback. "Of course you'll marry."

"Oh, really?" she scoffed. "Who? A white man? Sure! When we left town, I saw them lining up around the block. Hoping I would consent to bear their children."

Heath knew she was striking out at him because she hurt. "Not all white men are prejudiced. You sell them . . . and yourself short."

Her laughter was not a pleasant thing. "But you assume I want to marry a white man. I don't. Wouldn't have one on a silver platter. Nor an Indian. I would die first before I would marry an Indian and bring more Indian children into this world. More children to be spat upon and ridiculed for their ancestry." Tears streamed down her cheeks. She was unaware of this sign of weakness, so distraught was she. "I couldn't bear seeing my children treated like that," she finished in a whisper, dropping her forehead to her knees. "I just pray I can shield Winter from the worst of it."

Heath suspected that she was telling him things she had never told another living soul. Some, he imagined, she had never fully admitted to herself.

He didn't know quite how to respond. All he could think to do was pull her into his arms. She struggled at first, turning her back on him again. He pulled her against his chest and buried his face in her hair. "Shhh. Just be still and let me hold you." His voice was husky, gentle, filled with something that sounded awfully like affection.

She was silent long enough to rein in her emotions. That's when she noticed that he was caressing her jaw, his thumb coming closer to her bottom lip with each stroke. Her heart accelerated. She wanted him with an intensity that frightened her. And she could tell that he wanted her.

"I won't lie with you," she blurted out defensively. "If you want an Indian whore, you'll have to go to one of the saloons."

Heath stiffened, angered that she would cheapen what was passing between them. It was not just lust they were feeling for each other, but genuine affection. Surely she could sense the difference. She was just too damn stubborn to acknowledge it. He released her abruptly. "You overlook one very important fact, Miss Johns. I have not asked you to lie with me."

She spun around, gazing up at him. Her eyes sparkled with indignation. "What's wrong with me? Am I not good enough for you?"

Her change of heart was so abrupt, the look of righteous indignation so misplaced, all Heath could do was laugh. That was definitely the wrong thing to do.

"Don't you laugh at me, you green-horned, yellow-bellied, sap-sucking, toad-brained cardsharp!" She swung her fist and connected with his wounded shoulder.

He groaned, grasping his wound. Crimson oozed between his fingers as he fell back onto the blankets in agony.

She leaned over him. "I'm sorry, Lucky. I didn't mean to hurt you."

She looked so worried, so adorable that Heath reckoned the pain shooting down his arm was worth it. He chuckled wryly. "You're a crazy woman, you know that?"

"Here, let me check it." She unbuttoned his shirt.

He winced when she brushed against his throbbing flesh. "Dammit, be careful."

"There's no call for you to curse at me, Lucky Diamond."

He scoffed, this from the foul-mouthed angel of Mustang Mesa.

"Be still. I can't get to it with you floppin' around like a fish out of water."

"Owww. You're nursing skills are going to be the death of me yet."

"You're such a baby." She shook her head, but her examination was quick and rather gentle. She soaked the area of the dressing that had dried to his torn skin and eased the bandage back. His wound didn't look as bad as she expected. She wiped the oozing blood away, then applied light pressure until the bleeding stopped.

She sat on her knees at his side and peered down into his face. "It looks okay. But if you have to move, move slowly."

He covered her hands where they rested on the open buttons of his shirt. "I will if you don't hit me anymore."

"Well, don't laugh at me and I won't hit you." She fingered his top shirt button, careful to avoid eye contact.

He rubbed the back of her hand gently. "Deal."

The air around them crackled with sensual heat. With trembling hands she rebandaged his wound. The task complete, she started to rise.

He stilled her with a hand to her wrist. She kept her eyes riveted on the fire. "Sugar, look at me." She obeyed. "Despite what I said earlier, I can't think of anything I'd rather do than lie with you."

Her cheeks flamed, her heart accelerated, her mouth grew dry, while her innermost recesses grew moist. In spite of it all, her voice was fairly steady when she tossed her head and quipped, "If that's an offer to share your bedroll, no thank you very kindly. As shot up as you are, you'd probably just bleed all over me. Then blame me for hurting you afterward."

He smiled crookedly. "Care to give it a test?"

Her legs a bit wobbly, she moved to the other side of the fire, lay on her pallet, and wrapped herself in the blanket. "Good night, Lucky." As an afterthought she said, "Button your shirt against the evening chill."

"Yes, ma'am." He did as he was bid, still smiling. They lay in companionable silence, inordinately aware of the other's breathing.

"Sugar . . ."

"Hmmm?"

"If you change your mind, about . . . you know . . . I'm right here."

She threw a small pebble in his general direction and missed. "Don't hold your breath."

His deep chuckle raised the hair on her arms. She shivered delightfully. Turning over onto her back, she snuggled deeper beneath the blanket.

All of her senses were heightened. The stars overhead shone bright in a black velvet sky. The night sounds seemed unusually loud in the stillness. She was incredibly aware of the man cloaked in golden starlight. It was as if they were the only two people in the world. And she couldn't remember experiencing such a sense of peacefulness.

Ever.

Twenty-one

Naked, he slipped under her blanket, warming her with his body.

"I want you, precious," he confessed huskily, dropping kisses on her neck. "And I mean to have you."

She didn't argue. Instead—as hungry as he—she entangled her fingers in his ebony hair, bringing his mouth closer to her own.

He groaned low in his throat, aroused even further by the significance of her act. It told him as nothing else could that she wanted him. Now.

He kissed her again, not at all restrained. Ravenously, passionately, he crushed her lips with his own, thrusting his tongue into her mouth, in and out, over and over, a sure erotic rhythm that matched the instinctive movement of his lean hips as he pressed them against her.

He still wasn't close enough. Not until he was part of her. With trembling hands he divested her of her clothes. Rising high above her, he settled between her legs. The fire illumined her, a gilded goddess that he would soon make his own.

"Open for me, angel," he rasped, his breath warm on her cheek.

She obeyed gladly, baring her innermost recesses like a beautiful flower spreading its petals to the life-giving force of the morning sun. His lower body was flush with hers. His immense maleness branded her as his own. She could feel him throbbing against her with every beat of his strong, pulsing heart.

She gasped at the heady sensation, marveled at his magnificence when he lifted her thighs, settling them about his waist. He was glorious, limned in the moonlight: a wealth of midnight-black hair resting on bare, broad shoulders, a taut, corded abdomen that quickened at her shy touch, hard, muscled thighs pressing against her flanks firmly.

How she wished she could see his face. But he was cast in shadows with the moonlight and the soft glow of the campfire at his back. This need to see him became an obsession, filling her, flowing from the crown of her head to her toes. She twisted her head from side to side.

Reaching toward him, she tried to visualize him with her sensitive fingertips. She paused to still her shaking hands as first she touched his cheeks. Then slowly she caressed him from cheek to jaw to full sensual lips. He was beautiful! Ruggedly beautiful.

He captured one adventurous finger within the honeyed sweetness of his mouth, drew on it like a babe would his mother's breast. He sucked gently, then dropped his lips to hers once again. He kissed her tenderly even as he positioned his huge, aching need at the portal of her femininity.

"Look at me, angel," he instructed. "I want to see the look in your eyes when I make you mine."

Did he truly speak, or were the husky words transferred from his mind to hers? She didn't know. Frankly, she didn't care. All she could think of was the intense ache between her legs. He could ease it. She knew he could. He had to. She would die of want otherwise.

"It's time to make you a woman," he coaxed. "My woman."

"Please" was all she said, thrusting instinctively in invitation.

"My pleasure." His sexy chuckle turned into a groan as he entered her smoothly. He eased forward slowly, allowing her virginal body time to accustom itself to his invasion. When he reached the barrier that proclaimed her pure, he halted. He smiled with surprise and satisfaction to know that no one had ever touched her as he did now.

He tensed his hips and thighs, preparing to make the final thrust, the thrust that would make them one. Forever.

Stephanie jerked awake. A fine sheen of sweat covered her entire body, soaking her shirt and trousers, plastering the wet fabric to her aching body. Her breath was coming in short, rapid pants. To her horror and shame, there were tears in her eyes.

Quickly, she looked across the fire at Heath. She sighed relief when he shifted onto his side and snored softly.

Heath swallowed the painful lump in his throat. Stevie's low moans had awakened him. He had known instantly that she was asleep . . . and that she was in the throes of an erotic dream. The sensuous dance of her thrusting hips had raised a sweat on his brow. Other parts of his body rose to the occasion as well.

Stifling a groan, he knew that he would sleep no more tonight.

Sunrise found them tense, quiet, traveling farther into the mountains, carefully obliterating their trail as they went. After several hours of hard riding, they crested a peak. An emerald valley lush with grass and flowers lay before them. A craggy mountainside cradled the green carpet in its arms. Two magnificent waterfalls flowed down a precipitous slope, pooling into a reservoir of shifting, shimmering water.

Wordlessly, they crossed the valley, riding toward the falls, crossing a solid slab of rock to the pool.

"Eden." Stevie slowed her horse's pace; tears threatened. She and Jeff had visited this valley many times in their youth. They had dubbed it Eden. How she wished that he were riding at her side even now. "This way." She plunged her horse into the shallow water of the pool.

Heath followed close behind, heading straight for the falls on the left. They passed through the cascading water into a hidden cavern behind it, then entered a naturally formed tunnel. Picking their way carefully toward a brilliant light, they emerged onto the brink of another, smaller valley.

It too was lush with green grass and fragrant wildflowers, a smaller version of the valley they'd just traversed. A clear stream flowed through its midst, a blue ribbon providing water for the teeming wildlife that made the valley its home. The grassy plateau, about six square miles in size, was enclosed on all sides by mountains and cliffs. Except for the tunnel, it had no apparent access.

Heath drew up beside Stevie. He pushed his Stetson back on his head with two fingers and whistled through his teeth softly. "It's beautiful."

Stevie nodded. "We'll be safe here. There's plenty of water and game. The chances of Two Paws finding us are slim. When your wound heals, we'll head back to Adobe Wells."

She looked at him, and the full impact of last night's dream hit her. It unnerved her to admit how much she was looking forward to spending the next few days alone with Heath, how vulnerable she was to his charms.

Her cheeks flamed and her voice grew harsh when she ordered, "So hurry up and get well. You're no good to me like you are. And God only knows what Judge Jack's doing while we're away." Without waiting for a response, she sank her heels into her mount's flanks and galloped away.

He stared at her retreating back. "Now, what the hell brought that on?" he asked Warrior.

Warrior's responding whinny sounded remarkably like "Women!"

During their time in Eden, Heath recuperated rapidly. They spent much of their time relating anecdotes about their past. Examined one by one, these small slices of life seemed meaningless. But all told, they painted a canvas of their previous existence. As they learned about each other, they grew closer and more comfortable in one another's presence.

An overhang in the side of a cliff served as their shelter. It provided a cozy camp. Heath shot fresh meat for the cook pot with the bow and arrows Black Coyote had given him. Stevie went along with him as he stalked his prey, amazed at how skillfully he bagged game. She teased that he wasn't as good as an Indian but he would do in a pinch. Heath, being Heath, pinched her. She didn't scold him, just blushed becomingly.

When his shoulder was almost pain free, they were reluctant to leave. Their desire for each other was a personification of raw lust, a prelude to passion, their constant—if unwanted—companion. Both knew they had mammoth responsibilities awaiting them in Adobe Wells. Yet they sensed this time alone was an opportunity that wouldn't come their way again. By unspoken agreement they extended their stay.

To pass the long days, she taught him a game the Comanches played, using a ball of long grass pulled from the sides of the stream, tied together by two pieces of rawhide. The game involved a great deal of physical contact. When played by Comanche men, it bordered on violence. Such was not the case with Heath and Stevie; their touching was more provocative than injurious.

The sensual tension that characterized their relationship was especially high after each game. Stevie noticed that Heath took long, solitary rides when they finished playing. When she asked him about it, he said the exercise got his juices to flowing and the rides helped work off the excess energy. It didn't seem to work, she noted. He was just as tense when he returned, if not more so. But she refrained from pointing this out.

Each evening they bathed in the stream, first Stevie, then Heath. He invariably teased that he was going to slip down and watch her unaware. She threatened him with bodily harm.

One evening when their sensual tension was unusually high, like electricity building in the sky before a thunderstorm, Heath left for a hunt while Stevie bathed. At gloaming, he returned to camp. She was nowhere to be seen. He called to her, but she didn't answer. The sound of splashing water and her off-key rendition of "Camptown Ladies" drew him like a magnet.

Smiling, he picked his way down the path. She was standing in knee-deep water, her wet hair plastered to the gentle curve of her backside. Her gloriously nude body was bathed in rays of silver. Just as he halted, she turned toward him. Slowly.

He expected her to cover herself with her hands, but she didn't. Instead, she took a step closer to shore. The water shifted, caressing her satiny skin, swirling around her thighs, licking the soft flesh like a lover's tongue.

The breath lodged in his throat. His body responded to her sensual allure. He knew he should leave, but was rooted to the spot. His gaze traveled upward, past her most intimate place—lingering slightly—over her flat abdomen, up to her firmly rounded breasts. He stared hungrily at her rosy nipples. The rise and fall of her chest grew faster. He groaned softly when the dusky globes peaked under his gaze.

When he raised his eyes to hers, he saw fear mingled with desire. This was no seductive sea nymph, but a confused yet curious innocent. He should run like hell, for both of them. He managed not to run. Instead, he treated himself to one long, lingering glance, then turned on his heel and retraced his footsteps up the path.

He was throbbing with unfulfilled desire. A good dousing in the icy waterfall was what he needed to cool his heated blood. He jumped on Warrior's back and kicked him into a gallop.

Stevie crossed her hands over her chest and dropped down in the water. Guilt, embarrassment, frustration, and anger battled for prominence in her churning emotions. She had behaved like a common hussy, and had obviously repulsed Heath.

She couldn't blame him for being put off; she was disgusted with herself. Such behavior was unlike her. Why had she done it? she screamed silently.

The answer came to her with stunning clarity. She had fallen in love with Lucky Diamond. Instinctively, she wanted to give something of herself that she had given no other.

But he's a drifter, a gambler, her sensible self screamed, the kind of man who is here today and gone tomorrow.

Which made him the perfect man to have a brief affair with, since she never intended to marry anyway. The unprecedented idea took root and began to grow, becoming stronger, less shocking, and more enticing by the minute.

When Stevie returned to camp, she was clothed in a thin chemise and bleached buckskin pants made buttery soft by almost constant wear. Heath was resting against his saddle, cleaning his arsenal of weapons. She felt his eyes upon her but appeared oblivious.

Slowly, sensuously, she walked over to the fire and took a seat. Absently, she finger-combed her moist hair, stretching and thrusting her chest forward a bit more than necessary. Smiling softly, she was aware of every tense breath Heath drew.

He had taken two cold showers in the waterfalls, galloped over a three-mile area bareback, and was still throbbing with desire. It showed in his husky voice when he spoke her name. "Stevie."

"Hmmm?"

"I think we should head back to Adobe Wells tomorrow."

She was stunned into silence. How was she to seduce him if they left tomorrow? Exasperated, she turned her back on him.

He stared at her through the darkness. She was embarrassed by her actions, he knew. If he just had the words to let her know it was all right, that he had been flattered she would trust him enough to allow him to look upon her nakedness.

And he ached to tell her how beautiful she was, to confess how very much he wanted her, to admit he had never desired a woman as he desired her now.

But such conversation would lead places neither of them should go. And while she was just a kid—albeit a gorgeous, sexy kid—he was old enough to know better. "Well, good night, then," he said finally.

"Good night."

He failed to note that she did not agree to leave on the morrow.

Twenty-two

Nature conspired against Heath.

When they awakened the next day, the scent of a storm was in the air. Only a fool would leave shelter and begin a trip on such a day. He was a horny hombre who wanted nothing more than to seduce the innocent who had saved his life. But he wasn't a fool.

He went in search of Stevie. She was currying Whiskeypeat, studying the sky. "We'll have to wait till tomorrow to leave," he said.

She jumped as if she'd been struck by lightning. Gaining a measure of control, she spoke without looking at him. "Fine."

He hesitated as if he would say something more, then walked away.

She buried her nervous smile in Whiskeypeat's mane. One more night with Lucky, a voice chanted in her mind. Could she really go through with her plan to seduce him? More important, would making love to him change her emotionally as well as physically? The thought was exciting and frightening at once.

Clouds gathered above her head, mirroring her turbulent emotions. By late afternoon the sky was black, threatening. Lightning zigzagged across the astral dome, followed by drumrolls of thunder. Wind raced through the valley like a steam locomotive. Wild animals on the plateau prepared for the ominous scene about to be played out. Squirrels and rodents hid in their dens. Snug in their nests, birds ceased their chirping. All nature was subdued by the impending sirocco.

Heath was equally restrained. He had hardly gone near Stevie all day. Just the sight of her brought him to a state of arousal. And it was beginning to wear on his nerves.

If he wanted their relationship to remain platonic, he could ill afford to be shut up with her in a tight place, the elements of nature raging outside. But by late afternoon he knew they had to prepare for the upcoming storm. The need for safety overrode the danger of intimate contact.

Silently, he moved their bedding under the overhang. The alcove was so small, there was room for only one pallet. He patted the blankets in place, avoiding eye contact with Stevie as she stood in the entrance, staring at the narrow bed. He was the first to speak. "Not Willard's, but at least we'll be dry."

She stared at him blankly, never having heard of the plush Washington hotel. Then her gaze darkened as it slid down his body to the evidence of his desire.

The look in her eyes made him decidedly uncomfortable. "And safe." They would be safe from the electrical storm, he granted. But what about the carnal tempest engulfing them?

A man could withstand just so much temptation. . . .

Several hours past nightfall, the storm raged on. Stevie stood at the brink of their craggy home and blindly watched the wonders of nature unfold. Her mind and heart were filled with the man lounging on the pallet in the corner.

How did one go about seducing a man of the world? she wondered. It was a job Sandy Johns had neglected to prepare his daughter for, one he would tan her hide for even considering.

Outside, clouds billowed up into endless layers of black cotton, lost to the advancing darkness of night. Thunder boomed like muffled cannonfire. Lightning brightened the sky with brief flashes of midday illumination. Torrents of rain, great sheets driven by fierce winds, soaked her to the bone. Still, she was unaware.

When she shivered involuntarily from the wet and cold,

Heath rose and draped a blanket about her shoulders. She tensed at his touch. Misunderstanding her reaction, he attempted to reassure her. "I won't hurt you, hon."

Wide-eyed, she turned toward him.

He tapped her nose as if she were his kid sister. "And I don't bite." His arm around her shoulders, he led her to the blankets in the corner of the hideaway. When he seated her, he noticed the tension running the length of her. Suspecting she was afraid of him, a pensive frown knitted his brow. "I promised I won't bite, Stevie. Unless you want me to," he teased to lessen her tension . . . and his. He failed. Drawn by something in her eyes, he lowered himself to her side. Through a haze of confusion and desire, he whispered, "Sugar, if you keep looking at me like that, I'm gonna think you want me to bite. Or at least nibble on you a bit."

Her face flamed; she trembled. She hadn't meant for her need to be so transparent. Somehow, she grew passive, not yet ready to play her hand.

Standing, he picked up another blanket and tossed it to her. "Here, get out of those wet clothes and wrap up in this." Ignoring her quick intake of breath, he dropped down on his haunches near the entrance and began making a small fire. "You'll catch your death." When he heard no movement from her quarter, he threw over his shoulder, "Hurry up, sugar. I'll keep my back turned until you're decent."

Considering the wanton thoughts going through her mind, Stevie feared he was in for a long wait. In fact, the sight of his broad back, the muscles rippling under his shirt as he tossed kindling on the fire, she wasn't sure she wanted to be decent.

She had spent all day thinking about him. Or, more precisely, thinking about making love to him. At first she was horrified by the impropriety of such a notion. Then, as the hours passed, she warmed to the notion.

Discounting her lifelong beliefs and values, she wondered what would be so wrong with giving in to her desire for Lucky? Frankly, she was too full of life to imagine dying of old age, her maidenhead firmly intact. She had to know—just once—what it felt like to be a woman in every way. And since she would never want another man the way she wanted Lucky, and never have the opportunity of being alone in the wilderness with such a virile man, why not take advantage of the situation and enjoy herself?

The fact that he was a handsome drifter was to her advantage as well, she reaffirmed. She couldn't possibly have a long-term relationship—physical or otherwise—with any white man. So making love to a mysterious gambler who had more charm than the law allows, a heartbreakingly sensuous rogue who would undoubtedly leave town as soon as he escorted her safely back to Adobe Wells, was just the thing she needed.

Now all she had to do was convince him that he wanted her as much as she wanted him. His next words shook her resolve.

"Sugar, I want you to know you can trust me. I tease a lot about making love. Always have. But I would never do anything to dishonor you. Your virtue is safe with me, hon. Just think of me as a not-too-much-older brother."

Inordinately proud of himself for his gentlemanly attitude, he turned toward her with a familial smile pasted on his face. His smile froze, then disappeared altogether. He uttered a silent curse.

The sight before him heated his blood to the point of agony. Stevie, sitting in the corner, the firelight playing on her bare shoulders, her skin like brushed gold, made his fingers tingle with the need to touch her. Stevie, the blanket riding low on her breasts, was more provocative than a bride in a transparent peignoir on her wedding night.

He was in serious trouble here. "You look done in." Was that hoarse croak his voice? "Why don't you go on to sleep? I've gotta check the horses."

"But the storm . . ."

He waved her concern away. "A little water never hurt anybody. Don't wait up. I might be a while."

"Lucky." She half rose. The blanket covering her breasts slipped. A deep rose-colored half-moon peeked over the edge.

Perspiration popped out on his forehead. "Stevie, go to sleep," was his strangled admonition as he slipped out into the night.

"Dammit!" She slammed her fist down on the blanket beside

her hip. She might be an innocent, but even she knew it was next to impossible to seduce a man who wasn't in your vicinity.

Surely he would return before daybreak. And when he did, she would be waiting for him. If she had to hold her reluctant Romeo down and take him against his will, she was going to make love to Lucky Diamond. The prospect of attacking him while he was kicking and screaming, protecting his nonexistent virtue, made her giggle. Remembering her passionate dream, her giggle turned into a moan.

She dropped back on the pallet and drew deep breaths through her mouth. Marginally calm, she began planning her strategy. Mr. Diamond would soon discover that when Miss Stephanie Kay Johns put her mind to something—even seducing a reluctant lover—she did it.

Maybe even more than once. Innocent that she was, she wondered if that was physically possible. Before the sun rose over Eden, she planned to find out.

Renewed with determination, she paced the narrow confines of their shelter. The scratchy blanket rubbing against her naked flesh only heightened her need and frustration. It seemed like Heath had been gone an eternity when, exhausted, she sat. She drew her knees up and rested her chin on them. Second by second she became more frustrated . . . and more fatigued. Finally, just moments before Heath returned, she fell back on the pallet, slipping into a deep sleep.

She awakened to a very pleasant sensation. The blanket had fallen away from her naked form. In his sleep Heath's strong, hot body had taken its place.

She smiled instantly; that was the easiest seduction she had ever performed—'course, it was the only one.

Her smile disappeared as lips—soft, moist, searching—covered hers. Callused hands—caressing, teasing, exciting—spread over her, seeming to touch everywhere at once.

The reality of lovemaking was much better than a dream, she decided. One of Heath's expertly tutored appendages made the sensual journey from her shoulder, down her torso, slipping between her thighs, seeking the core of her femininity. She gasped sharply as maddeningly, tenderly, he caressed her inside and out.

She could feel his rapid, uneven breathing on her cheek. Her head fell back over his arm; her eyes, dark with desire, opened slowly. A low, guttural moan slipped past her lips. "Oh, Lucky."

He made no verbal response.

She raised her head slightly. "Lucky?" Awareness swept over her like a tidal wave. The rutting boar was asleep. He didn't know who she was. He was just acting on instinct.

She started to pull away from the exquisite torture, then hesitated. Wasn't this what she wanted? Sex—impersonal, temporary? No! Not like this. It was too degrading. If she were going to surrender her innocence, the *lucky* recipient was going to know what he was being given, and by whom. She placed her hand on his bare shoulder and squeezed. "Lucky."

His only response was to stroke her more aggressively.

What he was doing felt so good, she could barely think. She bit down on her lower lip to keep from moaning. Her hips strained toward his touch of their own accord.

Something velvety, hot, hard, and slightly wet connected with the inside of her thigh. She was momentarily distracted. Wide-eyed, she lowered her gaze. The muted light of the fire revealed a most provocative sight. His deep-bronzed hand was buried in the pale curls that hid her womanhood; his erect manhood brushed against her inner thigh with each instinctive movement of his hips.

She shook his shoulder harder. "Lucky, please wake up," she rasped.

Instinctively, he dropped a kiss to her lips. When she responded, he deepened the kiss and continued his bold stroking.

She reached out and touched him as he was touching her.

He jerked his hips and came fully awake in an instant. His eyes wide, glazed with desire, found hers. He made to pull away. "Sugar, I'm sorry. I didn't mean—"

She cut off his throaty denial by pulling his head down to hers for a long, satisfying kiss. Voracious, she sucked his tongue between her parted lips and drew on his lower lip, running her teeth lightly along its surface.

He hesitated for a moment, then groaned surrender. Capturing her head in his hands, he tilted it and fit his mouth over hers. As if he were starving, he put every pent-up desire he had experienced since meeting her in that one kiss.

Somewhere in the back of his mind a voice cautioned him to halt. But she tasted so good, felt so good. Where the admonition had once been a roar, it was now little more than a whisper, easily ignored, drowned out by desire's velvet thunder booming in his ears.

Twenty-three

Crushing her to him, he devoured her with his kisses.

The world beyond the circle of their arms ceased to exist. Passion, hot and pulsing, melded them together, heart to heart, soul to soul. They were both beyond rational thought, acting purely on instinct.

His searching fingers found one firm globe. Its dusky tip crested at his caress. He drew the pebbled tip into his mouth. As a babe at her breast, he suckled. All the while, his hands roamed intimately, expertly, from shoulder to ankle, stoking the fires of her desire.

An inferno, she writhed against him, moving sinuously, white-hot flames licking at his heated flesh. Tremors of arousal shook them both.

Shallow, rapid breaths escaped her lips, merging with his ragged moans. His conscience was burned away in the flame of her passionate response. Her desire for him overrode rational thought, maidenly modesty, and any semblance of control. All that mattered was that they become one.

Of their own accord, her thighs separated and circled his waist. She kissed his manhood with the core of her being. Lifting her hips, she ground against him. He uttered something that sounded quite primitive when she reached between their bodies and positioned his throbbing member at the portal of her femininity.

She whispered encouragement, first in English, then Comanche. "Now," she breathed. "Please."

Wrapping her slight body in his steellike embrace, he thrust into her, splitting the barrier that proclaimed her pure, capturing her brief cry of discomfort in his mouth. When he halted to ease her pain, she bucked against him. He plunged into her then, over and over, almost violently. Their mating was as wild, as out of control as the storm raging in the heavens. He cushioned her bottom in his hands and rode her as he would a bucking bronc. Rising and falling, she met him thrust for thrust.

It was over too soon. In a shattering crescendo Stevie reached her peak. Heath plunged over the edge a heartbeat later. With one last violent blast, the passionate storm consumed them.

Panting, she shifted slightly. He hardened inside her again. The seductive look in his sapphire gaze quickened the muscles in her belly and thighs, like a match striking stone, desire flared between her legs, flamed bright, burned hot.

When he slid from her honeyed warmth, she moaned her disappointment. His smile was masculine, hot. "This time I intend to take my time, sweetheart. And love every inch of you."

Slowly, patiently, he paid homage to her body, worshipping her with his hands and mouth. She was writhing beneath his maddening ministrations when his lips trailed over her stomach, lower. "Open wider, angel," he whispered against her silken curls, gently pushing her thighs farther apart.

"Lucky," she gasped, burying her hands in his hair.

His sexy chuckle vibrated against her core. "I'm more than lucky, sugar," he murmured, loving her with his tongue as he had with his immense maleness.

Had she not been overcome with desire, she would have been shocked at his action. This was an aspect of lovemaking she knew nothing about. But her attention was riveted solely to the part of her that was throbbing uncontrollably, to the sensitive nub that he was adoring with his mouth.

When she was certain she could take no more, he rejoined their bodies. He made love to her again, long and hard, guiding her on a sensual journey, where lovers go, always together, never alone.

Sated, their breathing slowed, their heart rates returned to normal. Sliding to her side, he pulled her against his body.

She still tingled from head to toe. "You're incredible," she said honestly. "Is it always like that?"

"Never."

Both in awe of what had passed between them, they fell into a deep sleep, safe in each other's arms.

Without their awareness the violent wind and torrential rain ceased. The clouds continued their journey across the vault of heaven until the sun's rays burst through, bringing morning to their mountain abode. A rainbow appeared in the sky, like a beautiful awning. Heady scents of freshly bathed grass and trees wafted across the valley on a light breeze. Peace reigned.

Stevie came awake slowly. Sliding out of Heath's embrace, she wrapped a blanket around her nude body and moved to the entrance of their hideaway.

For the first time in her life she felt whole. She leaned her head against the rock wall and silently thanked her white father's Christian God and her Comanche mother's Great Spirit for the serenity Lucky's loving had brought to her heart. He had touched her in a way that she would never be touched again. Now she knew what it was to be a woman. And she owed the wondrous discovery to a man she knew simply as Lucky Diamond.

He had awakened her and taken her on that sensual journey once again during the night, the last time more precious, more tender, than the ones before. Wrapped in each other's arms, they had fallen into an exhausted sleep.

"Come back to bed," a deep, sexy rumble caressed her ears.

She turned and found him smiling at her from their love nest. His ebony hair was tousled, a hint of a shadow on his strong jaw. Just the sight of him caused her knees to go weak.

Smiling, she hurried to his side. The morning air was cool on her bare skin as she dropped the blanket to pool around her feet. He lifted the cover and she slipped in beside him. He wrapped her in his embrace.

"Mmmm, you're warm." She snuggled against him. Hooking

one leg over his hip, she slid her foot up and down the back of his thigh. The contrast of their bodies felt delicious. Where she was soft and smooth, he was firm and hair-covered. Kissing his lips lightly, she trailed her fingers down his stomach and drew provocative patterns below his waist.

"Witch." The husky word sounded like an endearment.

When she wrapped her slender fingers around him and touched his lower lip with her tongue, he kissed her roughly and pulled her under him.

Once more he loved her with his body. But she noticed a new element to his lovemaking. More than passionate, he seemed respectful, almost restrained. She wondered at the difference. "Lucky?" was all she said after they shared a satisfying completion.

He offered her a gentle smile. "I have a confession."

She raised a brow, inviting him to continue.

"My name isn't Lucky Diamond."

She feigned surprise. "You don't say."

He chuckled, touching her cheek. "I do say. Name's Heath Turner, ma'am. I'd stand and bow properly, but since I'm naked, I doubt I'd look very impressive."

She grinned impishly and dropped her gaze below his waist. "I beg to differ."

He almost blushed. "Thank you."

"No, thank *you,*" she whispered.

"Me? What for?"

"For making me a woman."

"About that, honey, we need to talk."

She didn't like the chagrined look on his face. It told her that this was a conversation she did not want to have. "I'd say we communicate a whole lot better when we don't speak."

He was tempted to agree, but withstood the temptation. He had taken her virginity and that carried certain responsibilities . . . to a gentleman. The sooner he informed Stevie that he intended to live up to those responsibilities, the better. But he was a bit unsure of her response. She wasn't always predictable. "Maybe I can do this better with my pants on," he uttered to himself, rolling to his feet and shimmying into his trousers. They had grown cold and stiff during the night. Considering how much he wanted to make love to Stevie again, they were just what he needed. He looked down at the fetching sight she presented. "Aren't you going to dress?"

She stretched, the wool blankets feeling decidedly sensual against her bare skin. "No thanks. I'm fine, just like I am."

That was an understatement. Gorgeous, sexy, devastating, were the words that came to Heath's mind. But fine?

Turning his back to her, he stoked the smoldering embers of the fire. When his heated blood cooled somewhat, he joined her on the blankets, careful to maintain a respectable distance. A taunting voice told him it was too late for that, but he squelched it . . . and the accompanying guilt.

"Honey, about last night. I didn't mean for this to happen." He gestured vaguely at the rumpled blankets. Closing his eyes, he searched for the words to explain why he had assured her he would not take advantage of her and then proceeded to do just that. "When I got back from checking the horses, I was soaked clean through. I took off my wet clothes and wrapped up in a blanket. I planned to lie by the fire while my pants dried. Somehow, I ended up sharing your bed." He smiled weakly. "You know the rest."

It was apparent that Heath regretted making love to her. The most wonderful experience of her life, and he was apologizing for it. Her earlier joy evaporated, but she wouldn't let him see how much it meant to her. "We're both adults. You didn't exactly force me. There was no harm done. So let's just forget it."

He stared at her, openmouthed. She was so damned nonchalant about the whole thing. If he didn't have firsthand knowledge that she was a virgin, he would wonder at her virtue. "No harm done? I took your innocence. And I intend to do the right thing. We'll be married as soon as we reach Adobe Wells."

"Have you lost your mind?"

He fought to keep the exasperation out of his voice. "We're discussing your loss, Stevie. You lost your virginity to me and I feel honor bound to do the right thing."

"So I took your virginity too?"

Clearly, he found such a thought ludicrous, if not insulting. "Of course not."

"Well, do you marry every woman you've made love to? If so, I regret to inform you that there's a law against that sort of thing . . . having more than one wife. If there isn't, there should be."

"I'm not really certain what you're babbling about. And you needn't lecture me about the law." He produced his U.S. marshal's badge and brandished it in front of her face.

She jerked to a sitting position, the hem of the blanket crushed in her fists, pressed against her collarbone, hiding all the charms he had enjoyed during the night. "You're a lawman? And you let me think you were a gambler, a no-account drifter? Who I had to beg to help me deal with a crook?"

"Stevie, we're hell and gone from our original topic. Which was that I intend to do my duty by you. I ruined you, now I will marry you."

Her jaw tensed. "You have forgotten two very important facts, Mr. Turner."

"Pray tell, Miss Johns, enlighten me."

His calm in face of her anger made matters worse. "One, I do not intend to marry. Not you. Not now. Not ever. Two, you did not take my innocence. I surrendered it. Now, if you will take your pompous, overbearing, ignorant self out of here, I will dress and we can be on our way."

What was she so mad at? He was offering to do the right thing and she was throwing his chivalry back in his face. It wasn't as if he were dying to get married. He had a good many years left before he had planned to become leg shackled. Couldn't she see that he was making a monumental sacrifice . . . willingly? "I'm not ignorant! Maybe pompous and overbearing, but not ignorant. Furthermore, we're not leaving today," he informed her, slamming his hat on his head, grabbing his shirt, socks, and boots and stomping out into the beautiful morning.

The birds chirped gaily in the trees. He turned turbulent sapphire eyes on them. "Shut up!"

Heartfire
Romance

Twenty-four

Huddled deep in the blankets, Stevie withdrew into herself. Like the final note of a song, she turned off her mind; emotion reigned supreme, a myriad of emotions; regret—that she had given so freely of herself, love—for a man she couldn't have, and fear—that the loss of him would eventually destroy her.

Fear? The uncharacteristic emotion tasted like bitter ashes in her mouth. Stevie Johns, fearless hellion who needed no one to make her complete, had discovered the other half of herself in a valley nestled in the Sangre de Cristo Mountains. No. Not in a valley, but in the cradle of a man's arms—the man she loved now, the man she would love until she drew her last breath on this earth, the man she would cheerfully strangle at the moment.

And he wanted to marry her. Not because he loved her, but because he had ruined her. How could he not know that a forced proposal would insult any woman's pride?

Suddenly, she threw the cover off and surged to her feet. No good would come of lying in the dark, licking her wounds. She would face this latest challenge as she had all others in her life—head-on. Dressed, she emerged from the shelter to find Heath awaiting her.

"Can we talk?" he asked.

She regarded him warily, but followed him to a log by the fire and took a seat.

"Coffee?"

"Thank you." When she accepted the cup, their hands brushed.

Her sharp intake of breath restored a measure of his masculine pride. "I'm sorry if I came on too strong, Stevie."

She couldn't quite meet his eyes, but she relaxed marginally. "And I apologize for losing my temper. I'm not exactly world famous for my sweet temperament."

His soft chuckle raised the hair on her arms. "Oh I don't know. I think you're awfully sweet."

She colored furiously. "Awful anyway."

"Not hardly." He slid along the log until they were hip to hip.

She trembled at his nearness. Coffee sloshed over the rim of her cup, soaking into the jeans covering his muscular thigh.

"Here. Let me take that." He placed the cup on the ground beside his feet, cradled her cheeks in his palms, and lifted her face. She met his eyes then. Something in his heart broke free at the open, adoring, yet incredibly vulnerable look in her gaze.

The kiss he bestowed upon her opened the floodgates of passion and shut off the lifelong inhibitions their doting parents had nurtured. Lifting her high, he returned to their hideaway and loved her as if it were the first time, as if they hadn't been screeching at each other just moments before.

Over the next three days he loved her as often as his stamina would allow—beside the fire, on the shore, under the stars . . . and there was that unprecedented coupling on horseback.

Both were careful to avoid further mention of the future. By unspoken agreement, they were content to live in the present, to seize every moment of happiness they could. And by the third day they knew their time had come to an end. They were hopelessly in love . . . and helpless to confess it.

Lying in Heath's arms beneath a black velvet sky, Stevie sighed.

"What's wrong, angel?"

"I've been thinking"—she paused, reluctant to continue—"I need to get back. We should leave tomorrow."

"Is that what you really want?"

"It's what we should do."

He knew she was right. U.S. Marshal Heath Turner had never shirked his job before, not until he met the fiery, beautiful temptress snuggled against his heart. He loved spending time with her; more precisely, he loved her.

Still, the guilt of cavorting in paradise with a seductive sprite when he should be on assignment had begun to wear on him.

"Okay," he sighed. "But we still have tonight."

Dawn was a precious gift from God to the lovers lying snug in each other's arms. It loomed out of the darkness, grew more definite, then engulfed the slumbering world, capturing them in its panoramic embrace.

The morning sun shone bright overhead; rivers of gold streamed from the sky, gilding their naked bodies. A breathy sigh wafting through the valley swept them with a cool caress while the stream at their side bubbled musically down the mountain, serenading them in its wake.

But they were wholly unaware of the glorious spectacle. They were lost in a world of their own. Today was the day that they would leave their idyllic hideaway and face the future.

Together or alone, they didn't know.

As he told her, Heath had not meant to take her innocence, nor to fall in love with her. But now that he had, he would never let her go. Without a word he pressed his body flush with hers from shoulder to ankle. She shivered, reflecting his need, causing the breath to lodge in his throat.

Slipping into her body as if it were the most natural thing in the world, he looked down into her face and was struck anew by her incomparable beauty, beauty not limited to physical perfection, but beauty of the soul. Beauty, the depth of which, could be seen only by the man who had grown to love her deeply.

When had it happened, this all-consuming love? He didn't know. Stevie just sneaked up on his blind side, burrowed under his skin, then became an obsession. And he would never let her go, he vowed silently with every thrust of his body. This was the beginning for them. The beginning of a lifetime of love and happiness, together, forever.

Their passion blossomed to previously unimaginable heights. They moved as one, rising and falling, locked in an embrace that spoke of tenderness and desire in equal measure.

His pale hips ground against her bronze flesh. The contrasting color was ironic, perhaps even symbolic. She was Indian; he was white. Their people were at war while they were linked together body and soul.

Heath knew it would require courage to flaunt convention, strength to reach out and grasp what they both so desperately wanted. They would encounter opposition from society in general, and from individuals in particular, chiefly his mother.

But it wouldn't matter, he affirmed silently, kissing her feverishly. Turner men did not sound retreat once they entered battle. The general, Chap, and Rad would be disappointed in him if he turned his back on the woman he loved, simply for the accident of her birth.

But would she turn her back on him? He knew fear in the depth of his soul. Raw, stark fear that he might lose this woman he held close to his heart.

Inordinately disturbed by the thought, he engulfed her slender body completely and increased his efforts. He rained heated kisses on her dusky cheeks. It was then that he felt the tears coursing down her cheeks. Dear God, had his vigorous lovemaking hurt her?

He stared down into her eyes. The pain of loss, the resignation of defeat were evident in their watery depths. His heart lurched in his chest. Though they were still joined, neither of them moved. "Honey . . ." he began hoarsely.

Stifling a sob, she held him to her and shook her head. "Please, don't say anything." Stevie was not hurting physically but emotionally. When they rode out of the valley today, their love affair must end. And the prospect was breaking her heart.

But there was something she needed to express, a poignant feeling of gratitude. She twisted her head away and caressed his cheek in an attempt to cool his ardor . . . momentarily. More than his kiss, she needed to thank him for the past few days, for what he had taught her about love and life, for all that he had given her . . . for making her a woman. "The past few days have been the most wonderful time in my life. I'll never forget it. You made me a woman. Taught me what it was like to be loved by a man."

He looked at her with such love that her breath caught in her throat. Regaining a measure of her composure, she said as one wise beyond her years, "To be loved, not by a white man nor an Indian." She smiled wistfully. "Just a man. I can never thank you enough for that."

Eyes suspiciously bright, he blessed her with a sexy smile. "Truly, sweetheart, it was my pleasure."

She chuckled on cue. Their gazes met and held, stygian black, sapphire blue, each trying desperately to read what was in the other's heart.

Finally, Stevie's smile faded. Her voice barely broke a whisper. "But I don't want or expect anything else from you."

Unable to bear the hurt in his gaze, she stared unseeing at the scene around them. Finally, the beauty of nature faded into focus.

"Look around us, Heath. This isn't reality. It's . . . it's paradise," she breathed against his throat. "A place where race and society don't matter. Where everyone is equal and nobody has to apologize for the circumstances of their birth." Her arms tightened around his waist again. She was silent for a moment as he rocked against her. "Oh, God, it was wonderful, wasn't it?" Her voice broke as she met his gaze once more.

"It doesn't have to end, sugar."

"Yes, it does." There was the ring of finality to her agonized whisper. "But let's not talk anymore. Just make love to me. One last time."

Heath pushed down a surge of panic. One last time? Hardly. He would love her now as she requested, but that wouldn't be the end.

Taking note of her poignant resignation—and the hot, moist pressure below his waist—convinced him that this was not the appropriate time to discuss the future. Later, he would convince her that they would spend the rest of their lives together, that he would allow nothing and no one to tear them apart, not even her.

His hand trembled slightly as he tucked a stray curl behind her ear. The simple act, so sweet, so gentle, warmed her heart. He recognized the affection brimming in the ebony depths of her eyes. "I love you, Stevie Johns," he confessed, then kissed her with all the love in his heart.

She returned his kiss as if she were saying good-bye forever. "And I love you, Heath Turner," she surprised them both. "But that doesn't change who we are. And what must be . . ."

"Shhh. Just let me love you."

And he did.

Much later, they dressed, broke camp, and left their mountain hideaway in silence. The heady emotion they experienced as they topped the brow of the ridge made speech impossible. There were some things better felt than told, better shown than confessed.

When they halted side by side, the emerald valley a majestic picture in the distance, Heath pulled her over onto his lap. He cradled her in his arms. She snuggled deeper into his embrace. He tightened his hold as if he would never let her go. Still, they couldn't get close enough. It was as if they wanted to fuse themselves together.

The kiss he bestowed upon her then shook them emotionally and physically. His lips and tongue made love to her mouth over and over. Sipping, tasting, savoring, devouring, he kissed her until they were both trembling and breathless. It was the giving and taking of a vow.

Unwilling to commit, Stevie broke away abruptly. When she lifted her eyes, she noted with wonder his unabashed look of affection. It moved her even more than his passionate kiss. A soft whimper escaped her kiss-swollen lips as she threw her arms around his neck and pulled his mouth to hers.

His hands had a mind of their own. As if he were sightless, he sought to memorize her with his touch. From shoulder to knee he caressed her, paying homage to the flesh that caused his body to swell and ache.

Groaning, she squirmed on his lap, her bottom branded by the hot hardness upon which she sat.

His breathing grew shallow, fast, labored. "Whoa, sweetheart," he gasped. "We can't go on like this. I won't be able to stop."

"Guess you better put me back on my horse, then."

His body protested. But with thoughts of making camp early pacifying him, he kissed her one last time then shifted her over to her saddle. "Just don't be wiggling around in my lap like that anymore, young lady. Otherwise, you know what you'll get."

She blushed at his rakish wink. "I'll try to remember that." As if she could think of anything else.

Twenty-five

Heath's lusty plan for a night of unbridled passion was not to be.

Late that afternoon they heard voices coming from a clearing in the distance. Cautiously, they moved toward the sound. They dismounted and tethered their horses.

"Stay here," he whispered to Stevie. When she looked as if she would object, he kissed her soundly. "I'll be right back."

Slipping silently through the woods, he came upon three men and a woman grouped around an open fire. The woman was cooking. She limped back and forth from a large Conestoga wagon to the fire around which the men reclined. It appeared that her ankle was injured. Tears streaked her face; her clothes—of obvious quality—were tattered and filthy. It was apparent that she was being held captive. Heath imagined that beneath all that dirt she was probably very young and quite lovely.

A whinny from the edge of camp gained his attention. It came from a painted pony milling about a large remuda. No doubt these were the horses stolen from Black Coyote's camp

He swung his gaze back to the thieves. Two of them were comancheros, Mexican banditos dressed like Indians. In Heath's estimation, they were the lowest form of life on the face of the earth.

The oldest man, in his sixties, was dressed in a homespun shirt. His black breeches, faded and shiny with age, were held up by frayed suspenders. Sweat stains ringed his underarms and formed a triangle down his chest and between his shoulder blades. A disreputable red rag was tied around his forehead, holding his thin gray hair off his face. A moth-eaten eagle feather hung at a precarious angle, secured by his tattered headband.

The youngest man wore buckskin breeches and a printed shirt. His eyes had a slightly dull cast, as if he didn't have all his horses harnessed, intellectually speaking. If possible, he was even filthier than the old man. Heath could smell their unwashed bodies from twenty feet away.

The third man was an Indian. Large, swarthy, from the Northeast, Heath surmised, probably a Delaware. He stood off to one side, mesmerized by the fire. He was the single most savage-looking man Heath had seen west of the Mississippi. He was virtually naked, dressed in only a low-slung breechcloth and knee-high moccasins. Practically every weapon known to the American Indian hung from his body. But it was the string of scalps dangling from his bare, bronze waist that gave Heath pause.

As if feeling Heath's eyes upon him, he dropped his hand to the lethal knife in a sheath at his side. His predatory stance radiated danger, making Heath regret that Stevie was so close by.

The thought of Stevie caused Heath to return his gaze to the young woman. Even though she was in pain, she moved methodically, as if in a trance . . . or under the influence of drugs. Her hair, oily and drab, hung limp on her narrow shoulders. He felt a mixture of rage and pity at the sight she presented. Rage at her captors, pity for the girl.

He very nearly jumped out of his skin when Stevie touched his sleeve. Worry for her safety made his tone unusually sharp. "I thought I told you to stay put."

"I was worried about you." She lowered her eyes.

He angled her head toward him and murmured an apology against her lips. "I'm sorry I snapped. Give me a kiss and we'll get outta here"

"Now, ain't that touchin'?" a high-pitched voice sounded from behind them.

Stevie and Heath spun around. A teenage boy who bore a marked resemblance to the young man in camp held a rifle on them.

"Hey, Pa. Look what I found." He grinned like a jackass eating briars, revealing the decayed snags he no doubt called teeth. Roughly, he prodded Heath with the point of his rifle. He drew back a moccasined foot to kick Stevie.

Heath's next words forestalled him. "Touch her and die."

The look in Heath's eyes and his menacing tone convinced the kid. He lowered his foot without touching Stevie. "Move!"

Slowly, Heath helped Stevie to her feet. They stepped out into the open. His chest swelled with pride when she squared her shoulders and walked forward briskly. He had always considered her an exceptional woman, but never more so than now. As his sister Ann would say, the girl's got starch in her drawers.

The comancheros grabbed their guns and leveled them on the intruders. The half-naked Indian squeezed the hilt of his knife more tightly. The captive girl stared blankly at the couple entering camp.

"Hello." Heath's tone was deceptively cheerful. "Smelled your cook fire and thought you could spare some food."

"The hell you say," the old man growled with a hint of a Spanish accent. He aimed his rifle straight at Heath's heart. "That why you was layin' on the ground spyin' at us?" He cocked the trigger.

"Hold on there, friend. We don't mean any harm. Sorry if we bothered you. My wife and I will just be on our way."

"A moment please . . ." the Indian began in a sophisticated voice colored by a light French accent. It sounded so at odds with his appearance that Stevie whipped her head in his direction.

He returned her stare with undisguised lust. "I apologize for my uncivilized friend, *chérie*." When he snapped his fingers, the old man lowered his gun; the younger men did the same. "Come," the Indian continued. "You are welcome among us."

Heath hated the man with every fiber of his being. He tightened his arm around Stevie's waist.

"Don't you dare let that naked ape touch me," she whispered for Heath's ears only.

He smiled and moved his hand closer to his Colt. "Wouldn't think of it."

The Indian noted Stevie's reluctance and Heath's protective stance. Rage deepened his color, but his tone remained pleasant. He pointed to the pot of food bubbling over the cook fire. "Help yourself, *chérie.*"

Biding their time, Heath and Stevie each filled a tin plate with food and sat close together by the fire. The Indian filled tin cups from a blue metal pot. The air hummed with tension as he offered the coffee to Heath and Stevie, his eyes lingering on Stevie overlong.

When they had pushed the food around their plates for a sufficient time, Heath said, "Appreciate your hospitality. But we should be getting settled for the night."

Noting their still-full plates, the Indian challenged, "Not hungry? Won't you at least drink your coffee?"

A muscle twitched in Heath's jaw as the only sign of his displeasure. Who in hell was this savage? He acted as if he were receiving a peer of the realm in Queen Victoria's parlor. "Certainly." His lips barely moved as he spoke. He blew on the hot brew, then took a sip. Stevie followed his lead and drained her cup.

"Now we really must leave." The steel surety of Heath's voice was unmistakable. He grasped Stevie's hand as the world began to spin before his eyes, slowly at first, then faster and faster. He shook his head to clear his vision, to no avail. The hideous mask of his host's smiling face faded in and out. The sky changed places with the ground.

"Heath," Stevie groaned, slumping against him.

Heath was furious at himself for falling for such an amateurish stunt as having his coffee drugged. "You bastard." He leveled his Colt on the Indian. The weapon felt as if it weighed a ton in his hand. "One move and I'll kill you, you son of a bitch!" He waved his gun in the direction of the other men. "Tell 'em to drop their weapons or so help me God I'll blow your head off." When the men complied, he instructed the Indian to gather the guns. "Throw 'em in the back of the wagon."

He wrapped his arms around Stevie's waist and dragged her away from camp. Calling upon his waning strength, he hoisted her over his shoulder. He hated leaving the captive behind. But he feared he had only a few minutes of consciousness left. Silently, he vowed to return for her later, after Stevie was safe.

The world whirled around him like a top as he moved swiftly away from camp. He fought for control. Waves of nausea buffeted him; bile rose in his throat. He cast about for a place to hide, tumbled headlong into a gully, spilling Stevie onto the ground. Quickly, he gathered her against him and staggered on.

Finally, he came upon a small cave where a mountain lion had birthed her young earlier in the spring. Hoping that the den was empty, he backed into it. Luck was with them; it was uninhabited.

He moved deeper inside and laid Stevie on the ground. Returning to the opening, he piled dead branches, rendering the interior completely invisible from outside.

He could hear the comancheros searching in the distance. Fortunately, the sun had fallen. With a little luck they wouldn't pick up their trail in the dark. But he knew they would search again at daylight. Tomorrow would just have to take care of itself. For now, he whispered a prayer for Stevie's safety. Then, falling down beside her, he pulled her into his arms and kissed her cheek. Shadows of the evening crept across the land as he lost consciousness.

Twenty-six

When the morning wakened, a steady rain was falling outside the cave.

Stevie stirred in Heath's embrace.

"Are you all right, sugar?"

She moaned. "A little groggy. What happened?" She looked around her. "How did we get here?"

His smile was soft as dew. "You passed out. I dragged your lovely little hide in here. Which means that I saved your life. And I intend to be paid handsomely for my efforts."

She leaned back on his shoulder, blessing him with an innocent smile. "What's the current cost of rescuing a damsel in distress?"

He trailed a finger over her parted lips. "I'll let you know when I have time to collect. We need to get out of here and put as many miles between us and our hosts of last evening as possible."

She had almost forgotten the danger that threatened. Reality intruding, she glanced toward the entrance as if a heinous monster lurked beyond. "You don't think they're gone?"

"I highly doubt it, sugar."

She frowned, appearing more exasperated than frightened. "Couldn't you have lied to me and said they were in Texas by now?"

He chuckled and squeezed her till she squeaked. "I'm sure they're gone. No doubt they're in Texas by now. South Texas. Maybe even Mexico."

"From your mouth to God's ear."

He hopped up. "My sentiments exactly." Grinning, he pulled her to her feet. He stood there, gazing down into her shadowed face, thinking how incredibly beautiful she was. His fingers twined in her hair, smoothing the platinum strands over her shoulders. A fist took hold of his heart and simply refused to let go.

Reluctantly, she prodded him. "Heath, don't you think we'd better go?"

He stared a moment longer, then, shaking off the spell she had unwittingly cast about him, he nodded. "I guess we should."

He removed the branches from the opening of the den and looked outside. The rain was only a light mist now. He listened intently but heard nothing save the rain caressing the leaves strewn about the forest floor. Taking Stevie's hand, he led her out of the cave into a heavy fog hanging low to the ground. The earth's gray cloak made it virtually impossible to see more than fifty feet in any direction.

"I can't see my hand in front of my face," Stevie observed. "They could be close by and we wouldn't know it."

The eternal optimist, Heath responded, "True, but the fog conceals us too."

Carefully, he led her down into a gully. They followed the gully to where their horses had been tethered. The animals were gone. Hand in hand they headed north, walking briskly through the thicket. When they approached an open field, the fog lifted partially. The next wooded area was half a mile away.

"Damn, why couldn't it last a little longer?" he asked rhetorically, turning worried eyes on Stevie. "Hon, crossing here is gonna be dangerous. But we don't have any choice. Just keep low and stay close behind me."

She nodded.

They moved out into the open, crouching low in the tall grass. When they reached the woods without incident, they breathed a sigh of relief. But their sense of well-being was premature. A strong arm reached from behind a tree and circled Stevie's waist, jerking her back into the bony chest of the older of the two men.

Heath was on him in an instant. Grabbing him by the shoulder, he wheeled Stevie's abductor around and slammed his fist into his face. "Run, honey."

"No," she cried.

"Run, dammit. I'll catch up."

She shrieked then fell silent.

The sound of flesh striking flesh drowned out two sets of pounding footfalls as Heath put considerable weight behind his punch, sending the man down with a ground-shuddering thud. Young and wiry, he regained his footing, faced Heath with a knife in his dirty hand, and waved it back and forth.

Feinting to the left, Heath seized his opponent's wrist, pivoted, and gave a sharp twist. The bone broke with a loud snap. Howling, the man flipped over onto his back.

Satisfied that the man posed no further threat, Heath looked about for Stevie. A trail of broken branches led down into an arroyo that flowed with a swift-moving stream. He followed the arroyo at breakneck speed.

He hadn't traveled more than three hundred feet when he came upon the old man and his youngest son fighting over Stevie. Each holding one of her outstretched arms, they beat each other about the face, pulling on her as if she were a wishbone.

A red haze clouded Heath's eyes. He ran into them like a steam locomotive. Stevie flew in one direction, her assailants in the other.

Scrambling to their feet, the old man and his son dove for Heath simultaneously. Heath struck the old man in the jaw, then turned and smashed his fist into the boy's solar plexus. The boy hit the forest floor like a fallen tree, but the old man remained standing.

A bullet whizzed past Heath's head. Diving to the ground, he drew his Navy and shot the old man point-blank, the bullet piercing his heart, killing him instantly.

Stevie rushed into his arms. He hugged her quickly. "We have to keep moving, sweetheart." He led her down the arroyo for several hundred yards, where the narrow stream widened. White water rushed over protruding rocks. A mist hovered over the stream, creating a rainbow. It was a peaceful scene, deceptively peaceful.

They headed north, picking their way over boulders and slippery rocks. Heath searched for an exit from the arroyo, but its high banks hemmed them in. Tension mounted. One false step and they would perish in the rapids.

Suddenly, the Indian attacked from the high bank. The force of his fall knocked Heath and Stevie to the ground. Gaining his feet, Heath pushed Stevie behind him.

The Indian held his knife high in the air, slowly turning it, reflecting rays of sunlight, blinding Heath. A cruel smile on his lips caused the hair on the back of Stevie's neck to stand on end.

"This time you will not escape. The woman will be mine. After I gut you like a fallen deer."

Instinctively, Heath reached for his gun but found an empty holster.

"It's over there," Stevie called. The Navy lay close to the Indian's feet, partially hidden in a mound of leaves. She made a move toward it.

"No, little one. You will not help the white man. Your place is with me. With your own kind."

"I'm not your kind, you filthy snake. Your kind slinks around on the ground, eating the dust of decent men."

The vehemence in her voice distracted the Indian momentarily. Heath reached down, slipped his hunting knife from the sheaf tied to his ankle and held it behind his back. He angled his body, concealing the weapon from his attacker. "The woman has a point," he taunted.

The Indian's face clouded with rage. He rushed Heath, his head held high, rage making him reckless.

Heath took careful aim and threw his weapon with deadly accuracy. The blade sank into the Indian's neck, severing his jugular vein.

The man stopped in mid-stride, a look of horror in his eyes. He dropped his knife and slowly sank to the ground, his blood an ever-widening crimson circle. His eyes stared sightless into the towering treetops above him.

Quickly, Heath retrieved his gun and led Stevie away from

the stream. Climbing into an open field, they found the Conestoga beneath a spreading oak. Four mules were hitched to the wagon, while the horses, including Heath and Stevie's, grazed nearby.

The captive's feet and hands were tied to the front wheels of the wagon. She would be crushed by its weight if the mules moved. No longer under the influence of drugs, she held the reins tightly between her teeth.

The comancheros' intent was obvious. If they were killed searching for Heath and Stevie, they didn't want the girl to live. She would eventually weaken, release the mules, and suffer a cruel, painful death.

Heath cut the ropes and helped the young woman to her feet. She fell against him, sobbing. "It's all right now," he soothed. Glancing at Stevie apologetically, he awkwardly patted the girl's back.

Stevie's eyes were riveted to where the girl's lily-white hands clutched Heath's shirtfront. The sight was symbolic. Her hands were delicate, pale, needy, gentle, all part of something Stevie would never be—a white woman. Was that what Heath really wanted? No. He said he wanted her. But was it what he really needed?

Stevie hated herself for the intense feeling of resentment and jealousy that overwhelmed her then. To see any woman, especially a white woman, in Heath's arms, made her physically sick. She turned away lest they see the tears shimmering in her eyes.

Never let 'em see ya cry. Jeff's words of warning chanted in her mind like a mantra. He had always told her that as long as the townspeople didn't know they were hurting her with their rejection, they didn't have any power over her.

But Heath wasn't just anybody. He had great power over her—power she had given him by professing her love. She would have to disabuse him of that notion even if she had to lie. Then he would be free to find a wife like the helpless ninny hanging on to him like moss on a tree.

How would she live the rest of her life without him? Knowing that he was married to someone else, holding someone else in the night. Doing all the beautiful things he had done to her body—doing them to someone else. It was almost more than she could bear. She wasn't given to martyrdom.

But she was strong. She would do what had to be done just as she always had. No matter how badly it hurt, she would do what was right for herself, but more to the point, what was best for Heath.

Wasn't that what true love was all about? Caring for someone enough to set them free—free to find love and happiness with another? Stevie sincerely hoped she was woman enough to do that, for above all she wanted Heath to be happy.

Maybe the Indian was right. She should stick with her own kind just as Heath must remain with his.

Finally, the girl regained her composure. She didn't release her hold on Heath, however. Moving closer, she gazed up into his face adoringly. "How can I ever repay you for saving me?"

He extricated himself from her grasp and stepped back, leaving a good six inches of space and propriety between them. "Miss Johns and I were glad to help, Miss . . ."

"Hughes. Erica Hughes." She offered her hand.

Bemused at the formal gesture, he bowed over it. When she dipped into a light curtsy, he barely hid a chuckle. He looked toward Stevie, expecting to find her grinning and rolling her eyes at Erica's foolishness. Her back was facing them. There was something about her rigid stance that gave him pause. "Honey," he said softly, trying to gain Stevie's attention.

Stevie spun around, thinking that the endearment was meant for Erica. She found Heath looking at her, confusion knitting his brow. Embarrassed, she cleared her throat. "Shouldn't we be going?" She looked Erica full in the face for the first time. She was younger than Stevie had thought . . . and more lovely. "Would you show me where the food is? And our saddlebags," she requested quietly.

The girl couldn't seem to take her eyes off Heath. Somehow, she managed. "Come this way" was her flat order to Stevie.

Stevie followed Erica to the rear of the wagon and retrieved the supplies. Meanwhile, Heath saddled an extra mount.

Stevie approached him, struggling under the weight of the supplies that filled her arms. Erica trailed her, hands empty.

Heath frowned. "Here, sweetheart, let me take that." He secured the bags to the mounts, then caressed Stevie's cheek lightly. "You okay?"

She nodded and mounted, not accepting his hand-up.

Walking away, he released the mules hitched to the wagon. With a slap on the rear they gained their freedom. He returned to the women and found Erica still standing beside her horse, waiting for assistance. "Are you strong enough to ride, Miss Hughes?"

She lifted a delicate hand to her forehead. "I suppose I haven't any choice. Mother told Father I wasn't strong enough to make this journey alone. That a girl as pretty as me was fair game for unscrupulous men. But Father was so concerned about his duty to the army, he just wouldn't listen."

Where had all that come from? Suppressing the need to glance heavenward for divine intervention, he lifted her into the saddle. "Well, ladies, let's put this place behind us."

Without a word Stevie took the lead, providing Heath and Erica a good view of her horse's behind.

The ride was taxing that day. Erica was understandably weak. They stopped often to allow her to rest. Her strength returned as the day wore on.

And that's when her whining began. At first Heath shrugged off her incessant complaints as the result of being so young, having been through such a harrowing experience, and being a tad spoiled.

Mentally making excuses for her, he was the soul of comfort, assuring her that he would see that she reached her parents at Fort Bascomb safely at the earliest possible moment—a promise he intended to keep if only for his own sanity—that everything would be all right, that she would forget her experience as soon as she met the handsome, unattached officers at the fort.

As the day wore on, her complaints began to grate on his nerves. How could one woman find so much to her disliking? he wondered, amazed. She groused about the heat, the food, lukewarm water, dirty clothes, stringy hair, unsightly calluses, broken nails, lack of suitable gentlemen callers—as if she expected to find Casanova beneath the next toadstool—and a dozen other things.

She complained most vehemently that it had been ages since she'd had a bath. Heath wanted to offer to bathe her in the stream, but didn't trust himself not to drown the girl, especially when she started railing against the filthy Indians. For a moment he regretted rescuing her.

But Erica wasn't uppermost in his mind as the miles drifted by. He was puzzled by Stevie's behavior. No matter what he did, how many times he sought her comfort in the face of Erica's verbal harangue, Stevie ignored him. All he wanted was a kind word. If not a kind word, then a small smile.

Sighing heavily, he shifted in the saddle and tried to tune out Erica's wailing. Optimistically, he looked ahead to when he and Stevie would be alone. He would demand an explanation for her aloof behavior . . . and insist that she rush back into his arms as surely as she had rushed into his heart.

"Listen," Stevie whispered.

Heath pulled alongside her. "What is it, hon?"

"I don't hear anything," Erica whined. "How much longer before we stop for the night? I'm tired and hungry."

Heath and Stevie summarily ignored her.

Stevie turned her head sharply. "Hear that?"

"I'm hot," Erica groused.

Stevie and Heath both glared at her. "Hush," they hissed in unison.

Heath spoke over Erica's outrage. "Sounds like someone's crying. A woman."

Stevie slid from her mount and headed in the direction of the faint whimpering sound.

Heath dismounted and pulled his Colt. "Wait, sugar." She had disappeared. He followed her trail through the thick undergrowth. With each step the whimpering grew louder and—thank the good Lord—Erica's voice grew dimmer.

When Heath stepped into the clearing, he was smiling. For the first time in hours he couldn't hear the sound of Erica's voice.

But in the space of a second his expression jelled into one of shock, his mind trying desperately to deny the scene before him. Taut with tension, his heart slammed against his ribs. "Oh, my God!" he uttered, making his way across the clearing. "Honey?"

His luminous eyes widened. Stevie's actions claimed his undivided attention. He stood there, for how long he didn't know, shaken, mesmerized, fascinated, watching as she labored skillfully over a frail Indian girl . . . who was obviously in the last, agonizing throes of childbirth.

Twenty-seven

Robert Pridgen sat on the boardinghouse portico, drinking his morning coffee, watching the activities in town with a jaundiced eye.

To the dismay of Pridgen and the other permanent residents of Adobe Wells, the size of the miners' camp had doubled in a week. Speculators, prospectors, carpenters, freighters, and cowpunchers had streamed into town on horseback and wagons in record number. Striking tent on the first bare spot of earth they could find, each group was rougher than the last. All drawn by whispers of gold, silver, even diamonds.

A heavy rain the night before had turned the dusty road in front of Pilar's boardinghouse into a mud trough. Wagons along Main Street bogged down halfway to their axles, cutting deep ruts into the streets. Dangerous-looking men slopped in knee-deep mud, cursing the black gumbo.

Scantily dressed whores wended their way through the murky soup, trailing the men, in the event that some uncouth miner, successful in his efforts, would part with a bit of whatever it was that Judge Jack had promised him in this godforsaken corner of the country.

Pridgen suspected that all the fools would get for their labors was a stiff back. Then they would leave as quickly as they had come. Disappearing overnight, shaking the dust—or mud, as the case may be—from Adobe Wells off their feet.

The small western town would resemble a turkey carcass the

day after Thanksgiving. Bare, bereft, as if a hoard of scavengers had fed upon it and cast the slick, naked bones aside.

The prospect enraged Pridgen. But it was the foreboding that hovered over Adobe Wells, humming with violence, rank with the scent of death that frightened him. Scared the hell out of him.

A shrill scream drew his attention. The hair-raising sound came from across the plaza. Two drunk miners spilled into the street, pounding each other with bloody fists. They fought over a whore who had emerged with them, obviously to watch her suitors settle their dispute. Shouting obscenities, the brawlers battled feverishly.

Pridgen found the affair disgusting! He rose, leaned heavily on his cane, and limped down the portico to get a better view of the drunken brawl. Three men bounded down the courthouse steps, carrying a red, white, and blue banner, stretched it across the street, then attached it to buildings on either side.

Brawlers forgotten, Pridgen's lips moved as he read the banner silently.

Adobe Wells Welcomes Governor Ned Casson
August 10

"I'll be damned!"

Ted Reno poked his head out the door with a cup of coffee pressed to his forehead. "Morning, Mr. Pridgen." His western drawl was husky, slightly slurred.

Pridgen swung his gaze in Ted's direction. The man was tall, redheaded, freckle-faced, looked as though he should have a frog in his pocket rather than a six-shooter on his hip.

Squirming under Pridgen's perusal, the marshal surveyed his town with a nervous glance. The brawl that had gained Pridgen's attention was winding down, another one begun just as quickly. Ted hoped the paralyzing fear he experienced at seeing the violence didn't show on his face. "I'm surprised to see how much the town has changed in the few days I've been away . . . on business." His bloodshot eyes and trembling hands hinted at the nature of his business.

Pridgen tried to keep his voice light. "What kind of business?"

"Went to Santa Fe to see Sheriff Todd. Stopped off at Delgado's." Ted's lips curved in a boyish grin. "Got in a little fishing."

Pridgen couldn't help but return his smile. Marshal Ted Reno was a kid, pure and simple. Unfortunately, he was all that stood between the residents of Adobe Wells and Judge Jack. The town was in serious trouble. "Yep, things changed while you were gone. And not for the better."

Reno shifted from foot to foot. "So I see." He paused, searching for courage that was nowhere to be found. "Guess I better check in at the office," he said with little enthusiasm.

"Be careful, son," Pridgen advised.

He liked Ted Reno even though Judge Jack appointed him sheriff. The boy was honest as the day is long. If only he were a little more mature, a bit more accomplished with a gun, he mused. Damn. He would rest easier when Lucky and Stevie got back to town. The old man frowned harshly, wondering what was taking those two so long. Sandy was fit to be tied, understandably so.

Ted strolled across the plaza toward his office. His body tense, his eyes darted nervously about the town. Silently, he scolded himself for being fearful. Adobe Wells needed a brave lawman. Not a snot-nosed kid scared to walk the streets of his own town in broad daylight. Mentally shaking himself, he squared his shoulders. A shot exploded behind him and he almost lost control of his bodily functions.

A quick look told him that the blast had come from a couple of kids shooting off fireworks. "Chicken! Damn coward," he berated himself, his self-esteem a foot lower than a snake's belly.

Engrossed in self-chastisement, Ted failed to see a covered carriage stop in front of the courthouse. The driver jumped down from the box, quickly opened the door, and helped a brilliantly dressed female alight. How on earth could he have overlooked this woman? Ted would ask himself later. From the top of her fire-engine-red coiffure to the tips of her magenta leather slippers, she was a study of harsh color. She wore no soothing pastels as most ladies did, but brash, vibrant colors, the kind usually reserved for decorating high-priced bordellos.

Ted accidentally bumped into her as she made her way across the boardwalk. "Beg pardon, ma'am," he apologized, clutching her forearm in an attempt to steady her. "Guess I was day-dreaming and didn't see you." He blessed her with his boyish grin.

"Damn idiot!" She rapped his knuckles with her parasol. "Why don't you watch where you're going?"

The marshal was clearly taken aback, as was the disheveled miner watching the scene from the shadowy alley between the courthouse and the jail.

"I'm sorry I bumped into you, ma'am." Ted's voice cracked, whether from youth or embarrassment, the emerald-eyed miner couldn't tell. "But that don't give you no call to cuss me." Ted drew himself up with false pride. "I'm the law hereabouts."

Rachel drew back her hand and slapped him soundly across the face.

He cupped his stinging cheek. "You can't do that."

Just to prove that she could, she slapped him again on the other cheek. "If you're the law in this town, I pity the people who live here."

Ted's jaw fell open in shock and embarrassment. When he stared into her face, a flicker of recognition flashed in his eyes.

Rachel suddenly stiffened.

"Reno!" A loud voice boomed from the doorway of the courthouse.

Judge Jack and Henry Sims stepped down onto the board-walk. Twin scowls darkened their faces. "Is there a problem here, Rachel?" the judge asked softly.

"This boy accosted me right here on the street. If you hadn't come when you did, I shudder to think what he would have done." She summoned a delicate tremor.

Ted looked at her with genuine regret. "I'm sorry, ma'am. I wouldn't ever hurt a lady."

"Are you calling me a liar?"

"No'm. I mean yes—"

"Shut up, you stupid fool. And get out of here before I drill you right on the street," Sims threatened.

Ted looked from Sims to Judge Jack.

Judge Jack sketched a curt nod. "Do like he says."

Eyes downcast, Ted hurried off.

The hidden miner, having witnessed the entire episode, was disgusted. Things in Adobe Wells were worse than he thought. Somebody *had* to do something. But his hands were tied now that Rachel was in town. Where the hell was Heath? That was the question occupying his mind as he slipped into the courthouse, following Judge Jack and Rachel at a safe distance.

Judge Jack escorted Rachel through the courtroom to his chambers in the back. Closing the door behind him, he leaned against it. "My dear Rachel, to what do I owe this pleasure?"

"Ostensibly, I'm here to help prepare for the governor's visit. In reality, I'm here to pass on vital information . . . information that will affect our deal."

He gestured to a rose velvet tufted sofa. "Have a seat."

When they were settled, she continued. "Elanzo Welch's report created quite a stir with Governor Casson. Written on stationery from his San Francisco office, it squashed almost all skepticism about the mine. How did you convince Mr. Welch to lie?"

"He didn't lie." Jack was smug. "He examined the diamonds I bought from South Africa. The genuine diamonds. He merely reported what he saw. Of course, he didn't know that they didn't come from the cave in Adobe Wells." He winked. "That's our little secret."

"It may not be our secret for long. August ninth, one day before the governor's visit, a man named Layard Shackelford will arrive in Adobe Wells, requesting—on behalf of the governor—immediate access to the mine for a surprise on-the-spot inspection."

A muscle in Jack's eye twitched. "Who in hell is Layard Shackelford?"

"An engineer from the California Department of Mines. I don't need to tell you that he could cause us a hell of a lot of trouble. But if we can convince him that the mine is genuine, nobody, including the governor, will have any further doubts."

Jack rose and walked over to the window.

Unable to hear through the closed door, the miner trailing Jack and Rachel had exited the courthouse and hidden beneath the window at which Judge Jack stood. He barely had time to glue himself to the wall before the judge looked through the rain-streaked pane.

"Does anyone in the governor's office or in Santa Fe know Mr. Shackelford personally?" Jack asked.

"I don't think so. He never leaves California."

"Do you know his travel schedule?"

"I'm the one who arranged it."

Jack turned back toward Rachel in surprise.

She grinned like the proverbial cat who had eaten the canary. "Sometimes I help my husband by arranging travel plans for dignitaries. This time, I insisted on it."

"I knew I made the right decision bringing you in on this deal. You are proving to be very handy."

"As I recall, you didn't have much choice." Smiling, Rachel pulled a slip of paper from her purse. She joined Jack at the window and related Shackelford's schedule. "He'll arrive in Santa Fe on August seventh. Spend the eighth meeting with Governor Casson and Mr. Clark. Early on the ninth, he'll catch the stage to Adobe Wells, arriving here about noon."

"No, he won't."

The miner beneath the window listened intently, barely breathing.

"How are you going to stop him?" Rachel asked.

"James Filmore, disguised as Shackelford, will survey the mine and announce that it is the most productive diamond strike ever to have been made in this country."

"Filmore?"

"He's an actor I've retained on occasion. He's well educated and has all the sophistication of a San Francisco professional. And absolutely no scruples whatsoever."

"Dare I ask what you will do to Shackelford?"

"I won't do anything to him. 'Course, I can't speak for Sims," the judge quipped.

Rachel laughed low in her throat. The sound was pure evil. Her eyes sparkled with menace. "There's something else I want to tell you." She cocked her head to the side, as if mentally flipping through files of vital, top secret information.

Jack knew she was playing with him, wanting him to hang on her every word. He merely crossed his arms over his chest and waited.

She tried to hide her exasperation at his nonchalance. The information would get a rise out of him even if her dramatics didn't. "Governor Casson has persuaded a group of investors to buy out your interest in the mine, that is, if Shackelford gives a positive report of the mine." She smiled and watched Jack calculate the revenue his sale might bring.

"Casson thinks this diamond strike will bring the territory of New Mexico to statehood. But he doesn't want you to process the diamonds. He's afraid you don't have enough capital to follow through."

"I knew the pompous windbag was greedy."

"That he is. He's bringing the other investors with him on the tenth. They plan to form a ten-million-dollar corporation. The San Francisco and New York Mining and Commercial Company. The plan's to offer you two million dollars for your interest in the mine."

It would have been hard to say who was more pleased, Rachel or Judge Jack. Their plot was coming to an end more quickly and more successfully than they had anticipated. For a while they were silent, each contemplating what the future might bring.

Finally, they began speculating verbally on what they would do with their share of the money. They would go to New York. Rachel planned to buy a boutique, specializing in the latest fashions from Paris. She would change her name, dress like a queen, and move among the upper echelons of society. Jay Hampton would never find her there, she added silently.

Jack would belong to an exclusive men's club and become a well-known collector of fine guns and blooded horse flesh. His silent declaration was that he would seduce the kind of women who were not available to him now. Not sluts like Rachel, but ladies like the upstanding widow, Pilar Manchez, and the illusive Miss Stevie Johns. When he tired of them, he would reveal to the world what they were. He would prove that all women were whores at heart . . . a truism his prostitute mother had taught him all too well.

"There's only one other thing that would make this a perfect day for me," Rachel said.

"And what is that?"

"Kill the marshal." She spoke so dispassionately, she might have been asking him to step on a roach.

Jack's smile faded. "Reno's only a boy. Why do you want him dead? Surely not for that little altercation outside."

"I think he recognized me."

"How?"

"After you left Chicago, I embezzled two thousand dollars from that bank and got my face on a wanted poster." She didn't have to tell him about the other wanted posters on Rachel Jackson or the blond, green-eyed marshal who was hunting her as if she were a mad dog on the loose.

Jack shook his head. "I never kill lawmen unless I have to. It tends to encourage other lawmen to snoop around. And Reno's such a coward. He's just what I need here. As long as he's on the job, no competent lawman can come in and spoil my plans."

Rachel leaned against the sill, her hands knotted in her lap. "I'll go along with whatever you think's best. But if he blows the whistle on me, we could have U.S. marshals swarming all over the place."

Jack ran his fingers slowly along both sides of his mustache. Finally, he met her eye, his expression calm. "Don't worry about Reno. I'll have Sims and Jacobson give him a good scare. He'll be drunk for six months when they get through with him. By the time he sobers up, we'll be gone."

Rachel nodded. Fortunately, Elias Colt Jack was not her only ally in Adobe Wells. She would see Reno dead; she had come too far to let some tinhorn send her back to prison, much too far.

Unaware of her dire musings, the eavesdropper beneath the window heaved a sigh of relief, thinking at least the local law was safe. But Layard Shackelford was another matter. The geologist's life was in his hands.

If only he could reach him in time . . .

Ted entered his office. It was just as he had left it several days before. Donn Pedro was a good caretaker. He smiled at the thought.

The office was actually quite plain, furnished with a decrepit wooden desk and swivel chair. A splintered bench was pushed up against the front wall. The single crumbling jail cell was hidden in the back, behind a scarred door, an iron cot and porcelain slop jar in the corner of the cell.

Reno flopped into his chair and drummed his fingers across the desk, thinking. Donn Pedro came through the door.

The child was lame, just one more of life's throwaways. Reno had found him fighting stray dogs for scraps in the trash dump behind the town eatery. Knowing what it meant to have your pride insulted, Ted didn't offer the boy charity. Instead, he had gotten him a job at the stage office and allowed him to sleep in the jail in exchange for running errands. Reno was the only family the boy had. And Donn Pedro was completely devoted to him. The rest of the town might laugh at him, but he was Donn Pedro's hero.

"Buenos días, Señor Reno."

"Buenos días, Pedro."

The child's eyes sparkled when Reno spoke to him. He was clutching a packet of mail in his dirty fist.

When Ted looked into Pedro's worshipful gaze, his chest expanded with a measure of pride. Smiling, he took the mail. *"Gracias,* Pedro." He mussed the child's hair, studying him with feigned solemnity. "You look like a man who could use a licorice whip." He handed him a penny.

"Gracias, Señor Marshal." As fast as he was able, the child shuffled out the door, heading for Dowling's General Store.

Reno opened the packet and found a stack of wanted posters. Casually, as he thumbed through them, he leaned his chair against the wall, thoughts of Rachel teasing his mind. He almost tipped over when Rachel's likeness stared up at him from the third placard from the top.

"Rachel Baker," he read silently. "Wanted. Dead or alive. For embezzling $2,000 from the First State Bank of Chicago." He whistled through his teeth, then continued. "Aka Rachel Jackson. Wanted for murdering two guards during an escape from Arkansas Territorial Prison. Reward $1,000." He slammed the poster down on his desk. "Well, I'll be damned!"

The long day behind him, Ted carefully placed the wanted poster of Rachel in his desk drawer and headed back to the boardinghouse. As he passed the Golden Nugget, a harsh voice ordered him to halt.

On the boardwalk, Sims planted his feet and glared down at Reno. His hand blurred; his gun spat fire. A barrage of bullets plunged into the mud surrounding Ted's feet. Reno danced and screamed in alarm, expecting to feel the burning pain of hot lead.

"You damn sissy cur," Sims spat out, sending more gunfire in Ted's direction.

Ted's bladder emptied itself involuntarily, saturating his clothes with warm liquid. When he raised his head, his tearful gaze collided with Pedro's. "Don't," Reno shouted.

But it was too late. The child dove for Sims's legs. The brigand backhanded him, sending his small, broken body into the sucking mud.

Laughing harshly, Sims returned to the saloon.

Tears blurred his vision, but slipping and stumbling, Ted made his way to Donn Pedro. Kneeling, he gathered the boy against his chest. When he reached his office, he threw open the door, fell on the floor, and, still holding the child, sobbed quietly until he was claimed by a numbing sleep.

Pedro came awake slowly. Rising, he took a moth-eaten blanket from the back cell and reverently covered Reno's body. Then he curled up close to the man who was and always would be his hero.

No matter what.

Twenty-eight

Heath was wholly unaware of just how unique Stevie was. Among the Comanches, she was considered a healer. Whenever she touched someone who was ill, the powerful medicine would overtake her, flow through her fingers, soothing pain, spreading well-being. It was a mystical gift, wholly spiritual. She had not been with her mother's people long enough to learn their healing ways, how to employ the curatives of plants and herbs. All she had were her hands and the power the Great Spirit had imparted to her.

Even now, as she rubbed her flat palms over the maiden's belly, the girl's pain subsided. A warmth tingled inside Gentle Fawn, beginning in her stomach and spreading to her heart and mind. She breathed a Comanche prayer of thanksgiving for Stevie's gift.

"What's your name?" Stevie asked in Comanche.

"Gentle Fawn."

Stevie sucked in her breath. This was Black Coyote's wife and she hadn't recognized her. Her cousin's wife was so frail and thin. A life of danger and depravation had ravaged the beauty she once possessed. "Gentle Fawn, it is Yo-oh-hobt Pa-pi, Yellow Hair."

Just then Gentle Fawn felt the cruel fingers of another contraction. When it passed, she raised black, tortured eyes to Stevie. "Please save my baby," she whispered with her waning strength. "And raise him as your own."

"I'll save him. But he will have his *pia* to raise him," Stevie soothed, rubbing Gentle Fawn's stomach, easing her through another contraction.

There was so much Stevie wanted to ask. Why was Gentle Fawn out here alone? Where was Black Coyote? How long had she been bleeding so profusely? She settled for "How long have you been in labor?"

Gentle Fawn did not possess the strength to answer.

Heath stood riveted, unable to look away. The power surrounding Stevie was almost visible. She eased Gentle Fawn's pain with the touch of her fingertips. And her spirit soothed the girl's fear and despair as surely as her hands relieved the pain.

It was almost a spiritual experience, as if he were a part of Stevie, as if his love for her made him an active participant in the unnatural phenomenon he was witnessing. He was mesmerized and overwhelmed by this woman he loved more than life itself.

"What are y'all doing?"

The mystical spell was broken by Erica's nasal whine.

Stevie stiffened. For the first time since Heath entered the clearing, she lifted her gaze to him. "Get her out of here."

Their eyes met and held. "Don't you need me?" he asked.

Stevie regarded him for what seemed like forever. She had known he was there all along. And she had known he was participating in the healing process. It had been as if they were one. The power flowing through her fingers had never been so great. Heath had made her feel as if she could accomplish anything, as if they could accomplish anything, together.

But as she looked at him now, standing so tall and glorious in the waning light, with the small white woman pulling on his arm . . .

She wanted to shout, "No, I don't need you." But she couldn't bring herself to lie. So she said, "Just get her out of here."

Hurt, anger, and fear of a future without Stevie gripped Heath's heart. Wheeling around, he grabbed Erica by the arm and shoved her ahead of him. "Let's go. You can help make camp."

"But I'm tired. Let her do it. Why's she fiddlin' with that squaw anyway? She's just a dirty old Indian. It'd be better if her whelp died. And her along with it."

Heath jerked her to a halt and spun her around. "You say another word like that, just one more word, and I swear to God, I'll turn you over my knee and wallop the daylights out of you," he growled down into her face.

She spat, sputtered, and dredged up crocodile tears. "You wouldn't dare. Why, I've never been spanked in my life."

"That, madam, is abundantly clear. Now, come along. I'll start a fire and you'll cook while Stevie takes care of Gentle Fawn."

When the enraged marshal and the petulant belle arrived back at the horses, Erica stamped her foot and crossed her arms over her chest. "I will not put up with such abominable treatment."

Heath didn't trust himself to speak. Frustrated, he unsaddled the horses and gave each a vigorous rubdown. He hobbled them and turned them loose to graze.

Erica remained where he left her. The look she gave him when he returned would cook an egg in its shell. She was obstinately mute.

Thank God! "If you don't like our company, you are welcome to leave at any time," he threw over his shoulder as he headed back toward Stevie and Gentle Fawn.

The sound of Stevie keening, as her ancestors had done for generations, almost brought Heath to his knees. Never had he heard anything that moved him so. It floated on the wind. Mingled with the shrill cry of an infant, it wrapped around his heart and squeezed painfully.

He hastened his step, his long stride devouring the ground that separated him and Stevie. If he didn't touch her soon, his heart would burst, of that he was convinced.

When he reached the clearing, he found what he expected. Stevie, kneeling at the side of the still maiden, holding a blood-smeared baby in her arms. The life's blood from the mother had stained Stevie's platinum braid. A silver-gold rope tinged with crimson, it rested against the infant's glistening black head.

"Sweetheart," he said, hurrying to her side. He drew her and the baby into the shelter of his arms. "Gentle Fawn?"

"Suvate, it is finished," was all she said.

"The baby?"

"It's a girl."

Sitting beside Gentle Fawn's still, lifeless form, he rocked Stevie and the baby back and forth. Stevie's tears soaked the front of his shirt, warming his skin as the feel of her in his arms warmed his heart. He was unaware that he had dropped his hand to the infant's head.

But Stevie was quite aware of his action. She knew she should resist his comfort, draw into herself, but she needed him so much.

Settling her closer, Heath dropped his gaze. "What will happen to her?"

"I'll raise her with Winter. What did you expect?"

"Just that." He smiled down at her, caressing the baby's head. "She's so small."

When the child made a weak attempt to cry, a feeling of protectiveness slammed into his gut. The sight of the tiny scrap of life nestled trustingly against his body and Stevie's gave rise to a wave of love such as Heath had never experienced. It was the kind of intense feeling he had for Stevie, almost as strong, but different, the kind of love he imagined his father felt for his sisters, the kind of love that would make a man lay down his life for his child gladly, without a moment's hesitation.

Heath knew that he would kill for this Comanche baby. If anyone anywhere dared to hurt her, he would not be responsible for his actions. Retribution would be swift and sure . . . and harsh. And he had absolutely no idea why he felt this way. Emotions were like that, he supposed. They just sneaked up on you and you were powerless to do anything but feel.

He was unable to speak for a long time, so moved was he. Finally, he dropped a kiss on Stevie's brow. "Sweetheart, let me take you and the baby back to camp. Then I'll see to Gentle Fawn."

Tears started to streak down her cheeks again. "We can't even give her a proper burial." She leaned forward and kissed the still, peaceful form of Gentle Fawn.

Heath gathered her back against him.

"Oh, Heath, she was so beautiful. I remember when she and Black Coyote first married. She was so happy. And now her life's over."

The question uppermost in Heath's mind had to be asked. "What about the others? Her husband? Did she say?"

"The village was attacked. Everyone's dead. All the women. All the children. Black Coyote. Everyone." She wasn't prepared to tell him that she knew the identity of the men who had committed these atrocities. She would keep that information to herself. And somehow she would make them pay.

If Heath knew their identity, he would be obliged to turn them in. The murdering thieves would probably be given a reward for ridding the West of a bunch of filthy savages, she thought bitterly.

Her voice dropped to an agonized whisper. "Why? Why did they have to kill them?" She turned a tortured gaze on Heath.

His heart clenched at the pain in her eyes. He was unprepared for the sound of her harsh laughter.

"You know something? I've lived my whole life ashamed of what the Comanches have done to whites. But white men are no better. Not one bit. They're . . . they're worse." She buried her face in the baby's hair. "I hate them," she cried brokenly. "I hate them all. If there was a Comanche village nearby, I would go to it. I would live there . . . like an Indian . . . and never go back to Adobe Wells. Never. I would raid with the warriors. Kill the whites. I would kill them. I would kill them all." She dissolved into silent tears. The only sign of her distress was her shaking shoulders.

"Shhh, sweetheart. It's okay." He crooned nonsensical messages. He knew she didn't really mean what she said. For a moment he had been taken aback by her expressed hatred for whites, fearing that she would blame him for what his people—if indeed whites were responsible for the raid on Gentle Fawn's village—had done. But she was grief-stricken. She didn't hate all white men.

Dear God, he hoped she didn't.

* * *

When Stevie and Heath finally returned to camp, Stevie was inordinately subdued from exhaustion, physical and emotional. The baby lay listlessly in her arms, weak from lack of nourishment and the strain of a difficult birth.

"She's hungry." Stevie's voice was completely devoid of emotion.

Heath eased her down on the pallet he had placed close to the fire. He noticed for the first time that Stevie held a square, flat pouch. The pitiful mewling of the hungry child drew his attention away from the soft leather bag. "I don't have much experience with babies, but . . . can she drink sugar water? Until we reach Adobe Wells tomorrow?"

Stevie nodded, never taking her eyes from the baby's face. After her earlier outburst, she had grown almost as listless as the babe.

She was a far cry from the fiery hellion who had taken shots at him from Mustang Mesa. And it scared Heath spitless. "I'll get it." Worried about both Stevie and the baby, he didn't notice Erica approach, didn't see the hatred and disgust on her face as she glared down at them.

She motioned to the buckskin sack. "What's that?"

Stevie didn't answer, just clutched the baby closer to her body.

"It gonna live?" Erica asked in a low voice, gesturing toward the baby.

Heath didn't hear the question, but Stevie did. Still, she didn't respond.

"Did the squaw die?" Erica prodded.

Stevie looked up at the girl, violence blazing in her ebony eyes. She nodded tersely.

Erica tossed her head and huffed, "Too bad the brat didn't."

Stevie placed the baby and Gentle Fawn's pouch on the blanket gently. With a low growl emanating from her throat, she gathered her legs beneath her and lunged for Erica, claws bared. The words she shrieked in Comanche were unintelligible to Erica, but the message was crystal-clear.

The catfight was over almost as soon as it began. Dropping the cup of sugar water on the ground, Heath ran over to the women and grabbed Stevie around the waist. Holding her tight against his chest, he whispered into her ear, "Don't, sweetheart."

Stevie jerked around and stared at him, bewildered. She was crushed that he would protect Erica, a spoiled, selfish girl who could wish an innocent baby dead simply because she was an Indian.

Heath had not heard Erica's horrible words, but he had no doubt that she deserved any abuse she got. His intention was not to spare Erica as Stevie supposed, but to protect the woman he loved. Stevie was part Indian. Erica was the daughter of a white Army officer. The society they lived in would not allow an Indian to attack a white woman no matter the provocation. The fact sickened him, but it was a fact nonetheless.

Erica regarded Stevie as if she were a bug to be squashed. Pinning her gaze on Heath, she questioned, "She some kind of Indian lover or something?"

Stevie jerked free of Heath's hold and bent to pick up the child. "No. I'm not an Indian lover. I'm an Indian." She turned her back on the two white people in camp and went about the business of seeing to the Indian baby—her own kind.

"What did you say to her?" Heath growled low when Stevie was out of earshot.

Erica tossed her hair behind her shoulders and regarded him petulantly. "Nothing. Just that it was too bad the brat didn't die with the squaw."

Heath truly saw red, blood red. He wanted nothing more than to wrap his hands around Erica's throat and squeeze until her haughty face turned purple. When he spoke, his voice trembled with rage. "If you say one more word to offend Stevie, you will be camping elsewhere. Do you understand me?"

Without waiting for a reply, he turned on his heel and stomped away. He followed Stevie to the edge of camp, where he found her perched on a boulder, dribbling sugar water into the baby's mouth. His eyes and heart softened at the sight they presented. He moved closer, standing so near to Stevie their thighs touched. "She looks like a hungry little bird."

She swiveled her legs, turning slightly away from him.

He knew why she was angry at him, but it didn't make her rejection sting any less. "Honey, let me explain."

Stevie refused to meet his eye. "I'd rather you didn't."

He looked as if he would say more, then thought better of it. Stevie was too distraught to think rationally. She wouldn't appreciate his explanation, that society would judge her harshly for touching a white woman, even if that white woman deserved to have her neck wrung. "I'll check the horses," was all he said.

When he returned to camp, both women were lying on their blankets. Erica was snoring.

The only sound coming from Stevie was a soft snubbing sound like that of a child who had cried long and hard. He closed the distance between them quietly, dropped his gaze, and stared down at her slender form.

She looked so small, so helpless, little more than a child herself. Life was cruel, he acknowledged. This precious woman with a heart the size of Texas—though she tried to hide it—had been hurt time and again by all the Ericas of her world. He wanted to protect her, if only she would she let him.

"Stevie," he whispered. She pretended to be asleep. Placing his blanket close to hers, he lay down. Her back to him, he drew her into his embrace. "I love you, sugar," he whispered tenderly.

"Don't."

"Don't touch you?"

"Don't love me."

"Too late. I already do."

What could she say? She should move away from him, but couldn't if her life depended on it. She needed to be close to him tonight.

His body warming her back, she fought in vain for the mind-numbing oblivion of sleep. A lone tear slid softly down her cheek, disappearing into the sleeping infant's ebony hair as it mingled with her own white-blond tresses. Pressing the baby's tiny body against her breast as if she could keep her heart from shattering into a million pieces, she prayed for the strength to deny her all-encompassing love for Heath, love for a white man, a love that might well destroy them both.

Twenty-nine

Two hours outside Adobe Wells they saw a swarm of buzzards winging in the distance.

"I'd better check it out," Heath said.

"Not me," Erica whined. "I don't want to see anything dead."

Heath glanced back at Erica and noted the unpleasant smirk on her face. "Suit yourself."

"Unless it's Indians," she added spitefully.

Heath stiffened. When he looked toward Stevie, she acted as if she had not heard Erica's hateful statement.

"You coming, sugar?" he asked softly. Truth to tell, he didn't want to drag her to a scene of carnage—human or animal—after what she had been through with Gentle Fawn. Yet he didn't want to leave her to suffer Erica's verbal abuse either. He was in a dilemma.

Stevie took the matter out of his hands as she kicked her horse in a gallop and headed toward the circling carnivores.

Heath soon drew alongside her and they moved down the trail in silence. The stench that met them caused Stevie to gag over the side of her horse. He offered her his blue bandanna to cover her nose and mouth.

Stevie was not surprised at what they found, nor was she particularly saddened. Lying around a smoldering campfire, like wax figures, their scalps bloody and bare, with feathered arrows protruding from them like giant winged porcupine quills, were the men—minus Sims—who had pursued them into the mountains. The same men—Stevie knew—who had attacked Gentle Fawn's village. She sat her horse in silence, the sleeping infant clutched to her breast.

Heath dismounted and checked each man to determine whether he was alive or dead. They were all dead. After they had been shot with arrow or bullet, their throats had been slit. It looked as if they all had grisly smiles tucked beneath their chins.

He stood above Two Paws's lifeless body and raised his gaze to Stevie. What he saw in the ebony depths caused his stomach to lurch, accusation and distrust, directed at him. What had he ever done to her that would make her look at him that way?

"I suppose you'll report this to the army and they'll hunt them down like animals," Stevie said tonelessly.

Heath was hurt that she had so little faith in him. He pointed to the dead men scattered about him like fallen toy soldiers on a parlor rug. "This doesn't bother you?" he accused, striking back without thinking.

"These men attacked Gentle Fawn's village in the dead of night. They shot everything moving—men, women, children, animals. The ones they couldn't smoke out of their lodges, they burned alive. After everyone was slaughtered and the village was in flames, they found Gentle Fawn in the birthing lodge with the medicine woman, Cares for Everyone. They shot Cares, and while she was dying they cut her breasts off, bragging that the soft brown skin would make good tobacco pouches."

She stopped speaking and dropped her head back on her shoulders. After drawing a cleansing breath into her lungs, she was able to continue. "Then they started on Gentle Fawn. She was in labor, but that didn't stop them from taking turns raping her. One of these fine, upstanding men even raped the medicine woman. Gentle Fawn wasn't sure, but she thought Cares was already dead." Tears streaked down her cheeks. "Oh, by the way"—her voice rose hysterically—"did I tell you that Cares was seventy-three years old?" She laughed without humor. "And that she delivered me after the good people of Adobe Wells refused to tend my mother?"

"Stevie." Heath's voice was husky with emotion. He stepped toward her.

She raised her arm as if to ward him off. "No! Let me finish. They threw Gentle Fawn over the back of a horse then. By that time her pains were almost continuous and she was bleeding like a stuck hog. But they decided to take her along as sexual entertainment . . . for as long as she lasted. When they got word that there was a party of renegades in the area, they threw her off the horse while it was still moving, They didn't even slow down. We found her an hour later."

She clenched her teeth until her jaw ached. "And she died, what, an hour after that? So, what was your question, Heath? Oh, yes, does seeing these poor dead men lying on the ground bother me?" She wheeled her horse about. Over her shoulder, she spat out, "Not one damn bit!"

"The lady has a valid point."

Heath whirled and drew on Jay, reminiscent of the scene on Mustang Mesa moments after he had seen Stevie for the first time. How long ago that seemed now. Jay looked different this time. "What the—" Heath exclaimed.

If he had not recognized Jay's intelligent green eyes staring back at him from a face blackened with soot, he'd have shot his partner where he stood. To say that the gentleman from Georgia—who had given more than one fair maiden a fit of the vapors—looked disreputable would be a serious understatement.

And how had he blackened his teeth, making them look like decayed snags hanging precariously in a slack mouth? Heath wondered inanely. It was as if the gap-toothed smile mesmerized him. Heath shook free of the spell and sighed heavily. "What are you supposed to be?" he asked, holstering his gun.

"I'm supposed to be an undercover marshal. Which, if memory serves correctly, so are you. Why aren't you in Adobe Wells getting shed of Judge Jack and that gang of cutthroats he's surrounded by?"

Heath didn't answer Jay's question. Instead, he asked one of his own. "You've been in Adobe Wells? I thought you were hot on Rachel Jackson's trail. She give you the slip again?"

"Yes and no. Yes, I was in Adobe Wells. But no, Rachel Jackson didn't give me the slip."

"You mean Rachel's in Adobe Wells?"

Jay nodded.

"Damn! That's all I need. How am I supposed to avoid her?"

"You won't be able to. She's up to her double chins in the judge's diamond deal. 'Spect you'll run into her soon as you hit town."

Heath thought about the new obstacle to his job. Finally, he shrugged. He was so very weary, he didn't need another complication. "Guess I'll just have to convince her I'm on the other side of the law now."

"With your charm and Rachel's disposition you shouldn't have any trouble with her," Jay said, trying to wipe a layer of soot from his boyishly handsome face. "She always was a hot—" he began, shrugging. "Guess I'm still too much of a southern gentleman to say it. Suffice it to say that she's rotten to the core. She actually asked the judge to have Marshal Reno killed. Might've been orderin' a mint julep, for all the emotion in her voice." He shook his head. "Reno's so worthless, poor kid, I was tempted to shoot him m'self."

Heath was well aware that Jay didn't mean what he said about Ted. And he could tell his partner's brush with Rachel had affected him more than he let on. Jay's drawl always thickened when he was distraught. And it sounded like buttered molasses in January to Heath. "Please tell me he refused to kill the kid."

Jay reassured Heath that the marshal was safe for the time being. Then he filled him in on the remainder of Judge Jack and Rachel's plan. "So I'm on my way to warn Shackelford. Obviously, Rachel's not goin' anywhere till money changes hands. But just the same, keep an eye on her for me. Hear?"

Heath nodded, hiding a tired smile. When Jay said "hear," it sounded like he'ah. He *must* be upset. "How do you plan to protect Shackelford without Jack knowing we're on to him?"

"I don't know." He smiled and continued. "But I'll think of something between here and Santa Fe."

"I have no doubt that you will. Meantime, I'll head on back to Adobe Wells, keep the marshal's fat out of the fire, and deal with Rachel." Then abruptly, he asked, "Do you have your grandfather's watch?"

Jay looked at him suspiciously. Anybody who knew Jay Hampton knew that his granddaddy had given all three of his grandsons ornate pocket watches with their initials engraved on the back. He was never without it; none of them was. Sliding the expensive timepiece from his breeches pocket and handing it to Heath, he asked, "You wanta know the time of day, or you just got a hankerin' for my property?"

"Neither. Rachel knows that you wouldn't part with this while there was still life in your body. So I'm going to show it to her as proof that I got tired of working for pennies as a lawman"—his voice was dry, a twinkle lit his eyes—"and stole this from you after I put a few dozen bullets in your hide."

Jay smiled his appreciation for Heath's plan. It was simple enough to work. Still, he couldn't help teasing Heath. "Nobody'd believe that you could shoot me. I'm such a fine fella and all."

"Somehow, I don't think Rachel would agree. You did put her in jail once, and she has to know it's only a matter of time before you do it again."

"If you don't let her get away."

"I'll keep my eye on her."

Reassured, Jay said, "Do we have to bury these bastards?"

Heath glanced around at the corpses for the first time since he and Jay began speaking. "I'd let them rot where they lay, but if the army found them, there'd be hell to pay for every Indian north of the Rio Grande."

Jay agreed. "I was afraid you'd see it that way."

But the earth was too hard to penetrate with a shovel. So one by one they dragged the bodies to a deep ravine and sent them hurtling over the side of the cliff. They threw branches into the hole after them. Silently looking down, they were satisfied that the men would not be found.

Stretching his stiff neck, rotating it from side to side, Heath raised his gaze. The sun was low in the sky, casting a rosy glow over the mountains. A red veil draped from peak to peak. It looked like the whole world was tinted with blood. Sangre de Cristo—the blood of Christ—these mountains were aptly named, he decided.

Considering the bloodshed that had occurred in the past twenty-four hours, the name was even more apt. Not to mention the bloodshed that had occurred for the past several years, with whites attacking Indians, Indians raiding whites.

He was beset by a series of questions that seemed to have no answer. Where would the struggle end? With every renegade Indian dead or imprisoned on a reservation with the rest of the Comanche nation? And how long would the battle go on? How many innocents—like Stevie, Winter, the new baby, and even himself—would get caught up in it?

Genocide or freedom—which would be the Indians' fate? Manifest destiny—the battle cry of the white masses.

Who would triumph? Who would lose? The answer was painfully clear. The Indians would lose in the end. But they would not give up easily. Admiration and sadness swept over Heath in equal measure.

As he bid Jay good-bye and made his way back to Stevie, he was sure he had never yearned for New York quite as much as he did now. But an even stronger motive for leaving the West was his desire to take Stevie home with him, to whisk her, the baby, and Winter away from this violent country, away from the racial war that would break Stevie's gentle heart.

"What was it?" Erica asked as soon as Heath rode into the makeshift camp. She jerked her head in Stevie's direction. "She wouldn't say."

Heath felt Stevie's eyes on him. The tension was thick enough to cut with a knife. "A pair of jennies. Both had broken a leg. The owner put the animals out of their misery. But he was too lazy to bury them where scavengers couldn't find them. I took care of it."

Stevie exhaled, unaware that she had been holding her breath. "You buried them where they can't be found?" The silent words "by the army," hung in the air.

"Nobody will ever find them."

Bored with the conversation, Erica moved over to her horse, rummaging around in her saddlebags for a hairbrush.

Heath's eyes met Stevie's. They looked at each other for a moment, communicating with their eyes. Understanding passed between them. The renegade band had dispensed its form of justice—killing the men who destroyed Gentle Fawn's band of peaceful Comanches. They would not be hunted like animals and executed for doing something that had to be done.

Stevie smiled tentatively at Heath and mouthed, "Thank you."

He sketched a slight bow, his heart suddenly light. Stevie's gentle smile could make his day. Dare he be so dramatic as to say that the lack of it could break his heart?

"Let's go home," he told her softly.

The gloaming cast a silver shadow over the threesome as they made their way back to Adobe Wells. Stevie and Heath both remembered their brief, beautiful stay in the majestic Sangre de Cristo mountains. In ways they could scarcely imagine, this idyllic time had changed them drastically, irrevocably.

They would realize in the days to come just how much. They would learn that they needed each other more than air to breathe, water to drink, or food to eat. And they would both realize what they already suspected, that apart, they were only half alive.

Thirty

A mile outside of town, Heath noticed four men riding hell bent for leather toward Santa Fe.

A more disreputable bunch he had never seen. They were brigands, up to no good. He'd bet his badge on it. Fearing that Jay's cover had been blown and the gang was in pursuit of him, he took Stevie and Erica into town and dropped them at Pilar's before heading over to the jail.

He would get the marshal and they would go after the men. It was time someone taught the young lawman how to go up against the opposition. And Heath was the man to do it.

Inside the jailhouse, he found Donn Pedro alone, his lower lip trembling, mumbling something about the three men who stole the marshal. A sob escaped the child's lips, but he held back the tears.

"Damn!" Heath uttered. Dropping down onto one knee, he pushed his hat back with two fingers and looked Pedro in the eye. "What's your name, son?"

"Donn Pedro."

"Where do you live, Donn Pedro?"

Pedro settled his gaze on the floor. "Here."

"Okay. You just stay here and don't tell anybody about this—" Heath began quietly. "And don't worry. The men who took Marshal Reno won't hurt him. I promise. I'll bring him back. Safe and sound. If you need anything while the marshal and I are gone, go to Miss Pilar's boardinghouse and ask for Stevie Johns. Do you know her?"

"Sí." His voice was very small.

"Stevie's a friend of mine. She'll help you. Okay?"

Pedro drew himself up, trying to hide his fear. "You will help the marshal." It sounded quite like an order. "And I will do as you say." As an afterthought, he added, "Who are you?"

"Can you keep a secret, Donn Pedro?"

Pedro eyed Heath with a hint of indignation. Of course he could keep a secret! He nodded tersely.

Heath reached into his pocket and drew out his U.S. marshal's badge.

The child's eyes widened and darkened with respect. He stretched forth a shaky finger and touched the metal that had been warmed by its proximity to Heath's body. "I won't tell nobody," he promised reverently. "Just bring the marshal back." His voice quivered. "Please."

Something broke loose inside Heath. He gathered the child in his arms. Pride stiffened Donn Pedro's back momentarily, then he caved in and accepted the comfort the big gringo freely offered.

Heath patted the child's head awkwardly. This land was too harsh and unforgiving for the weak, and this boy was weak. He was an orphan, alone in the world except for Reno. If the marshal were killed, the boy could starve to death. Pedro had to know that; Heath couldn't begin to imagine how that would make a child feel.

Well, he would do what he could for Donn Pedro. First, that meant going after the marshal. While the abductors didn't plan to kill Reno now—according to the information Jay had overheard—they might hurt him. Heath would trail them and stay close in the event that things got out of hand.

When their guard was down—when they stopped for the night—he would steal into camp and rescue the marshal. He would bring Reno back if it was the last thing he ever did.

Telling Pedro as much, he rushed back to the boardinghouse. Stevie was sitting in the rocking chair on the portico. He knew that she was waiting for him, and the knowledge warmed his heart. “I have to throw some things together. Come up with me.”

She nodded, rising from the chair.

He halted with his hand on the front door. “Where’s Erica?”

“A lieutenant from the fort arrived moments after you left. Sent here by her doting papa. With an escort of twenty. They took her away.”

Heath grinned, taking Stevie’s hand in his own. “There is a God.”

Smiling, she followed him up the staircase.

When they entered his room, he found his saddlebags packed with sufficient food, clothing, and ammunition for a lengthy trip. He pulled her through the doorway and closed the door firmly behind them. He tossed his hat on the bed, leaned back against the door, settled her into the cradle of his thighs, and looked down into midnight-black eyes. “You packed for me.” It wasn’t a question, rather a statement of fact.

“You’re going after them.”

“I have to. They’ve kidnapped Ted Reno. And while the kid may not be worth a spit in the river, he’s still the marshal. I have to go,” he repeated. “Now. Before they get away.”

Cupping her head in one large palm, he took her lips beneath his own. He kissed her with all the love in his heart. Then his mouth brushed hers softly as he spoke. “I wish we had more time to say good-bye, sweetheart.”

The hot hardness pressing against her belly told Stevie what they would do if they had more time. More than anything, she wanted him to stay. But perhaps it was best that he leave quickly. His absence would give her time to shore up her defenses, time to convince herself that she could live in a world without him.

Frustrated longing shook her body at the thought of never being held by Heath again. Hungrily, shamelessly, she burrowed her arms beneath his leather vest and circled his waist. Silently, she cursed her own weakness.

His arms closed about her more tightly, one hand in the small of her back pressing her to him. The ensuing kiss was urgent, frantic, ravenous. It was brilliant light, vibrant heat, melding them together, mouth to mouth, heart to heart, soul to soul.

Fused, he rocked her slowly against him, massaging the part of him that was trying to make him forget about outlaws, kidnappers, marshals, promises to orphans, anything, everything but Stevie. Loving her long and hard was uppermost in his mind as he fed on the passion of her kiss.

Pulling away, he tried to tell her how much he loved her, how much he would miss her. And between each vow of devotion, each declaration of need, he showered kisses on the tip of her nose, her eyelids, her cheeks and jaw, her bare, slender neck.

"Will you think about me while I'm gone?" Heath asked against her heated skin.

At a loss, she buried her face in his hair. She breathed in the scent of him, wanting his aroma, the very essence of him to be captured inside her. She held her breath. When her lungs would burst, she exhaled grudgingly.

He massaged the rise and fall of her chest. Again he asked her, "Will you think of me?"

"No."

"No?" He pulled back and tilted her face up.

She kept her expression carefully blank. She should tell him now that there was no future for them. She knew she should. It would be easier on both of them. Quick and clean, cut him out of her life like a cancer.

But the way he was gazing at her—hopefully, lovingly, with more vulnerability in his eyes than she had ever expected to see—she couldn't bring herself to voice the words. He was not a cancer that killed, but a force that gave her life. Despite her best efforts to the contrary, a slow smile lit her face. Then his in response.

"Yes," she breathed. "I'll miss you." She cleared her throat and blinked against the water forming in her eyes. Small fists pounded the wide muscled wall of his chest. "But I don't want to. Damn your black heart."

Chuckling, he captured both her hands in one of his own. His smile was so sexy, it made her want to throw him on the floor and jump on top of him, so patently self-satisfied, she wanted to break the slop jar over his head. She did neither.

Instead, she whispered, "Kiss me again, you wretched man, then go catch the bad guys."

"Yes, ma'am."

She expected a quick kiss, little more than a vigorous peck. What she received was a full frontal assault on all her senses, over her entire aching body. He employed lips, hands, body, and voice in his seduction of her. And he met with unparalleled success; she melted and pooled at his feet.

If he had to leave her indefinitely, he would give her something to think about while he was gone. He mapped her gently with his touch, his husky voice praising each part of her body, raising her desire and heart rate accordingly.

His tongue and lips were everywhere at once. On, in, and around her mouth, over her face, in her ear—she giggled, then moaned at the heady sensation—down her neck, pausing on her pulse point. He nipped it, then soothed it with the tip of his tongue. When he laved it flatly, he felt the blood surging beneath her silky skin.

He slid his knee between her thighs, and the pounding beneath his tongue increased. He raised his leg a bit higher, nestling his bulging thigh at the V in her legs. The pulse at her throat grew erratic as she ground herself against his leg. His sharp breath dissolved into a deep groan.

It was then that Heath questioned the wisdom of his actions. Stevie was writhing against him passionately, making those sounds in the back of her throat that never failed to drive him crazy. If her uninhibited response was an indication, she would think of him while he was gone . . . just as he had intended when he began his skillful seduction.

But he had gotten caught in his own net. He was so aroused that he would be lucky if he could sit his horse. He didn't even want to consider being unable to love her for days on end. What had started as a way to keep his woman enticed had ended as a means of self-torture. And Heath was no sadist. So after a kiss that was so heated it left them both momentarily stunned, he disentangled himself from her embrace and held her away from him.

It took her a few moments to regain her composure. "Wow," she said, a little break in her voice. Her sense of humor was intact despite the fact that her whole body was screaming for release. "You sure you gotta go? So soon?"

His laugh turned into a groan when she ran a finger over his moist, puffy lips. He sucked it into his mouth as if he were an infant suckling on her breast. He groaned again at the mental picture he had drawn. "I'm sure I've gotta go . . . while I still can."

She smiled sweetly.

"But I can barely stand the thought of leaving you behind. If it wasn't dangerous, sugar, I would take you with me."

She sobered instantly. "You will be careful, won't you?"

He cursed himself for worrying her even as the concern in her ebony eyes thrilled him. His callused palms gently cradled her face. "Stephanie Johns, nothing in this world could keep me away from you and Winter and that new baby girl. I'll be back." He tilted his head, suddenly intense. "I swear it on our children's lives." He grinned. "Our present and future children's lives."

The thick fringe of lashes that shaded her eyes flew up. She blushed instantly, helplessly. Her heart pounded in her chest. The need to bear his child was a living, breathing desire inside her. Even now she could be carrying his baby beneath her heart. She was speechless. "Dear God, please make it so," she prayed silently.

Unaware of the desperate prayer, he said as prayerfully as she, "I love you, sugar." Then he kissed her one last time. Long, deep, and heartbreakingly sweet.

She couldn't say the words back to him. It would be too hard to tell him good-bye later if she did.

Pretending not to notice, he told her about Pedro, retrieved his hat, hefted his saddlebag over his shoulder, and together they left the room.

"Please, be careful," she whispered against his lips, squeezing the hand that held her own.

"I promise." He kissed her gently, mounted his horse, and headed out of town.

The sight that would sustain him in the hard times ahead was Stevie, standing on the portico, waving to him, one arm wrapped protectively around her waist.

Thirty-one

He left town at a full gallop, heading southwest for the Santa Fe Trail.

Soon the lush green llano gave way to bunchgrass, mesquite bushes, mounds of dust, and craggy canyons. He shifted his Stetson low over his forehead to block out the bright rays of the sun.

Squinting his eyes, he surveyed the ground beneath his horse's hooves, looking for sign. The men who had taken Marshal Reno weren't even bothering to hide their trail. Arrogant bastards, it was considerate of them to make his job so easy, he thought wryly.

A hot wind blew across the basin, kicking up weeds and dust. He pulled his bandanna over his nose and mouth against the grit and grime. When the silken material brushed his lips, his mind and heart went back to Stevie. Lord, how he hated to leave her!

Suddenly his attention was captured by four riders about two miles away. Their swiftly moving forms were silhouetted against the skyline as they disappeared into a thick copse of trees. They were the men he pursued.

He left the trail and pushed Warrior to the limit. Taking a shortcut, he managed to get ahead of them. He positioned himself several hundred yards off the beaten path. Dropping behind a clump of mesquite, he tethered his mount, then crouched out of sight, waiting.

When they came alongside him, he saw a Mexican riding a roan in the lead. The cartridges in his bandoleer glistened in the sun as he shifted in the saddle. His sombrero was pulled low, giving him a sinister look. He resembled many of the lowlife crooks that Heath had gone up against in the last two years. They were all basically cowards, most insane. Therefore, they could be unpredictable. Heath would have to watch them all closely.

The second rider held the reins of his bay mare in a gloved hand while a carelessly rolled cigarette dangled from his mouth. Unlike the others, he wore rawhide chaparreras over his denim trousers. He looked like a typical cowboy riding the range in search of strays.

The third rider, a tall young man, was the prisoner, Marshal Reno, no doubt. He was mounted atop a buckskin gelding, his feet tied to the stirrups, his hands secured behind his back. A full mop of red hair topped a face made boyish by a swarm of freckles roaming over his nose. His dirty cheeks were hollow, his back straight. He was obviously trying to hide his fear. So this was Donn Pedro's hero. Heath smiled sadly.

The fourth man, wearing a filthy wampus, rode a muscled black stallion. His face was harsh, jagged, set by a life of murder and mayhem. At a glance Heath knew he was the one to watch most closely.

After the riders passed, they turned off the trail, heading west, and descended into a canyon. Heath mounted and rode over to the rim of the canyon. He watched them snake their way down a winding path into the arroyo. Reaching the floor of the canyon, they followed a stream, single file, until they disappeared around a bend.

Keeping a distance between the men and himself, Heath pursued them through a maze of ravines that led off the first canyon. The mountaintops rose high above. The path slowly descended into a fault.

Although it was midday, the walls of the ravine closed in around Heath, casting shadows all about. The surrounding hills blocked off the wind, but the lack of sunlight made the air cool.

A strong sense of foreboding raised the hair on the back of

his neck. The feeling was too strong to go unheeded. He picked up his pace.

The riders twisted and turned, following winding canals. Finally, they approached a precipitous talus slope. Heath halted Warrior with a slight tug on the reins. When the three brigands stopped and dismounted, he backed his horse around a bend, slid from the saddle, and peered around a boulder.

The Mexican untied Reno's feet and shoved him to the ground. The Marshal cried out in agony when he hit the rocky surface of the ravine. Heath released the loop around his gun.

The men ringed Ted like a pack of wolves circling a wounded fawn. Heath's mouth grew dry at the murderous looks on their faces. Acting on instinct, he ran down the path, gun drawn.

Reno begged his abductors for mercy, but to no avail. The third brigand kicked Ted in the teeth, yanked out his six-shooter, and emptied it into the young man's chest. His body jerked convulsively with the impact of each bullet.

"God no. Dear God, no," Heath panted, throwing himself behind a boulder. He pressed his cheek against the cool rock.

Why did they kill him? Jay said Judge Jack wanted him alive. He groaned, railing against fate, against his own sense of failure. It wasn't supposed to happen this way. It wasn't. How could things have gone so horribly awry?

Spurred by the need to avenge Reno, Donn Pedro, and every other poor defenseless soul the judge and his band of bastards had hurt, Heath rode back through the canyon. He came to a ravine that led off from the main channel. He followed the ravine, slipped off the trail, then waited for the killers to pass him by.

He had underestimated them the first time, but he would not be caught unawares again. If it took him forever, he would see that they paid for what they had done to Reno, more to the point for what they had done to Donn Pedro. But he had to see to the marshal's body. He couldn't just leave it lying there.

Shortly, he heard horses' pounding on the rocky terrain in the main canyon. Before long the brigands passed his hiding place. The rhythmic clacking of hooves, the creak of saddle leather, faded in the distance.

As Heath returned to the scene of the murder, Reno's buckskin gelding met him on the path. Taking the gelding's reins in his fist, he led it back to the site of the carnage.

Heath slid from his mount and approached a shallow mound of rocks. One pale, blood-smeared hand was visible beneath the mound. It almost seemed to be pointing an accusing finger at him. With a voice he scarcely recognized as his own, he told the buckskin that he had one last duty to perform for his master.

The bastards hadn't even buried Reno properly, though they had obviously been instructed to hide the body. Heath hefted the rocks and threw them aside, not even feeling the sharp edges cut into his skin, the heavy strain tearing at his muscles. He released Reno's bonds, placed his body over the gelding, and tied his hands and feet together underneath the horse's belly.

Numb now, Heath began the long journey out of the ravine. An hour before sundown he rode up to Delgado's. It consisted of several adobe buildings, all connected by portals. Stopping before the general store, he tied the horses to the hitching rail and sauntered inside, out of the late afternoon sun.

When he entered the store, the smell of leather, denim, and tobacco filled his nostrils. It was a familiar smell, a smell he always connected with the West.

A heavyset Mexican with an open, friendly face greeted him. He introduced himself as the proprietor, Ricardo Delgado. With a heavy Spanish accent he offered Heath a room.

Heath accepted, not opting to return to Adobe Wells that night. The trail would get cold if he took Reno back to town before pursuing his killers. Perhaps luck would be with him and he would find them quickly. Otherwise, he would have one helluva time picking up their trail.

His thoughts reversed. Considering how little time he had spent on his assignment in Adobe Wells, he didn't need to be distracted by a killing that might have nothing to do with Judge Jack and his bogus diamond mine, no matter what he had promised Donn Pedro.

A sense of guilt and the desire for justice reversed his thoughts again. He had to find the men who killed Ted Reno. They had to pay for their crimes. Determined, he wheeled around and left the store as quickly as he had entered.

Delgado followed him out onto the porch. He gasped when he saw Reno's bloody corpse. *"Madre Dios.* It's Marshal Reno. Who did this to him?"

"I don't know. But I intend to find out. Do you have somewhere I can leave him tonight?"

"Sí, Señor. In the shed out back." Delgado regarded the grisly body riddled with blue whistlers and covered his nose and mouth with a handkerchief. With his other hand he made the sign of the cross.

Heath placed Ted's body in the shed Delgado indicated, then followed the proprietor to the room that would be his for the night. Automatically, he washed the blood and dirt from his hands, face, and arms. He pulled a comb from his back pocket and ran it through his long black curls.

A glance in the cracked mirror told him he needed a haircut and a shave. His own mother wouldn't know him. His gaze slid down the front of his body; his clothes were filthy, but he was too weary to change.

He went down to the saloon, ordered a steak with all the trimmings, and devoured it like a pack of wolves feasting on a fallen doe, somewhat surprised at his appetite, considering the day he'd had.

His hunger sated, he tossed a coin on the table and made his way back to the general store. It was illuminated by several lanterns, as empty as it was before. Muttering appropriate but noninformative responses to Delgado's incessant questions, he purchased a new Winchester. Almost asleep on his feet, he bought a shirt to replace the bloodstained one he still wore.

The smell of liquor wafting through the door of the saloon was tempting, but the thought of a clean bed held even more appeal. If only Stevie were there to share it with him. He was truly exhausted, but he knew if she were within arm's length, he would summon sufficient strength for something more than sleep.

But she wasn't here. The ensuing depression her absence caused sapped the faint flicker of strength he had left. Sighing heavily, he made his way to his room, fell into bed, boots, filthy clothes, and all. He lapsed into a deep sleep as soon as his head hit the pillow.

His dreams were anything but restful. Visions of Stevie running from Judge Jack, crying out for Heath to save her, tormented him. He awoke during the night, sweaty and shaken. "Stevie," he whispered thickly. He had to see her, to make sure she was all right. Someone else could go after Reno's killers; he was on another assignment, after all.

But he was honest enough to admit that Judge Jack and his diamond scheme weren't his main concern. His thoughts were of Stevie, his precious, beautiful, delicate, gutsy Stevie. She needed him. And more than he ever thought possible, he needed her. With thoughts of holding the woman he loved in his arms, he drifted into a dreamless sleep.

The next morning Heath awakened as the sun rose over the white peaks of the Sangre de Cristo Mountains. He washed up quickly, eager to be on his way.

Shouldering his saddlebag, his first stop was the shed. He loaded Reno's blanket-draped corpse on his horse, then led the buckskin around to the stable, where Warrior stood cropping hay.

As he saddled his mount, the animal whinnied, whether in response to Heath's stroking reassurance or the marshal's mare's proximity, Heath didn't know. Maybe the old boy was smitten with Reno's horse.

When he approached the saloon, he found three horses tied to the hitching post; a roan, a bay, and a black. He recognized the horses as those the killers had been riding. He'd hit pay dirt!

Heath tied Warrior and the buckskin to the rail, checked his Navy Colt, and slowly entered the saloon. He paused long enough for his eyes to become accustomed to the dim interior. One by one three men came into focus. But they weren't the men Heath sought.

The Mexican barkeep and two cowpunchers in range clothes glanced at Heath absently. If their appearance was an indication, the cowboys had ridden all night and were sipping whiskey before turning in at the hotel.

They looked as tired as Heath had last evening. He nodded

sympathetically. They returned his wordless greeting then turned back to their drinks.

"Buenos días," the barkeep greeted him.

Heath said good morning by ordering a cup of coffee. Moving to a table in the rear of the room, he sat with his back to the wall.

As the barkeep placed a cup of the steaming brew on Heath's table, the double doors of the establishment squeaked on their hinges, drawing both men's attention.

"Madre Dios." The words rushed from the barkeep's chest as Reno's abductors stepped into view, guns drawn, trained on the room at large.

Heath remained seated and silent; every nerve ending in his body tingled with anticipation. The cowboys halted their glasses in midair.

The Mexican desperado—obviously the leader—sauntered in first, wearing jingle-bob spurs. Their large silver rowels glistened when a ray of sunlight struck them through an open window. A bandoleer of cartridges crossed his broad chest, lending him an ominous air. A brilliantly colored sombrero was suspended behind his neck by a piece of stiff rawhide. The brace of Walker Colts, usually tied low on his stringy thighs, were aimed at the cowboys and barkeep in turn.

His partners trailed him, also wielding their weapons indiscriminately. The big man who actually pulled the trigger on Marshal Reno stepped into the room immediately behind the Mexican. With the sun at his back, his face was cast in shadows. His ruddy complexion, unkempt hair, waist-length beard, and massive shoulders and arms gave him the appearance of an orangutan. The wampus he wore made him look larger than life.

All Heath could think was that this was the bastard who had actually pulled the trigger, over and over, snuffing out the life of a man who was little more than a boy, a man who was about as threatening as a puff ball tossed in the wind.

The cowboy entered next and stepped up beside the Mexican. He had a thin, mousy face with cruel eyes. His chaparreras made the bottom half of his body look much too large for the top. He was small, wiry, and unlike his friends, harmless-looking. But Heath knew that looks could be deceiving.

The brigands backed up to the bar. They ordered whiskey and again stared at each man in the room in turn. Finally, they turned their attention toward Heath.

"What are your names?" Heath asked almost conversationally, catching them off guard by speaking first.

The leader raised a questioning brow. He shrugged as if he didn't see any harm in revealing their names since he didn't plan to allow anyone in the saloon to leave alive. "I'm Chi Chi. This is Jones"—he pointed to the ape—"and that's Montana." He indicated the cowboy. "Who wants to know?"

As Chi Chi spoke, Jones lumbered over to the window, away from the Mexican. Montana stationed himself halfway between the two.

Heath acknowledged silently that the gang had played this scene before. Three to one, that was probably their usual odds. They were too gutless to face a man one on one.

The barkeep and the cowpunchers sympathized with Heath, but none was interested in dying that day. Men in the untamed West learned early on that minding their own business was vital to staying alive. Smiling at Heath apologetically, the cautious threesome made for the door.

Heath understood. Too bad he had never learned the lesson of minding his own business, he thought drolly. He inclined his head in tribute to their pragmatic spirit.

He turned his full attention on the brigands then and watched with shock as they wheeled away from him and coldly shot the three men in the back. He was horrified, enraged. Still, he resisted the urge to do the same to them. Heath Turner was not a back shooter.

Chi Chi turned a hideous smile on Heath. "Now we will have to kill you." He feigned reluctance. "Such a pity to kill a man of honor," he sneered, making reference to the fact that Heath didn't shoot them in the back when he had the chance.

"It doesn't take a great deal of honor to refrain from shooting a man in the back. No matter how lowlife the man is. It's the code of the West. Or hadn't you heard? Only a coward takes advantage of a man with his back turned. But then, I had you three figured for cowards all along."

Anger sculpted the faces of all three men. "Your first mistake, *mi amigo*"—the Mexican bit off harshly—"was that you didn't leave the marshal where you found him."

Heath stared coldly at him, unblinking. "Killing him was your first mistake." He paused for emphasis. "And your last."

Montana raised his weapon. It shook slightly in his black-gloved hand. His voice was defensive when he spoke. "We found him on the trail and did our Christian duty by burying him."

Heath's gaze hardened as he released a snort of disbelief.

"You think he's lying?" Jones interjected.

Heath stared at him silently. He rose to his full height with the grace and menace of a great predatory beast. Tucking the bottom of his vest behind his back, he revealed his Colt—shiny, deadly, loose in his holster. "I don't *think* he's lying, you filthy piece of garbage. I *know* he is. I saw you murder Reno in cold blood." He hitched his head toward Chi Chi and Montana. "While your gutless partners stood by and watched." His voice was steady, his eyes burning like hot pokers, damning. He flicked the Mexican a glance. "You're not only cowards and murderers, you're liars as well. The list of your attributes grows long. Unfortunately, my patience for this conversation has grown short."

Montana's mendacious grin faded, and something fierce flickered in his eyes.

Heath recognized the sign. He kicked the table over, dove behind it, and drew his gun in a blur.

As if on cue, the brigands aimed and fired as one.

Thirty-two

Heath came up on one knee and fired a slug straight through Montana's eye, killing him instantly. The outlaw whirled around upon impact and jerked backward. His head crashed through the window, shards of glass cutting to pieces what was left of his face.

An instant later Heath turned his attention to the Mexican. They both fired, Chi Chi a second behind Heath. A burning-hot slug slammed into the brigand's shoulder; his own shot buried itself in the wall behind Heath's head.

Chi Chi fell heavily behind the bar, joining Jones. Heath slipped one leg around his side of the bar and shook the table he had overturned. Instantly, the men blew the table into fragments.

Heath leapt up and threw himself atop the counter, scattering empty glasses as he went. The Mexican, staring at the table, was surprised to hear Heath sliding along the bar. Finding the strength to swing his guns upward for a kill, he felt more hot lead enter his body. Then blackness descended upon him a breath after Heath shot him clean through the heart.

Jones slipped around the edge of the bar.

Heath slid down and stood before the Mexican as thick, hot blood spewed from the dead man's body. Bullets began flying like fireflies on a summer night. Heath hit the floor and returned Jones's fire, wounding him in the side.

Clumsily trying to reload an old Allen pepperbox .45, the

big man grunted when a second bullet plunged into his thigh. He fell heavily and overturned a brass spittoon. Moaning, he pretended to surrender.

Cautiously, Heath approached him. Despite his grave injuries, the big man surged to his feet and caught Heath around the chest in a bear hug.

Heath felt the breath whoosh from his lungs, but he remained standing. His arms penned at his sides, he planted his feet solidly and pushed backward, slamming his attacker against the wall.

Jones grunted but hung on tenaciously, tightening the pressure around Heath's chest. Again and again Heath slammed him against the wall, but the big man held tight.

A sharp piece of wood protruded from the center post of the room. Heath swung around and crashed his assailant backward, trying to impale him on the knifelike splinter. Jones's thick wampus took the brunt of the impact. But the splinter jabbed into his back like a straight pin piercing a tough side of beef. He twisted away from the post and the pain, but continued to hold tightly to his prey.

Heath whirled his assailant back around and pressed him against the splinter twice more. Finally, the big man loosened his grip.

Heath turned on him and landed several cutting jabs to Jones's face. The man, virtually superhuman in strength, was slow and torpid, almost lethargic in his movements. Heath moved smoothly, expertly, gracefully, almost as if he were dancing, ducking, parrying, jabbing, while the ape followed him sluggishly.

Just when Heath thought his opponent was finished, Jones threw a fierce uppercut, catching him by surprise. The force behind the punch sent Heath stumbling backward. He tripped over Montana's lifeless body. The floor rose up to meet the back of his head.

Jones advanced on him, enraged by staggering pain and the flow of hot blood. He kicked Heath repeatedly, sinking the tips of his pointed boots in Heath's belly. He showered Heath with a barrage of oaths and threats. Pink-tinged spittle flew from his mouth with every vile invective.

Heath rolled away from his insane nemesis and crawled behind the bar, hoping for a moment's respite. Before he could get to his feet, however, the monster bounded over the counter and fell on top of him. Heath felt as if he were trapped beneath a ton of bricks. Claustrophobia and the will to survive provided him unnatural strength as he fought to dislodge Jones.

There was little room for maneuvering behind the tightly enclosed bar. Jones wrapped his forearm around Heath's neck and held him in a death hold. Heath was unable to breathe, unable to break free. Frantically grasping about, his fingers encircled the neck of a broken bottle. He brought it over his head like a club. Jones shrieked and released him when the sharp point sank into the tender flesh beneath his left eye.

Heath couldn't imagine how the man could take much more. He was bleeding like a butchered hog. Still in all, Jones remained conscious.

Hearing a lionlike roar, Heath turned his head slightly and saw Jones on his knees. His face was swollen beyond recognition.

"I'll kill you, you rotten bastard, if it's the last thing I ever do!" he thundered, trying to rise.

"Damn!" Heath cursed, casting about for his gun. It was across the room, lying on the floor beside the empty coffee cup the barkeep had brought him before all the bloodletting had begun.

Out of the corner of his eye he saw an ax leaning against the cold black stove. Jones let forth a hair-raising yell and rushed Heath. Grabbing the ax with both hands, feet planted squarely, Heath lifted it high over his head. He threw it with his remaining strength. Following through, his body hit the floor, belly down.

The ax sank into Jones's chest with a sickening thud. The metal sunk into his breastbone up to the handle, knocking him on his back with a thunderous crash. The floor vibrated beneath Heath's cheek where he lay.

Onlookers entered from the hotel and general store. They stared wide-eyed at the carnage, six men, all dead.

Heath raised his head and saw Delgado in the crowd. When the stunned proprietor entered, Heath angled into a sitting position. He pointed to Chi Chi's, Montana's, and Jones's corpses. "Put these bodies on their horses. They killed Marshal Reno. I'll take them back to Adobe Wells. Soon as I get cleaned up." He added silently, if I can walk.

"Sí, Señor," the owner replied, inordinately relieved that his buildings would soon be corpse-free.

Later that day Heath entered Adobe Wells, leading four horses, each carrying a corpse.

News of the macabre parade down Main Street spread like wildfire. Merchants and shoppers exited the stores. Merrymakers filed out of the saloons, all eager to view the morbid scene.

Heath held the reins to Ted Reno's mount. Ted's red hair bounced from beneath the blanket with each step his horse made. The Mexican's reins were tied to the mare's saddle horn. Jones and his horse followed in like manner. Montana and his mount brought up the rear.

Pilar, Sandy, and Preacher Black watched in varying degrees of surprise from their vantage point on the boardinghouse portal. Pilar and Preacher Black took down the street after Heath. Not entirely recovered, Sandy followed at a slower pace.

Pilar caught up to Reno's horse as Heath halted the animal in front of the jail. Throwing the blanket back, she lay her cheek against the marshal's back and wept bitterly. She had thought of Ted as a son, and now he was gone.

Preacher Black stepped to Pilar's side and placed a comforting arm around her shoulders. "There, there, child," he soothed dramatically. "All of us are bereaved over the loss of our dear brother. Prayer and fasting will ease the emptiness."

With quiet authority and a doubtful glare Sandy pushed the good reverend aside and took Pilar in his arms. She fell against him and cried as if her heart were broken.

Heath sympathized with Pilar. But he was more concerned with Donn Pedro. He had promised the boy that he would bring the marshal back safely. He had failed. Casting about, he searched the crowd for the child. He came up empty.

Judge Jack, Rachel, and Henry Sims stepped out onto the

boardwalk as Heath continued his visual search for Pedro. They joined the others in front of the jail.

There was genuine surprise in Judge Jack's voice. "What's the meaning of this, Mr. Diamond?"

"Brought you some bodies" was all Heath said.

"Who killed them?" the Judge asked.

"All except the marshal, I did," Heath answered.

Jack examined each corpse. When he came to Jones, he pushed the man's shoulders up and jerked a nod toward the mass of dried blood surrounding his breastbone. "What did that?"

"An ax."

The judge shrugged, unconcerned. When he reached Ted, his expression changed. Heath tried to read it. The emotion reflected on his face was irritation. This surprised Heath.

"Who killed Reno?" Judge Jack asked.

"They did."

The judge ordered that the dead brigands and Marshal Reno be taken over to Radner Banks, the undertaker. His command was carried out with incredible speed. Preacher Black stepped forward, raised his hands in the air, and addressed the crowd as it began to disperse.

"We have seen the effects of evil and violence today, my friends." He regarded Heath with a condemning glare. "All of us"—he paused—"should confess our sins and be mindful of the brevity of life."

Again his gaze settled on Heath. Tension was thick. Black flashed Heath a look he couldn't define. Finally, he concluded, "There will be a special service for Marshal Reno tomorrow at the church. All of you are invited to come and pay your last respects to this poor boy."

Heath looked away from Reverend Black's pious face. That's when he saw Rachel staring at him. The shadow of a self-satisfied smile flickered across her face.

"Oh, shit," he muttered. She had recognized him. He waited for her to blow his cover. She didn't. Instead, she smiled at him. Her smile was a invitation that no red-blooded male could fail to interpret. Well, he would have to play along for the time being. He returned her lustful smile with a slight bow, mutely promising a future liaison.

Turning in the saddle, he caught Stevie's eye. She had joined her father and Pilar without Heath's notice. The look of stark betrayal on her face told him that she had seen Rachel's smile and his uncharacteristic response.

His gut ached with a sense of guilt that he didn't really deserve. He hadn't done anything improper with Rachel—the very notion sickened him. He didn't intend to do anything improper with Rachel. But he doubted Stevie would be easily convinced of that.

He wanted to reassure her, to tell her how much he missed her, to hold her and to love her, to never, ever let her go. He realized, however, that was not advisable, not just now. There would be time for them later. He had to find Pedro first, tell him of Reno's death. He also had to deal with Rachel . . . somehow.

That done, he would go to Stevie. She would just have to trust him until then. He smiled at her, trying to communicate how he felt about her.

She did not return his smile.

Heath watched her retreat with a foreboding sense of loss. When she disappeared into the boardinghouse behind Sandy, Pilar, and Preacher Black, he tore his eyes away from them and slid from the saddle.

His boots were unnaturally loud on the boardwalk. He pushed the door to the jail open and stepped inside. Dust motes danced in a stream of light pouring from the hole in the wall that served as a window. It didn't take but a moment for him to determine that Donn Pedro was not inside.

Dreading the coming confrontation, Heath made his way to the stage office where Pedro worked part-time. The shingle outside the plain wood building read: SOUTHWEST STAGELINES/ASSAYERS/TELEGRAPH OFFICE/UNITED STATES POST OFFICE. Drawing a deep cleansing breath, Heath entered the multipurpose establishment.

He would rather square off against Billy the Kid with nothing but a slingshot in his hand than tell this child his hero was lying on a slab at the undertaker's. But there was no help for it. He had made Donn Pedro a promise. And now he had to face him.

Heath's gaze took in the room in one quick glance. Pedro was nowhere to be seen. His shoulders relaxed slightly.

"Could I help you?"

Heath had not even noticed the slight, bespectacled man standing behind the counter. He was as colorless and nondescript as the office in which he worked. "I'm looking for Donn Pedro. I'm afraid I have some bad news for him. Regarding Marshal Reno."

"You must be Mr. Diamond."

Heath nodded.

The man stepped from behind the counter and offered Heath his hand. "I'm Josiah Shelter. Donn Pedro works for me."

Heath shook Josiah's hand. He was impressed with the strength of his grip despite his small stature. The general always told Heath and his brothers to shake a man's hand like they meant it. And that they should never trust a man with a weak-wristed handshake.

If that bit of advice was valid, Josiah Shelter was trustworthy. The sympathy in his eyes and affection in his tone when he spoke Donn Pedro's name reassured Heath as well. The boy would need someone to replace Reno in his life. Heath imagined that Josiah Shelter would be that man.

"Can you tell me where to find the boy?"

"He's probably over at Miss Manchez's boardinghouse. He and Miss Stevie's little boy are thick as thieves." He smiled, looking like a doting grandfather.

Heath nodded his thanks. He had not planned to go to the boardinghouse so soon, wanting to get his duty to Pedro and his dealings with Rachel out of the way before he talked with Stevie. But now that he would see her sooner rather than later—maybe she would help him break the terrible news to Pedro—he could hardly wait.

"If you will excuse me." Heath headed for the door.

"Mr. Diamond."

He halted with his hand on the doorknob. "Yes?"

"I almost forgot. You have a telegram from Santa Fe."

Heath returned to the counter. As he supposed, the message was from Jay.

It read:

LUCKY. STOP. I WAS TOO LATE. STOP. ON MY WAY BACK TO A.W. STOP. WATCH MY GIRL CLOSELY. DON'T WANT HER TO GET AWAY AGAIN. STOP. AND WATCH YOUR BACK. STOP. SIGNED, THE MINER.

Heath crumpled the missive in his fist. Another man was dead; Jay had been too late to save Layard Shackelford's life. The innocent man was a geologist, for heaven's sake. A peaceful, law-abiding citizen, a well-known scientist. And the judge's men had killed him as if he were a wild dog on the run.

"Mr. Diamond, are you all right?"

Heath nodded, but accepted the chair Josiah offered him nonetheless. How many more innocent bystanders would die before Judge Jack was stopped?

He wanted to rush into the courthouse and arrest Jack, Rachel, and anyone remotely involved with them. Actually he wanted to kill them, but that would make him no better than they. He could charge them with the death of the two miners found in the cave on Sandy's property, Marshal Reno, Layard Shackelford, the three innocent men at Delgado's, and for shooting Sandy and him as well, not to mention grand larceny, conspiracy, and Lord knows what else.

But the time wasn't right. He didn't have the evidence to put them away for life. He would continue his surveillance and in the meantime try to keep as many people alive as he could.

He left the office in a semidaze brought on by blinding rage. In his present frame of mind it was just as well that he didn't notice Judge Jack, Rachel, and Sims standing on the boardwalk outside the courthouse.

"I should have killed that bastard the first time I saw him," Sims growled.

Judge Jack shot him a derisive look. "As I recall, you weren't too anxious to draw on him face-to-face." He paused for effect.

"And it wouldn't be wise to shoot him in the back in broad daylight. Or any other time without my permission."

"Can't we arrest him? He killed those men," Sims said.

"If he hadn't taken care of the fools who shot Reno, I would've killed them myself. I wonder who hired them? Men don't usually kill a marshal without good reason," he finished as if he were speaking to himself.

"Unless there's money to be made," Rachel pointed out.

The judge waved Sims away and turned to Rachel. He looked like a man with a bone to pick. "Or a secret to hide."

She looked affronted at his accusing tone, splaying her hand over her chest. "Are you implying that I had something to do with Reno's death?"

"Did you?"

She looked him full in the face. "Of course not. You told me that you would handle the marshal. I took you at your word." When he was still clearly skeptical, she stepped closer to him and placed a beseeching hand on his forearm. "Honest, Jack. I had nothing to do with this. I wouldn't cross you. I swear."

He shook off her arm. "See that you don't!" He left her staring after him.

The muscle in Rachel's jaw twitched. She was furious at Jack's high-handed manner, yet frightened nonetheless. He was a man who didn't issue idle threats. But she was a woman who didn't cotton to submission. And she certainly didn't enjoy intimidation.

Squaring her shoulders, she lifted a stubborn jaw. What she needed was insurance, perhaps an alternate plan—more to the point—a strong ally, a predator. Her gaze settled on Pilar Manchez's boardinghouse, her mind on one of the men therein.

The smile that lit her face did not reach her cold eyes.

Thirty-three

Stevie sat in Pilar's antique rocking chair, her new daughter slumbering against her breast. She was humming a soft lullaby that brought poignant memories of her mother to mind.

Standing in the doorway to her bedchamber, mesmerized by the tender scene, Heath was certain he had never seen such a heartwarming vision. The picture she presented was sufficient to drive all thoughts of Donn Pedro from his mind.

"Are you just gonna stand there? Or did you have something to say to me?"

Stevie's soft voice surprised Heath. He pushed away from the door jamb and closed the distance between them. "You're not sore at me?" He was still uneasy about the look that she had witnessed between him and Rachel. Kneeling at her side, he covered her hand as it stroked the baby's head. Unconsciously, he dipped his head and placed a kiss on the infant's tiny cheek.

"No, I'm not sore. I'm furious." She was unable to meet his eyes. Emotion lodged in the back of her throat at his tender treatment of the baby.

"You don't sound furious."

"Oh, but I am. I truly am." She paused as if she didn't care to finish her thought. "But I'm also glad that you're safe." She cleared her throat twice. "That your dead body wasn't brought back thrown over a saddle." Her voice quivered on this last.

The thought of Heath, so big, so strong, so full of life, lying cold and still on Warrior's back, was almost her undoing.

He noticed that her eyes were unnaturally bright. "Honey—" he began.

"Shhh. Let me finish." She met his gaze then, bewildered and exasperated. "Why do you have to go chasin' after every man on the dodge?"

"Because it's my job."

"Can't you quit? It's so dangerous . . ." she trailed off.

His heart swelled. She was concerned for his safety. Her next words stopped him cold.

Not wanting Heath to know just how frightened she was for him, she maintained control of her emotions and runaway tongue. "Just go home, Heath Turner." She stiffened in the chair, pulling away from his touch. "Back to New York, where you belong. Before you get killed."

Heath was stunned. She was telling him to leave. And it was obvious that she didn't plan to go with him. Had he noticed the pain darkening her ebony eyes, he would have taken heart. But he didn't. All he heard was the woman he loved telling him good-bye, with little or no emotion in her voice.

If he lost Stevie, he would lose the children as well, children he barely knew but thought of as his own. Somehow he had begun to think of Stevie, Winter, and the baby as his family. And a man without his family was truly lost.

He allowed himself to wallow in self-pity a grand total of ten seconds. Then, with the Turner stubborn streak a mile wide and spreading, he tamped down his hurt and swallowed his pride. Women like Stevie came along once in a lifetime. He would fight for her. She was worth it. "Trying to get rid of me?" he taunted thickly.

Stevie's eyes snapped with fire. "I'm trying to keep you alive."

He rose to his full height. "Thanks for your concern. But I can take care of myself." He walked to the open window and looked out at the red hills in the distance. Even this stark, open wilderness had begun to feel familiar, downright homey. "I've managed on my own so far." Why was he saying one thing and thinking another? He lifted his arm to rest against the wall. He winced at soreness caused by fighting a man the size of a mountain.

"What's wrong? Are you hurt? Has your wound opened up?" Stevie asked all at once. Quickly, she surged to her feet, placed the sleeping child in a cradle beside her bed, and joined Heath at the window. She unbuttoned his shirt. "Let me see."

Unbuttoning his shirt was such a natural, unconscious act for her that he was momentarily nonplussed. Her inconsistent messages, verbal and otherwise, had him slightly off balance, as usual. "As much as I'd like you to take my clothes off, sugar, I hardly think this is the time or the place. And I haven't opened my wound. I'm a little sore, that's all. One of the desperadoes at Delgado's fell on me." This last was spoken with a self-deprecating chuckle. "The lumbering ox."

"Is anything broken?"

"Just bruised, I imagine." He shrugged like the big, tough cowpoke he was and almost groaned at the pain.

She saw the agony clearly etched on his face. Her hands fisted on the fabric covering his chest. "This proves my point."

Sensing he was losing control of the conversation, he said, "Honey, it's nothing. Just let it drop." Heath knew he'd said the wrong thing before she started raving. But it was too late to recall his blasé reassurance. So he endured her tirade with grace.

"How can you say it's nothing?" Her voice rose in volume and intensity with every word. "You could have a—a broken rib. You could puncture your lung, you idiot! You could die. Now do you see what I mean?" She gestured wildly, speaking to the ceiling. "You're just not cut out for life in the West," she accused him.

If Heath had not been so insulted by Stevie's conclusion, he would have been amused. "I beg to disagree." He gripped the sill at his back so he wouldn't be tempted to shake some sense into her.

"You can beg all you want, but I'm right and you know it."

Heath shook his head. Had he ever won an argument with Stevie? He wasn't certain how the talk had turned to his ineptitude in the West, but he was as offended as Hades at the grossly unflattering implication. Much to his dismay, Stevie was about to make it worse.

"Who do you think you are? The Rough Riders, Texas Rangers, and Fifth Cavalry all rolled into one?"

Typical of Stevie when she was on the scrap, she didn't wait for him to answer. Not that anyone could find an intelligent response to such an outrageous charge anyway.

"Well, you're not, Heath Turner. You're a fancy easterner who got bored with civilization." She tossed her hands in the air and threw her head back on her shoulders. "So bored, you needed to flex your great big muscles"—she actually flexed her slender arm, brandishing the slight hump she called a muscle in his face. Heath almost took a nip out of it—"and tame the Wild West in one fell swoop. You came out here, the law in your holster, a badge on your chest, champing at the bit to take on all the bad men west of the Pecos."

She regarded him with such anger that he feared she might shoot him for no other offense than crossing the Mississippi. But he saw much more in her eyes. Anger, yes, but also fear and something that looked a heck of a lot like love. He grew unnaturally calm. This infuriated her even more.

"They'll kill you, you stupid clod, just see if they don't!" She bit on her lower lip and hugged herself to keep from flying into a million pieces. "Well, say something!" she ordered him.

He stood silently, staring down at her; an exceptional specimen of a man, perfectly proportioned, deep-chested, lean-loined, splendidly muscled, arrow-straight. She was shrieking at him like a banshee and terrifying the baby to death—the baby, who was now wide awake and crying, thanks to her hysterical outburst.

He walked over to the cradle and took the infant in his arms gently. She quieted at his touch. Carrying the babe, he returned to Stevie, moving as graceful as a panther, his muscles rippling smoothly under his skin.

His larger-than-life presence called her unflattering assessment into question. Embarrassed at her irrational outburst, she surrendered and stepped into his open embrace.

He looked down into her upturned face. His eyes told her that she had exhibited no more sense than a snake has fleas, but he loved her anyway. And he understood the cause of her attack—whether she did or not. She was frightened for him. And dammit all, she loved him!

He wanted to make her admit both her fear and her love. But he decided to wait until she did so voluntarily. "I'm just a lawman doing what I'm paid for."

She tightened her grip on him. Oh, you're much more than that, she thought. But she said nothing.

Heath smiled and hugged her tightly. He knew her mind as well as his own. "I love you too," he whispered in her ear. Then straightening, he asked, "Have you named her?" He clearly referred to the child in his arms.

"Mmm-hmm. I call her Summer."

He smiled. "Well, she *will be* Winter's sister."

"I thought it seemed logical."

His smile faded. "Hon, have you seen Pedro?"

"You've come to tell him about Reno?"

He nodded.

It was obvious to Stevie that Heath dreaded the duty he was about to perform. She slipped her arms around his waist again, a wordless offer of support. "He's at the creek with Winter. Blue took 'em on a picnic. They shouldn't be gone long. You can wait here."

Heath flicked a glance at Stevie's bed. Sensual heat crackled in the dry desert air like lightning in a spring thunderstorm. "I'd better go. If Pedro comes into town, he might hear that the marshal's been killed. It's my place to tell him."

"You're a good man, Heath Turner."

Heath waved away her praise. "I promised to bring Reno back alive. I failed. The boy's my responsibility now. I owe him."

His eyes told her that his responsibilities didn't end with the orphaned Mexican child. She knew that he considered her, Summer, and Winter his responsibility as well. She wasn't quite certain why he felt that way. But she was awfully glad that he did. This last thought caused her a moment of uneasiness. Shrugging it off, she reached for the baby. "I'll take her to Pilar. I'm goin' with you."

"Let's take the baby with us. I'll carry her."

"Okay. I'll get her shawl." There was definitely a smile in her voice.

Heath heard it and didn't mind at all.

Heath and Stevie stood side by side, watching Winter and Pedro chase butterflies beside the creek. Blue was nowhere in sight, but Stevie knew she was nearby, undoubtedly sitting in the shade, watching the boys with an eagle eye, hiding from any townsfolk who might pass by. The saloon girl turned nanny absolutely doted on the boys. She would give her life for them, of that Stevie was certain.

The tranquil display lulled Heath into a momentary sense of well-being. Childish laughter bubbled musically in the summer air, as musically as the brook beside which the boys romped. Even though their world was teeming with violence, the orphaned children had found a haven of peace.

It was a sight that would melt the heart of the most resolute cynic. But cynicism was not a characteristic shared by Stevie and Heath. They carried within their souls the seeds of hope—hope for the future, hope for a family of their own, hope for a world that would be safe for them all. Unknowingly, the frolicking children watered those seeds and brought new hope to life.

"I wish they could always be this happy." Stevie's heartfelt sigh broke the idyllic spell the children had woven.

"I do too, sugar." He placed Summer into her arms. "Let's get this over with." On leaden feet he moved into the clearing.

"Señor." Pedro was excited to see the tall man who had promised to bring Ted Reno home. He could hardly contain himself as he and Winter ran to meet Heath. "The marshal, he is at the jail?"

Heath knelt between the boys. Stevie stood silently at his side, Summer in her arms, a hand resting lightly on Winter's head.

Winter was young, but he sensed that something was terribly wrong. His mother was wearing her sad face. He moved even closer to her reassuring warmth.

Pedro knew something was wrong as well. The man called

Lucky Diamond was stiff, though his face was kind. "Where is Reno?" Pedro asked again.

Heath tried to hide the tremor in his hand as he raised it and grasped Pedro's shoulder. "I'm sorry, son. He's gone."

Pedro drew in his breath sharply. Tears pooled in his black eyes. He wanted to cry, but he couldn't. He was a man now. Marshal Reno had told him so many times. And men did not cry. He would shame the marshal's memory if he did. "He's not gone, *señor.* He's dead," the brave boy corrected Heath. His voice was flat, lifeless.

Had Pedro sobbed hysterically, it would not have been as pitiful as the boy's valiant attempt to fight back tears. The child widened his eyes, bit his lower lip, and took deep, cleansing breaths. He was clearly devastated. Yet not one tear touched his cheek.

Not until Heath pulled his frail, trembling body into his embrace. "Go ahead son," he whispered against Pedro's sun-warmed hair. He cupped the child's head with one broad hand and covered his narrow back with the other. "It's all right."

Pedro couldn't hold back any longer. He pressed his face against Heath's shoulder and sobbed.

Winter whimpered, frightened at his friend's emotional outburst. Stevie bent to her knees and Winter hid his face against her chest. Her thin printed shirt absorbed the Indian child's tears.

Blue watched the heartrending sight from beneath a shade tree. Unable to bear it, she turned her back on the scene and leaned her cheek against the scratchy bark. Self-consciously, she dried her eyes with the end of her apron.

Why did good people have to be hurt? she wondered. First Jeff, then Marshal Reno, and now Donn Pedro.

Judge Jack was the answer.

Heath, Stevie, and the children headed back to town in silence.

Winter and Donn Pedro walked hand in hand no more than two paces in front of the adults. They didn't want to get too far away. It was as if the boys thought Heath and Stevie might disappear if they were out of sight. And it frightened them.

Blue was sitting on the portal with Nellie when the weary band approached the boardinghouse. "There are oatmeal cookies and a fresh pitcher of lemonade waiting on the kitchen table for you two," Blue said to Winter and Donn Pedro.

In tandem, the children looked at Heath first, then at Stevie. "It's all right," she told them. "I'll be right out here."

"Señor Diamond, will you stay?" Pedro asked.

"I'm sorry, son. I've got to go. But I'll be at the Brass Tumbler Hotel if you need me."

Donn Pedro nodded tersely. He stiffened his spine and mounted the steps, entering the house without so much as a backward glance.

Heath couldn't escape the feeling that he had let the child down again. But leaving the boardinghouse was for Pedro's own good; he didn't want the child close to him when violence erupted. Too many innocent lives had been forfeited already.

Stevie placed a hand on his forearm. "He'll be all right."

Heath nodded, grateful that Nellie and Blue had left him and Stevie alone. He touched Stevie's cheek gently, marveling at its softness even as he marveled at her inner strength.

"Why are you leaving us?" she couldn't help but ask.

"This thing is coming to a head. I don't want you or the children near me when it does. I'll keep an eye on you." He smiled apologetically. "From a distance."

Stevie studied the ground beneath her feet and shifted Summer up onto her shoulder. "That woman . . . the redhead, is she staying at the hotel?"

Heath's smile spread. Stevie's jealousy was very apparent, and it pleased him. "Probably."

His answer was honest, if not the one Stevie wanted to hear. "Is she a friend of yours?"

"An acquaintance," he hedged. Heath had kept his own council for so long, it didn't occur to him to explain his unpleasant past with Rachel. Actually, he wasn't thinking too clearly. The late afternoon sun playing on Stevie's platinum tresses had gained his rapt attention.

Blinded by jealousy and disconcerted by Heath's vague answer, Stevie assumed the worst, that Rachel and Heath were former lovers, that they would become lovers again, and that he didn't consider it any of her business. Had she been thinking with her head instead of her heart, she would have realized that he had never done anything to deserve this lack of faith. But her heart overruled her head. Her voice was cool when she said, "I'll pack your things and have Donn Pedro bring them over."

"Whoa." Heath grabbed her arms when she turned her back on him. She wouldn't face him. "This isn't necessary, sugar." He meant her jealousy and withdrawal.

She thought he referred to Donn Pedro. "It'll give him something to do. Activity is the best antidote for grief."

"Honey—" Heath began.

Summer chose that moment to awaken and announce to the world that she was wet, hungry, and in need of immediate attention. "Good-bye, Heath," Stevie whispered.

Before he could protest her abrupt departure, she was gone. He considered going after her, explaining about Rachel, but decided against it. Somewhere along the way she was going to have to start trusting him.

Now was as good a time as any.

Thirty-four

That evening Heath ate supper at the Brass Tumbler Restaurant, located just off the lobby of his hotel. The dining room was plush according to western standards, all polished wood and crystal chandeliers. He couldn't help but admire the elegance and beauty of his surroundings.

But it was nothing compared to his stomping ground in New York. Delmonico's, now, that was a restaurant! Allowing his gaze to wander the room, he realized how much he missed home. He dismissed the thought as soon as it came. He didn't need to be distracted. As he told Stevie, this job was rapidly coming to an end. He needed to concentrate, without allowing anything to pass his notice.

He scanned the restaurant with a professional eye. It catered mostly to businessmen and cattle barons, the wealthy men who were pouring into town in droves, eager to invest in Judge Jack's diamond mine.

In the past five minutes he had seen emissaries from such warring notables as Major L. G. Murphy, Alexander McSween, J.H. Tunstall—and the king of the Pecos himself—John Chisum.

He had overheard that these four men—the stuff of which legend was made—would arrive in town on the ninth along with the governor. He sincerely hoped not.

The vast expanse of New Mexico Territory was virtually a war zone, had been since shortly after the Civil War, when men like Chisum gathered up great herds of wild Texas cattle and headed south, carving their own private kingdoms out of the wilderness.

Chisum, McSween, and Tunstall had been fighting Murphy in the newspapers to this point, but the factions of these powerful cattle barons weren't content to sling words. They would sooner put a bullet between one another's eyes than eat when they were hungry.

One story in particular, involving a hot-headed kid, popped into Heath's mind. The boy was young, thin, fresh-faced, and innocent-looking. His name was William Bonney. Among other things, he was called Billy the Kid. In the beginning the Kid worked for Tunstall—a friend of Chisum's.

Billy quarreled with Chisum and subsequently declared a vendetta against the cattle king. He dropped into a cow camp in the Panhandle one night. It was a typical scene. Young boys—as wild and unruly as the herd they drove—were cooking supper, just going about their evening chores.

One poor soul was standing apart from the others, hobbling his horse. Billy approached the lad and asked him his name to which he replied, "Bennett Howell."

Congenially, Billy asked Bennett whom he rode for.

Howell responded just as friendly, "Chisum."

Billy smiled and said, "So. Then, here's yore pay." He pulled his six-shooter, shot the cowboy in the head, and rode away, still smiling. The whole incident happened in less than two minutes, but when it was over, a boy lay dead, for no other reason than he was working for the wrong man.

It was enough to give Heath a heart seizure. Men like William Bonney were drawn to riches such as the judge promised like flies to an outhouse. Enforcers, Heath called them, men who looked out for their boss's interest, and their own. Having these men in such vast numbers and in such proximity was a nightmare.

Heath shifted uncomfortably in his comfortable chair. He hated to admit that the foul taste in his mouth was caused by stark fear. Not for himself, but for the innocent residents of Adobe Wells, especially Stevie and the children.

He had made some dangerous enemies. From here on in it would only get worse. Just being a lawman set him against the likes of Billy the Kid and Peg-Leg Smith. He was fair game. As he told Stevie, it would be better for her and the children to be as far away as possible.

But he didn't have to like it. Depressed and lonely, he had a negligible appetite. He ordered his customary dinner of beefsteak, potatoes, pie, and coffee, with little enthusiasm. While waiting for his food, he sipped a glass of red wine, pondering the events of the past two days.

He had assumed the three desperadoes he brought in were Judge Jack's men, that Jack had paid them to kill Marshal Reno. Now he thought differently. Jack had been surprised to see Reno dead.

But if the killers didn't work for Judge Jack, whom did they work for? Hired guns like Chi Chi, Montana, and Jones rarely shot anyone unless there was money to be made, or unless their prey posed a threat. And Ted Reno hadn't posed a threat to anybody. The boy was innocence incarnate.

Heath's musings were interrupted by Rachel's entrance into the restaurant. The hair on the nape of his neck rose in unison with his well-honed defenses.

As with any opponent, he studied her from head to toe. She was dressed in a closely fitted gown of crimson taffeta. Flaming red hair was piled high atop her head, decorated with magenta ostrich plumes and a spray of dog roses. Nestled between blue-veined breasts, she wore an exquisite diamond-and-ruby pendant. Matching earrings dangled from thick earlobes. The gown and jewelry were obscenely extravagant. The woman wearing them looked cheap.

Not aware of Heath's unflattering assessment, Rachel glided toward him. She knew her entrance had created a stir. The room had quieted as soon as she stepped to the door. Perhaps the diners wanted to get a good look at Judge Jack's lady friend. She preferred to think that they were stunned by her uncommon beauty. She was wrong on both counts. They were struck blind by her bright clothing and dyed hair.

Heath knew that she always dressed like this to call attention to herself. Why she would want to do that, he couldn't fathom. She wasn't beautiful in his eyes. She was repulsive. But he didn't allow this to show as he rose perfunctorily and bowed over her hand. She smiled down at his glistening black hair like a predator . . . or a gambler who held all the cards.

Heath straightened and met her eyes. Obviously she had not revealed his true identity to Judge Jack. He couldn't help but wonder how and when she would.

He needed to buy time until Jay could arrive from Santa Fe. In the next few minutes he had to convince Rachel that he was no longer a lawman, that he was as low, conniving, greedy, and evil as she. It would be the performance of his life. He prayed to the theatrical muses for artistic aid even as he pulled out a chair and imagined Rachel Jackson with a noose around her neck.

"Thank you, Mr. Diamond." She tossed her head seductively.

The waiter approached as soon as Rachel was seated. "Will the lady be joining you for dinner?" He faltered slightly over the word "lady."

"The lady will." Rachel snatched the menu from the waiter's white-gloved hand and glowered at him. Crisply, she ordered white wine and fish baked with lime.

The man retrieved the menu and beat a hasty retreat.

Heath leaned back in his chair, appearing absolutely relaxed. Nothing could be further from the truth.

Rachel was the first to break the heavy silence. "What brings you this far west, Mr. Diamond?" she taunted, licking her rose-tinted lips. "Last I heard, you and your partner were combing the Nations for a dangerous escapee." She rested her elbow on the table and leaned forward, giving him an unobscured view of her bosom.

For a moment Heath stared, not because he cared to see her breasts, but because he was sure she was going to fall out of the dress and he had never seen a woman's breasts land in a butterdish.

Mentally shaking himself, he listened to her factious prattle. She was laughing at him, there was no doubt about it. The bitch had killed two men, broken out of prison, eluded capture, and now sat, laughing at him. It was almost more than he could take.

But he maintained control and chuckled. "My partner is still there." Slowly, he removed Jay's pocket watch from inside his coat and placed it on the table in front of Rachel.

She looked as if she'd been hit in the face with a shovel. "I never thought he'd part with that."

Being from Athens, Georgia, and knowing the Hamptons since she was a child, Rachel was well aware of how much they treasured their watches. Jay almost died during the war when it fell out of his pocket during his escape from Danville Prison. The fool had actually risked capture going back for it.

"He didn't part with it." Heath laughed harshly. "Voluntarily."

She raised her carefully tweezed eyebrows, inviting him to continue. "Why, Mr. Diamond, you sound positively evil."

"Even lawmen can change." He lowered his voice. "Miss Jackson."

She glanced around them frantically, hoping that no one heard him. "Don't call me that. My name is Mrs. Smyth. And what do you mean, even lawmen can change?"

"I mean, Mrs. Smyth"—he hesitated for emphasis—"that I tired of staying on the right side of the law." He pulled a cheroot from his inside coat pocket and lifted it to her for permission to smoke. When she nodded like Queen Victoria acknowledging a commoner, he lit the cigar and took a deep puff, squinting his eyes against the blue plume of smoke he exhaled.

"Barnes Elder's gang robbed the River City Mining Company. Got away with the payroll to the tune of fifty thousand dollars. Jay and I gave chase. Found 'em holed up in a line shack. I killed Barnes. Jay got Barnes's little brother, Emmett. The others, Shotgun Taylor and Bullwhip Parnell, surrendered. We arrested them and confiscated the money. I didn't mind turning the prisoners in, but decided to keep the payroll. I offered to split it with Jay. Fifty-fifty. But you know the Hamptons. Honorable till the end. Well, Jay met his end." He tried to look menacing, cold, and self-satisfied all at the same time. Most of all, he hoped he looked convincing, not an easy task considering that he was inventing the criminals and the crime even as he spoke. "Facing the wrong end of my six-shooter."

Rachel sat and studied Heath intently. He made a conscious effort to relax, to breathe normally. When her rouged lips spread into a depraved smile, his answering grin was genuine. She'd bought it!

"What did you do with the money?"

Heath threw his head back and laughed. He hoped it sounded more sincere to her than it did to him. "I spent it. Fifty thousand doesn't go very far, especially when one wants to keep the ladies happy."

Rachel began a slow perusal of Heath, starting at his head and sliding over every inch of him. "Why don't you come up to my room after supper. We can share a bottle of champagne. And whatever else comes up."

Heath fought the urge to gag even as he cursed beneath his breath. How was he going to get out of this without insulting the slut?

"That sounds mighty good, Rachel." He tried to look disappointed. "But I have to see a man about a horse." Oh, Lord, he groaned silently. How stupid could he get? A woman was offering him her body and he turned her down in favor of a horse. That really oughta do her self-image good.

Rachel's face flamed. Men never turned her down! Well, not too often. "Maybe later," she said without moving her lips.

"Absolutely," Heath enthused.

For the rest of the meal they spoke infrequently and merely about inconsequential matters. Heath finished eating before Rachel did. "I'm sorry, but I really must go." He rose, bowed gallantly—or mockingly, depending upon one's point of view—and left the spurned woman glaring at his back as he made his way from the restaurant.

He went up to his room and stood in the dark, looking out the window. In a few minutes he saw Rachel walk down the street, heading in the direction of the courthouse. He quickly retraced his steps to the ground floor, slipped out a side exit, and made his way to the courthouse too. From the shadows cast by the hulking building, he observed her enter.

He strolled back down the boardwalk toward the Silver Dollar Saloon. The walkways and streets were full of men going from one saloon to another. Some of them were drunk or well on the way; others were sober, just arriving in town for a night of merrymaking.

When he entered the Silver Dollar, he took a table next to the front window and ordered a drink. He had a clear view of the courthouse. Lights coming from two upper-level windows showed him that Judge Jack was in his living quarters.

The silhouette on the drawn shade was of a man and a woman. They talked momentarily, then came together in a heated embrace. Shortly thereafter, the lights went out.

Heath returned to the hotel somewhat relieved. He had confirmed what he had suspected all along. Rachel and Judge Jack were lovers. He seriously doubted they were talking about him at the moment. For reasons known only to Rachel, she was keeping Heath's identity a secret.

Entering the hotel lobby, he bounded up the stairs and turned left toward his room. From the corner of his eye he caught sight of a small form standing in the shadows at the end of the hall.

He dropped down into a crouch and pulled his weapon. Leveling the gun, he ordered, "Drop your gun and step out into the light."

A very familiar wolf ambled forward. From somewhere behind the animal, an amused female voice said, "Don't shoot, he's not armed."

Thirty-five

Stevie strolled up beside Sweetums and scratched his head. "Neither am I." She drew closer to Heath, who had not yet leathered his gun. Looking pointedly at the weapon, she quipped, "You wouldn't shoot an unarmed lady, would you?"

"Stevie, what are you doing here?" That didn't come out exactly as he meant it. He sounded angry. Rather, he was frightened that he might have shot her and her four-legged pal.

"Well, excuse me for living. I'll just be going."

That was when he noticed the pain in her eyes. Something was wrong with Stevie's world, something new, and she had come to him for help. "You're not going anywhere. At least, not yet."

He held on to her hand while he unlocked the door. He pulled her into his room and into his arms. He kissed her sweetly, hoping to distract her from her troubles. Passion took over, and soon they were both breathless. He gave her a lopsided grin. "To what do I owe the honor of this visit . . . after I'm trying my damnedest to stay away from you?"

Stevie's eyes burned with rage. "Our cook, Pepper, told Pa that Judge Jack's burned the ranch house down."

Her obvious anguish aroused deep emotions in Heath. He took her hands in his own. "I'm sorry, hon. When all this is over, it can be rebuilt." He bent his head until they were eye to eye. "I'll even help."

Smiling gratefully, she regained control of her rage and nodded. "Thanks. I'll remember that." The silence that ensued was uncomfortable. Unable to help herself, Stevie glanced at the bed that seemed to dominate the room. "I want to show you something."

He arched his brows twice. "And I'd love to see it."

"Ha-ha." She withdrew a sheet of paper from her shirt pocket. "I gave the rock we found in the cave to Pepper. He took it over to Fort Union and got back this report. What do you make of it?"

He accepted the paper and dropped onto the bed. Standing close in front of him, she watched as he scanned the report.

"The stone is a partially cut diamond. Obviously imported from somewhere else. Africa maybe."

Stevie nodded agreement. "So how can we prove it's a hoax and get our land back?"

"I don't know yet. Let me think about it." He seemed to forget her presence. "What we need is tangible proof." He sat a moment more, thinking. "Ted Reno's funeral is tomorrow, isn't it?"

"Yes."

"The judge will attend the services for appearance's sake. I'll search his quarters while he's gone. If there's proof to be had, that's where it'll be."

"No."

"No?" He smiled incredulously.

"No. It's too dangerous."

"I appreciate your concern, sugar. But I assure you, I can take care of myself."

"You might end up like Ted."

"No, honey. I won't end up like Ted."

"You might," she whispered.

He didn't see the point in arguing further, so he changed the subject. "How's Pedro holding up?"

Stevie was well aware that Heath had just made a switch. She let him get by with it since she wasn't getting anywhere with the obstinate male anyway. "He's trying very hard to be brave. Blue's a big help. They've become very close. She won't let the boy out of her sight. If we could find her a husband, they could be a regular family."

Heath chuckled softly. "That might take some doing in this town, given her former profession." He pulled Stevie between his thighs. "You know you shouldn't be here, don't you, sugar?"

She shook her head. "I know. And I'll go. In a minute. There's something else I want to say."

"What is it, sweetheart?"

She was careful to avoid his eyes. "I had no right being jealous of that woman." Clearly, she referred to Rachel. "I mean, you and I both know that I can't be a part of your future."

"We do?"

"Yes. So I don't have the right to begrudge you other women. Everyone needs companionship. I understand that. And I want you to be happy . . . and find somebody to love." Her voice broke. She regained control almost immediately. "That's all I wanted to say."

It was obvious she didn't mean a word of it. At least not the part about wanting him to find somebody to love. Heath tried unsuccessfully to hide his grin. God, how he loved this woman! It was a good thing her head was still bowed, otherwise she would see the skeptical, indulgent, knowing gleam in his eye and crown him for sure. "You're a very understanding young lady. I appreciate that you feel that way."

Stevie's head jerked up. "You do?"

Heath kept his face carefully blank. He hadn't ridden the Mississippi posing as a gambler for two years without developing an effective poker face, after all. "Certainly. Most women wouldn't be so selfless. I really admire that in you."

Admiration be damned. Stevie would rather hear a confession of love. Even if she couldn't allow herself to return the sentiment. "It's nice . . . being admired."

"I thought you would appreciate the sentiment."

Her expression could have curdled milk in a cow's teat. But she cleared her throat and tried to appear nonchalant. "So you'll be seeing her again?"

"What do you think?" The little imp; he had told her he loved her, three simple words that didn't come easy for him. Did she think he was so fickle that he would profess his love, then throw her over for the likes of Rachel Jackson? He couldn't help but be insulted. It would serve her right if he let her stew in her own juices.

"Do you think she's pretty?" Stevie asked.

"What do you think?" he asked again, maddeningly.

She clenched her jaw and tapped her foot rapidly on the hardwood floor. To say that he was irritating her would be an understatement. "Well, truthfully, I think she's a little old for you." Actually she's too old for anybody, she muttered beneath her breath. Aloud, she observed, "And she's kind of . . . pudgy. And loose." She gestured appropriately. "Everything on her just kind of hangs there."

She tossed her head defensively. "I know I'm no fashion plate, but really, Heath, the clothes the woman wears . . ." She trailed off when Heath's laughter drowned out her *glowing* assessment of Rachel. Jerking her hands free of his and balling her fists, she planted them firmly on her hips. "Heath Turner, don't you dare laugh at me."

Heath fell backward onto the bed and hooted. Stevie dove on top of him, scrambled up his prone form, sat on his stomach, and hit him squarely in the chest with the flat of her hand. "Stop laughing at me, you pea-brain!" She thumped him again for good measure. "I don't know what you have to be so happy about. If my girlfriend was a fat old toad, I wouldn't be laughing. I'd be downright depressed."

The thought of Rachel Jackson as his girlfriend was so ludicrous that Heath laughed even harder. Stevie grasped him by the shoulders, tightened her thighs around his waist, and shook him vigorously. "Hush, you imbecile. You're going to alert everyone in the hotel. And if I'm caught in your room, Pa will sprain his brain trying to decide which of us to shoot first."

He would have continued laughing had she not slid her derriere south just a tad so that her most intimate place was in warm contact with his most intimate place. His laughter turned into a groan, her righteous indignation into a gasp of desire, a situation her pa would not like one bit.

He wrapped his arms around her waist, and flipping over, pulled her under him. Their bodies fit together like a hand in a well-worn glove. It seemed the most natural thing in the world to be lying in bed, kissing, cuddling, rubbing against each other.

Stevie reached up and touched his cheek gently. "We can't do this, Heath," she whispered.

He closed his eyes and pressed his forehead against her own. "I understand."

"Do you? Do you really understand why I can be no more to you than a friend?"

"I know your reasons. But I hope you don't mind if I disagree with them."

She decided to try again. "You can't tie yourself to an Indian for the rest of your life. I won't let you."

Heath's heart plummeted. He would tell her how he felt . . . just one more time. There was a fire in his sapphire gaze that she hadn't seen before. When he spoke, their was a depth of sincerity that she had not heard. "Stephanie Kay Johns, I love you dearly. I want you to be my wife, the mother of my children. I want to be a father to Winter and Summer. I can't even imagine a future without the three of you. My life would be hell on earth. Please, sweetheart, you can't sentence me to that."

Tears brightened her eyes, but when she clenched her jaw, Heath knew he had lost. Sighing heavily, he released his hold on her.

"I have to go," she said quietly, slipping from the bed. "The children need me."

"I'll walk you back to Pilar's."

Stevie nodded. They made the trip home in heavy silence. When they mounted the steps, Stevie moved aside for Heath to open the door.

He placed his hand on the knob, then turned to her. "Sugar," he whispered down to her.

She angled her head back. "Hmm?"

"Do you love me?"

The question was so simple, so vulnerable, so poignantly pitiful, she couldn't deny him. "Yes. I love you."

He released the knob and swept her against him. Their hearts beat as one. They stood in the darkness, entwined, like two halves of a whole, for how long neither of them knew.

"But I can't love you," she said, then pulled away and slipped into the house.

He stared at the closed door. The haunting call of a coyote

broke the silence. The wild, predatory animal sounded as lonely and empty as Heath felt. For the first time since he fell in love with Stevie, he considered the possibility that he would face the future alone. His gut ached at the prospect.

Fortunately, the general had not taught his sons to retreat. Heath simply didn't know how. Wheeling about, he strode back to his hotel. No matter what it took, he was going to marry Stevie.

And if anyone opposed their union, that was just too damn bad.

Thirty-six

The next day at precisely one o'clock, the townsfolk of Adobe Wells turned out for Marshal Reno's funeral. Even some of the miners, freighters, and businessmen who had never met the boy attended.

Preacher Black's eyes sparkled with delight when he looked out over the congregation. The church was filled to the rafters. It was hot, stuffy, and those parishioners who weren't acquainted with soap and water made the atmosphere unpleasant for those who were.

The regulars knew their reverend loved the sound of his own voice. And today he had a captive audience. It was going to be a long afternoon, they feared.

Since Reno had no living relatives, Pilar, Sandy, Pedro, Stevie, Sully, and the Pridgens were the closest thing to a family he had. After everyone was seated, they made their way to the front of the church.

Blue had cared for Reno as well, but she remained at the boardinghouse, minding Winter and Summer. Try as she might, Stevie was unable to coax Blue out into society. Once a whore, always a whore; that was Blue's perception.

Stevie told her that she was stupid to allow the townspeople's misguided prejudice to control her life. But when Blue pointed out that Stevie was giving up the man she loved because of society's prejudices, Stevie walked out on her. She couldn't argue with the truth.

Pilar entered the pew first, dressed in a black bombazine gown, her tear-ravaged face covered by a heavy crepe veil. Sandy, looking ill at ease in his Sunday suit, was by her side, offering emotional support even as she gave him the physical support he needed due to his slow-healing gun wounds. Nellie and Pridgen entered next. Sully slipped in behind them.

Hand in hand, Stevie and Donn Pedro brought up the rear. Stevie wore her black leather trousers, fringed vest, and print blouse. It was the same outfit that she'd had on the first time she saw Heath. The matrons of the church gasped at the sight of a woman dressed like a man—in church—but for once Stevie was oblivious of their disapproval. Her thoughts and concerns were centered on the grieving boy at her side.

Donn Pedro was dressed like a little man, wearing the dark frock coat, trousers, and white shirt Stevie had purchased for him early that morning at Bret Dowling's general store. New leather shoes encased his feet for the first time in his life. They pinched his toes, but he was unmindful of the physical pain. He would much rather be barefooted and dressed in rags, sitting beside the stream, a fishing pole in his hand, his hero, Ted Reno, big and strong, telling him tall tales about the ones that got away.

As he took his place by Stevie's side, he fought desperately to maintain control of his emotions. He would not cry as he had when *Señor* Diamond held him in his arms. He would not shame Marshal Reno's memory. His piercing black eyes never left the plain pine box at the end of the aisle. He wanted to scream. It was unfair. Reno couldn't be dead. He needed him! Didn't God know that? Tears threatened and the child trembled with the effort to keep them at bay. He bit down on his tongue until blood pooled in his mouth.

Stevie sensed his inner turmoil, and her heart ached for him. She remembered sitting at her own mother's funeral, trembling from head to toe, tears cascading down her cheeks. She had felt cold and hot at the same time. Her teeth chattered from the chill while perspiration pooled under her arms.

The only thing that saved her that awful day was the warm, secure presence of her father and Jeff. Her pa had placed his arm around her shoulders and Jeff had held her hand. Somehow, the two of them had kept her from flying apart.

When she slipped an arm around Pedro's frail shoulders, he leaned against her gratefully. She tucked his head beneath her chin and glanced toward the minister, signaling him to begin.

Heath stood watching them from the rear of the church. He smiled sadly at Stevie's gesture of support. He had never loved her more than he did at that moment, when she offered comfort to this child who was heartbroken.

But he wasn't surprised at her act. Stevie was the kindest, gentlest, most giving woman he had ever known. His heart was full of her. How could she possibly think marrying him would hurt him? Didn't she know that losing her would destroy him?

Preacher Black's thickly pious voice drew Heath's attention. The reverend droned on, extolling the virtues of their dear, departed brother.

Heath stared at the pine box, then sighed heavily. It always angered him when a lawman was killed, any lawman. But Reno had been little more than a kid. "Damn," he cursed silently. Placing his hat firmly on his head and nodding respectfully to the lifeless marshal resting in the coffin, he slipped from the room and hurried to the courthouse.

Quickly, he searched Judge Jack's living quarters. He swept the obsessively neat room and found nothing out of the ordinary. Even when he gave close attention to the judge's desk, he came up empty.

Undaunted, he moved to the dark mahogany chifforobe. The open doors revealed a number of expensive suits, robes, hats, and boots. The lingering smell of expensive cigars rose as he patted the frock coat and waistcoat pockets, one by one, absently noting the quality of the fabric.

"Well, well, well, what have we here?" He pulled a sheet of thick paper from the breast pocket of a charcoal-gray frock coat. It was a letter from Johannesburg, South Africa, addressed to the judge.

It read:

Judge Elias Colt Jack
Adobe Wells
New Mexico Territory
United States of America

Dear Colt:

It was good to hear from you after so many years. I hope this letter finds you well.

As requested, I am forwarding two hundred uncut industrial-grade diamonds. The funds sent with your request were adequate. I assure you that these diamonds have the same appearance as those found anywhere in the world, including your own country.

Best wishes in your new business venture.

Sincerely,
George W. Stiphelmont, Esquire

A grin the size of his aunt Louise's fanny spread across Heath's face. He tucked the folded letter into his vest pocket and quit the room. Finally, he had tangible evidence of the judge's scheme. With the letter as leverage, he hoped to make him confess his other unlawful deeds. If the judge wouldn't cooperate, they would arrest him for conspiracy to defraud. The man's accomplices would run up one another's backs to sing like canaries, just to save their own sorry hides.

Or his name wasn't Harrington Heath Turner.

* * *

When the heavy blanket of night cloaked Adobe Wells, Heath left the hotel, making his way to Pilar's rooming house. He slipped around the house and approached from the rear.

Silently, he peered through the kitchen window. It was a cozy scene reminiscent of the times he, his brothers, and sisters would gather around the kitchen table and coax Hattie, their housekeeper, who was more like a mother than a servant to them, out of ginger cake and spiced cider.

He smiled at the nostalgic tug. As he had so often in the past several weeks, he yearned for home.

He shook his head to clear his thoughts and allowed his gaze to wander the kitchen idly. From the tranquil picture within Pilar's house, one would hardly know that brigands and murderers roamed the streets of Adobe Wells. Thank God these people who had come to mean a great deal to him were safe inside.

Motherly in the extreme, Pilar was alternately washing dishes and making sure that everyone was properly fed. Sandy, Pridgen, Nellie, Stevie, and Preacher Black were sitting at the table in the middle of the room, assuring Pilar that they'd had quite enough.

Blue sat beside Summer on a pallet near the cold fireplace. The baby was lying on her back. Pedro and Winter were dangling brightly colored wooden objects just out of her reach. She was too tiny to pay them any mind, but Winter didn't seem to notice. Despite what he'd been told about babies not being able to see clearly at Summer's age, he was enthralled with his little sister, sure she could see him if no one else. Donn Pedro had a vacant look in his eyes, more hopeless and grief-stricken than any child should look.

Heath automatically returned his gaze to Stevie, drinking in the sight of her. She was dressed in her usual boyish attire, but her hair was loose about her shoulders. It brought to mind ebbing and flowing waves of corn silk. The lantern light played across it, giving it the appearance of a cloud upon which fireflies flirted and skittered about.

Stevie felt his gaze. She looked toward the window and saw his strong profile limned by the full moon at his back. Drawn to him by a silken cord, she slipped through the back door and joined him on the porch.

He smiled broadly, starlight dancing in his clear blue eyes. "Hello," he mouthed, leading her into a corner away from the window.

"Hello," she returned with a thready whisper.

They stood still and drank in the sight of each other.

Stevie shook herself free of his seductive spell. She cocked her head and tried for a wry smile. "For a man who wants to stay away from me, I sure have seen a lot of you lately."

Not as much as I'd like you to see, he thought, then raised one thick brow, feigning arrogance. "Well, missy, I had some interesting news to tell you . . . about Judge Jack. But I think I'll just keep it to myself now." He bowed chivalrously. "A good evening to you, madam." He made to leave.

"Get back here." She grabbed his hand, whirling him toward her. "Talk."

He looked meaningfully toward the kitchen door. "Not here."

Nodding, she took his hand and led him to the front porch. Golden illumination bathed them from the porch light like rivers of cream flowing over fresh fruit. His next words were spontaneous, spoken without conscious thought. "I've never known a woman as beautiful as you."

She actually blushed. Thoughts of Judge Jack were forgotten in the heat of Heath's perusal. "I swear to heavens, Heath Turner. Charm just oozes out the pores of your skin." She was truly perplexed. "Do you practice that, or does it come naturally?"

He shook his head, setting his shiny hair in motion. Stevie was so taken with the way the ebony strands brushed his strong bronze neck that she barely heard his reply. "It's a Turner family secret. How we charm our women." His voice dropped to a husky caress. "I could tell you, but then I'd have to shoot you. You're far too precious to shoot." He slid a finger over her dusky cheek.

Such a simple act, but so devastating to Stevie's senses. She scoffed to hide her reaction to his touch. "I think we've gone far afield from the purpose of your visit."

He smiled down at her a moment more, then shook his head, dashing away the heady effect of moonlight and amour. He handed her the missive from South Africa without speaking.

She read the letter and smiled. Throwing her arms around his neck, she kissed him soundly. "That's it," she enthused. "You've got your evidence." Her brow furrowed before her heels hit the floor. "Why haven't you arrested him yet?"

He pointed to the scrap of paper she clutched in her hand. "This implicates the judge. But he's not in it alone. I'll let him play the scheme out. It won't be long now. It's almost over."

"But what if he gets away?"

"Trust me, sweetheart. Judge Elias Colt Jack is not going to leave town without his ill-gotten gains. He's far too greedy." He gave her a barely perceptible wink. "But just in case I'm wrong, I'll be watching him like a hawk."

She squared her shoulders and nodded tersely. "I'll help."

Fear slammed into his gut. "You will not."

Her mouth fell open at his harsh tone. Eyes wide, she seamed her lips together and affected the picture of innocence. "You're right, of course. It would be entirely too dangerous." She smiled sweetly. "I'll just leave that nasty business to you." She actually had the audacity to shrug her shoulders and wrinkle her nose.

He chuckled, tapping her nose with the tip of his finger. "Good try, sugar. But I'm not buying it. You've never given up that easily in your life."

"I'm sure I don't know what you mean." She stepped closer to him and laid a slender hand on his shirtsleeve. "Of course, you can believe what you want. I would never try to dissuade you. But I told you I'll stay away from the judge, and I shall."

The little minx, he knew what she was about. She stepped closer, so close their thighs were flush. It was hard to think with her pressing against him, and she knew it. Ah, well, he would enjoy her nearness and think later. "Good." He circled her waist loosely and pulled her with him into the shadows. "But remember, while I'm watching the judge, I'll be watching you too."

She tossed her head flirtatiously. "Watch all you like, Heath Turner." She leaned toward him and flicked his bottom lip with her tongue. His sharp intake of breath pleased her inordinately. She enjoyed the sensual power she had over him almost as much as the sensual power he had over her. "I'll have to remember to draw my shades at night." She stood on tiptoe, planted a chaste kiss on his cheek, and slipped out of his embrace.

Heath let her go. "Don't go to any trouble on my account," he called after her.

The laughter that floated back to him fluttered across his heart.

Thirty-seven

She stepped into the foyer and her smile froze. She halted abruptly, as if she ran headlong into a brick wall.

"It won't be long now. It's almost over," Heath had said.

Her heart plummeted. He would be leaving soon. Dizzy, she clutched the entrance hall table. How would she ever let him go? Now that the time was drawing near, she couldn't imagine life without him.

"Stevie, I've put the baby down," Pilar told her, but Stevie was unaware.

She moved in a daze. Through the foyer, up the stairway, into her bedchamber, she floated like a wraith. Once inside, she didn't bother to light the lamp.

An hour later Blue found her, sitting in the dark, in a rocker beside Summer's cradle, staring blankly at the infant, holding a strange leather pouch in her lap. The baby slept soundly. Stevie cried softly.

Blue crossed over to Stevie on silent feet. She lit the lamp at her side. "What's wrong, honey?"

Quickly, Stevie hid the evidence of her weakness, brushing her cheeks with the backs of her hands. "He'll be leaving soon." The words were torn from the depths of her heart.

There was no doubt in Blue's mind to whom she referred. She pulled the velvet-tufted vanity chair close beside Stevie and took a seat. "And you're just gonna let him go? Just like that."

"What else can I do?"

"You can fight for him."

Stevie turned wild eyes on her new friend. She stretched her hands out at her sides. "Fight who? His family? Society? The whole world?"

"No, sweetie." Blue's demeanor was calm in light of Stevie's outburst. "Yourself. Your own insecurity." She paused and lowered her voice for emphasis. "And maybe even your own prejudice."

Stevie was stunned. "What's that supposed to mean?"

Blue patted Stevie's shoulder gently. "You're a smart girl. You figure it out."

Stevie was deep in thought when Blue left the room. Was it possible that she was a bigot? she wondered. Was she reluctant to pledge her life to Heath not because she was Indian, but because he was white? Did she harbor so much hatred and bitterness against the whites who had caused her mother's death that she was unable to give herself freely to one of their race? The possibility tortured her.

Later, when Blue returned to check on Summer, Stevie was pacing the room frantically. "I've got to find out," Stevie said.

"Find out what?"

Stevie halted in front of the window, absently pulling the shade. She turned and narrowed her eyes on Blue. "Don't play innocent with me."

Blue feigned horror. "Me, innocent? Have you forgotten where we met?"

Stevie giggled. It was good that Blue could tease about her past. The children had healed her emotions more quickly than anything else could have. Pushing the thought aside, Stevie returned to the matter at hand. "I've got to find out if I'm a . . . a bigot."

"How do you propose to do that?"

Stevie's brow furrowed. "I don't know. Any suggestions?"

"Well, there's the barn dance. You could attend just like the other single ladies in town. Then, when Heath asks you to dance, accept. Act natural. And let nature take its course."

Stevie considered the suggestion and decided it was perfect. She ran across the room, tossed the package she had been holding on to the bed, and threw her arms around Blue's shoulders. "You're brilliant."

Blue was taken aback by Stevie's display of affection. She returned Stevie's hug, reluctant to let her go. "I've been called many things, honey, but brilliant wasn't one of them."

Stevie chuckled. The thought of dancing in Heath's arms lightened her heart. She threw her head back on her shoulders, whirled about the room in a waltz. Moonlight illumined her willowy frame. Catching sight of herself in the mirror, she stopped mid-twirl. She moved to within inches of the swivel mirror. "A boy." She met Blue's gaze in the mirror, clearly horror-stricken. "I look like a boy."

For the first time since her mother's death, she wanted to look feminine, desirable—God help her—like the finely dressed ladies in town who crossed to the other side of the street to avoid her and whispered behind their lace-gloved hands when she passed.

"That can be remedied," Blue soothed.

Doubt dulled Stevie's eyes. Dreams of dancing with Heath, of having everyone recognize that she was his woman, died in the reality of the tomboy who stared back at her from the looking glass. How could anyone transform that creature into a femme fatale? Unable to bear the sight of herself, she lowered her eyes. Her gaze fell to the package on the bed. She moved to the bed and picked up the pouch. Untying the rawhide strings, she dumped the contents onto the eyelet comforter.

Both women gasped at the beautiful garments. Stevie ran her hand beneath Gentle Fawn's wedding dress and lifted it to her cheek. Like melted butter, the platinum doeskin slid down her fingers. The only hint of color atop the bed was provided by the blue-white glass beads decorating the neckline, fringed sleeves, hemline, moccasins, and headband.

"Try it on," Blue suggested.

Stevie shed her leather attire. Silently, reverently, she slipped into the exquisite clothes. The doeskin sheathed her naked body like a lover's caress. The floor-length dress fit her like a second skin. She slipped the moccasins on her slender feet, slid the finely beaded headband over her head. It was impossible to determine where her waist-length hair left off and the velvety buckskin began, so identical was their color.

"Oh, Stevie. look at you."

This time, when Stevie studied her reflection in the mirror, she didn't see a tomboy. She saw a slender yet voluptuous woman, a fair-haired Indian princess.

"You have to wear that to the dance."

A short, sharp burst of laughter escaped Stevie's lips. She covered her mouth with her hand, happiness and mischief darkening her eyes. "Can you see old Mr. Mac when I walk in dressed like this? He'll curse a blue streak, rail against the godless savages, and warn everybody to mind their scalps."

She pretended to hitch nonexistent trousers beneath her armpits. With her tongue in her cheek, mascarading as a plug of tobacco, she effected a western twang. "Galldern heatherns." She limped around the room, aping Mr. Mac. "Steal the silver dollars off'n a dead man's eyes. Oughta hemp the lot of 'em. Galldern murderin' redskins."

Blue laughed heartily. "Every man there will give his right arm for a dance with you. Including old Mr. Mac."

"That I've gotta see."

Blue came up behind her and placed her hands on Stevie's shoulders. Gently, she turned her until she was once again facing the mirror. Her voice was a heartfelt whisper when she declared, "But Heath won't let another man near you." Blue left then, taking Summer down to the kitchen for her bottle.

Stevie's moccasined feet moved of their own volition. The beaded fringe made a musical swish with each step. Slowly, she removed Gentle Fawn's precious clothes, laid them aside as if they were a prize of great price, and dressed in a voluminous white nightgown.

She moved to the window. With a gentle tug she raised the window shade halfway. Heath was on her mind and in her heart. "Good night, sweetheart" was her heartfelt whisper.

He couldn't hear her hushed good-night. But leaning a broad shoulder against the cottonwood beneath her window, he released a deep sigh into the darkness.

Thirty-eight

The morning of August 9 found Adobe Wells bursting with barely contained excitement.

Layard Shackelford was coming to town to inspect the mine, and tomorrow the governor would arrive in time for a barn dance to be held at sundown. Men, women, and children packed the sleepy little town.

Judge Jack watched the activities from his courthouse chamber overlooking Main Street. Buckboards, wagons, carriages, and saddle horses jammed the streets and lined the tie rails. Literally hundreds of miners, cowpunchers, reporters, businessmen, and gunslicks joined the townsfolk. Rowdy ruffians and stalwart citizens alike came from throughout the territory, anticipating the public announcement of the biggest diamond strike in the country.

The judge had informed the miners that their jobs depended upon Shackelford's report. That they would be rich, if the mine were judged genuine. And they believed him.

Everything was going as planned, down to the venders and hawkers who filled the plaza, selling coffee, food, and souvenirs. The saloons had opened early to accommodate the merrymakers. The gambling tables and brothels were doing a booming business. And though it was still early in the day, he could see that many of the revelers were already drunk or well on the way.

All according to plan . . .

Out of the judge's line of vision, Heath stood beside the hitching rail in front of the Silver Dollar Saloon. When the judge took a step back and dropped heavy curtains in place, Heath turned his attention to several old codgers sitting on a bench fronting the saloon. They had formed a musical group—fiddles, juice harps, and base jugs. In anticipation of the following days barn dance, they were practicing exuberantly. The musicians weren't exactly the New York Philharmonic, but the carefree music was mildly distracting.

Ted Reno had been replaced by Jerky McGahee—a gutless wonder who made even Reno seem brave—as marshal of Adobe Wells by Judge Jack. There was no one to stop the sporadic scuffles that kept breaking out along the streets and boardwalks. Nobody seemed to worry about the violence, Heath noted, tensing as the fistfights grew in intensity and frequency. And he couldn't intervene without revealing that he was a marshal. All he could do was watch with growing disgust.

Just after sunrise he had attended a duel between two attorneys. The best he could figure, they'd fought over a woman. What else? Seems the lady in question couldn't decide which man she wanted, said she would take the one left alive.

Scores of onlookers had lounged on the grassy knoll down by the creek to witness the grisly proceedings. When the smoke cleared, one man was shot clean through the heart, the other gravely wounded. Again, nobody cared. The crowd just melted away, in search of other mischief. Heath could hardly understand such apathy, but was powerless to do anything about it.

"Stop, thief!" A call rang out, drawing Heath's attention. In front of Bret Dowling's general store, a man was making for his horse, carrying a bag close to his chest. Heath rounded the railing, but before he could cross the street, Bret's son, William, appeared on the portal, leveled his shotgun, and virtually blew the bandit's head off.

"Damn!" Heath exclaimed, halting in mid-stride.

Two passersby carried the bloody corpse to Radner Banks, who stood in the doorway of his mortuary, rubbing his hands together. Two men dead since sunrise, with the prospects of more before nightfall. After that, it was anybody's game. The greedy mortician looked as happy as a dead pig in the sunshine.

Revolted, Heath turned away, centering his attention on the boardinghouse. He caught sight of Stevie and relaxed instinctively. She, Pilar, Pridgen, and Sandy were watching the bedlam from the hotel portal.

Pridgen's face was beet red and darkening. The hustling, bustling town bore little resemblance to the lifelong home the old man knew and loved, and the change was taking its toll on him.

"Mr. Pridgen, wouldn't you like to sit down?"

He ignored Stevie's offer. "The whole town's gone crazy. Shackelford'll probably be trampled by a mob of drunks when he gets off the stage. If he knows what's good for him, he'll just keep right on going." He slammed his fist against the wall.

"Might as well," Sandy interjected. "There's nothing but bats, rocks, and dirt in that mine!" No one responded, as he had declared this sentiment nearly every waking hour since Judge Jack had run him off his ranch.

"Now, Sandy," Pilar soothed. "Don't get so excited. You know what Sully said. You have to take it easy. You mustn't tax yourself."

Sandy calmed instantly at his ladylove's touch. He glanced at Stevie, who was watching Heath on the boardwalk watching her. Satisfied that he wouldn't be overheard, Sandy leaned close to Pilar's ear. "I don't recall you warning me about overdoing last night."

Pilar's face flushed. Her lecture to Sandy on the propriety of teasing one's lover within earshot of one's daughter was forestalled when the stage rumbled into town.

The jehu cracked the whip sharply to attract the crowd's attention. The mob roared when they saw the shiny Abbot-Downing Concord coach and stampeded the express station. Drunks and malcontents cursed and elbowed their way to the front. Several more fights broke out.

Henry Sims and Carlos Garcia exited the courthouse and began clearing a path to the stage for Judge Jack and Rachel. They elbowed what they considered the scum and riffraff out of their boss's way.

Judge Jack wore his best black suit and Stetson. With his black eye patch and blond hair, he cut a dashing figure.

Rachel was dressed in a lemon and ebony striped silk gown,

complimented with jet pendant, bracelet, and ring. Her brilliantly colored red hair bulged from beneath a black leghorn straw bonnet that was tied at her throat with lemon grosgrain ribbons.

Against the backdrop of the tattered townsfolk and ragged miners, the exquisitely attired couple looked like they'd dressed to effect a striking picture. They had.

His best politician's smile in place, Judge Jack grasped the newcomer's hand when he stepped off the stage and gave it a hearty shake. "Mr. Shackelford, welcome to Adobe Wells."

Shackelford returned Jack's greetings, then cut his eyes to Rachel.

"I'll introduce Mrs. Smyth when we get out of this crowd," the judge said close to Shackelford's ear. "But I must make a brief announcement before we retire to my quarters."

Shackelford smiled, nodding his agreement.

The judge climbed to the box of the stage, held up both black-gloved hands, and waited for the unruly mob to quiet. His knee-length frock coat flared open, revealing a double brace of pearl-handled pistols tied low on his thighs. The picture Judge Elias Colt Jack presented was one of unequaled power and uncompromising menace. It was a daunting combination.

His sophisticated northern tone coupled with the fire burning in his pale eye completed the image. "Friends and fair citizens of Adobe Wells, we all know the importance of Mr. Shackelford's visit here today. He will inspect the mine and—I fully expect—will confirm its genuineness."

At that, the crowd went wild. The alcohol-crazed men fired their weapons in celebration, setting horses to bucking, asses to braying, babies to crying, and mamas to shushing. Fights broke out like bursts of popcorn, but were quickly broken up by Sims, Garcia, and their underlings.

When a semblance of order was restored, the judge continued. "I'm taking Mr. Shackelford inside to allow him a few minutes to recover from his arduous trip from Santa Fe. At one o'clock we'll all go to the cave, permit Mr. Shackelford to examine the mine, and then hear his report."

Judge Jack, Rachel, and Shackelford started for the courthouse. Again, the judge's ruffians cleared a path through the riotous crowd. When the door to the courthouse was firmly closed behind him, the judge turned to the man masquerading as Layard Shackelford. "James, permit me to introduce my partner, Rachel Smyth. Rachel, this is James Filmore."

Filmore bowed politely over Rachel's outstretched hand. He was a tall, handsome man who looked to be in his early forties. A large dimple in his chin caught Rachel's eye. She smiled seductively at him.

When he saw Rachel's smile, Filmore winked at her. "Judge, I didn't know you had such a lovely associate. It must be a pleasure doing business with one as beautiful as she. I confess that I envy you."

Before Jack could speak, Rachel seized the conversation. "Why, thank you, Mr. Filmore. We're fortunate to have an actor of your stature." She batted her long eyelashes at the performer.

It occurred to Jack that Filmore wasn't the only actor in the room. In fact, he would pit Rachel's theatrical abilities against Filmore's any day. He shrugged mentally, more interested in his scheme than Rachel and Filmore's dubious fascination with each other.

"We'll leave for the mine in an hour. I'll blindfold you in front of the crowd. I trust you have your speech prepared?"

"Yes, sir, indeed." Filmore tapped his breast pocket. "When I get through with my announcement, the whole world will believe that your mine is unimpeachably genuine."

"That's what I'm paying you for," Judge Jack finished dryly.

An hour later the three conspirators descended the stairs to a covered carriage awaiting them in front of the courthouse. The judge's carriage led a long procession of conveyances—wagons, buckboards, horses, even dog drawn carts—to the mine.

Many of the liquor-crazed miners stumbled behind on foot, arm in arm, singing as they went. They were oblivious of the relentless summer sun beating down upon their bare heads, oblivious of the fool's errand they were on.

Riding Warrior, Heath was situated about halfway in the procession. From his high perch, he was provided an encompassing view. The festive air reminded him of a Fourth of July picnic in New York. The vendors and hawkers, who accompanied the crowd, continued to peddle their food and merchandise, lending a holiday spirit to the throng.

Most of the rough westerners clutched a bottle of rotgut in their hands. He suspected correctly that some had spent their last pennies for the mind-altering libations. And those who had money remaining in their pockets were easy targets for the thieves and tricksters working their way through the throng.

Uneasy, he scanned the crowd for Stevie. He didn't find her.

When the parade arrived at the mine, Judge Jack went through the ceremony of blindfolding Filmore. "This is to protect all of our interests in the mine," he explained to the unnaturally quiet crowd. "No one knows where the mother lode is located but me. And for your sake, I intend to keep it that way."

Spontaneously, the deluded believers began to chant, "Judge Jack, Judge Jack . . ."

One big miner boomed, "Judge Jack for governor." Another close beside Heath threw an empty bottle of Red Eye in the air and shouted, "Judge Jack for president."

Heath almost laughed. He shook his head, amazed at how desperate these people were for a hero. Just human nature, he guessed absently, searching the crowd for a sight of black leather and platinum braids. He hoped to God that Stevie'd had the good sense to remain behind at the boardinghouse. Even as the thought occurred, he discounted it. She was close by, he could sense it.

With ostentatious pageantry the judge led the blindfolded inspector into the cave. They returned thirty minutes later. The judge stood on a flat-bed wagon and signaled for attention.

Standing in the shade of a nearby cottonwood, Heath awaited the judge's report, though he knew what it would be. For the third time he made a visual search for Stevie. Predictably, he came up empty. She was so tiny, there was no way she would stand out in this gathering of rough and tumble miners. He sighed his frustration and listened to the judge's announcement.

"Friends and citizens of Adobe Wells"—the judge began formally—"our mine has now been inspected by an official representative of Governor Ned Casson." The judge smiled benignly at the representative. "Mr. Shackelford comes to us with impeccable credentials. As both a geologist and a mining engineer from the California Department of Mines." Every second that passed excitement mounted, just as the judge intended. "He is one of the greatest diamond experts in the world. So it is with great pleasure and personal pride that I present him to you."

The onlookers roared in expectation. Judge Jack allowed several minutes for an ensuing celebration before attempting to quiet the mob again. Finally, he motioned Shackelford forward.

Heath's sapphire eyes were as cold and hard as a blue diamond when Shackelford replaced Judge Jack at the front of the wagon bed. He could hardly wait to arrest the impostor—the man who was a co-conspirator in fraud, murder, and God only knew what else.

But he would have to bide his time.

Thirty-nine

The actor turned geologist held a large crystallike stone high in the air, quicting the assemblage. "This is the largest diamond I've ever seen." He gestured to the arched opening in the hillside. "I cut it out of a wall in that mine. I've never seen a more spectacular or productive mine in all my life. There are diamonds on the floor, diamonds in the walls, and diamonds in the ceiling." He spread his arms expansively. "This is the greatest geological discovery in recorded history."

The crowd was mesmerized. Stock-still, they breathed as one. Out of the corner of his eye Heath caught a slight movement. It was Sandy Johns pushing his way through the crowd. His intent was obvious. He was going to reveal that Jack and his cohorts were lying crooks. The fool would be torn apart. Heath jumped atop Warrior and headed in Sandy's direction.

At just that moment the crowd went wild, stamping, shouting, firing their weapons into the air. Stevie ran along behind her father, yelling for him to stop. Sandy couldn't hear her, but it wouldn't have mattered if he had. He was determined to expose the man who had stolen his home, and the devil take the hindmost.

When a drunken miner swung his elbow and accidentally knocked Stevie to the ground, Heath's heart felt as if it would explode. He feared she would be trampled to death. "Stevie," he cried. The word was snatched from his lips, lost in the deafening roar. He slapped Warrior's flanks with the tips of his reins, spurring him along. But it was slow going through the thick crowd. It seemed an eternity before he reached her.

He sailed from the saddle and dropped down on one knee. She was lying unconscious, being kicked and jostled by the shifting rabble. He cleared a ring around her. Kneeling again, he gathered her to him. Her head dropped back on his arm, a fall of platinum tresses pooled on the ground like melted snow.

"Sweetheart," he uttered, pushing wisps of hair from her face with a gentle hand. The drop of blood glistening beside her swollen lip, the telltale bruise forming on her high cheekbone, caused rage to tighten his chest. The thought of Stevie experiencing pain, the real possibility that she could have been killed, was almost his undoing. He pulled her unconscious form to him and held her close. Then he whistled for Warrior, rose to his feet, and mounted, never jostling his precious burden.

High above the others, he searched absently for Sandy. He sighed relief when he saw Pridgen and Sully leading Sandy toward town. Stevie's pa was shaking his fist and cursing to beat the band, but he was in one piece. Apparently, he had been unable to reach the judge and his entourage before they rode away.

Heath wanted to throttle Sandy Johns. Didn't the man know that his foolish outburst would put his daughter in harm's way? Didn't he know that Stevie would follow him . . . to protect him from Judge Jack?

He gritted his back teeth and pulled her closer to his chest. The warmth of her body pressing against his heart calmed him and allowed him to think more clearly. Sandy had lost his son, his home, even his dignity to Judge Jack. And Heath knew the man loved his daughter. So he allowed him one lapse in judgment. "But just one," he muttered.

By the time he arrived at Pilar's, Heath knew Stevie was all right. Her breathing was slow and even, the pulse in the hollow of her throat regular. He halted Warrior by the dismounting block. Dipping his head, he placed gentle kisses on Stevie's eyelids. "Baby," he murmured against her smooth skin.

She was semiconscious now. When she burrowed against him, he traced her lower lip with his tongue. Instinctively, she parted her lips, inviting him inside.

He kissed her gently at first. She returned his kiss with surprising hunger. He deepened the caress, employing lips, teeth, and tongue. He swallowed the moan that began low in her throat, shared his life's breath with her. She shifted against him, unwittingly massaging the aching hardness between his thighs. He groaned more loudly than he intended, awakening her fully.

"What, where . . ." she began.

"Feel okay, sugar?" His voice was husky.

Sooty lashes fluttered up to reveal passion-glazed midnight-black eyes trying to focus on the concerned face above her. "Heath?" she whispered vaguely.

"Of course it's me. Who else kisses you awake and lets you wiggle on his lap?"

She smiled slightly, then gasped. "Pa," she rasped, jerking up. "Ohh," she groaned, and fell back against him as the world spun before her. "Pa, he was . . ."

"Your pa's fine."

"That he is. And wondering why you're holding his daughter like that, Mr. Diamond," Sandy Johns said from the shade of the portal.

Despite Heath's best efforts, he couldn't meet Sandy's eye. Nor did he respond to his pointed remark. Uncomfortably, he wondered how long the man had been standing there. And if he recognized the aroused state he was in. And if he planned to shoot him because of it.

A strange notion entered Heath's mind at that point: What would he do to a man who held Summer—after she was grown—like he was holding Stevie? The answer was immediate and unexpected; he'd shoot first and ask questions later.

Unaware that Heath's thoughts had gone far afield and unmoved by the censure in her pa's voice, Stevie smiled up into Heath's face. "Why are you carrying me?"

Gently, Heath caressed her bruised cheek. "You were hurt." She winced at his touch, and he felt her pain sharply.

Seeing the compassion in his eyes, she smiled. "I'd better put some ice on my face. I don't want to go to the governor's dance tonight looking like I've been in a barroom brawl."

Neither Heath nor Stevie were aware that Sandy continued to watch them with a bemused expression on his face. Shrugging, he decided the smitten couple couldn't get into too much trouble on the back of a horse in broad daylight. Besides, he reminded himself, it was past time the girl got herself a husband. And Lord knows she was taken with the gambler. He was all she ever talked about anymore. A hopeful papa, he slipped unnoticed into the house.

"You still feel up to going to the dance tonight?"

"Mmm-hmm," Stevie said.

"Save me a dance?"

"Just one?"

Heath dropped a kiss on her lips. "All of them."

She dimpled sweetly. "I'll see what I can do."

"Are you flirting with me, Stephanie Johns?"

"If you have to ask . . ." She trailed off, shaking her head from side to side. "I thought you were such a charmer that you'd written the book on flirting."

"I didn't write it, sweetheart. But you can believe I read it," he growled, nuzzling her neck.

Her laughter was like dove feathers stroking his heated skin. He swooped down on her again.

But with surprising energy she eluded him, slid from his lap, and landed on the dismounting block solidly. Despite the incessant pounding in her brain, she hopped to the ground. Once on the portal, she turned to face him. "See ya tonight." She smiled, wiggled her fingers in his direction, and sailed through the front door.

"Little imp." His smile remained in place all the way through town. "You idiot," he murmured to himself. It was unwise for his love for Stevie to become common knowledge. He had made some dangerous enemies, and they wouldn't hesitate to use Stevie to get to him.

Well, it was too late now. Half the town had seen him rescue her, not to mention the passionate scene in front of the boardinghouse. He would have to watch her more closely now. The prospect pleased him more than it should have.

The streets were full of buggies and saddle horses again. With no room on the boardwalks, people poured out into the streets. Heath's going was slow as he strove to avoid trampling the pedestrians beneath Warrior's hooves.

Lanterns hung at the entranceways to all the shops and stores, inviting trade. If Heath had not known these people were being set up for a fall, he would have enjoyed the carnival atmosphere. But he did know. Accordingly, it was incumbent upon him to keep his eyes open and watch out for their interest. He must remember that he was a marshal on duty for his country.

And he was supposed to be undercover as a gambler. With this in mind, he headed toward the Raw Hide Saloon. It wouldn't hurt to be seen around the disreputable watering hole. He might even play a few hands of Jacks or Better, just in case anyone was sober enough to wonder why a professional gambler had scarcely touched a deck of cards since he hit town.

Shouldering his way through the batwings, he disappeared into a mass of coarse, drunken miners. The mixture of foul body odor, cheap alcohol, and even cheaper tobacco assaulted his nostrils. He squinted against the thick gray fog that hovered over the room.

The atmosphere was even less pleasing to his ears than to his eyes. A man who looked better suited behind a general-store counter than seated at a dance-hall piano was banging out a lively tune. A scantily clad dance-hall girl stood beside the meek-looking musician and tried—emphasis on tried—to sing "Sweet Betsy from Pike:"

> Oh, don't you remember sweet Betsy from Pike,
> Who cross'd the big mountains with her lover Ike,
> With two yoke of cattle, a large yellow dog,
> A tall Shanghai rooster and one spotted hog.

The girl may well have been calling the one spotted hog for all her musical ability. Unable to bear the entertainment and doubtful that anyone was lucid enough to notice his presence or lack of it, Heath left the saloon as quickly as he had entered.

He untied Warrior's reins from the post. "Come on, boy." Humming "Sweet Betsy from Pike"—on key—he led his mount toward the livery. Just as he reached the shed, he heard someone shout "Fire!" Instantly, he turned and saw smoke pouring from the Raw Hide Saloon. He ran toward the men who were stumbling out of the smoke-filled hall. They were coughing and gasping for breath.

He ran inside. The building was an inferno, but it was empty. Surveying the crowd of coughing, wheezing men outside, Heath tried to form a bucket brigade. But they were too drunk or too apathetic to follow his instructions. There was little to do but watch the saloon burn. The clapboard building went up like a box of matches.

Donn Pedro approached Heath moments later. There was nothing left of the Raw Hide Saloon but smoldering ashes. *"Señor."* Pedro gained his attention, handing him a telegram.

"Thanks, son." Heath held the missive in his hand, observing the drunk miners staggering back to their shacks and tents. August 9 would long be remembered by the men who scratched a living out of the earth—Heath suspected—as one helluva day. He shuddered to think what tomorrow would bring.

Shaking his head at the prospect, he ripped open the telegram.

It read:

> LUCKY. STOP. WILL ARRIVE AUGUST 10. STOP. MEET ME THREE MILES EAST OF AW ONE HOUR BEFORE SUNRISE. STOP. SIGNED, MINER.

Heath smiled. The telegram's message was obvious: Jay would arrive tomorrow morning. And they would rendezvous outside of town an hour before sunrise. That's when they would plan their strategy.

Heath surmised that whatever the judge had in mind, he would wait until the governor arrived. He folded the telegram and placed it in his vest pocket. "Come on, son." He placed a strong hand on Pedro's shoulder.

Pedro fell into step at his new hero's side without a second thought.

Forty

The next afternoon Stevie sat on the back porch stoop, finger-combing her waist-length hair. The scent of warm lilacs rose from her damp tresses as the bright golden haze of sunlight embraced and dried each silken strand.

Winter and Sweetums rolled about on the fragrant summer grass, cavorting with gay abandon. The child's musical laughter blended with the wolf's low growl, bringing a smile to Stevie's lips.

Abruptly, Blue dropped down beside her onto the step. "Bet I can guess what you're smiling about."

"Them." She jerked her head toward Winter and Sweetums. "What else?"

Blue laughed warmly, placing Summer in Stevie's outstretched arms. "I thought maybe you were thinking about a certain blue-eyed gambler."

Stevie settled Summer in her lap. Unconsciously, she ran her fingers through the baby's midnight-black hair. It was so fine, so thin, so silky that it arrested her attention momentarily.

"No comment?" There was a definite hint of laughter in Blue's husky voice.

Stevie frowned. She hated to think that she was so transparent. Did everyone know she was mooning over a man she could never have? "As I said, I was smiling at Winter and Sweetums."

Blue enjoyed teasing Stevie just as she had enjoyed teasing

Jeff. As always, the memory of Jeff hurt. Pain flickered across her face.

Assuming that she had unwittingly hurt Blue's feelings, Stevie was quick to explain. "I didn't mean to sound cross. This time I *was* smiling at Winter and Sweetums. Honest." When Blue continued to stare at the ground beneath her feet, Stevie was chagrined. "Blue, I wouldn't hurt you."

Blue placed a hand on Stevie's arm. "Don't you think I know that, honey? You've been so kind to me. It's just . . ." She trailed off. More than anything, she wanted to confess her tender feelings for Jeff. And who better to share them with than his sister? But she didn't want to tarnish his memory. To make Stevie think less of her big brother because he had given his love to a whore? Tears filled her eyes and she blinked them away.

"Blue, what's wrong?"

"It's something that happened before we met." She cleared the emotion from her voice. "I don't think you'd care to know."

Blue made to rise. Stevie stilled her with a gentle word. "Stay."

Blue settled in a cloud of black crepe.

Ever since she left the saloon, she had worn nothing but black. Stevie hadn't paid much attention to the fact, didn't think it had any significance. But coupled with the grief on Blue's face, it made her wonder. "You've lost someone you loved." It wasn't a question.

Unable to speak, unwilling to meet Stevie's questioning gaze, Blue merely nodded.

"Your parents? A child? A husband?"

At each of Stevie's questions, Blue shook her head, no. She hesitated slightly when Stevie mentioned a husband.

"A man you loved?" Stevie hazarded.

Blue nodded, the motion releasing the tears that clung precariously to her lashes. A large wet spot appeared on the black crepe covering her lap. She topped it with her folded hands, as if she could hide the evidence of her weakness.

Stevie flattened a dusky palm over Blue's pale, porcelain hands and squeezed comfortingly. "If you talk about him, it might help."

Blue raised her eyes and found Stevie's ebony gaze. Those deep, fathomless eyes, so like the man Blue loved, were full of compassion. Blue spoke without thinking. "It was Jeff."

"Jeff? My Jeff?" Shock registered on Stevie's face and in her tone. Jeff in love with Blue? Her brother Jeff, with his devil-may-care demeanor, had fallen in love with a fallen woman. Stevie was speechless.

Blue took her silence as censure. Grasping her skirts in both hands, she surged to her feet and ran as far and as fast as she could. She never heard Stevie calling her name, pleading for her to return.

Stevie cursed beneath her breath. Unable to pursue Blue since she held the baby, and berating herself for hurting the woman whose only crime was to love her brother—a man who deserved to be loved—Stevie herded Winter and Sweetums inside. There was nothing to do but dress for the dance and hope that Blue returned soon, so that she could apologize for being such a mindless ninny.

When Blue returned, Pilar informed her that Cook had offered to care for the children. Blue planned to dismiss Cook for the night, as soon as the others left for the party.

The Pridgens and Sandy joined Blue and Pilar in the foyer. The women were decked out in their party finery. The air of anticipation was contagious.

"Stevie, if you don't come on, we're going to leave without you." Sandy Johns's threat rang false to all assembled.

"Go ahead, Pa. I'll catch up," Stevie called down from her room.

Sandy hesitated.

Pridgen thumped him on the back. "Come on. It's still daylight. She'll be all right. Anybody who'd bother her is already too drunk to pay her any mind."

Sandy hesitated. Pilar smiled her agreement and handed him her shawl. Laughing, he lay the wispy scrap of lace across her bare shoulders. "I've been taking care of her so long"—he shrugged self-consciously—"old habits die hard."

Blue suspected that Lucky Diamond would fill that position before long, but she kept her own counsel.

"You comin', Blue?" Sandy queried.

Assuring him that she would have more fun minding the babies, she bid them all good-night. She drew a deep, cleansing breath and mounted the stairs. Now was the time to face Stevie, else she would lose her courage. "Stevie." She tapped lightly.

The door swung open on its hinges. Stevie was bent over Summer's cradle, a gentle breeze fluttering the curtains at her back. When she straightened, the dying sun limned her willowy frame. It appeared as if her pale hair and gown were living fire, a silver-white heart cradled in crimson hands.

"If Lucky could see you now," Blue breathed appreciatively, "he would think he'd died and gone to heaven."

Gently, she smoothed her hands down the creamy soft doeskin clinging to her gentle curves. "I wouldn't go that far, but it is a pretty dress, isn't it?"

"It's almost as pretty as you are."

"Thank you." Stevie was equally awed by Blue's beauty. The lantern in the hallway illumined her picture-perfect profile. Seeing Blue as she was now, so gentle, so hesitant, so unsure of herself, her large eyes softened by grief, Stevie could well imagine that her brother had loved her with every beat of his heart. Stevie was warmed by the knowledge. For the first time in her life, she felt as if she had a sister. Mutely, she crossed the room and hugged Blue.

"I'm sorry" was all Stevie said.

"You don't hate me?" Blue asked needlessly.

Stevie laughed. "You goose. Of course I don't hate you." She stepped back and fidgeted with the fringe hanging from her sleeves. Both girls were embarrassed by the emotion hovering in the room. "Jeff loved you. That's good enough for me." She smiled sweetly. "Will you tell me about it? About the two of you."

Blue returned her smile. "I would be happy to. But first, young lady, you have a dance to attend."

Stevie's smile widened. With the promise that they would talk long into the night, she left the boardinghouse, each step taking her closer to the dancing torches and lighthearted music she saw and heard in the distance. Closer to the man she thought of every waking moment of the day, the man who haunted her dreams, the man who was her reason to awaken in the morning light.

Heath was standing beside the makeshift refreshment table that held nonalcoholic punch, ginger cakes and all manner of aromatic confections. Watching for Stevie, he conversed absently with Pat Garrett, a fellow lawman who was passing through town. Pat and Heath had known each other since Heath and Jay came west, following the war. Pat was a former buffalo hunter, Heath knew, one of the few men who had killed the great beasts that he respected.

"Looks to me like the hardcases have decided to find their amusement elsewhere tonight. Those who are still conscious."

Absently, he nodded agreement to Pat's statement, all the while searching for a glimpse of Stevie. When Sandy and Pilar had arrived earlier, he had been sorely disappointed that Stevie wasn't with them. Since then, he had waited for her with all the patience of a new father awaiting the arrival of his firstborn child. The waiting was making him uncharacteristically nervous and fidgety.

It didn't escape Pat's keen eye. "You expecting trouble?" was his lazy question.

There was a moment of silence before Heath swung his gaze back to Pat. "Hmmm?"

"I asked if you were expecting trouble." Pat tried to hide his amusement. He knew Heath's reputation as a lawman. The man was fearless when it came to pursuing outlaws. Fact was, Heath had become somewhat of a legend, known far and wide for riding into danger with hardly a second thought to his own safety . . . and returning unscathed, brigands in tow. The only thing that could unsettle him like this had to be a woman. Pat would bet his tin star on it.

Heath read Pat's thoughts as if he'd spoken them aloud. He chuckled at himself and relaxed slightly. "No. I'm not expecting trouble. Not tonight."

Pat scrutinized the good citizens of Adobe Wells with a professional eye. "Not from this bunch."

Heath hadn't really noticed the people milling around him until now. They were a laughing, gay, sober bunch. Families: husbands, wives, teenagers, toddlers, babies. And they appeared to be having the time of their lives. "Well, I'll be. With the exception of Mrs. Manchez's boarders, all I've seen since I've been in town were Judge Jack's gunhands and a few drunks."

"That's the way it is when trouble comes to town. Most of the law-abiding folks stay away." Pat spoke from experience.

The atmosphere altered slightly then. The crowd grew hushed; the musicians ceased playing. The stillness was broken only by the crackling fire.

From their vantage point Heath and Pat couldn't see what everyone was staring at. But when the partygoers parted, they revealed the single most glorious sight either man had ever beheld.

"Well, I'll be damned," Pat exclaimed appreciatively. Now he understood the source of Heath's impatience.

Heath's mouth fell open at the vision before him. He was physically unable to move. It was as if roots had grown from the bottom of his boots, anchoring him firmly to the patch of grass beneath his feet.

Stevie seemed to be suffering similarly. The bonfire at her back, she stood with her head held high, arms straight at her sides, not moving a single rigid muscle.

To Heath, she looked like a gilded Indian princess in her wedding finery. Her ethereal beauty mesmerized him. As always, he was struck by her uncommon radiance, body and spirit. She was an enigma exuding purity and passion, serenity and seduction, calling forth love and lust. He had never known a woman like her, and as always he renewed the vow to make her his . . . forever.

Raising her chin fractionally higher, she met his eyes.

When he read the insecurity in their ebony depths, his heart stirred in his chest. Nothing could have kept him from her side. Quickly, he closed the distance separating them. He took her hand and brought it to his lips. "You're the most exquisite creature I've ever seen."

She bowed her head shyly, releasing a shimmering curtain of platinum silk. It hid her oval-shaped face from his view.

Unaware that they were being watched by everyone in attendance, Heath stepped closer to her. Smoothly, he slid his hand through the hair veiling her face, cupped her jaw, and lifted her head until her eyes met his once again. "What's this? Don't tell me my courageous Indian princess has turned shy on me?"

For once, she was speechless. The intensity of Heath's love for her was written clearly on his face. It was frightening and thrilling all at once.

"Always said she were a galldern perty Injun," old Mr. Mac observed loudly in a voice tinged with awe.

The unexpected compliment broke the tension surrounding Heath and Stevie. He chuckled and she blushed.

"My thoughts exactly," he tossed to the half-deaf old codger.

"What'd he say?" Mr. Mac shouted to his bemused son-in-law. The men standing around them laughed and teased the old man mercilessly.

Taking Stevie's arm, Heath led her to the dance area. The plethora of frontier musicians struck up a rousing tune. But the sweetest music being played was the love song passing from Stevie's heart to Heath's and back again. They danced time and again, falling more in love with each moment that passed.

To Stevie's surprise, Heath wasn't the only man who wanted to dance with her. Many of the white men she had kept at arm's length—assuming they would disdain her Indian heritage—tapped Heath's shoulder boldly, nonverbally asking if they might have a moment of her time. His reluctance to release her each time pleased her more than their fawning attention.

She was also pleased by the reaction of the women of Adobe Wells. Most of the prim and proper matrons who had looked askance at her before were almost civil tonight. She couldn't imagine why they had changed their behavior toward her. Perhaps it was because they sensed a change in her, a change brought about by the love of a good man.

An hour later Heath stood just beyond the circle of dancers, watching Stevie whirl about in Pat Garrett's arms. Jealousy threatened to choke him as he watched her throw her head back on her slender shoulders and laugh at something Pat said. When her hair brushed Pat's tanned hand as it rested possessively on the small of her back, Heath clenched his jaw.

But he didn't interfere. It was important for Stevie to realize she could be accepted into white society, that she had in fact been accepted by most of the townspeople without her knowledge, that it had been her choice to remain isolated on the ranch and not their intention to shun her.

However, when Pat instinctively pulled her closer, so close her breasts brushed the leather fringe on his vest, Heath bolted. His long strides eating up the ground in a blur, he was standing behind Pat in mere seconds. He breathed deeply before tapping Pat on the shoulder more forcefully than he ought.

The only thing that calmed his jealous rage was the brilliant smile Stevie turned on him as she moved willingly into his arms. "That's it," he whispered fervently against her ear. "No more dance partners for you."

She tilted her head back and raised a brow, clearly amused, obviously delighted.

Heath smiled down into her face. "Except me, of course."

She moved her hand from his shoulder and brushed the hair off his forehead lightly. "Of course."

They were unaware that they had stopped dancing. Standing in the midst of the whirling, circling throng, they might have been a boulder in the center of a white water rapid. But they were oblivious of all else save the fire, the passion, the raw desire embracing them from roots to arch.

Stevie's world consisted of Heath. At this moment she existed for him alone. She loved him as she had never loved another. And she wanted him more than the next breath she drew. She didn't care what the morrow would bring. For tonight, she wanted him. It was as simple as that.

Reading the staggering need in her eyes and feeling the same ravenous desire, Heath took her trembling hand in his and led her into the night. As soon as they were cloaked in darkness, he leaned her against a tree and covered her body and mouth with his own.

Forty-one

While Heath and Stevie were lost in a world of their own, the governor, accompanied by three august personages and a host of armed men on horseback, pulled up to the courthouse.

Governor Ned Casson and the famous cattle king John Chisum emerged from the first carriage.

Judson Smyth, Alexander McSween, and J. H. Tunstall alighted the second carriage. Judson went to Rachel and dropped a cold peck on her cheek. Then, turning to the judge, he introduced his guests.

Even Judge Jack was impressed and intimated by coming face-to-face with three of New Mexico's most powerful citizens. Compared to Chisum, McSween, and Tunstall, the judge, the governor, and Smyth were of little consequence. The label living legends came to mind.

In for a penny, in for a pound, Jack chanted silently. Smiling to hide his uneasiness, he stepped forward to greet the men who would happily skin him alive for what he planned to do to them.

He started slightly when still another carriage entered town, carrying three men, led by John Carrington of Santa Fe. Carrington, the judge remembered, was Governor Casson's administrative assistant.

"Judge Jack." Carrington used his official voice. "Allow me to introduce Theodore Howard and Victor Patton, attorneys for the San Francisco and New York Mining and Commercial Company."

"Welcome to Adobe Wells. All of you." Jack spoke to everyone assembled at once. "Mrs. Smyth has made the necessary arrangements for your comfort. She has prepared a place in my chambers where we can meet privately before attending a little dance the town is giving in your honor."

"We'll talk, then leave," Chisum stated flatly.

To a man, they nodded agreement.

Jack was nonplussed but careful to appear calm. "Certainly. Governor Casson, you and your party will want to meet with Mr. Shackelford alone first, I'm certain."

Casson nodded.

Judge Jack eyed the men warily. "I'll be waiting in the courtroom."

Rachel led the gentlemen to the judge's chambers. She'd had the plain pine furnishings removed and replaced by a large mahogany table surrounded by deep leather chairs. She had personally selected and arranged cut-glass ashtrays and delicate crystal glasses and silver pitchers of water for the convenience of the participants. They took no notice whatever of her careful preparations.

A bit nervous now, she waited until they were all seated, then left the room, closing the door firmly behind her. She raised a questioning brow at Jack, who sat in his official chair. He shrugged negligently.

Trying to appear as nonchalant as he, she said, "It'll all be over soon. Then we'll be rich beyond our wildest dreams."

"We leave tonight" was all he said.

In a few minutes Judson Smyth opened the door.

"Judge, I believe we're ready to do business."

With false bravado Judge Jack sauntered into his chambers and took the remaining seat. He quickly perused the men. He couldn't read their expressions.

Governor Casson was the appointed spokesman. "We're prepared to offer you two million dollars for your interest in the mine."

It took conscious effort not to sigh relief as Jack inclined his head graciously.

Money changed hands, and less than twenty minutes later the governor and his party left for Santa Fe. Rachel remained behind to aid Judge Jack in tying up loose ends.

With all the fanfare of purchasing a glass of lemonade, Chisum, Tunstall, and McSween, the major shareholders in the San Francisco and New York Mining and Commercial Company, believed they had just acquired the greatest diamond mine on the North American continent.

And Judge Jack was two million dollars richer. He should have felt unparalleled elation. Instead, he knew a fear that was almost paralyzing in its intensity. If those men ever found him—after they discovered the swindle—they would make his life hell on earth. He would beg for death before they finished with him. Of that, he was certain.

Shrugging off the terrible foreboding, he and Rachel headed for his chambers. Henry Sims passed them in the hallway.

He flashed the judge a look Rachel couldn't define. She laughed uneasily and congratulated Judge Jack on a job well done.

Once inside his room, he patted two large leather cases full of money where they rested on the floor beside the valises holding his clothes.

In a few minutes they would leave for Delgado's, where they would catch the morning stage to Kansas City. There, they planned to catch the train to St. Louis, then travel to Cincinnati, Baltimore, Philadelphia, and finally New York. It would be several weeks before their fraud would be discovered, and by then they would have new identities, disappearing among the masses of the big city. They hoped.

Suddenly, there was an explosion along Main Street. "Stay here," Jack ordered Rachel as he ran from the room.

After the judge's hasty exit, Judson Smyth entered through the rear door.

Rachel surged to her feet. "I thought he'd never leave."

Judson looked toward the door as if Judge Jack would burst back in at any moment. "Quick, let's get the money and get out of here."

Rachel grabbed her husband around the neck and squealed, "We've done it. While he untangles that mess you set up outside, we'll rob the stupid son of a bitch. We'll be on the night stage to Kansas City before he knows were gone."

"Hush. Someone might hear."

Rachel rolled her eyes. "You worry too much, Judson."

He didn't think so. Hurriedly, he grabbed the leather money bags and rushed for the door. He had already placed a small travel bag for each of them in the small carriage waiting in the alley behind the courthouse. When they arrived at the carriage, he automatically opened the door for his wife.

"Going somewhere?" a familiar voice growled from behind them.

They turned and saw Judge Jack holding a gun on them. A deadly smile stretched across his face.

"I'm disappointed in you, my dear." He spoke to Rachel but was watching Judson for sudden moves. "You surely didn't think I would allow you to get away with my money, did you?"

Rachel spat a string of oaths that would embarrass a sailor. She reached into her pocket, withdrew a Remington Vest Pocket .22, and with the quickness of a rattlesnake shot Jack in the chest. The judge's gun fell from his hand as he crumpled to the ground.

"Rachel, you killed him. You promised there wouldn't be any killing."

"You're damn right I killed him," she snarled at Judson. "What do you think he planned to do to us?" She regarded first her husband, then Judge Jack, with utter disgust. "I hope he burns in hell. Now, put the money in the carriage. Or you're next." She pointed her weapon in his direction for emphasis.

Head down, Judson did as he was told.

Before they could board, Carlos Garcia ran out the door of the courthouse. His gun was drawn, but Rachel ducked behind the carriage door and shot him through the heart.

"You killed him. How could you kill him?" Judson groaned as his wife shoved him into the carriage ahead of her.

She pulled the door shut behind her. "I killed my own father, two prison guards in Arkansas, and others I don't even remember."

Leaving both bodies where they lay, the harsh woman and her white-faced husband headed toward Delgado's.

Heath and Stevie heard the shots from the portal, where they stood clenched in a passionate embrace.

"Señor." Donn Pedro spoke from the front yard. "Henry Sims said to tell you he's waiting."

So this is it, Heath thought. He had known since his first night in Adobe Wells that he and Sims would square off against each other. Actually, he was surprised Sims had waited this long to force a gunfight.

Stevie followed Heath's train of thought and stiffened in his arms. "I'm going with you."

He knew there was little use telling her to stay behind. She turned, facing town, only to be restrained by his tightening embrace.

Her eyes blazed. "Don't dare say I can't go, Heath Turner. You need my help. He won't be alone, you know."

Stevie was a good gunhand for a woman, better than most men, Heath acknowledged. But she was no match for Henry Sims and Bear Jacobson. Besides, she was unarmed. He had been close enough to her tonight to know. Cupping her chin in his hand, he stared deep into her eyes, so deep he touched her soul. "You're my heart," he whispered. "I can't let anything happen to you."

"It's not your decision to make. I do as I please. Or have you forgotten that?"

"Come on, sweetie," he cajoled.

Her jaw was set at a mutinous angle. He brushed a kiss against that stubborn jaw. She stiffened in his arms. In a blur he released her and retrieved the rope hanging around his saddle horn. Turning back, he wrapped it around her arms and body. She kicked and screamed and cursed, but in the end he succeeded in tying her to the post.

Just as she would damn his soul to everlasting hell, he covered her mouth with his own, pressing his body flush with hers. He kissed and caressed his fiery love until she went limp against him. Lifting his head, he smiled triumphantly down into her face.

"Damn you, Heath," she spat out through her teeth when the sensuous haze cleared.

"I'm sorry, sweetheart. But I don't have time to argue." He

looked at Donn Pedro squarely. "Stay with her and keep her safe. But don't untie her unless the house catches on fire."

"Sí, Señor."

Heath chuckled at the venomous look Stevie shot Pedro. "Don't look at the boy like that, doll. You'll scare him." Heath kissed her thoroughly again, but quickly. "You'll thank me for this after we're married." As he headed toward town, Stevie's curses floated in his wake. The last thing he heard her say was "Be careful, damn you."

He smiled and waved without turning around. When he reached the plaza, he saw Henry Sims on his left, standing in front of the courthouse. The porch lantern and the lights inside the saloon washed over him, revealing his smug smile. Bear Jacobson stood across the street in front of the Silver Dollar Saloon. Both men were set to draw. Their accomplice, a gunslick Heath knew as Shorty, was crouched in the alley on the far side of the Gold Nugget, sporting a long gun, probably a rifle, making the picture even more dismal.

Sims fired his rifle into the air, supposedly to rattle his opposition.

Heath didn't flinch. He stood stock-still for a full five minutes. Then, drawing a deep breath through his nose, he edged toward the Gold Nugget Saloon. The thick white posts of the portal blocked him from Sims's view, which was his intention.

He spoke first to Jacobson. "All right, fat man. You've spent your life bullying people weaker than you; let's see what you can do with me."

Bear glanced at Sims and saw him hold up his hand but failed to recognize the signal as a warning that Sims didn't have a clear shot. Thinking the two of them could take Heath, Jacobson edged his hand toward his 1848 Dragoon Colt and made his move. Heath fired before Bear could clear leather. The bullet hit the fat man in the belly, throwing him backward onto the boardwalk. Dust flew a foot high and boards cracked and splintered as he broke through the walkway.

Heath ducked and took a hopping step back. He expected Shorty to shoot any minute. But Shorty never raised his gun.

Mortally wounded but not yet dead, Bear rolled over and emptied his gun in Heath's direction. The shots went wild.

Heath took aim, put another bullet into Bear, shattering his skull. The big man's body convulsed as he performed the final lethargic dance of death.

Heath reloaded and holstered his Navy. Then he stepped out into the street and faced Sims.

"Hey, Shorty," Heath shouted. "I'm going to kill Sims first, then I'll get to you. So hold on and don't go gettin' impatient." He paused for emphasis. " 'Course, if you want to live, you can throw down your gun and move out here, where I can see you. It doesn't really matter a whole hell of a lot to me either way."

"Now, Marshal Turner, that doesn't sound very professional."

The soft southern drawl drew reaction all around.

"Marshal?" Sims croaked, his eyes darting to every shadow and crevice, trying desperately to discover who had spoken.

Shorty made to turn toward the voice, but a gun barrel was shoved in his back.

Heath just smiled. "You're a day early. Must've known I'd need you."

"I was camped on the edge of town, just bedded down for the night, when I heard that rifle shot. Somehow I knew you'd be knee-deep in whatever was goin' on. But it looks like you got things pretty well under control, to me," Jay complimented, a smile in his voice. "Sorry I left that nice warm bedroll now."

Heath chuckled, never taking his eyes off Sims.

"I quit, Marshal," Shorty interjected. "You remember that when this is over. Okay?"

Heath nodded toward Shorty when he stepped out into the street from the shadows of the alley. "Smart man."

Grinning, Jay followed less than a foot behind. "He didn't really have much choice."

Sims cursed beneath his breath. He was all alone. And not facing a fancy gambler as he'd supposed, but a lethal-looking lawman.

Heath stood in front of him, feet planted, half crouched. His eyes were cold, the promise of death in their depths. Sims knew he had to kill or be killed. He had forced the confrontation and now there was no way out.

Suddenly, he went for his gun. He was very fast, but Heath was faster. As Sims pulled the trigger of his Army Colt, he felt hot lead sink into his neck. The impact threw his aim off slightly so that his shot grazed Heath's left shoulder, spinning him around like a top.

Sims fell to the ground. His heart gave several strong propulsive beats, squirting blood from his jugular; it finally stopped when he was stone cold dead.

When Heath recovered, Shorty was standing in front of him, holding out his bandanna for a bandage.

"Where's Judge Jack?" Heath asked, ignoring his wound.

"He's dead," Shorty explained, telling Heath and Jay what had become of the money . . . and Rachel.

Jay cursed long and loud. "Will I ever catch that bitch?"

"We'll get her," Heath said.

"Heath," Stevie cried, running up the street toward him.

Heath opened his arms and caught her up in a tight hug. "I'm all right, sweetheart."

"I failed you, *Señor.* I untied her." Donn Pedro looked so fatalistic that Heath almost smiled. The boy raised guilt-ridden eyes to Heath's sapphire orbs. His voice held a tint of bewilderment when he shrugged and said, "She cried."

Heath nodded. The man had not been born who could resist this beautiful woman in tears.

Stevie's husky voice broke into their conversation. "Is it over?"

"Almost, sugar." He stroked her back. "Judge Jack and his men are dead or have surrendered. But we still have to go after Rachel and her husband."

"But you're hurt. Can't you let someone else go?"

"She's right, Heath. I can finish this," Jay offered.

Stevie's head jerked toward the blond marshal who had spoken. She had been so concerned with Heath's safety, she had not noticed his partner.

"No, Jay. Adobe Wells is my assignment. I have to finish it."

Jay nodded. He had expected no less. "Can you use a little help?"

"Always, partner."

"I'm going too." Stevie steeled herself for Heath's refusal.

But he knew his time with her was growing short. And he couldn't keep her tied up the whole time he was gone. Hell, she was so persuasive, he couldn't keep her tied up for fifteen minutes, not as long as there was a red-blooded male in the vicinity.

He and Jay exchanged glances. Jay nodded almost imperceptibly. Heath smiled. Together, they would keep her safe. And maybe along the way, he would convince her to be his wife. "All right," he said softly.

She smiled incredulously. "Honest? You mean it?"

"Honest."

Jay grabbed Shorty by the arm and pushed him toward the jailhouse. "Come on, my good man. Let's give the lovebirds a little privacy. I have a few questions for you."

Donn Pedro followed close on Jay's heels. Seems there was no shortage of heroes in Adobe Wells these days.

Forty-two

Rachel and Judson Smyth drove the horses that pulled their private carriage with a vengeance. Granted, they had escaped with the money, Judge Jack was dead, and the others were engaged in a gunfight. But they doubted seriously if the victors of the shootout would let them get away with two million dollars unchallenged. Whoever remained alive would be after them soon.

Not accustomed to hardship—at least not lately—Rachel found the ride horrendous. The road was a grainy ribbon of mud ruts, gopher holes, and rocks the size of the Sangre de Cristoes. Dust particles blew through the window in heavy sheets, coating her face. She spat, sputtered, cursed, and damned every mile that passed beneath the horses' hooves.

The coach bounced, the stay chains rattled, the springy layers of leather thoroughbrace slings squeaked, the churning wheels clattered. Had she not been a homicidal maniac before the trip, this endless ride would have turned her into one.

Just when she thought she couldn't bear another moment, they arrived at a way station for the stagecoach. Solicitous as always, Judson bought coffee and sandwiches for them while Rachel stretched her legs and refreshed herself. But before long the stage arrived, they left the private carriage behind, and boarded the coach. They were its only passengers.

As they continued down the dirt road, only one of them was aware of the tall man in dark clothes who followed on horseback. He kept in the shadows, well off the beaten track, as was the plan.

The next evening they pulled into Two Forks, a small mining town in Colorado. Rachel announced that they would spend the night and continue on in the morning. "I want a hot bath and a decent meal."

"Do you really think we should wait for the morning stage?" Judson was inordinately nervous. "If somebody trails us here, it'll be impossible to hide."

"If you're afraid, you can go on alone. But the money stays with me." Rachel's harsh, matter-of-fact statement ended the discussion.

Judson engaged a room in the town's only hotel. While Rachel soaked in a steaming hot bath, he brought the luggage, including the money bags, up to their room. Later that evening, they dined downstairs in the hotel restaurant.

Rachel was dressed to the teeth. It wasn't so much the style of her clothing that drew every eye in the room, though the cuirass bodice of her gown fitting tightly over her ample hips wasn't exactly demure. It was the color of her clothing that gave the more sedate matrons in the room pause. Her apron-fronted overskirt, puffed at the back over a giant bustle, was the brightest crimson any of them had ever seen. And her vivid pink satin underskirt was sufficient to strike them blind. Add orange-red hair fringed beneath a pink ostrich-plumed hat, and she was an arresting—if not visually painful—sight to behold.

Judson noted that his wife's mood was as bright as her clothing. Uncharacteristically, she laughed at everything he said, no matter how inane. When she ordered a second bottle of wine, a sense of foreboding flooded him. He suggested gently that they return to their room.

She vetoed the suggestion. And that was that.

After what seemed an eternity to Judson, Rachel indicated that she was ready to leave. He sighed relief and followed her upstairs.

When he unlocked the door and stepped inside, he was grabbed from behind by powerful hands. His assailant held him in a death grip. He gasped for breath, kicked and fought, but his struggles were futile against the strong arms that held him. His body convulsed in paroxysms and his eyes bulged. He wanted to scream for help, but he couldn't.

Fear for Rachel's safety all but paralyzed him. He twisted frantically, hoping to communicate to her to escape while the maniac held him. That's when he saw her, sitting in a wing chair beside the double windows, enjoying the macabre scene being played out before her.

The impact of her perfidy hit him as if it were a physical blow. She had planned his death and tarried in the restaurant to give his murderer time to prepare for their return. Tears blurred her hateful mask before his eyes. He had loved her, loved her with all his heart, and now she sat, watching him die, with a smile of betrayal sculpting her face.

The fight left him then. He went absolutely limp. His attacker twisted his head, breaking his neck with a loud snap. His body slid to the floor. Judson Smyth was dead.

"I've been waiting for you," Rachel purred, not sparing her husband's corpse so much as a glance.

The smile that lit Preacher Black's face caused the hair on Rachel's nape to rise. "You have, have you?" He bore down upon her and slapped her across the face. "Where's the money, bitch?"

"In the bags. There on the floor." She was truly bewildered. "What's wrong? Everything's gone just as we planned."

Black struck her again, then hauled her to her feet. "I'll kill you just like I killed that worthless husband of yours if you don't stop playing games with me. Where's the money?" He shook her like a rag doll. Her head snapped backward, loosening a torrent of fiery red hair.

She tried to fight him, but her struggles were useless against his superior strength. When he struck her repeatedly about the face, her nose spurted blood onto his pristine white shirt. Pulling his Colt from its holster, he crammed the barrel into her mouth and cocked the hammer, breaking two of her front teeth with the force of his thrust.

Her eyes teared from terror and pain. Instinctively, she pulled a small knife from her waist pocket and jabbed it into his neck. Blood bathed her white-gloved hand, turning it a curious pink.

Black shoved Rachel's body away as he fell to the floor. Screaming like a wounded animal, he jerked the knife from his neck. He withdrew a handkerchief from his waistcoat and pressed the small cloth against his wound. Immediately, the cloth was saturated with blood. The room dimmed before his eyes. His hearing wavered, but he thought he heard footsteps in the hallway growing louder.

Rachel heard someone approaching. Satisfied that Judson and Black were dead but unable to retrieve the money from beneath Black's body, she slipped out the double windows and disappeared into the night.

The door opened slowly. Black stirred with his ebbing strength as three people entered the room. "Please, get a doctor."

"I'll go." Before Heath could object, Stevie ran from the room.

"Where's Rachel?" Jay demanded of the dying man. Black's gaze swung toward the double windows. Weapon drawn, Jay slipped through them.

Preacher Black and Heath were left alone in the room. "Want to clear your conscience and tell me your part in all this, Reverend?"

His voice low and thready from pain, Black began. "Rachel and I both worked for the First State Bank of Chicago when Colt Jack robbed it. We knew that sooner or later he would pull another job. So we followed him west. Rachel married Smyth about the time Colt came to Adobe Wells."

Black coughed up blood. With his waning strength, he pressed the cloth to his neck.

Heath felt the quickening of sympathy. But remembering those who had died, he ignored it. "Keep talking."

"When Judge Jack showed up in Santa Fe, Rachel confronted him. He cut her in on his diamond scheme. Then she convinced her husband to help her steal the money from Jack."

Again Black coughed. His body was growing cool from the loss of blood. His teeth chattered as he continued. "I came to Adobe Wells shortly after the judge, disguised as a preacher. I trained for the ministry as a young man . . ." Black trailed off with a look that might have been contrition on his face.

"Tell me about Ted Reno."

"Reno discovered that Rachel was wanted for embezzlement. I was afraid that if he called in a U.S. marshal, it would blow the scam. So I hired the men who killed him."

Stevie returned with the doctor. A squatty man, barely sober, he entered the room and knelt beside Preacher Black.

Black's eyes were fixed and glazed. He stared blankly at the ceiling and began to whisper, "Dear Jesus, forgive my sins. Jesus, sweet Jesus, please have mercy on my soul. Wash me white as snow. Receive my spirit into your heavenly bosom . . ."

And then he was dead.

The doctor summoned four men to remove the dead bodies of Judson Smyth and the man known to Heath only as Preacher Black.

Heath stared at the pool of blood that remained where Preacher Black had lain. It never occurred to him to rush to Jay's aid. If his partner found Rachel, he would be able to handle her alone. Instead, he sat on the bed, sickened by the wanton killing Judge Jack's greed had caused. Taking his hand in her own, Stevie sat quietly at his side.

They were still sitting silently when Jay entered the room through the doorway thirty minutes later. Heath raised a questioning brow.

His face white with rage, Jay shook his head. Once again Rachel Jackson had slipped through his fingers. Silently, he crossed the room. He knelt beside the money bags and opened them.

So many had died—for two bags filled with newspaper clippings.

Forty-three

A whooshing air current as sweet as lilac perfume brought mid-morning to the sleepy little town of Adobe Wells.

The cornflower-blue sky above was accessorized by a gold-white sun, ringed by a profusion of swanlike clouds. The sea of blue flowed over and around the land, embracing it as far as the eye could see.

Delicate shafts of light dropped through the clouds, warming the threesome as they rode into town. Heath and Stevie rode side by side; Jay brought up the rear.

Heath was unaware of the beauty surrounding him. He shifted nervously in the saddle, drawing Stevie's notice. He smiled at her weakly, then quickly looked away before she saw the guilt in his eyes. The plan was to leave her safely in her father's care. Then he and Jay would replenish their supplies and go after Rachel. Stevie, of course, was not privy to the plan. Dreading the confrontation that was sure to arise when he told her she wouldn't be part of the posse was the source of his discomfiture. If he considered Rachel as part of the conspiracy, then so would Stevie. And she would deem it her right to bring Rachel to justice. He just had to convince her it wasn't in her best interest. Riding into town, he turned his attention to the people milling about, anything to preoccupy his mind.

Stevie noticed Heath's strange behavior and decided it was because they had come to the end of the road. It couldn't be because he suspected she was pregnant. She had just come to that realization herself a few days ago. And she had been very careful to keep the fact from him. His problem was undoubtedly that the threat to Adobe Wells was over, his job was complete, and he would be leaving soon.

She might never see him again. Her heart felt like a lump of coal in her chest. "I can hardly believe it's the same town," she observed absently. "I never dreamed things would return to normal so fast."

Instead of the brigands and gunslicks she had become accustomed to seeing, the local folks were going about their normal day: farmers and their runny-nosed broods, cowboys in town for supplies, ladies doing their weekly marketing. It should have been a comforting sight, but it wasn't. Normalcy meant that they no longer needed the handsome U.S. marshal who had stolen her heart. At least she would have his baby to remember him by.

"When the money dries up, bad men go elsewhere."

Stevie barely heard Jay's observation. Her thoughts were full of the change that had come over Heath since last evening. He had been polite to her at best. She shouldn't be surprised that he wasn't his usual charming self, she scolded herself. Since his job was finished and he was leaving town, he wanted to erect an emotional barrier so their parting wouldn't be more painful than necessary, she reasoned. Actually, she should appreciate his efforts, not be hurt by them.

Just as she shouldn't be hurt by the fact that he had stopped proposing marriage to her. After all, how many times could a man be rejected before he gave up? Obviously, Heath had reached that limit. She wished he would ask again, if for no other reason than to reassure her of his love. Still, if he proposed right now, she doubted her answer would be yes. What a fickle woman she had become!

Confused and disheartened, she rode ahead of him. Reining in at Pilar's boardinghouse, she slid from the saddle without waiting for Heath's aid.

He was still frowning when she disappeared into the house. Moments later, Donn Pedro brought him a telegram. He thanked the child automatically and smiling Pedro went on his way. "What now?" Heath groused, staring at the telegram as if it were a two-headed viper.

Jay understood his partner's ill humor and ignored it. "Probably from the captain, calling us to Santa Fe for our next assignment."

"We haven't finished this job yet," Heath verbalized the obvious harshly, casting an unconscious glance toward the house.

Jay's expression soured. "Don't remind me." He took the reins of all three horses in his hands. "I'll find fresh horses while you tell her you're leaving."

Heath nodded and closed his eyes for a moment. He didn't want to leave Stevie, but he would be back. He tried to reassure himself. When he opened his eyes, he was alone. He shoved his hat off his head with two fingers and moved to the porch swing, out of the brilliant sunlight. He remained standing as he ripped open the telegram.

It read:

> HEATH. STOP. THE GENERAL HAS TAKEN A TURN FOR THE WORSE. STOP. COME HOME RIGHT AWAY. STOP. YOUR BROTHER, CHAP.

It was dated the day they left town, four days earlier. His knees weakened and he sat abruptly. The swing creaked under his dead weight. Fear, stark and vivid, swept through him. His stomach clenched into double knots of denial. Icy panic twisted around his heart. For a moment he feared he might faint. He drew deep, cleansing breaths through his mouth until his physical world righted itself somewhat.

He knew Chap was no alarmist. And he was a damn good doctor. For him to send such a telegram, their father must be gravely ill. Panic returned like a monstrous swell.

A thought—quick and devastating—drained the color from his tanned face. Like a poised cobra, it rose unbidden in his mind, striking before he could erect a defense against it; *perhaps his father was already dead.* The possibility tore at his insides, threatening to shatter his fragile control.

A groan of despair slipped past his lips. He dropped his head into his hands and stared at the flooring beneath his booted feet with unseeing eyes. He didn't just love his father, he worshipped him. The real possibility of losing him was almost more than he could bear.

"Heath?"

Stevie's concerned voice came to him as if from a long way off. He raised his head slowly, met her concerned gaze, but couldn't speak.

She stood before him, frowning. "What's wrong?"

Her tender concern was his undoing. He wrapped strong arms around her waist and pulled her to him roughly, burying his face in the pillow of her breasts. She was the only solid object in his voidless world of despair.

He embraced her so tightly that she could scarcely breathe. When she sifted her fingers through his hair and whispered nonsensical reassurances, he relaxed slightly.

She tried to absorb his mental anguish and make his pain her own.

After what seemed an eternity, he regained full control. He handed her the telegram as an explanation of his strange behavior.

Taking a seat beside him, she read the message quickly.

"Oh, Heath. I'm so sorry." The sight of him struggling to hide his fear gripped her heart in a vise. "I'm sure he'll be all right."

Her simple reassurance was surprisingly convincing. He held on to the solace and reached for her hand.

Giving his hand a gentle squeeze, she offered him a bolstering smile. "You did say he was invincible."

Heath realized then how much he needed Stevie. Not just for love or lust, sex or seduction, but as the other half of his being. He didn't want to face the future without her. More to the point, he didn't want to face what awaited him in New York without her. His voice was raspy with emotion when he said, "Come with me."

Stevie was awash with conflicting emotions. "Why?"

"Because I need you." He remembered a long-ago promise he had made to himself, to remove Stevie and the children from this area before Indians and whites engaged in all-out war. This was his chance to do that. And God knows he couldn't bear the prospect of leaving her behind.

Stevie could think of a million reasons to refuse, but all that came to mind was "The children need me too."

"We'll take them with us."

"You're not thinking clearly. We can't take two children to New York." The unspoken words, *two Indian children,* were thick in the air.

He misunderstood her hesitation purposefully. "Blue can go along to help."

The picture of Heath waltzing into his New York mansion with his pregnant half-breed paramour, two Indian children, and a reformed hurdy-gurdy girl in tow was almost enough to make Stevie laugh. Almost. But too much was at stake to make light of the situation. "Have you forgotten that I'm part Indian?"

"I've told you I don't care about that, dammit." He sounded more harsh than intended. His nerves were raw pieces of meat. His father needed him and he needed him now. He didn't have the time or patience to argue with her. She had to go with him. That was the beginning and the end of it.

"I'm sorry about your father. But, Heath, I can't go home with you. You have to leave right away. There's just too much unsettled between us. I'm not sure of my place in your life—if I even have a place in your life."

"You know damn well that you do." His voice was so full of conviction, Stevie was momentarily speechless.

Finally, she found her voice. It was very soft when she said, "Then maybe when your father is better, you can come back. Then maybe . . ." She trailed off.

Not willing to let it lie, he pushed his advantage. "I love you, Stevie. I've made no secret of that. And I know that you love me. I want to spend the rest of my life with you. If you'll stop being so stubborn, you'll admit that marriage is the only logical conclusion to our love affair. Why should I have to come back? Why can't you come with me now?"

She opened her mouth to argue, but he placed his fingers over her lips.

"I'm sorry that we don't have time to marry before we go.

My family in New York needs me." He smiled at her gently. "But I need my family in New Mexico. I need you, and Winter, and the baby. Please say you'll go."

Stevie couldn't hide the confusion in her eyes. She wanted to say yes. God knows, she did. Especially when she remembered the baby slumbering beneath her heart, Heath's baby.

She had been reared by one parent for most of her life. And she was the only parent Winter knew. She wanted better for her baby. She wanted him to have every possible chance in life, not just financial, but emotional as well. Most of all, she wanted him to know both his parents. But she couldn't go with Heath, not now, maybe later. "I'm so sorry." Her voice broke. "I just can't. Not now."

Heath's pain was visible. But he wouldn't beg. "No, Stevie. You can. You just won't."

She knew she should say something. But what could she say?

"Maybe I was wrong. Maybe you don't love me," Heath said.

She covered her sob with a hand and ran into the house.

Heath stared at the floor through a mist of emotion. Whether he was hurting for Stevie, his father, or himself, he didn't know; perhaps it was for all three.

Jay cleared his throat, announcing his presence, allowing Heath a moment to regain his composure before he stepped up onto the porch.

Silently, Heath handed him the telegram Stevie had thrown on the floor when she made her exit. Jay read it silently. "I'm sorry, buddy. But he'll be all right. You'll see."

Heath merely nodded.

Jay rested a hip against the portal railing, crossing his feet in front of him. "Judge Jack's body's missing."

This got Heath's attention, took his mind off his personal problems. "What did you say?"

"Judge Jack's body's missing. But I think I know where he is."

"Hell?" Heath supplied.

"Afraid not. McGahee said he heard the judge and Rachel

talking about going to New York after they pulled off the swindle."

"Surely, you don't think the bastard's still alive."

"That's exactly what I think. It would explain the paper clippings in the valises. He fooled Rachel and made off with the money himself."

Heath had to admit that it made sense. His analytical mind whirred. "When I wire Chap that I'm on my way home, I'll send a message to the New York office to be on the lookout for the judge."

"When do you leave?"

"Soon as I say good-bye to Stevie. I'll reach Delgado's by nightfall. Take the morning stage to Kansas City, then continue by rail." He told Jay each of his stops, in case he had news of Rachel.

Jay's soft drawl hardened with contempt at the thought of Rachel. "I'd better get packing if I'm to reach Two Forks by dark. I don't intend to let her trail get cold."

Inside the house, Stevie—the snoop, she derided herself—gripped the doorjamb. Judge Jack—the rotten bastard—was still alive. The man who had killed her brother, had her father shot, and stolen their home. He was alive. More than likely, living the high life in New York with money stolen from decent people. She took the stairs two at a time. Her decision was made before she burst through the door to Blue's bedchamber. "I need your help."

"Sit down and get your breath," Blue said. "Now. Who do I have to kill?"

"Don't tease me now, Blue. This is important."

Blue's smile slipped away. "Anything. All you have to do is ask."

"Will you take care of Winter and the baby for me?" Her voice broke, the thought of leaving her children tearing her apart. But she'd never be able to face them—or herself—if she didn't see this thing out with Judge Jack.

"You know I will. Where are you going?"

"New York."

Misunderstanding, Blue's smile was genuine. "With Heath?"
"Not exactly."
"Stevie?" she invited her to continue.
"Judge Jack's alive. Jay and Heath think he's in New York."
"And Heath plans to catch him."
"I suppose."
"And he's going to let you go with him and help?" Blue's voice was incredulous.
"He won't know I'm along."
"You've lost me."
"I figure if I can keep him in sight, I can follow him to New York. Sight unseen. Once I get there, I'll find the rotten bastard." There was no doubt she referred to Judge Jack. "And when I do, I'll kill him." Blue looked as if she would argue. "For Jeff" was all Stevie needed to say.
"What'll you use for money?"
"I still have the five hundred dollars I withdrew from the bank to hire Heath."
"That'll take care of your finances. But what'll you tell your pa?"
"Nothing. Now that we've got the ranch back, he's out scouring the countryside, searching for hired hands. By the time he returns to Adobe Wells, I'll be long gone."
"Pilar will sit on you if you try to leave again."
"She won't know I'm leaving. She rode out to the Boone's with Sully before daybreak. Mrs. Boone's having her baby. By the time Pilar gets back to town, I'll be gone." She continued methodically, telling Blue that she planned to throw her few belongings in a soft-sided valise, find Heath and tell him a final good-bye, then take a carriage to Delgado's after he left town. She would hire a horse when Heath boarded the stage, and follow him to Kansas City. She would catch the same train as he and keep him in sight all the way to New York. She wasn't a complete fool. She knew women didn't travel cross-country alone. With Heath nearby, albeit unaware of her presence, she should be safe.
"Are you going to tell him you're carrying his child?"
Stevie gasped. "How did you know?"
Blue merely smiled. Instead of answering Stevie's question,

she asked one of her own. "Stevie, why can't you trust Heath? As far as I can tell, he's never done anything to deserve your mistrust. And if your problem is that you're Indian . . . well, I heard how the townspeople accepted you at the dance. Why can't you just commit to him, take the train with him, and go to New York as his fiancée?"

Those were excellent questions, questions Stevie had no good answers for.

Just then Winter entered the room, saving her from having to reply. Sympathetic to Stevie's dilemma, Blue left them alone. It was nigh onto impossible for Stevie to tell her child good-bye without breaking down. "I must do this. Judge Jack has insulted our honor and I must make him pay."

Winter tried to be brave. "Please let me go with you, *pia*. I will protect you."

Stevie wrapped him in her arms and sat on the end of the bed. "I know you would. But I need you here, to help Blue with your little sister. Can you do this for me?"

Both mother and child were crying freely now. "I can do this for you," Winter vowed with a raspy whisper. His next question nearly broke her heart. "Will you bring Heath back when you come home? He lives in my heart."

She couldn't make promises regarding Heath, promises that she might not be able to keep. So she hedged, "He lives in my heart as well." Smiling sadly, she brushed Winter's tears away. "We have to go tell him good-bye. You must not tell him that I plan to go along and help him. It might insult his honor."

Winter understood. Sliding to the floor, he took her by the hand and led her to Summer's cradle. With the baby snug in her arms, they went in search of Heath.

Heath stepped inside the foyer as Stevie and the children topped the staircase. They moved slowly toward him. He noticed that both Winter and Stevie had been crying. For a moment he feared that his hard-won equanimity would dissolve and he would embarrass them all.

"We've come to say good-bye," Stevie said more calmly than Heath would have wished.

Heath dropped onto one knee before Winter. With love shining in his sapphire eyes, he touched the child's cheek. "I will miss you."

Winter covered his heart with a small hand. "You will be in here."

Heath wrapped the child in his arms and held him close. "That pleases me," he said against Winter's hair. They held each other, man and boy, for a moment. Heath leaned back and stared down into eyes as black as midnight. "I will come back. You have my word."

Winter nodded tersely before wrenching away and running out the door.

Stevie stood breathlessly still. The guilt of leaving her children warred with the elation that she was not really saying good-bye to Heath. "He'll be all right."

He came to his feet. Smiling off center, he quipped emotionally, "But will I?"

She smiled sweetly. "Yes. You'll be fine."

With a low moan issuing forth from his lips, he wrapped his arms around her and Summer just as he had Winter. Rocking back and forth, he dropped kisses into Stevie's hair. His hand trembled as he stroked the baby's head. "I'm going to miss you so damn much. But I *will* be back. I don't know how long it'll take me, but I will be back." He kissed Stevie almost violently, dropped a kiss on Summer's head, then held Stevie at arm's length. "You promise to wait for me?" Unaware, he shook her shoulders for emphasis.

"If you mean do I promise not to get married while you are in New York, then yes. I promise."

"Promise," he asked again against her lips.

"I promise," she breathed into his mouth.

He held her so tightly, he felt her heart beat. "I love you. You know that. Don't you?" There was an edge of desperation to his voice.

She almost told him that she planned to go along. "I know."

His heart aching, he released her, pushed through the door, mounted his horse, and rode away.

He couldn't bear to look back.

Forty-four

As Heath made his way to the telegraph office, he realized he missed Stevie already. But years of forcing himself to do what lesser men found impossible provided him the wherewithal to leave his heart in a dusty western town. Temporarily.

Stevie bid Blue a hurried farewell, thanking her for watching after the children in her absence. Satisfied that Heath was on his way to Delgado's, she made the short walk to the Silver Dollar and boarded a hired carriage.

A newly married couple sat across from her. The thin young man tapped on the roof of the carriage and the conveyance lurched forward. Stevie leaned out the small square window and watched Adobe Wells until it was a mere speck on the horizon.

The ride to Delgado's was far from comfortable, but Stevie was unaware. She squeezed her eyes shut against the tears and emotions that threatened her composure. One by one she mourned the family members she left behind. Doubts and fears assailed her, but through it all the single thought burning in her mind was that Judge Jack was responsible for her brother's death.

On the backs of her lids she saw her brother Jeff, smiling back at her, mischief shining in his black eyes. She rubbed her closed lids, trying to banish the vision. She had to stop torturing herself like this. He was gone. All she could do now was avenge his death.

But they had never found his body, a hopeful voice reminded her. Shaking her head against that futile hope, hope that would only tear her apart, she whispered good-bye to him in her heart just one more time.

Then she renewed her vow to find Judge Jack and make him pay. If it was the last thing she ever did . . .

As she told Blue, Stevie had thought to hire a horse at Delgado's and ride along behind the stagecoach upon which Heath traveled—at a discreet distance of course. But there were no horses for hire at Delgado's.

She needed to catch a different stage from Heath. There were two stages per day, morning and night. But she couldn't let Heath get too far ahead of her. Traveling alone would be too dangerous. So how was she going to take the same stage without him recognizing her? She couldn't imagine. Tired and disheartened, she took a room for the night.

She spent an almost sleepless night, fearing that the ruffians downstairs would burst through her door at any moment. Or worse, that Heath would discover her presence, discern what she was about.

But the night passed with Heath unaware of her presence . . . and her person mercifully unmolested by strangers. The coach rolled in just before sunrise. She stood at the side of the main building, waiting for Heath to emerge.

She had yet to formulate a plan, when a group of women floated out the front door. Her eyes widened into ebony moons. They were nuns. Apparently, on their way to the outhouse. For some reason, it never occurred to her that nuns used the outhouse.

Shaking herself free of the inane thought, a plan formed in her mind. A quick glance through the swinging doors reassured her that Heath and the other men were still occupied with their breakfasts. She hurried down the path behind the building, close on the sisters' heels.

As good nuns are wont to do, they were waiting their turn single file outside the small wooden building patiently, three outside, one inside. Stevie approached them at a dead run, dressed in her buckskins, her hair tucked beneath a pert Stetson.

Seeing her, the nuns cloistered together for protection, supposing that she was a marauding male with libidinous designs on their chaste persons.

Stevie skidded to a halt, casting a harried glance over her shoulder. "Could I have a word with you?"

The sister Stevie supposed was the head nun spread her hands and addressed her companions en masse. "There's no need for concern, Sisters. It's a girl."

Stevie was insulted. "Well, of course I'm a girl." She tried valiantly to ignore her wounded pride. "And I'm in terrible trouble." She affected her best poor, pitiful, frightened orphan look. "I have to take the stage. But I'm all alone." She dredged up a crocodile tear and silently asked God's forgiveness for manipulating these brides of the church. "I'm scared of all those men."

That set them in motion. As a unit they swarmed over her, clucking and cooing like soothing winged creatures. They all spoke at once.

"Poor dear."

"There, there."

"We'll help you."

Even the sister relieving herself had miraculously appeared at Stevie's side.

Fast talking and fifteen minutes later, the party of four nuns had swelled to five. But none of the men, least of all Heath, noticed the newest addition. Men didn't regard nuns very closely. It was almost as if they feared giving offense by just touching the Lord's vessels with their worldly eyes.

Had they paid scant attention to the fifth nun, a painfully shy child, they would have seen that she was quite small. Her headpiece rode low on her forehead.

Even if they had been inclined to view her closely, the other sisters kept her all but hidden from their sight. Stevie appreciated the nuns' help, but they were almost suffocating her. Everyone aboard would have been scandalized to hear the irreverent oaths the little nun uttered to herself, cursing what she called these infernal holy clothes. A nun's habit might be comfortable if one were born on the sun, she decided. Otherwise, it was damned hot, a tool of torture. Long before she reached Kansas City, she told the good Lord that these kind women deserved his richest rewards if for no other reason than wearing such horrendous uniforms without complaint.

She was not as self-sacrificing, however. When they reached Kansas City, she thanked the women profusely and assured them that she would be quite safe now. She donned her buckskin outfit in the depot outhouse, passed the black wool habit through the door to Sister Mary Christopher, and bid her saviors a muffled farewell.

Once alone, she followed Heath to the Kansas City Hotel. He stood looking cool as a cucumber in the lobby of the elegant building, much to her irritation. From her vantage point behind a large potted palm, she studied her environs and declared the room a thing of beauty. Black marble floors covered with exquisite Oriental rugs. A chandelier overhead sparkled with hundreds of tiny gas jets, casting flirtatious lightning bolts down upon the elegantly clad ladies who perched lightly on the deep wine brocade settees and matching wing chairs.

Unconsciously, she brushed the worst of the dirt from the seat of her trousers as one person in particular caught her eye. He was a middle-aged gent who carried himself as if he were royalty—or at least in the employ of royalty. She decided that he was the cleanest man she had ever seen. From carefully coiffured hair to glossy slippers, he looked like he'd been spit-shined and polished. Totally out of place in the West.

His knee-length frock coat was of the finest cloth, as ebony as Summer's eyes. His blinding-white shirt and elaborately tied neckcloth rested against creamy pale skin that had never been kissed by so much as a ray of sunlight. He glided across the carpeted floor as if he floated on air, heading Heath's way.

When he reached Heath, he bowed at the waist. "Master Heath. May I say, you're looking well." He spoke with a decidedly British accent, just loud enough for Stevie to overhear his greeting.

Heath glanced down at his worn jeans, leather vest, and scuffed boots. He grinned and slapped the man on the back. "If you say so." He didn't dare offer to shake his valet's hand.

Poor Jeevers would die of heart seizure if his employer behaved so familiarly. "It's damn good to see you, Jeevers."

"And you, sir. Dr. Turner received your telegram. I arrived this morning. You'll find everything is in order." The report was crisp, concise, yet not totally impersonal.

"Good man."

Something flickered across Heath's face that Stevie read as anxiety. Her heart warmed.

"My father?"

Jeevers's expression never changed. "General Turner is much improved."

"Really?" Heath could scarcely believe the welcome news.

"Certainly, sir. He told both Drs. Turner that he would make a full recovery. Of course, they did not dispute him."

Heath's face broke into a grin. He uttered something that might have been a curse or a prayer.

"He asked me to convey a message to you, sir."

When Jeevers reddened slightly, Stevie suspected that the show of emotion was unlike him.

He cleared his throat. "He said to tell his wayward son to get his sorry a—" Uncomfortably, he halted and glanced at the ladies milling about them.

"You needn't finish the message, Jeevers. Knowing the general, I can imagine the rest." Heath's grin widened. "I'm hungry as a bear."

"I anticipated your needs, sir. Regretfully, your usual suite was unavailable"—Jeevers sniffed disdainfully—"but I've engaged comparable accommodations. Room 202." He handed Heath the room key. "A bath and a light repast have been ordered."

"Whatever you ordered to eat, double it."

"Very good, sir."

Stevie studied Heath intently. This was a side of him she had not seen. To have a servant anticipating his every whim . . . and to watch him accept . . . no, expect, the fawning attention was disconcerting. It occurred to her then that this was his real life, not the hard existence in the West. Obviously, he had been born with the proverbial silver spoon in his mouth. The difference in their upbringing was even more diverse than she had thought. She felt very sad.

"Heath darling!"

Heath, Jeevers, and Stevie turned toward the enthusiastic voice as if their heads were connected by a string. Bearing down upon Heath was an exquisite creature dressed in emerald-green tulle. Stevie wanted to cut her into little pieces and feed her to Sweetums. Heath just wanted the woman to disappear. Jeevers discreetly moved away.

When Stevie turned back toward Heath, she saw that he was standing stock-still, a strained smile on his face. The beauty walked right up to him and kissed him full on the lips. He pulled away, but not as quickly as Stevie thought he could have.

He held the woman at arm's length. "Christina, what are you doing here?"

Blood coursed through Stevie's ears. She failed to hear the displeasure in Heath's voice.

"I was visiting your mama when Chap sent Jeevers after you. It's been so long . . . I couldn't wait to see you. I thought you might like some company on the trip home."

Stevie almost choked on jealousy and rage. Had Heath really pined for her all the way to Kansas City, all the way to his floozy? One look at the woman wrapping herself around him, and Stevie sincerely doubted Heath ever meant to return to Adobe Wells. Had all those sweet professions of love been a lie? Even what he told Winter? A small voice deep in her heart said that she was being ridiculous. That she should trust Heath. And she almost had her jealousy under control so that she could think rationally when Christina launched herself into Heath's arms again.

Unable to bear more of the touching reunion, she turned to flee. Her boot caught the rim of the planter, upsetting the shiny hunk of brass, dumping dirt, greenery, and herself on the marble floor. The sound reverberating through the room sounded as if the roof were caving in.

Along with everyone else in the lobby, Heath and Christina turned toward the noise. "Stevie," Heath breathed, a myriad of emotions coursing through him: elation, rage, anticipation, confusion, suspicion.

Stevie scrambled to her feet. Just as she tried to burst through the front door, a strong hand circled her arm, pulling her against a chest as hard and wide as a brick wall.

"Let me go!" she snarled.

"Unless you want me to tan your hide in front of all these people, you had best keep your mouth shut and come with me."

Without responding, she allowed Heath to guide her through the lobby, up the carpeted stairs, Christina's irate voice ringing in their ears. When they reached Room 202, he unlocked the door, shoved her into the suite, and slammed the door behind them.

Stevie refused to look in Heath's direction. Instead, her gaze wandered throughout the room. She noted with disgust that the place was fit for a princess.

It was certainly too grand for her—a half-breed hellion who had been raised on a cattle ranch with no one save a rough-cut pa, a Comanche orphan, a half-breed brother, a crotchety old cook, and a host of malcontent and ne'er-do-well cowboys to call family. She engaged in a full thirty seconds of self-pity before she mentally pulled herself up by her bootstraps and turned and faced Heath head-on.

He was leaning against the wide oak door, arms crossed over his chest. He looked as impenetrable as Sherman's front line. "You have some tall explaining to do."

"Drop dead" was all she said.

Forty-five

He noted her courage in the face of discovery. Didn't like it a hell of a lot, but he noted it. Just as he noted her jealousy. He could hardly blame her. If he had seen a man kiss Stevie the way Christina—damn her soul—had kissed him, he would shoot first and ask questions later.

Just the thought of a man kissing Stevie sharpened Heath's voice. "Before we discuss why you're so mad at me, I demand an explanation. Why did you refuse to travel with me, then show up here in Kansas City?" His tone softened. "Dare I hope you changed your mind?"

"You can hope all you want. Far as I know, it's not against the law. But some of us have learned there's not much benefit to it."

Heath winced. The air was thick with her unspoken accusation. She had hoped that he would return for her. It was painfully obvious that due to Christina's untimely arrival, Stevie now considered her hopes for a future with him futile. Guilt warred with indignation. If she had wanted him so badly, all she had to do was accept his invitation to New York. She really had no right to be angry at him about Christina. Just as he was about to reassure her on that score, she pulled a snub-nosed derringer on him.

"Now, get out of my way," she ordered, pointing the patently unimpressive weapon at his chest.

"Take care, sugar." He chuckled, enraging her further. "If

you shoot me with that and I find out about it, I might get mad."

That he would make fun of her made her even angrier. "Move," she spat out through clenched teeth.

He stood there for a moment. "Oh, hell!" With two strides he was in front of her. "Give me that damn thing before you hurt yourself." He grabbed the gun and tossed it on the bed. Wrapping his arms around her, he kissed her hard. At length, she relaxed against him. He raised his head. "Are you going to tell me what you're doing here, or not?"

She stiffened. "I'm on my way to New York."

"Care to tell me why you turned me down, then struck out on your own?" He had a pretty good idea what she was after. It was the same thing she had been after since the first moment they met. Judge Jack. When she remained mute, he prodded her, "You didn't eavesdrop on a conversation between Jay and me, did you?"

She considered confessing all and asking his help. Now that he had discovered her, there was little need for secrecy.

A sharp rap came on the door. Heath crossed over and admitted Jeevers. A string of hotel employees filed into the room behind him, some carrying buckets of hot water, some platters of food. He instructed the water bearers to fill the tub in the other room, the food bearers to set the table in front of a pair of partially open French doors.

"Our train leaves within the hour. Do you want to bathe or eat first?"

Stevie was put off that Heath assumed she was traveling with him. All the while she was pleased that he didn't press her for further explanation.

When she didn't answer, he said, "I have a matter to attend to. Feel free to use the bath. We can eat when I return."

Stevie knew good and well the matter had to do with Christina. Indignant, she turned on her heel and disappeared into the other room.

Refreshed and replete, Stevie still not speaking, they piled into a carriage shortly before sunset for the ride to the depot.

When they arrived, it took conscious effort for Stevie not to gape at the spectacle before her. The sight was even more awe-inspiring—and intimidating—than the elegant hotel.

What a country bumpkin she was! She had never seen such a mass of people. It seemed as though everyone west of the Mississippi were catching the train to St. Louis. Despite her pique, she stepped closer to Heath's side as he made his way through the crowd with ease, guiding her the length of the train, arriving finally at the most exquisite Pullman rail car Kansas City had ever seen.

Stevie lost the fight for nonchalance then. There was no way she could appear unimpressed when they broke through the crowd ringing the exquisite mode of travel. "It's beautiful," she breathed, her first word to Heath in an hour.

"Wonder whose it is?" a heavyset woman behind them asked her pencil-thin husband.

Stevie wondered the same. Pictures of European royalty dining inside flashed upon the stained glass windows in her mind. A richly clad lady smiling across a candlelit table at her lover was another of her fanciful musings.

She was drawn to the car by her whimsical flights of fantasy. That's when she noticed the ornate gilt initials painted on the side of the car. H.H.T. She jerked her head in Heath's direction. Surely not.

Jeevers directed the carriage driver to load their luggage inside the Pullman, keeping his own luggage by his side.

Stevie stared at Heath's profile, wide-eyed. She felt a sense of betrayal. The hotel and Jeevers were one thing, but this . . .

She had known that he was well-to-do; financially comfortable was the way he had explained his family's economic status. But he must be a flaming millionaire to own a rail car such as this. Once again the impossibility of their union loomed in her mind, large and threatening. In one instant of painful honesty she had to admit that she was afraid.

Afraid? She was terrified. She had faced a striking rattler with nothing more than a garden hoe for defense and not felt the depth of fear that was clawing at her now. This was too much. She was out of her element, in over her head. Mentally, she searched for further clichés even as she entertained the notion of running as far and as fast as her fancy tooled boots would carry her.

Just as she would have made her cowardly getaway, Heath's unborn child chose that moment to keep her rooted in place. A twenty-foot tidal wave of nausea flowed over her, drenching her in misery from top to bottom. "Ohhh," she moaned as the sky above her head and the platform beneath her feet changed places. She bent at the waist and fought desperately for breath.

She was about to faint for the first time in her life. She would probably be trampled by the masses gawking at the evidence of Heath's wealth. Her panic rose to the degree that her consciousness wavered. She moaned.

"Honey?" Wheeling toward her, Heath wrapped his arms around her. She lost consciousness and he lifted her high against his chest. Beset by worry, he carried her aboard.

Forty-six

Stevie's first impression was that heaven was made of brocaded satin, polished wood, shiny brass, and pastel pink light.

Her second was that paradise rocked back and forth. She would have to speak to His host of angels about that. Continual motion was not heavenly in her estimation. Not when a gal suffered the evils of morning sickness.

She struggled upright, only to be assaulted by another wave of nausea. This was not heaven. Hell maybe, but not heaven.

Alerted by her sound of distress, Heath crossed the Pullman and knelt at her side. "Honey?" Replacing the cool cloth on her brow, he kissed her cheek lightly. "How do you feel?"

"Sick to my stomach." She wanted to bite back the words as soon as they slipped past her lips. The last thing she wanted Heath to know was that she was pregnant.

His brow furrowed. "Was it something you ate at the hotel?" Not giving her time to answer, he continued. "We've already left Kansas City. But I'll have the conductor unhitch us in St. Louis. I know a doctor there. He studied with Chap and Rad."

Stevie opened one eye. She was concerned by the worry and fatigue clouding Heath's visage. "No. I'm all right. We'll go on to New York."

He wanted to disagree; she could see that. But he also wanted to hurry to his father's side. "I'm fine, really."

"Why did you faint?"

She tried to sit again. This time she noticed that she was

naked beneath the sheet. Clutching the sheet to her chest, she demanded, "Where are my clothes?"

"Gone."

She looked as if she would do him physical harm.

He arched his eyebrows twice and gave her a seductive grin He had discarded his vest, pulled his white shirt from the waistband of his jeans, and unbuttoned the shirt hallway down his chest. He was bootless, sockless, and looked like he had been through hell. But sexy and gorgeous just the same.

She experienced the desire only he could call forth. Looking away, she tamped down the inclination to throw her arms around him. "By the way," she began dryly, "what did you do with Christina?"

"That depends on when you're talking about," he teased unmercifully.

"Never mind. I don't want to know." She groaned and fell back to the bed.

He frowned again. "Are you sure you can wait till New York to see a doctor, sugar?"

Alarm bells clanged in Stevie's head. "I didn't say I'd see a doctor in New York."

He affected a look that was very like Pepper's favorite jackass. "You're not going to see a doctor. You're going to see two doctors. My brothers."

She narrowed her eyes. "Okay. If you say so, I'll see them."

He was suspicious of her capitulation, given the mulish look in her eyes.

"But I don't intend to let them see me. Professionally, that is."

Just as he would argue with her, she declared that she was about to be sick. He wrapped the sheet around her and carried her from the sitting room, through the bedroom, into the bathing area. It held a white porcelain hip bath, chamber pot, and basin. It was the warmest area of the car, too warm given her present condition.

She allowed him to hold her head while she paid homage to the porcelain pot. Mentally, she cursed every male with the equipment to get a woman in the family way.

"Are you comfortable on the lounging sofa, or do you want me to put you to bed?" His smile could only be called a leer.

"The sofa." Wide-eyed innocence, she added, "It's perfect for one."

Heath might have told her that two could lie on it quite nicely. But she would undoubtedly ask how he had come about that knowledge. And since gentlemen didn't kiss and tell . . . and she was undoubtedly still smarting about Christina, he decided to keep that information to himself. Smiling mysteriously, he carried her back to the sofa.

"What will Jeevers think if we share this car all the way to New York? I don't want him to think I'm just another of your Christinas."

"He won't. I told him you're my wife."

She frowned. "And what do you intend to tell him when we reach your home and he finds out the truth?"

He ignored her question. "I'll think of something. Until then, we're sharing this car and I'm going to take care of you. So you may as well accept the inevitable and save your energy."

Her frown grew in size and intensity. How would she keep her pregnancy a secret from Heath if they were cooped up in such close quarters day and night? "I don't need a nursemaid . . ." she began. "I can hire a berth in another part of the train and take care of myself." As if to dispute her bold claim, she turned a curious shade of green.

"Can you make it to the bath this time?"

Lips clamped together, she shook her head, no.

He dove for the shiny brass spittoon across the room and thrust it beneath her face just in time.

The contents of her stomach made a hasty exit. She was desperately ill, terribly confused, and terminally embarrassed, but still in possession of a wry sense of humor. "You sure you wanta share this car with me?"

Heath failed to appreciate the jest. "You're not leaving my sight until I turn you over to Rad and Chap."

She wanted to disagree, but was too busy being sick to argue.

* * *

Stevie confided in the maid who cleaned their rooms that she was pregnant and wanted to keep it a secret from her "husband." The kind woman smuggled her an ample supply of salty crackers and instructed her to eat several upon awakening, before raising her head off the pillow.

After the first morning, Stevie was quite convinced the woman was brilliant. The crackers worked wonders, temporarily. She was able to make it all the way to the privacy of the bathing area before retching her insides out.

With Heath none the wiser.

Sitting in the dining area, perusing the morning paper, Heath took a sip of lukewarm coffee.

"More coffee, sir?" the oversolicitous waiter at his elbow asked.

Heath replaced his china cup in the saucer and nodded. He sighed, marveling at how easily he fell back into the role of wealthy gentleman. Turning his head to the side, he caught his reflection in the window. An ebony-haired, sapphire-blue-eyed gunslick smiled back at him. Dressed in jeans, shirt, vest, and boots, his Colt tied to his muscular thigh beneath the table, he looked anything but an aristocratic gentleman. But he would be dressed fit for a morning at his exclusive gentlemen's club when they disembarked in New York. His mother would be scandalized otherwise.

He couldn't help but wonder what Stevie would think of him, all decked out like a Wall Street banker. His smile widened at the notion. As if his thoughts summoned her, she approached. He stood and seated her. His smile disappeared.

"What's wrong?" she asked.

"I don't like the way you look."

Hormones on the rampage, Stevie drew herself up as if she were insulted. "I'm sorry you don't like my clothes." In her men's attire, she had been stared at ever since they boarded the train. It was beginning to wear on her nerves. "I'm getting good and damn tired of being gawked at. You'd think these people have never seen a woman in breeches before."

He hadn't been talking about her clothes, but her tirade distracted him. "They probably haven't. It's against the law, you know."

"What's against the law?"

"For a lady to dress in men's clothes."

"You're making that up."

He laid his hand over his heart, covering his U.S. marshal's star. "Swear to God. It's a misdemeanor."

"You mean you could arrest me for what I'm wearing."

"Technically, yes."

Unease settled on her face.

"Don't worry, hon. When we reach New York tomorrow, I'll have Ann outfit you first thing with one of her frocks." He shook his head when she began to rebut. "But I wasn't referring to your clothes, and I suspect you know it. I was talking about your skin color."

Eyes wide, she tossed her head back and opened her mouth to speak.

He seamed her lips with his fingertips. "Don't even think of turning that remark into a racial slur. I declare, you're as ill as a sore-tailed cat. I hardly know what to say to you anymore." Like most men when confronted with an emotional, irrational female, he was totally at a loss, and utterly bewildered.

Stevie was properly chastised. She knew her emotions were running amuck these days, that it took next to nothing to reduce her to tears . . . or anger. She snapped like an irascible turtle with little or no provocation. "I'm sorry."

"There's no need to apologize, sugar. I'm just worried about you. You don't look well. You have no color whatever in your cheeks."

"I'm all right." She had told him as much a dozen times since leaving Kansas City. "Really." Her voice quivered and she cursed her missishness.

He reached across the table and covered her hand. "Poor baby."

A month ago she would have considered the endearment condescending and put a few holes in his hide. But now it touched her. She had become a stranger to herself. Of late, she was unsettled, emotional, unreliable. How was she to get the best of Judge Jack if she couldn't control herself any better than this? Breathing deeply, she looked out the window, pretending to study the countryside rushing past at a rapid twenty-five-mile-an-hour clip.

Heath released her hand as the waiter approached.

"Madam. May I serve you?"

She didn't even turn around. "Tea and dry toast."

"Sir?"

"I'll have a tall stack of flapjacks, three eggs, biscuits, buttered toast and orange marmalade, oatmeal, sausage, and bacon. And bring us both some orange juice," Heath ordered his usual breakfast automatically.

Once they were alone, Heath covered her hand again. "Sweetheart, you haven't eaten enough to keep a bird alive on this trip."

She met his eyes then. "I guess I'm just nervous about meeting your family."

He nodded, appearing unsettled by her response. An uneasy quiet settled over them until they were served.

"Thank you," Stevie said weakly, not touching the meager meal before her.

Heath studied her surreptitiously. Instead of diving into his hefty breakfast, he pushed back in his chair.

Stevie raised her gaze and discovered him watching her intensely. She paled. He knew about the baby. She was convinced of it. Dear Lord, what should she do, confess? She still couldn't accept his marriage proposal. Though their love was undeniable, his wealth made her feel as if they were further apart than ever. She needed more time; she just wasn't ready for a lifelong commitment.

But Heath would never give up his child. She knew that as surely as the sun rose and set.

"About my family . . ." he began at length.

Stevie almost collapsed with relief. "What about your family?"

"I feel that I should warn . . . I mean, explain to you about my mother."

Stevie's brow furrowed. "What about her?"

"She's . . . she's different."

"And I'm not?" She tried to shrug his concern off.

He searched for words to describe India Turner, words that wouldn't frighten Stevie and send her back to Adobe Wells on the first train traveling west. "Mother's very straight-laced. Some would say intolerant. If she disapproves of a person, she doesn't take great pains to hide the fact. And far as I know, there aren't many people she deems . . . suitable."

"And you think she won't find me suitable?"

Heath raised his gaze. "Frankly, sweetheart, I doubt it."

Stevie was surprised. She had been certain that he would lie. That he would reassure her, tell her that his mother would love her, or at least tolerate her.

She wanted to defend herself, persuade him that old people—red and white—usually found her quite worthy of their esteem. The elderly, babies, and animals, they all liked her. Pa said that was to her credit. You couldn't fool old people, babies, and animals. If they liked you, your good character was unquestionable. And they did. They liked her. Old people, babies, and . . .

Heath broke into her silent ravings. "But you must not take anything she says or does personally"—he paused—"you can't imagine how awful she was to Kinsey, Chap's wife."

"Your mother doesn't like your sister-in-law?"

"Actually, she doesn't like either of them."

"Whyever not?"

"They're Southerners."

Her expression was blank. "And?"

"Mother has very strong feelings about class and geographical distinction."

"And equally strong feelings about the kind of women who are good enough for her sons?"

Acknowledging her insight, he nodded. "But it really doesn't matter what she thinks. It certainly didn't to Rad and Chap. All that mattered to them was that they loved Kinsey and Ginny." His voice softened. "As I love you."

She closed her eyes momentarily. How could she fight his mother and her own feelings of insecurity at the same time? And were there other Christinas she would have to deal with? She pushed the unpleasant thought aside. "What about the rest of your family? Will they hate me too?" The emotions she was trying so desperately to hide were evident in her husky tones.

"Absolutely not. And, honey, Mother won't hate you. Precisely."

"Precisely?"

"I'm not explaining this very well. You've got to understand how mother was raised. Strictly. By an English nanny. You can't imagine some of the notions the woman instilled in her."

Her open expression invited him to continue.

He searched his mind for pertinent examples. "Silly things really. Like one must not place books written by male authors and those by female authors on the same shelf in the library."

Stevie appeared stunned, then burst out laughing. "You're just making that up."

"I'm not. I swear. That's not even the strangest rule of propriety that Mother and her cronies cling to." He had been living in the West so long, it was hard to remember the rules of society that had once been as natural to him as breathing. Before long it all came rushing back. "She won't let us back up to a fire and warm our . . . well, you get the picture."

"Warming your cold butt's not proper?" Stevie asked irreverently.

"Heavens no. And a lady"—the way he emphasized "lady" made her squirm—"never says *butt.* In fact, a lady doesn't say many seemingly innocent words in mixed company. Such as *stomach.* And one would never utter such personal words as *shirt, trousers, breeches.* They're called *inexpressibles.*" Heath was warming to his subject. "And one never reports that they're going to bed." He leaned closer and lowered his voice. "Too sexual. One retires. That's proper."

Speaking of bed, Stevie regarded him with a mixture of longing and incredulity. A slow smile spread across her face. "I can hardly believe that you're her son."

Heath felt as if Stevie had just complimented his masculinity. He sat a bit straighter in his chair. "Thank you."

"You're welcome." A mischievous light brightened her eyes. "Don't suppose I should request son-of-a-bitch stew for supper."

"Not unless you want Mother to faint."

"That might be worth remembering," she mumbled to herself.

"Actually, there are any number of foods she considers improper. Apples, artichokes, chestnuts, chocolate, garlic, leeks, dates. The list goes on and on."

Stevie was clearly thunderstruck. "What on earth is wrong with them?" She was strangely fascinated with this world of propriety of which she was sadly ignorant.

"They incite lust, make one virile."

"How did you get so big?" she blurted out.

Heath almost choked on his coffee. "Excuse me?"

"I'm not talking about that!" She colored becomingly. "I mean, how did you grow so big if there were so many foods she wouldn't allow you to eat?"

"Oh, we ate them." He winked at her. "The general insisted that his sons be given double portions." His smile dimmed. "Mother abstained, of course. And she forbade my sisters to partake of such foods . . . as long as they were respectable, asexual females."

"I shudder to ask. But what's a respectable, asexual female?"

"A fancy word for a virgin."

She widened her eyes, looking as innocent as a downy-faced tot. Then for Heath's ears only, she whispered, "Thanks to you, that leaves me out."

"Mmmm. It sure does."

Sexual sparks shot between them, sufficient to ignite the white linen cloth covering the table. The fact that they were in a public place dawned on them at the same time.

Stevie cleared her throat. When she spoke, her voice was noticeably thick, however. "It might be educational meeting a person like your mother."

"That's one way to put it."

"As long as I refrain from warming my butt by the fire, swilling hot chocolate, and eating artichokes and chestnuts."

They chuckled together. He lifted her hand to his lips and brushed it lightly with his kiss. His stomach growled loudly. Having the matter of his mother behind them, he attacked his breakfast. When the delicate china plates were empty and he was full, he noticed that Stevie had yet to touch her toast. "Honey, aren't you hungry?"

She was silent for a moment, pleating the tablecloth with her fingers. "How does your mother feel about Indians?"

There was no need for him to answer. His strained expression said it all. "Actually, I doubt she's ever seen one," he hedged finally.

Mentally, she winced, then shrugged as if she were unaffected. "Well, she's about to come face-to-face with one."

"And a very beautiful one at that."

It was their last night alone in the rail car. The curtains had been lowered for privacy, the Tiffany lamps lit. The rosy glow of the compartment lent their close environment a romantic quality that was apparent to both Heath and Stevie.

Heath reclined on a tufted sofa, smiling at the picture she presented in her black leather breeches peeking from under one of his soft blue shirts. The shirt came to her knees, the shoulder seams rode her elbows, and she looked so damn sexy that he reconsidered asking Ann to provide her with a dress.

She turned to him abruptly and caught the unguarded desire in his eyes. Her smile was almost shy.

He patted the sofa upon which he sat. "Come sit with me."

His invitation was unmistakable, but Stevie was not looking for romance. Yet. Today was the day for heart-to-heart talks. First Heath's disclosure of his difficult mother. Now Stevie had something of import to discuss with him.

Slowly, very slowly, she closed the distance between them. She halted in front of him, their knees almost touching. He took her hands and drew her between his legs.

He noticed her reticence. "What's wrong, sugar?"

She was silent for a moment. When she looked him full in the face, she exhaled. "Since that first day in Kansas City, you haven't asked me why I'm here."

His expression never changed. His only movement was the circular caress of his thumbs against her knuckles. "I figured when you were ready, you would tell me."

They both spoke quietly, almost reverently.

"You want me to be honest?"

He nodded.

"Revenge." She could see that she surprised him with her frankness.

Though he suspected as much, her response was less than flattering. "Against whom? As if I didn't know."

"Judge Jack."

"So, you *did* overhear Jay and me talking about the judge going to New York." He released her, rubbing his palms on his thighs.

She sat at his side. "I've made no secret of my plans regarding the judge since the first day we met. But—"

He cut her off. "That's true." His bitter laugh skittered down her spine. He couldn't look at her. "You want to hear a joke? I actually convinced myself that you were coming along because you couldn't bear to be away from me."

When he did turn his gaze on her, she wished desperately that he hadn't. Pain mixed with accusation dulled his sapphire orbs.

"You should have been honest with me from the first, Stevie." He surged to his feet. Crossing over to the bar, he sloshed fine Kentucky bourbon into a crystal glass. "And not let me think you cared for me as I care for you."

Stevie rushed to his side. She grabbed his arm. "You know I have feelings for you."

He wanted to shake her off. But instead he turned and looked down at her. "Do you? Then why do you continue to refuse my proposal of marriage?" His words were harsh, almost a challenge.

Tears filled her eyes. "Don't you know how much I *want* to accept?"

"No, I can't say that I do."

She breathed deeply, as if a band tightened around her chest. "Well, I do. But I can't. Not yet."

He turned back to the bar.

"I wish I could make you understand."

She watched with admiration as he forcibly regained a measure of his control. He placed his glass on the bar, then took her hand and led her back to the sofa. "Give it a shot," he said softly.

She took a deep breath, gathering the scattered bits of her

thoughts and feelings into a manageable whole. "I know it doesn't matter to you that I'm an Indian. And I"—she paused, clearing the emotion from her throat—"I love you for that."

His hand tightened on hers.

"But you have to know that you're unusual. Your family probably won't accept me as you do. It's for sure that white society doesn't."

"You've told me all this before. And again, all that matters to me is being with you."

"I know I've told you." She surged to her feet. Pacing before him, she shoved the shirtsleeves above her elbows with frustration. "But you haven't listened!" She wheeled around, knelt before him, and cradled his face with trembling hands. "My whole life I've held myself aloof from outsiders. I haven't allowed myself to love anyone, not any man, anyway. Certainly not a white man." She grasped his hands in both of hers and held them to her breast. "But I love you, Heath! I do. With all my heart. And I couldn't live with myself if by marrying you I caused anyone to think less of you."

"What others think doesn't matter to me, sweetheart."

"How do you know? How can you possibly know it doesn't matter?" She stood. "Have you been shunned, laughed at, spat upon, considered less than human simply because of your ancestry?"

He joined her. "Of course not . . ."

"Well, if you marry me and take two Indian children to raise, you will." She dared not pause and give him entry to disagree. "Have you given any thought to our children, the ones who will be born of our union?" She tapped his chest with her finger. "Your sons and daughters, Heath. Boys and girls who will be more white than Indian? How do you think they'll feel, always having to defend their Comanche mother and brother and sister?"

Her eyes burned with conviction; her heart ached from a lifetime of prejudice. "And there's no doubt in my mind that any children of yours will defend their family." She smiled sadly at him, obviously proud of the man she loved. "How will you feel when those innocent children come home with black eyes and bloody noses? Will you love me and Winter and Summer as much then? Or will you regret marrying some little half-breed that you stumbled over on the edge of nowhere?"

He grabbed her, holding her against him fiercely. "Don't you dare talk about yourself that way." He suspected that their conversation regarding his mother brought this on, at least in part. Having told her about India, how could he convince her that her fears were groundless? He had to try.

"Honey, you could never, ever be some little half-breed to me. You're the other half of my heart. And the notion that I would blame you, Winter, or Summer for the actions of bigots is ludicrous. You really hurt me, babe. That you don't have any more faith in me than that."

Stevie clung to him with all her strength. Burying her face in her neck, she groaned, "It's not you I don't trust. It's me."

He leaned back and stared down into her face.

She spoke before he could respond. "I can't explain it. Let's not talk anymore. Not now. Please. Just make love to me."

Groaning, he swept her up in his arms and carried her over to their bed. Later, he would find the words to convince her that he could not bear a future without her. For now he would do as she asked. Love her physically. All night long. Fortifying them both for the uncertainty that tomorrow would bring.

Forty-seven

The morning they arrived in New York, Stevie was having a good day, pregnancy speaking. After munching three crackers, she crawled off the end of the bed and pressed her cheek against the cool post. She stood perfectly still, expecting the morning sickness viper to rear its ugly head. When it didn't, she whispered a prayer of thanksgiving and crossed to Heath's side of the bed. Silently, she watched him as he slumbered.

She pulled a light sheet up over his naked torso. Her waist-length hair slipped over her shoulder, brushing his cheek like a lover's caress.

He smiled in his sleep, but didn't appear to awaken. She tucked her hair behind her shoulder, bent to kiss his parted lips lightly, and whispered against them, "I love you."

She straightened and stood above him for a moment. Her heart swelled with love. He seemed so young lying there, so incredibly vulnerable in his sleep. How could she bring pain into his life? But how could she bear losing him?

As she stared at him, she massaged her naked abdomen absently. She hoped that the baby she carried would grow up to resemble his father . . . more important, that he would grow up to *be* like him, fine, honorable, strong, gentle, and above all, loving.

After last night there was no denying that she and Heath were desperately in love. So why couldn't she commit her life to him? She wanted to, oh, how she wanted to. But just when she teetered on the brink of final capitulation, paralysis struck. She just couldn't take the final step. Her throat thick with emotion, she eased away from the bed.

Lack of self-esteem. It had become her defense against the world. If one didn't think highly of oneself, nothing much could be required of them. It was high time she gathered her courage and shook off the bonds of the insecure. Otherwise, she would lose the most important person in her life.

On silent feet she walked to the window and brushed the drapes aside. Dawn rose in the sky like a glorious rebirth, painting her naked form a glowing pink. She was surrounded by all things new and exciting, yet terribly frightening. The most frightening, however, was the prospect of life without Heath. Dare she risk hurt, put her own desires above all else and yoke herself legally to the man she had already joined with physically and emotionally?

"Yes," she whispered from the depths of her soul.

Committing to Heath would be the height of selfishness even if it demanded personal courage, her conscience warned again. Such a monumental decision would affect the innocent for generations. Heath's descendants from now till the end of time would have Indian blood flowing through their veins, and the stigma associated with it.

Her hands tightened on the draperies she held aside. Was her Indian ancestry so bad? No, she proclaimed vehemently. Unconsciously, she straightened her bare shoulders. Could they teach their children—and perhaps society along the way—about the Comanche's proud heritage?

She smiled wryly. As a matter of fact, the American Indians were the first inhabitants of this country. The cream of New York society were the interlopers. She bet that tidbit would shock Mrs. Turner smack dab out of her prim, proper inexpressibles.

Suddenly, the future didn't look so forbidding after all. She wanted Heath and she would fight the entire human race for him. Muffling a giggle, she reminded herself that the Comanche had been fighting the White Eyes for generations. Starting today, she would mount a campaign that made the efforts of the proud war chiefs of yesteryear look tame.

She needed to look her best. For the first time in almost

eleven years, she wished she had a dress to wear. She considered wearing Swan's wedding gown, but decided against it. Arriving dressed like an Indian maiden might prejudice Heath's family against her. Not good strategy, she decided.

So she pulled on her black leather outfit. The one she had worn the first day she met Heath.

Instead of wearing the Stetson, she decided to do something special with her hair. Taking a seat at the vanity, she plaited her silken tresses, then wound the glistening braid in a coronet at the back of her head. She secured it with a few precious hairpins. With a fingernail she loosened wayward platinum curls at the nape and temples, softening the hairstyle fashionably.

A white lily had miraculously appeared on the vanity that morning. She attached it to the side of the coronet, lending the coiffure an overall effect of elegant simplicity. Pleased with her appearance, despite her manly attire, she tiptoed past Heath and headed for the dining car.

"Good morning, madam." Jeevers bowed gallantly as he passed her in the hallway.

"Good morning." She and Heath had seen little of the manservant on the trip. But they had seen evidence of his presence almost continuously.

Whenever they were hungry and didn't care to go to the dining car, trays overflowing with all manner of food would arrive magically, many of Heath's favorite aphrodisiacs included. When they wanted a bath, servants would appear with buckets of hot water without being summoned, day or night.

It was as if the man were their fairy godfather, on duty twenty-four hours a day, but invisible. This morning, however, he was making an appearance in the flesh.

"Mr. Turner's still asleep." Stevie expected Jeevers to change course and leave Heath to his rest.

"Very good, madam." He continued on, heading for the private car.

She stood arrested in the hallway, mouth agape.

"Is he going to dress him?" she asked the empty hallway. She had read sufficient romantic novels to know the goings-on between valets and their lords. And Heath and Jeevers qualified as such in her mind. They might have been servant and peer of the realm for all of their aristocratic splendor.

"I can't imagine anyone dressing Heath." Undressing him, yes. Despite her bawdy thought, she affected a haughty, disdainful expression. "Surely he can find his way into his inexpressibles by himself."

She chuckled all the way to the dining car. Nausea-free, she enjoyed a normal breakfast for the first time in days. When she consumed the last morsel, the train pulled into Grand Central Station.

Butterflies the size of steamships fluttered in her stomach, making her regret the hearty repast. Her confidence and determination wavered. Like a condemned horse thief marching to the gallows, she made her way back toward the rail car.

The tall, handsome man coming toward her stopped her dead in his tracks. Her first thought was that he was beautiful! Not just his clothes, but the man himself.

Though he *was* dressed exquisitely! His cutaway coat was single-breasted, mid-thigh in length. It was made of a deep sapphire-blue linen, hugging the contours of his muscular torso, matching his eyes to perfection. Underneath, he wore a double-breasted vest of linen pique, also sapphire in color, with pale yellow stripes for detail. His lemon silk ascot was fastened around his wide neck by no less than a diamond stickpin. A yellow handkerchief peeked out of his breast pocket flirtatiously. His trousers were of the same rich material as the cutaway. They fit his waist like a second skin. The buttoned fly bulged, unable to disguise his virility. The tubular pant legs had no cuffs or creases. On a lesser man they would have appeared loose, undoubtedly quite proper. But on Heath they skimmed thighs made enormous by hugging the sides of a galloping stallion.

Heath tried not to fidget under Stevie's unwavering perusal as she raked him from head to toe, missing nothing in between. He tucked his ebony walking stick beneath his arm and nervously withdrew a pair of yellow chamois gloves from his deep blue top hat. Characteristically, he ran his fingers through his hair, then set the impressive-looking headgear firmly in place. He forced a disarming smile. "What's wrong? Have I got shaving soap on my face? Tooth powder on my lips? Are my trousers . . . my inexpressibles on backward?"

"Who are you?" she croaked.

"I'm the same man you covered with a sheet this morning." His eyes darkened with desire. "The same man you kissed." He stepped closer. "The same man whose heart nearly burst at your confession of love." His voice deepened. "The same man who made love to you most of the night." He spread his arms to his sides. "This is just window dressing, sweetheart. Just fabric and thread. It doesn't change what's on the inside."

She wasn't quite convinced.

"Master Heath." Jeevers spoke from behind Heath.

"Master?" she mouthed. In her estimation, the title fit.

Heath responded to Jeevers, smiling down at Stevie. "Yes?"

"Dr. and Mrs. Turner are waiting on the platform beside the rail car."

"Please tell them we'll be right along."

"Very good, sir."

Once they were alone, Heath donned his gloves and cradled Stevie's chin in his palm. The look in her eyes was quite like that of a rabbit he had found snared in a trap when he was just a boy. "You're really afraid, aren't you?"

"No."

"Liar." His soft accusation failed to elicit the smile he sought. "Where's the hellion who took shots at me from Mustang Mesa?"

"I think you left her west of the Pecos." Her voice sounded very small.

He hugged her warmly, affectionately, not with the heated passion that they had shared in the night. He spoke into her hair. "Don't worry, hon. Everything'll be all right. You'll see."

"Will it?" Silently, she cursed the quiver in her voice.

Chivalrously, he offered her his arm. "I swear. Just trust me, sugar."

Renewing her earlier vow to fight for the man she loved, she placed her hand firmly in the crook of his arm.

Together, they exited the train.

Forty-eight

The gathering on the platform did little to ease Stevie's sense of insecurity. If Heath looked well-to-do, the couple awaiting them looked downright wealthy.

She would have known Dr. Turner anywhere. His resemblance to Heath was undeniable. He was slightly older than Heath and almost as handsome. But not quite, in her besotted estimation.

His hair was blond, unlike Heath's black tresses. And it rested on shoulders that were extremely broad for a doctor—extremely broad for anyone. Like Heath, his brother was built like a brick wall.

She didn't know whether the man staring at her with a friendly smile on his face was Rad or Chap. Heath had told her that no one—except their wives—could tell the twins apart. But the appropriate sister-in-law standing very close to her husband's side obviously tipped Heath off.

"It's Kinsey and Chap," he informed her, unable to contain his excitement. His voice was husky when he whispered the single word "Chap." The brothers embraced unashamedly. It wasn't the quick hug, that Stevie expected from two such manly creatures. They held on to each other tightly, as if they were reluctant to let go. Obviously, they couldn't care less that they were in public.

When Heath released his brother, he turned immediately to the tiny woman standing at Chap's side. Kinsey Turner was perhaps the most beautiful woman Stevie had ever seen; less than five feet tall, one hundred pounds of delicate female, rich mahogany hair, big emerald eyes, and a compact, curvaceous figure that the rest of the female species would gladly kill for.

And the tears in her eyes made it obvious that she loved Heath dearly.

His strong feelings for her were equally evident when he enveloped her in his strong arms. Actually, he held her closer and longer than Stevie thought necessary, but Chap didn't seem unduly concerned.

What Stevie didn't know was that Kinsey, the infamous Vixen in Gray, had saved Heath's life during the war. The small, frilly package of courage that he cradled close to his heart had broken him out of a Confederate prison at great risk to her own personal safety . . . not to mention going against her people—fellow Southerners like herself who were zealous believers in the Glorious Cause.

Kinsey's emotion overflowed as she pulled away. Heath touched her cheek and brushed away a tear. He glanced down at her exquisite silver gray watered silk gown. "Still wearing gray, I see."

"Kinsey's convinced the South will rise again," Chap put in, circling his wife's wasplike waist with his arm and pulling her back to his side.

Though the love between Chap and his wife was apparent, she elbowed him in the ribs with a good deal of force. "It would rise if we could get rid of you damn Yankees." Without missing a beat she turned on the man she had just squeezed to within an inch of his life. "Harrington Heath Turner, I swear and declare you have the manners of a warthog." She popped his chest with her reticule. "Are you going to introduce your friend, or not?"

Her heavy drawl oozed like thick molasses in January, quite unlike the western twang to which Stevie's ears were accustomed. Drawn to Kinsey instinctively, Stevie presented the southern belle her hand. She doubted gently reared ladies shook hands, but it was too late. "I'm Stevie Johns, Mrs. Turner."

Kinsey didn't seem to be offended in the least as she accepted Stevie's hand, then covered it with both of her own. "I'm pleased to meet you, Stevie. But you mustn't call me Mrs. Turner. When we're up north, Ginny and I reserve that exhalted title for our mother-in-law." She actually rolled her eyes heavenward.

Chap smiled at his incorrigible wife.

"You must call me Kinsey."

Introductions complete, Heath asked the question that he could put off no longer. "How's the general?"

Before their very eyes, Chap turned into the professional picture of a physician. His dimples disappeared, and, if possible, he stood even taller. "He's greatly improved, I'm pleased to report. But if he were to suffer a setback . . ." He trailed off, looking about, locating the Turner carriages. "Rad's with him now. But I'd like to hurry back." He squeezed his baby brother's shoulder. "Everyone's eager to see you." Taking his wife's arm, he turned. "The carriages are this way."

Kinsey fell into place beside her husband, Stevie and Heath close on their heels. Stevie couldn't help but feel ill at ease. Everyone they passed nodded respectfully to the elegantly attired couple ahead of them. Then, when she and Heath drew alongside them, they looked at him with the respect wealth demands. As for her, they just gaped.

Heath saw the unguarded desire in the men's eyes as they took in Stevie's incredible beauty, skimming her with their gaze, lingering on her snugly clad derriere. He glared at them and reminded himself to purchase a suitable wardrobe for her posthaste. That firm little derriere belonged to him, and it wasn't for public view.

All Stevie noted was the disdainful way the fashionably clad ladies regarded her. Though she felt uncomfortable under their scrutiny, she was determined to hide it. She carried herself as if she were Queen Victoria decked out in royal splendor.

When they reached the carriage, Kinsey was already inside.

"May I?" Chap held his hand out to Stevie.

Heath dipped his head and placed a chaste kiss on her cheek. "Chap, I forgot to instruct Jeevers. Would you accompany me?"

Chap lifted Stevie aboard. "Certainly. We'll be right back, hon," he told Kinsey.

Once they were out of earshot of the ladies, Chap broke the silence. "This must be serious. I've never seen you kiss a woman like that." He grinned over at his brother. "Such a proper gentleman." He shook his head in astonishment. "Even Mother would be impressed."

Heath stepped inside the depot and turned toward Chap. "I have my doubts that anything about Stevie would impress Mother. But you're right. This is serious. I plan to make the lady my wife."

Chap realized then that Heath did not want to tell Jeevers anything. He wanted to talk to him, away from Stevie. Though she had platinum hair, Chap doubted her dark skin was the result of the hot sun of New Mexico. With those cheekbones and slightly tilted eyes, her Indian ancestry was unmistakable.

Heath read his brother's expression, if not his mind. "That's right. Stevie's part Comanche. And nobody better say one damn word against her."

Chap was astonished. His devil-may-care brother had found someone to care for, someone to fight for. Well, it was about time Heath settled down, he reckoned. Maybe if he and the lovely Miss Johns married, they would live east of the Mississippi, where they would be safe. He sure as hell hoped so. "Whoa, brother. I'm not the enemy."

Heath had the grace to appear chagrined. "Sorry. It's just that she's sure the family will send her packing without giving us a chance." Before Chap could offer assurance, Heath addressed the real reason he had detained him. "I want you and Rad to examine her first thing. She's been sick ever since we left Kansas City."

Chap frowned. "Symptoms?"

"Vomiting, fatigue, irritability. She's hardly eaten enough to keep a sparrow alive. And she seems close to tears most of the time. It's a complete reversal of the woman I first met." He smiled with remembrance. "She tried to shoot me before I even reached town."

Chap was pretty sure he knew what ailed Miss Johns. If Heath weren't acting so strange, so protective of the girl, he would have asked if the twosome were lovers. But he didn't want to get his head bitten off again.

Still, he was pretty sure that the Comanche maid who held his brother's heart was not sick but pregnant. He found the prospect of being an uncle again eminently pleasing.

"I'll check her out."

Inside the carriage, Kinsey came to the same conclusion as Chap. She and Stevie were talking softly about nothing in particular. Kinsey noticed the dark circles under Stevie's eyes and the slightly nauseous look that crossed her face every now and again.

Remembering her own passionate courtship with Chap, a knowing smile crept across her face. She'd bet the plantation that the Turner brothers were alike in more than physical appearance. In less than nine months, her heartthrob brother-in-law would be a papa.

Furtively, she glanced at Stevie's left hand. The girl had not so much as an engagement ring on her finger, much less a wedding band. Kinsey stifled an indignant huff. She would have to take Heath in hand. It was time he made an honest woman of the beautiful blonde sitting across from her, the poor child who was obviously carrying his baby. Overcome with sisterhood, she reached over and patted Stevie's hand.

Stevie smiled hesitantly. Just then the men joined them. Heath's brow furrowed when Kinsey regarded him as if he were a bug under a glass.

Stevie found the ride from the depot pleasant. She didn't have a clue that Kinsey was put out with Heath. She was put totally at ease by the gregarious southern belle, which was Kinsey's intention.

When they pulled up in front of the mansion, however, Stevie's sense of well-being disappeared like brittle leaves in the midst of blue-hot flames. The carriage passed through ornate wrought iron gates that had to be fifteen feet tall if they were an inch, she decided. A host of servants dressed in blue and white livery awaited them at the foot of twelve marble stairs that led up to the most ornate mansion she could have imagined.

Sensing her tension, Heath began describing the mansion as

if she were a potential buyer and he were a real estate agent. Turner House was an exceptional example of Gothic Revival architecture, he explained. The layout was cruciform. The steep-pitched roof was broken by sharp gabled windows. Their colored panes were diamond-shaped. The siding was board and batten, the porch roof arches on clustered piers. The overall form was asymmetrical.

Stevie didn't understand his description. It just looked like a very ornate church to her, not at all like a home.

"Isn't it awful?" Kinsey exclaimed. "The first time Chap brought me here, I thought I had slipped back in time. But the gardens are exceptional and the inside of the mansion is really quite lovely."

"If there's one thing Mother knows how to do, it's spend money," Chap added.

Kinsey nodded agreement. "The furnishings are beautiful."

The carriage halted. Chap and Heath alighted. An imperious-looking gentleman separated himself from the other servants. "Master Heath, may I be the first to say welcome home?"

"Thank you, Smithers."

Chap addressed the family butler, "Where is everyone?"

"General Turner is napping, sir. Dr. Turner has taken the opportunity to see about Miss Ginny. Mrs. Turner insisted that your sisters accompany her shopping."

Kinsey uttered something that was less than complimentary about her mother-in-law. Heath's telegram had informed them that he was bringing a female friend with him. Obviously India Turner wanted him to know she was displeased from the onset.

The snub was not lost on Stevie. But it just made her all the more determined to win the old bat over.

"It's all right, Smithers. I wasn't expecting a brass band," she heard Heath say. As an aside, he asked Chap, "What's wrong with Ginny?"

Chap lifted Kinsey down first.

"She's pregnant again." Kinsey's happiness for her sister-in-law was palpable in her voice.

As Heath helped her from the carriage, Stevie wondered if Kinsey would be happy for her.

There was a smile in Heath's voice when he said for Chap's ears only, "Sounds like he's already seen to her, to me."

Hiding his laugh behind a discreet cough, Chap waved the servants away. He and Heath led the women inside.

The foyer was so large that Stevie was certain it would hold the Rocking J's lower forty. Heath stood close at her side. Noticing the purple smudges beneath her eyes, he frowned down at her. "Are you all right?"

"I'm fine."

Heath was clearly skeptical. But he didn't challenge her. "I think I'll run up and look in on the general. Chap, do be charming and entertain Stevie. I'll be right back."

"I'll do my best." Pointedly, Chap looked at Kinsey. "Honey, why don't you look in on the hellions."

Kinsey knew that Nanna had their two children under control, but she took the hint that he wanted a moment alone with Stevie. "Certainly, dear. How kind of you to remind me."

Stevie thought she detected a note of sarcasm in Kinsey's voice, but perhaps it was her imagination. Before she knew how it happened, she found herself alone in the foyer with Chap. It was then that she remembered his profession. And she knew that she had been ambushed.

Chivalrously, he offered her his arm. "May I escort you into the parlor?"

Sighing, she placed her hand on his arm. They entered yet another exquisite room. She was very sure that she had never seen so much beauty in her life. She felt like a fish out of water. Gently, as if her slight weight would somehow damage the fragile rose damask, she allowed Chap to seat her in a Queen Anne chair. All the while she watched him warily.

Dropping down onto the hassock in front of her, he didn't waste any time getting to the point. "Heath said you've not been feeling well."

She tensed visibly. "Just a little stomach upset is all. He worries too much."

"Does he?"

Chap's piercing gaze made her squirm. He appeared to move closer without changing position. Was that challenge, mocking, or simply knowing she detected in his voice? Finally, she smiled. "If I were a betting woman, I'd wager that you're a very perceptive doctor."

He chuckled lightly. "And if I were a gamester, I'd wager that you're not sick." His silent invitation for a confession was louder than his verbal declaration.

She considered her options. Lie, run, spill her guts. "You'd be right," she said at last.

"You know Heath wants me to examine you."

"Just you? I thought he wanted both of his doctor brothers to check me from head to toe."

"I have no doubt that after I'm finished with you, he'll drag Rad in for a second opinion. So what shall I tell him?"

"If I tell you the truth, will you reassure him?" She widened her eyes. "And get him off my back?"

"Guess that depends on the truth."

"I'm pregnant with your brother's baby."

The uncle in Chap smiled hugely. The doctor maintained his professional air. "And do you intend to tell him?"

"Eventually."

That was good enough for Chap. He had meddled in this little lady's private affairs sufficiently for one day. "Well, everything that passes between a patient and her physician is confidential." He patted her hand in a familial gesture. "But a man can reassure his brother that the woman he loves is healthy."

"Thank you, Chap."

"Don't mention it."

Charm *was* an inborn trait in the Turner men, Stevie decided.

Forty-nine

Heath stood just inside the general's door. The suite was cast in semidarkness, the early morning sun barely penetrating the closed potierres.

At the far end of the large room, his father's bed was curtained off. Though he couldn't see the general, familiar scents that he associated with him alone filled his nostrils: fine tobacco, expensive leather, spicy cologne.

A myriad of emotions flowed over him. Weak in the knees, he gripped the knob at his back. The memories of a lifetime flashed before his mind's eye. He and the general hunting, fishing, talking. Most of all, talking. Whenever he'd had an important decision to make, the general was always there, always understanding, always interested, and always able to help him find his way.

He hadn't known how much he depended on his father until now. Like most children, he'd taken his father for granted, expected him to be there when he needed him, thought him invincible. Even now he couldn't imagine life without him.

Heath was closer to his father than to his brothers and sisters. They had dubbed him "the little general" as soon as he was old enough to toddle around after their patriarch.

"Well, are you gonna stand there all day, or are you gonna come over here and say hello?" a deep, familiar voice called to him out of the dark. "And open those damn drapes. This place looks like a tomb."

"Yes, sir." Heath smiled and did his father's bidding. When he reached the bedside, it took great effort to keep his pleasant expression in place. His usually larger-than-life father looked thin and pale propped against a half dozen pillows. Not thin for a normal person, but certainly frail for the general.

"Good to see you, son." The old man's voice was husky, his once-snapping eyes sunken and faded.

"It's good to be home, Dad." As long as Heath could remember, none of the general's children had ever called him "Dad." But the emotion welling in his heart overflowed. Somehow "General" was too impersonal. He bent and wrapped his arms around his father's shoulders. They were thinner than Heath remembered. But the strength of his returning embrace belied his frail appearance.

The general's voice was gruff with emotion, his eyes unusually bright when Heath finally released him. "Hell, am I dying?"

"Sir?"

"You hugged me like you were saying good-bye for the last time."

"No, sir. I wasn't saying good-bye." He blessed his father with an off-center grin. "I just got home. You running me off?"

"No, son." The general straightened as much as he was able. "Fact is, I need you."

Supposing that he spoke of emotional support, Heath declared fervently, "I'm here, sir."

"Good." The general adopted a business-as-usual air. As much as he was able, sitting in bed, dressed in a nightshirt, he assumed control. "We'll talk specifics later, but I want you to take over our businesses. Soon the twins will head back to Richmond." He coughed until Heath thought he would choke.

After a long draw of water, he continued where he left off. "Which is as it should be. They have their medical practice to think of. And the girls"—Heath surmised his father referred to Ginny and Kinsey—"have family who need your brothers' help. But there are families here that depend on us. More than you know. The Turners employ a large number of people, and I want a Turner looking out for their interests—as well as our own."

The general noted the incredulous look on Heath's face. "Your mother has found some pantywaist she's bound and determined to marry Ann off to. You know the kind, impeccable breeding, rich as Croesus. But the man couldn't blast his way out of a wet paper bag with a twenty-pounder cannon. He'll be no help to me at all. And Emily's still grieving for Ross. I have my doubts she'll ever marry again. Though her children need a father." He waved the thought away and faced Heath seriously. "Son, I know you enjoy your marshaling. But your family needs you. It's time you took your rightful place as head of Turner Incorporated."

Heath was stunned. He'd had no idea he was walking into this. Truth to tell, the prospect of wheeling and dealing on Wall Street appealed to him. His days of roaming the Wild West were beginning to wear thin, the bloodletting nightmarish.

But there was Stevie to consider. He could scarcely imagine her as a New York socialite. And the children, Winter and Summer, he wondered how they would be treated in the East?

The general detected interest, surprise, and hesitancy on his son's face. In all, he was pleased. Having planted the seed, he decided to water it later. "But we can discuss business tonight, after dinner. Tell those overprotective twins of mine and your mother that I will be joining my family after tea. You brought a young lady home with you?"

"Yes, sir." Heath was still somewhat distracted, and inordinately intrigued by his father's proposal.

The general hid a smug smile. "I assume she has a name."

"Yes, sir. Stephanie Johns. But she likes to be called Stevie."

"Well, tell Miss Stevie Johns that I look forward to meeting her at dinner. Now, run along," he said as if Heath were still in short pants, "and tell your mother's cook if she serves me anything that remotely resembles gruel, I'll fire her on the spot."

Still in somewhat of a daze, Heath nodded to his father.

"Son?"

Heath halted in the doorway.

"Pass the word that I want to see my grandchildren this afternoon."

"All of them, sir?"

There was definitely a note of paternal pride in his voice when the general responded, "Every last hellion on the place."

Heath quit the room wondering if the general hadn't exaggerated his illness just to get him home. Surely not. Chap and Rad would have had to be in on the scheme, and they were far too professional for that.

Weren't they?

A scant hour later Stevie was still seated in the parlor. Heath had replaced Chap on the hassock fronting her chair. When he returned from his father's room and reported on his visit, Chap mumbled his excuses, claiming an inordinate interest in the general's remarkable recovery.

"I'll show you upstairs for a rest. You must be exhausted." He winked. "I bribed Smithers to put you in the room next to mine."

"What will your mother think of that?"

"I'm not masochist; I don't intend to tell her."

"Won't she just see me there?"

"It's doubtful. The boys—as she still calls us—and the general sleep in the east wing. Mother's suite is in the west wing. She never comes into our part of the house, something about men giving off vapors when they sleep. In fact, she's horrified that Ginny and Kinsey insist upon sleeping with their husbands. If we're lucky, she'll not think to ask where you are."

She feigned apprehension. "About these vapors . . ."

Stevie was unable to finish her sentence as the parlor doors were almost wrenched off their hinges. They hit the wall with a deafening bang. Nothing could have prepared her for Ann Turner, Heath's youngest and most affectionate sister.

"Heath," Ann squealed, flying across the room like a whirling dervish in a Worth gown. She tackled him before he could rise, knocking him backward off the hassock. Brother and sister hit the floor, disappearing in a flurry of silk, satin, and lace.

Heath wrapped his arms around Ann and tried his best to cushion her fall. Squeezing the breath out of him, she placed kisses on both of his cheeks, his forehead, and his chin. "I've missed you, you idiot," she cried breathlessly, thumping him in the chest.

He edged to the side of her, pulling them both to a sit on the floor. "Stevie honey, may I present my sister Ann." His arm still around Ann's shoulders, he paused for breath. "As you can see, Mother's attempt to turn her into a lady failed miserably."

Stevie found herself being scrutinized by beautiful pale blue eyes. "Hello, Ann . . ." she began. She was soon to learn that one rarely completed a sentence around Ann Turner.

When Ann surged up onto her knees, her skirts spread about her. She looked as if she were sitting on a pale pink cloud. She stretched forth her white-lace-gloved hand and touched Stevie's knee with wonder. "Oh, I love your leather trousers." She looked past Stevie's shoulder. "Em, don't you just love her trousers?"

"They're pretty on her."

Heath and Stevie turned toward the calm, kind lady gliding across the room. Heath rose smoothly to his feet and met her halfway. He enfolded her in his embrace. "Emmy."

He spoke her name so tenderly that Stevie knew this was yet another beloved Turner sibling. She was the opposite of Ann. Where Ann was pretty and full of life, her older sister was rather plain and sedate. She didn't possess her brothers' good looks or their vivid coloring. In fact, there was nothing physically attractive to distinguish her.

Until she smiled. Her face was transformed. The only word that came to Stevie's mind was *radiant.* Emily possessed something more entrancing than physical comeliness; she possessed inner beauty. But it was the pain in her eyes that touched Stevie's heart. Grief was an emotion she recognized from experience.

Arm in arm, Heath escorted Emily over to Stevie. "Honey, this is my sister Emily. Em, may I present Miss Stephanie Johns."

Emily greeted her warmly. "Miss Johns, welcome to Turner House."

"Thank you. But please call me Stevie."

Ann rose with Heath's aid. "How wonderful. A boy's name and trousers too. Oh, she's just wonderful, Heath."

Heath regarded his youngest sister, wondering at her strange behavior. He shook off the thought. Ann had always been a tad strange. That was what set her apart from the other young, beautiful socialites in New York. "Annie, since you and Stevie are close in size, I've offered her the use of one of your gowns until she can see a modiste."

"Certainly. You'll need to be wearing a gown when you meet Mother." The fervent way Ann said that made Stevie uneasy. "Let's go up now. That'll give you time to find more than one. You'll need an outfit for tea and another for dinner."

"Hon, I have some business to attend. I'll leave you in Annie's capable hands."

Stevie had a notion that Heath's business concerned Judge Jack. She didn't want to be left behind. "I wouldn't want to be an imposition."

"Oh, pooh. It's not an imposition." Ann linked her arm with Stevie's and escorted her from the parlor.

Stevie glanced over her shoulder at Heath. He winked and nodded. Sighing, she accepted her fate.

From the open doorway Heath and Emily heard Ann say, "Would you permit me to try on your trousers?"

Stevie's muffled response was lost in the distance.

"When did Ann become so fascinated by masculine affectations?" Heath asked Emily. "Not that there is anything manly about Stevie." Thinking about Stevie's feminine charms, he didn't meet Emily's eyes.

"Since Mother betrothed her to a man who has so few masculine traits of his own."

The harshness in Emily's tone arrested Heath's attention; he had never heard her sound so unpleasant.

"Annie fully plans to be the one to wear the pants in the family . . . if Mother is able to make her go through with the wedding."

"So when do I meet this specimen of masculinity?'

"Tonight at dinner, unless we're lucky and he doesn't show."

"Sounds like you don't like him either."

"Either?"

"The general told me about him. He wasn't too complimentary of—"

"Eugene." She almost spat the name. "And I'm not surprised the general doesn't think much of him. If Father were stronger, I should think he would get his gun and shoot the worm."

"What on earth has the man done, Emmy?"

"It's what he hasn't done. Dear Eugene didn't fight in the war. Asthma, you know. Unsubstantiated by any medical man Chap and Rad have been able to find. Nevertheless, he paid an immigrant to take his place. The man was killed at Bull Run."

"Cowardly bastard," Heath uttered, acknowledging one more obligation to his family. Ann Turner would marry Eugene over his dead body.

No matter what their mother said.

The gentlemen's club was virtually deserted when Eugene Prickle entered, making his way to his usual table. Only one other table in the richly appointed common room was occupied. But Eugene didn't spare the man so much as a glance. He was too angry to concern himself with strangers.

It was those damn Turners. Despite his best efforts, he feared that the clan as a whole would indulge Ann's spoiled wishes and oppose their marriage, despite their mother's dictate to the contrary.

He couldn't let that happen. He had to marry Ann Turner and he had to marry her soon. Everyone—India Turner included—assumed he had access to his father's fortune. But after Eugene's unfortunate incident, one which involved his sister Eugenia, his father had left the country, instructing them both to be out of his house, out of his life, by the time he returned.

Thankfully, the old man had not told anyone that he was disowning his children before he left town. So Eugene had been able to put his creditors off for a time. But that time had come to an end. He needed access to the Turner fortune, and the only way to do that was marry the bratty chit.

The general was sick but improving. The Turner doctors would leave soon, he'd been told. He could handle the women once he married into the family. Eugenia didn't like the thought of him marrying Ann. But it was the only way. . . .

"Pardon me, sir."

Eugene started as if the man speaking to him discerned hi thoughts. The afternoon sun limned the intruder. Eugene shifte in his seat to get a better look at the man interrupting hi thoughts. He was middle-aged, tall, handsome, with blond hai He was dressed smartly in unrelieved black. But it was hi black eye patch that intrigued Eugene. It lent him a sinister ai "Yes?"

Judge Jack gestured toward an empty chair. "May I?"

Eugene nodded.

Judge Jack broke the tense silence. "I believe we have common interest."

Eugene lifted his weak chin disdainfully. "Since we are com plete strangers, I can't imagine what that might be, sir."

Jack had paid dearly for the information regarding Eugen and his sister. He needed a local partner, someone who had th run of Turner House. And the prissy gentleman peering dow his aristocratic nose at him was his best bet. "We both wan something from the Turners. And we want it badly. In fact, would venture to say that our very survival depends on it."

A frission of fear and anticipation skittered down Eugene' spine. The man across from him was ruthless, he could se that. But desperate times called for desperate measures. "I'n listening."

"I know Mama would lock me in my room for the next yea if she knew." Ann sighed dramatically, lying across her bed "But I want to have one last lark before I'm sold into slaver to that sorry excuse of a man. I'm going to do it tonight Stevie." She paled as if she had said too much. "Please don' tell Heath. He'll sit on me if he finds out."

"I don't know anything about gentlemen's clubs, Ann. Bu they don't sound like the place you should be."

"I imagine they're like your western saloons. Have you eve been in one?"

Stevie remembered her eventful visit to the Silver Dollar "Once. And Heath almost drowned me afterward."

"Tell, tell," Ann chortled, coming up on her elbows.

Stevie related the incident with a great deal of embellishment. She left out the fact that she had caught Heath in the act of kissing a soiled dove. After all, Blue was reformed now, and it had been an innocent kiss in the first place.

Ann wrapped her arms around her waist and flopped over onto her back. Her pink gown disappeared in the fluffy pink bedspread and post drapes that billowed at her every movement. "Oh, I envy you." She bounded off the bed. "I have a disguise. Wait'll you see." Ann's top half disappeared into an enormous armoire. She withdrew a small suit of men's clothing. It looked somewhat like the ensembles worn by both Heath and Chap.

Stevie had to smile. The look in Ann's eyes was absolutely devilish.

"I can get another suit. You could go with me. The men will closet themselves in with the general after dinner. Heath won't know you're gone. We'll slip into the club and just hide and watch. Don't you want to know what goes on in those bastions of male domination?" she finished theatrically.

Stevie now knew what it meant to be between a rock and a hard place. Mentally, she listed the pros and cons of participating in Ann's daring escapade. The gentlemen's club sounded like the kind of establishment that would draw Judge Jack like flies to a pile of cow manure. If he weren't there, she could ask around. Oh, she wouldn't speak to the patrons. But surely there were serving girls she could question. At least she guessed there were. Her experience with gentlemen's clubs was rather limited, she reflected wryly.

If she discovered the judge's whereabouts, she wouldn't confront him. She would come back and tell Heath. They could capture him together. With the judge behind bars where he belonged, she and Heath would be free to begin their new life.

Also, she would take her derringer and bowie knife. She could protect Ann. There's no telling what would happen if the girl went alone. Heath's sister was precocious, but she was green as a gourd. Stevie would be doing the Turners a favor, watching out for their sweet if somewhat willful daughter. That might even get her in India Turner's good graces.

Despite her rationalization, she knew good and well that Heath would wear her fanny out if he discovered what they were up to. He was protective of her in the extreme. And he didn't even know that she was carrying his child. In the end, Stevie decided to go. Her pa always said people did exactly as they pleased; this was no exception. "All right. I'll go."

"Oh, Stevie, you won't be sorry. It'll be great fun."

"First we have to get through tea and dinner." And I have to meet the formidable India Turner, Stevie added silently.

"I'll run dress for tea. Be back for you in a flash."

Stevie was hardly aware of Ann's exit. She was planning ahead. Soon she would begin her campaign to convince Heath's mother that she was good enough to marry her son.

She sighed heavily, thinking of the monumental task before her. After tea and dinner with Heath's mother, infiltrating the gentlemen's club should be like a walk in the park.

Fifty

Heath was standing at the bottom of the floating staircase when Stevie and Ann came down to tea. He had eyes for Stevie alone. Usually unflappable, he stood with his mouth agape, watching the vision approach.

Seeing her dressed like a woman, he vowed to burn every pair of trousers she owned. Her voluminous gown of lemon tulle brought out her ethereal beauty in a way that men's clothes never could. The skirt was fashionably flat in the front, showing the outline of her firm thighs with each step she took. It was drawn up into a soft bustle in the back, flaring into a short train.

The bodice skimmed her slender torso, the low décolletage edged with double rows of seed pearls. Her softly curving breasts rose high above the neckline, providing an arresting contrast of pale fabric with smooth, dusky skin.

Ann's maid had twisted Stevie's platinum hair into long curls at the back of her head, ornamenting the silken tresses with small yellow bows. Pearl drop earrings dangled from her delicate lobes, a single strand kissed the dark shadowy cleavage that drew Heath's eyes like a magnet.

"You're breathtaking," he whispered, taking her hand and bringing it to his lips.

Ann couldn't stifle a giggle as she stood on the step above them.

Heath raised his gaze to her. "You too, short stuff," he complimented Ann. His sister looked like a fairy princess in pale blue taffeta. Much too lovely for the likes of Eugene Prickle "Shall we?" Offering each lady an arm, Heath escorted Stevie and his sister into tea.

Stevie steeled herself against meeting his mother. But she needn't have worried. India Turner was nowhere to be seen.

The only sign that Heath noticed his mother's continued slight to Stevie was the muscle twitching in his jaw. He had visited her in her rooms earlier and specifically requested that she come to tea and meet Stevie. It appeared that she didn't intend to honor his request.

Teatime at Turner House was a joyful affair. The fact that Heath's mother still refused to put in an appearance had unsettled Stevie at first. But Chap, Kinsey, Emily, Ann, and a host of Turner grandchildren were so open and accepting, she soon dismissed India from her mind and just enjoyed being part of Heath's family.

"Sorry we're late," a masculine voice intruded on the outlandish tale of life in the Wild West Heath was spinning for his nieces and nephews.

Stevie turned to see an exact, life-size replica of Chap. Clinging to his arm, Ginny Turner appeared the flesh-and-blood epitome of southern womanhood. And she was at least six months pregnant.

Heath surged to his feet. "'Bout time you two showed up." He hugged Rad, then carefully embraced Ginny.

"It's my fault. Seems all I want to do these days is sleep," Ginny's drawl was very like Kinsey's. She rested her hand on her stomach. Just touching where Rad's child slumbered appeared to give her pleasure.

"And being the good husband that I am, I have to keep her company."

Chap and Heath laughed knowingly. From the blush on Ginny's face, Stevie doubted that her handsome husband allowed her to sleep a great deal when they were in bed together. Stevie found herself blushing as well, remembering what she and Heath had done in his bed just the night before. Reading her expression, he winked slightly.

Rad wasn't reserved like Chap. He was much more gregarious, blatantly flirtatious, incredibly charming, like Heath. He walked up to Stevie, wrapped his arms around her waist, and lifted her off her feet. He hugged her so tightly that her borrowed corset creaked. When he placed her on her feet, he planted a firm kiss on her cheek. "Has that kid brother of mine made you my sister-in-law yet?"

"Damn, Rad, you could've at least let me introduce her before you swept her off her feet." Heath made the necessary introductions, then took Stevie's hand. Unconsciously, he ran his thumb over her knuckles. "And no, she's not your sister-in-law. I haven't been able to get her to accept my honorable proposal. That's why I brought her home. Hoping that we could all gang up on her and force her into it."

Ginny and Kinsey exchanged glances. "Hah," the southern ladies said at the same time. They knew from experience that God had not created the woman who could refuse a Turner when he set his mind to winning her. The love shining in Stevie's eyes told them that she was no different from the rest of the female race. She was a goner.

Kinsey stepped forward and took Stevie's hand from Heath. She led her to a low sofa. "You'll get no help or pity from us, you scoundrel," she said to Heath. "You haven't even bought her a ring."

"Pitiful," Ginny clucked, taking a seat on Stevie's other side. Emily and Ann voiced sisterly support of the other women. Stevie just blushed.

"What's got their back up?" Rad asked.

Heath shrugged, bewildered. Chap looked away guiltily. He had told Kinsey about Stevie's pregnancy. Obviously, she had told Ginny. If he didn't watch his plain-spoken wife, she would be calling Heath on the carpet and demanding a wedding within twenty-four hours. That wouldn't do at all. Stevie would never forgive him. And since she would be his sister-in-law for the next fifty years or so, he hoped they could be friends.

Intent on charming them out of their pique, the men joined their ladies.

Kinsey served tea as the children ran wild. When the hellions grew quiet, it drew the adults' attention.

India Turner walked through the door. She spared her grandchildren not so much as a glance. It was as if all the air were sucked out of the room. Slowly, she made her way to the circle of adults. Her first words were not of welcome, nor did she sit. Rather, she regarded Ann harshly and spat out, "You did ask Eugene and his sister to tea as I told you, didn't you?"

Ann squared her shoulders and lifted her chin defiantly. "No, Mother. I did not. I wanted to spend a pleasant afternoon welcoming my brother and his lovely friend. Eugene will join us for dinner. As for dear Eugenia, frankly, the woman gives me the creeps. I didn't invite her to dinner. Nor do I ever intend to invite her into this home."

Heath stood stiffly and pulled Stevie up beside him. "Mother." He paused until he gained her attention. "May I present my fiancée, Miss Stephanie Johns. Stevie, my mother."

Stevie excused Heath for introducing her as his fiancée. In the face of India Turner, she needed all the legitimacy he could lend her. When she found a pleasant smile and pasted it on her face, her lips felt numb, along with the rest of her. "I'm pleased to meet you, Mrs. Turner."

India took her time, scrutinizing Stevie from head to toe. She did not return her cordial greeting. "You failed to tell me that she was an Indian." Her observation sounded quite like an indictment.

Heath stiffened but Stevie stilled him by gripping his hand. "Yes, ma'am. I'm Indian. Comanche." There was such pride in Stevie's voice that everyone in the room admired her even more than they had a moment before.

Everyone save India Turner. India pulled her skirts aside, as if she couldn't bear the thought of brushing against Stevie. Hardly necessary considering she still stood some six feet away from her.

"Ann, inform me when Eugene arrives. And do change out of that blue gown. It does nothing for your sallow complexion." With that, Heath's mother turned on her heel and quit the room.

They all stood in stunned silence for a moment. When Stevie was certain that she had given India time to make her way back to the east wing, she made her apologies. Head high, she walked from the room.

"Excuse me . . ." Heath began.

Kinsey restrained him. "Don't, Heath. Give her some time alone."

The look of rage mingled with hurt on Heath's face touched them all. Ever supportive, Emily patted his arm.

"Stevie's strong," Kinsey continued. "It'll take more than a snub from the old bat to do her any real harm. Besides, it wasn't so bad. As I recall, she had me kidnapped. And I survived . . . and even married her son."

Rad chuckled flatly. "Just in case Mother's up to her old tricks, we'll all keep a close eye on Stevie." It was a sad state of affairs, but they all realized Rad's jest held some merit.

Heath nodded and resumed his seat. But his attention was not on the conversation his quick-witted siblings batted back and forth as a means to regain some of the earlier joy that had characterized their reunion. His thoughts were upstairs with Stevie.

He closed his eyes and dropped his head back on the chair. If Stevie needed proof that white society wouldn't accept their marriage, that they would be persecuted for her ancestry, his own mother had just provided it.

That evening, when Stevie joined the family in the parlor, she was not dressed in the lovely silk gown Ann had loaned her. During the afternoon she had decided that if she were to be accepted, it would be for who she really was.

Proudly, she entered the room dressed in Gentle Fawn's wedding gown, her platinum hair braided into one long, silken rope, tied at the end by a short length of rawhide, a beaded headband circling her forehead. Nestled between her breasts was the necklace containing a lock of her mother's hair.

As Heath approached her, she noted that he was impeccable in black evening wear. Love, pride, and masculine approval was shining in his sapphire eyes. She relaxed visibly. "I'm glad you changed. You look beautiful." He hugged her affectionately and whispered into her hair, "Your mother and Gentle Fawn would be very proud."

The evening passed in a blur. The highlight for Stevie was when she met General Turner. The consummate gentleman, he had stood to his feet—albeit a bit unsteadily due to his ill health—bowed over her hand, then much as Rad had earlier, engulfed her in a bear hug.

"Now I see why you spent so much time out west, son." He squeezed Heath's shoulder. "You've chosen well."

Those simple words pleased Heath and Stevie as no other.

After the general's sound endorsement of Stevie, Mrs. Turner sat quietly in her chair, aloof, sullen. The only time she spoke the entire evening was when she greeted Eugene Prickle.

As for Ann, she ignored her lackluster fiancé altogether. Until dessert, when she announced to her family—and Eugene—that she had no intention of marrying him, now or ever. It was immediately apparent that she had the unspoken but tangible support of the Turner men.

Red-faced, Eugene informed Ann that he would give her time to reconsider, then left the house. Her mother cast her a fulminating glare and retired to her room without a word. Needless to say, the evening was over. As Ann predicted, Chap and Rad closeted themselves in the library with their father.

Heath said he'd join them in a minute, after he escorted Stevie to her room. He was unusually quiet, she noticed. When they stood facing each other outside her door, he took both her hands in his own. "Hon, about Mother . . ." He trailed off.

"There's no need to talk about it. I understand. And it really doesn't matter to me what she thinks."

"All the same, I must apologize for her."

She squeezed his hands. "Apology accepted."

He kissed her then, soundly, with an air of desperation. It was as if he were trying to convince her how much he loved her.

She responded in kind. Despite what she said, she was hurt by his mother's ill treatment. The feeling of insecurity that plagued her was foreign but understandable. She was far away from home, missing her children and her father, pregnant, and unmarried. She had definitely felt better in her life physically and emotionally. And was it any wonder?

Heath sensed her need and sought to fill her with his love. He kissed her hungrily, his mouth open and giving. He thrust his tongue into her dark, sweet cavern, over and over, mimicking what he wanted to do with his maleness.

She was instantly caught up in his passion. Grinding her lower body against him, she stood on tiptoe and threaded her fingers through his hair.

They were ravenous, starving for each other. For a time they indulged themselves. Heath skimmed her body with his hands. She was nude beneath the bleached animal skin, so he could feel every curve and crevice. Bunching the buckskin in his clenched fists, he raised the fringed hem to her upper thighs. Instinctively, he slipped his thigh between her legs.

Moaning, she ran her hands across his shoulders, over his back, down his spine, flattening her palms over his tensing buttocks. She dropped her head back over his arm, giving him greater access to her throat. He trailed hot, wet kisses down the sleek column. Wrapping his arm around her waist, he lifted her until her soft, moist, skin rested on his thigh. She raised her head and gasped. Over Heath's shoulder she saw Ann just inside a doorway, watching them, wide-eyed.

Stevie had never moved as quickly in her life. She lurched backward, righted her dress, and placed her palms on Heath's chest as if she were holding him off.

He was lost in the throes of passion. The jolt back to reality momentarily stunned him.

She raised a hand to his cheek. "Honey, your brothers and father are waiting for you downstairs." His eyes were somewhat dazed. "What will they think if you're gone too long?"

"You're right." His voice was thick with unappeased desire. He blessed her with a smile that curled her toes inside her soft moccasins. "I could come back later."

Stevie wanted to groan at least, cry at most. Heath had set a fire in her that was raging out of control. But she had promised Ann. She couldn't allow Heath to come back tonight. Maybe, after they got home, she could sneak into his room. "As much as I'm tempted, sweetheart"—she lowered her voice so Ann wouldn't hear—"as much as I want you, I'm really exhausted. I fear I'll be dead to the world as soon as my head hits the pillow."

"Oh, I'm sorry. How thoughtless of me."

She could see that Heath was disappointed. When sh opened her mouth to reassure him, he bent to kiss her again this time tenderly. It moved her more than the passionate em brace they had exchanged earlier. He lifted his head and sh dropped her lashes to hide the unfulfilled desire shining in he eyes.

He touched her cheek gently. "I love you, sweetheart. Sleep well."

She nodded. "Good night." Raising her gaze, she watched him as he walked away. Before he disappeared around the cor ner, she ran to him. "Heath, wait."

"I knew you couldn't resist me."

She could see that he was teasing her. "I just wanted to say"—she lowered her voice—"I love you too."

His smile lit up her heart. Brushing her lips with a gentle kiss, he vowed his love again, then whispered, "Good night sugar."

By the time she reached her room, Ann was standing outside the door, dressed in a man's three-piece suit, holding her top hat, gloves, and cane with one arm. With the other she held a similar outfit for Stevie.

Stevie blushed furiously.

Ann actually laughed. "All I've got to say is you two had better hurry and get married" was her sage advise. "Mama says society frowns on babies born out of wedlock."

If only she knew . . .

Leon, the young driver who had provided the gents' clothing for Ann and Stevie, halted the carriage outside the gentlemen's club. The street front was cluttered with expensive carriages drawn by blooded horseflesh, the owners spending a relaxing evening at their club.

"Pull around the corner and wait for us," Ann instructed. "We won't be more than fifteen minutes. I just want to see what it's like inside."

The boy regarded her worshipfully. "Before you're leg-shackled to Eugene?"

Arm tossed her head defiantly. "Over my dead body."

When Leon was out of sight, Ann and Stevie mounted the stairs. They never made it inside the club. Soaked handkerchiefs covered their noses and mouths as strong hands dragged them back down the steps into the discreet black carriage that awaited them.

The last thing Stevie saw before she lost consciousness was a black eye patch.

Fifty-one

Sitting at the breakfast table, Heath dropped his head into his hands. His eyes were gritty from lack of sleep. His back ached; his legs throbbed. The heaping plate of eggs and crisp bacon under his nose made him queasy.

He shoved his breakfast away forcefully and downed a brimming tumbler of whiskey. Stevie and Ann had been missing for five days now. The two women had disappeared without a trace. He, Chap, Rad, and half the law-enforcement agents in New York had been searching for them around the clock.

Heath's first thought when he discovered Stevie missing was that his mother'd relied on an old plan and had her kidnapped. The voice of reason, Chap had pointed out that Ann was gone too. No matter how hard their mother was, they doubted she would harm her own daughter, at least not physically.

Unconvinced and crazed with worry, Heath had said some things to his mother that she would never forgive. But he couldn't worry about that now. All he could think about was finding Stevie and Ann.

Stevie had been so sick on the train. He kept picturing her in some dingy hole, sick, cold, starving. It was almost more than he could bear.

Once he admitted to himself that his mother was not to blame, he decided that Judge Jack had kidnapped Ann and Stevie, undoubtedly to wreak vengeance of both him and Stevie. When he found the man—and he would find him—he would tear him apart with his own two hands. Hanging would be too good for him. The judge had gone beyond the barrier; he had dared to touch Stevie.

If he lost her now— Heath couldn't finish the thought.

"Mr. Heath, can I have a word with you?"

Heath raised red-rimmed eyes. He clenched his jaw and tried to maintain a shred of composure. "Leon, I don't care to speak with you right now. I know I shouldn't blame you, but if you hadn't indulged Annie, she and Stevie might be safe at home."

"I don't blame you a bit, sir. If I was you, I'd give me a strappin'." The boy could see in Heath's turbulent gaze that he was tempted to do just that. "But I might have some information that can help you find Miss Ann and your fiancée. I was talkin' to my cousin that works down on the docks—"

Heath surged to his feet, grabbed Leon's arm, and propelled him from the breakfast room. "You can tell me on the way."

When they reached the foyer, they ran into an unexpected confrontation. Smithers was instructing two of the footmen to physically remove a dark-haired young man from the premises. The stranger was mad as hell.

Chap and Rad entered the hallway, coming to investigate the ruckus; their wives were right behind them. The general stood at the top of the stairs. Everyone seemed to be shouting at once.

Heath didn't give a damn what the man was doing there, didn't care if he burned Turner House to the ground. He just wanted to get past him and go find Stevie and Ann. The young man pointed at Heath and called over his shoulder, "Is that him?"

The soft answer in the affirmative was lost in the din. The stranger called Heath an unpleasant name and lunged for him, catching him around the middle. They crashed to the floor.

Heath banged his head on the polished marble. The room faded out of focus. He raised his gaze to the man sitting on his chest. He looked vaguely familiar. But he shrugged off the thought. From somewhere deep inside him Heath knew he had to get to Stevie. He feared that if he didn't find her soon, it would be too late. Desperate, he struggled to remove the man sprawled atop him.

Heath's assailant was big and strong. His strength almost

superhuman, fueled by anger and righteous indignation. Heath fought just as hard, from desperation. They were an even match. It took both of the footmen, Smithers, and Rad and Chap to pull the combatants apart. Under the general's supervision, of course.

When General Turner thundered for quiet, miraculously everyone obeyed. He turned toward the intruder. "Now, young man, what in hell has made you so mad that you would invade my home and attack my son?"

He spat at Heath's feet. "That son of a bitch got my sister pregnant and kidnapped her. Without marrying her."

"Jeff Johns, I presume," Heath hazarded. No wonder he looked familiar. Heath gasped suddenly. "Did you say pregnant?" He looked at Chap for confirmation. Chap nodded. "Oh, God," Heath uttered, wiping blood from his face with the back of his hand.

Blue wound her way through the gaping crowd and stepped up to Jeff's side. She grabbed his arm roughly. "You idiot. Heath wouldn't hurt Stevie." She turned pleading eyes on Heath. "I tried to tell him. So did Pilar and Sandy. But he just went off half cocked."

Jeff shot her an exasperated look. "I want to see my sister. Now! I'll believe it only from her."

"I'm afraid that won't be possible, son," the general said.

Heath turned toward his father. "It will soon." He pushed Leon forward and called back to Jeff. "You can beat the hell out of me later if you want. Right now I'm going after Stevie."

Jeff jerked a nod. "I can wait. I'm going with you."

Just then Jay sauntered through the front door. Heath looked as if he were expecting him. "We goin' after the judge?"

"That's the plan," Heath said, leading the way.

Rad and Chap followed Heath, Jeff, and Jay. As they rode down the street, it occurred to Blue that the men looked like a bloodthirsty posse on the chase.

That's exactly what they were.

Eugene entered the warehouse, waving a marriage license over his head triumphantly. "I finally got it." It was what they had been waiting for, risking capture for, the license that would make his marriage to Ann legal. It had taken some time to grease the right palms. But as Judge Jack assured Eugene, just about anything could be had if the price was right.

Seated in the corner of the room on a makeshift pallet, Stevie and Ann were bound and gagged. Ann's eyes widened, giving her the look of a frightened doe in the sights of a hunter.

Stevie shifted closer to her, trying to reassure her with her presence.

"As soon as the judge gets back, sweet dear, you and I will be wed," Eugene taunted Ann from across the room.

Ann's back stiffened. Her eyes shouted, "Go to hell!"

Stevie's mind raced ahead. The bastards would release them for this forced wedding. That's when she would make her move. She tried to smile at Ann around her gag. The rough cloth and her bruised and swollen jaw made the effort futile.

The night they were abducted, Judge Jack had confiscated her derringer. Fortunately, he had not discovered the bowie knife tucked inside her chemise. She couldn't do much with it, but perhaps she could hold them off until Heath could get there. And he would get there. Isn't that what heroes did? Rescued the women they loved?

The thought of Heath brought tears to her eyes. She turned toward the wall, not wanting to worry Ann, not wanting her captors to see her weakness. Men like Eugene and Judge Jack thrived on weakness in others. Probably because they were so weak themselves.

She and Ann had been a disappointment to them. Though they were totally at the brigands' mercy, they had managed to hide their fear. It was undoubtedly why they had fared as well as they had. One show of vulnerability, and the men would swoop down on them. Ann had realized that as surely as she.

Stevie leaned her head against the rough-hewn wood, absently caressing her locket for reassurance. If they could just hold on a little while longer, Heath would find them. She knew he would.

* * *

The men dismounted two blocks east of the warehouse indicated by Leon's cousin. They could see the building clearly from where they stood. The sun was bright overhead. Nestled between the towering buildings, the group was cast in shadows, unaware of the cool breeze blowing off the Atlantic. Bloodlust raged hotly through their veins.

Leon's cousin wiped his sweaty forehead with a grimy fist and addressed the men who towered over him. "It was five days ago, like I told Leon. I saw two scrawny-lookin' swells. They was bound and gagged, bein' dragged through that door by a big man with a black patch over one eye and another man, a prissy sort, looked like a mama's boy to me. One of the prisoners kicked the prissy one in the shin. That's when her hat fell off and all that blond hair spilled out. The man with the patch cuffed her on the jaw. Knocked her clean out. He threw her over his shoulder and carried her inside."

Heath uttered a vile oath.

"Think the mama's boy could be Eugene?" Chap asked.

Rad responded, "Wouldn't put it past the bastard."

Chap turned his attention to Heath. "You're the marshal, brother. I assume you have a plan."

The look in Heath's eyes as he exchanged a glance with Jay did not bode well for the patched judge or the mama's boy.

Judge Jack returned to the warehouse just before noon. Looking over his shoulder, he unlocked the door and slipped inside. Arrogant, he didn't bother to lock the door.

It's about time you got back," Eugene whined.

Jack ignored the complaint. "Let's get this over with. Miss Johns and I have a ship to catch."

Stevie kept her face blank as Judge Jack untied her wrists. As soon as her gag dropped, she asked flatly, "Would you do me one favor before this goes any further?"

He laughed in her face. "What? Let you go?"

She was not amused. Her voice remained even, almost emotionless. "No. Tell me why you kidnapped me. It's obvious why the twit over there had to steal Ann. How else would someone like him get a wife? But why did you take me? I would think that with all Heath and I know about you, you would want to stay as far away from me as possible."

A strange look came over his face. "Years ago I traveled out west to Comanche country. I was a trader." He grimaced. "No money in that. It's hard work. But there was this squaw. As soon as I saw her, I knew I had to have her. One day when she was down at the river, I took her. Unfortunately, her brother found us. I could tell from the look on his face that he would have my scalp on his belt before sundown. So I lit out. Never knew what happened to her until I came to Adobe Wells. Seems her people deserted her and she married a white man. Sandy Johns."

Stevie's face blanched. "You're not . . ."

"Your father? No. Fortunately, the timing's not right.

"But you're so much like Swan—except you have more spirit—and I never got my fill of her."

"And Jeff?"

"No. I'm not his father either. Might've saved his life if I had been."

Bright spots of crimson warmed Stevie's cheeks. "You killed him?" her voice was a husky whisper.

"Sims shot him."

Enraged, Stevie lunged at him. Just then the door burst off its hinges. Simultaneously, solid bodies came hurtling through the windows. Chap backhanded Eugene, knocking him unconscious. Rad untied Ann and wrapped her in his arms.

By the time Heath and Jeff got to Judge Jack, Stevie was sitting on the judge's chest, the point of her knife pressed against his neck. A single drop of blood glistened in the morning light.

"I'd shove it in," Jeff hissed.

Heath wrapped his arms around Stevie's shoulders and pulled her up against him. "He's not worth it." He turned toward Leon and his cousin. "Go for the police."

"Heath," Stevie cried, burying her face in his chest.

Jay bound and gagged the judge, then stood to his feet.

At his side, Jeff said, "Don't I even get a hello?"

Stevie stiffened in Heath's embrace. He dropped a kiss to the top of her head and swiveled her toward her brother.

She gasped, cried, and threw herself against Jeff with such force that he almost lost his footing. "Whoa, don't be so rowdy." He patted her abdomen.

She reddened. "You know?"

"That I'm to be an uncle?"

She nodded. Eyes hard, he raised them to Heath. Stevie clamped her hand over her mouth and turned around. "You know?"

A smile lit his face. "That I'm to be a father?"

The mist glistening in Heath's eyes was her undoing. Choking a sob, she stumbled into his embrace. He lifted her chin with a tanned finger. "Stephanie Johns, will you marry me?"

"You're damn right she will," Jeff said harshly.

Heath shot his future brother-in-law a hot glare. "I would hear it from her." His voice gentled. "Will you, sweetheart?"

"Yes," she breathed.

The ensuing kiss was long and filled with promise. With one arm around Stevie's shoulders, Heath stretched his hand out to Jeff. "Satisfied?"

Jeff saw the unadulterated joy on his sister's face. He shook Heath's hand firmly. And his voice was gruff when he said, "You're damn right I am."

Six months later Heath received a telegram.

It read:

HEATH. STOP. I FOUND RACHEL. STOP. WILL INFORM YOU OF FURTHER PROGRESS. STOP. JAY HAMPTON, U.S. MARSHAL.

Epilogue

Ten years later

Hungrily, Heath reached for Stevie. "Alone at last."

Clutching a child's pale pink frock in her hand, she leaned against her husband. "I swear and declare that daughter of yours will be the death of me."

There was no doubt in Heath's mind which of their children she meant. His lips twitched. "What's she done this time?"

"She absolutely refuses to wear a dress."

He pulled her closer against him. "Now, I wonder who she gets that from."

As always, her heartrate accelerated at the nearness of her husband. At forty-five, Harrington Heath Turner still had more than a few women panting after him, especially his wife.

For the past ten years he had run Turner Incorporated expertly, wheeling and dealing on Wall Street. She had half expected him to get a little soft around the middle, sitting behind a desk in his plush Manhattan office. But not her husband. No sir. If possible, he was even harder and more muscled now than the day she married him.

He took the garment from her and dropped it at their feet. "Why does she have to wear a dress anyway, sugar? It's just a family get together."

They were leaving Manhattan on the noon train, their ultimate destination, Adobe Wells. It would be the first family reunion they had attended in two years. And being the doting mother that she was, Stevie wanted her children to make a good impression. And that meant the boys impeccably turned out like their father and the girls clothed in feminine attire.

Even she wore nothing but women's clothes now, ever since the day she married Heath. Absently running her hands down the elegant traveling suit she had donned earlier, she regarded her bemused husband. "You know you've spoiled her rotten."

He took her hands and cradled them against his chest. Dipping his head, he nipped at her bottom lip.

"Don't think you can distract me by getting me all hot and bothered."

He rubbed against her suggestively.

"Well, maybe you can." She smiled seductively, causing the breath to catch in his throat. She was thrilled to her toes when his eyes darkened with desire. "Two can play this game, husband," she whispered against his lips.

"I'm not playin', wife," he growled, and kissed her deeply.

"Oh, yuck. Is that all you two ever do?" the hellion in question wanted to know.

Heath held Stevie even tighter as he smiled at Heather, their nine-year-old daughter, standing just inside the door to their suite. "Would be if I had my way, puddin'."

"Yuck," Heather declared again.

"One of these days you'll meet someone wonderful like your daddy and you'll want to attract his attention." Stevie bent to pick up Heather's frock. She gasped when Heath pinched her fanny—hidden from Heather's view, of course.

"If it means dressing like a girl, forget it." Heather crossed her arms across her chest.

Stevie looked to Heath for moral support. He just grinned and shrugged. There was no help coming from that corner. "I give up."

Summer ran into the room, resembling a lightly bronzed porcelain doll. While Heather looked the ruffian in jeans and a flannel shirt, Summer was an angelic vision in a mint-green pinafore. No two children could be any different. But they were both incredibly beautiful.

Winter entered next, towering at his sisters' backs. His voice was very deep. "What's this, Dad? A family meeting?"

Stevie smiled with pride. Her first child was a handsome lad, almost seventeen now. His Comanche ancestry was evident in his dusky complexion. His hair was neat, as shiny and black as a raven's wing, not unlike his adoptive father's. He was dressed like a true Turner gentleman and he carried himself with a sense of self-pride, just like Heath.

Close on his heels, Winter's shadows—as Heath and Stevie called their six-year-old twin boys—followed. "What's going on?" they asked in unison. The twins often spoke in unison.

Heath regarded his brood and grinned like a self-satisfied fool. They were a good-looking bunch of kids even if they were his. "I was just telling your mother that our family isn't large enough. We get lonesome with only the five of you to keep us company."

Blushing, Stevie regarded her husband as if he had turnips growing out his ears. Winter, old enough to get his dad's meaning, chuckled.

In case there was any question, Heath's next remark confirmed Winter's suspicions. "Who thinks it's time your mother had another baby? Raise your hands."

"Heath!" Stevie was stunned. Six hands—including the wide one of the husband she was going to strangle at her first opportunity—shot into the air.

"That settles it. Nine months from today your mother will present us with a new baby."

"Or two," the twins speculated in tandem.

"Boy or girl?" Summer wanted to know.

Heath spread his arms expansively. "Maybe both."

Stevie stifled a groan.

Heath gave Winter a man-to-man wink. "Son, I have something to discuss with your mother. Would you see to your brothers and sisters for a bit?"

Winter blushed as furiously as Stevie had earlier. Nodding, he ushered his siblings out and closed the door firmly behind him.

A wise man, Heath didn't give Stevie an opportunity to

speak. He sealed her lips with his own. By the time they came up for air, she had forgotten why she was so outraged.

Nodding toward Heather's pink frock, she asked, "What about the dress?"

He purposefully misunderstood. With deft fingers he attacked the pearl buttons of her bodice. "Just hold on, sugar. I'll have you out of it in a second."

She tried to hide her smile. "This really isn't necessary, you know."

Moving his lower body against her, he whispered, "Honey, I find it very necessary. Besides, I really do want another baby."

She smiled up into his face. "But, darling, I'm already pregnant."

Whooping like a Comanche on the warpath, he lifted her in his arms and carried her to the bed. "Then this time we'll do it just for pure pleasure."

The solitary figure high atop Mustang Mesa drew Heath by invisible cords.

Stevie stood looking out on the land that had belonged to the Comanche for as long as anyone could remember, the land that belonged to them no more. She closed her eyes and allowed the spirit of her ancestors to wash over her. Tears slipped silently down her cheeks. They'd been there for only a week, yet it still seemed like home. And though they lived in the East, and followed the path of the white man, she had infused pride of their Indian heritage in her children.

Winter, Summer, Heather, and the twins were accepted by most of their white acquaintances. Those who didn't, the men, women, and children who disdained the Indian blood flowing through their veins, found themselves being pitied by the Turners. Heath and Stevie's family believed that one day all races would live together peacefully, in full acceptance, if not appreciation of their varied ancestry. Until that day, they took pride in all that they were, Indian and white.

"I thought I'd find you here," a deep, familiar voice spoke from behind her.

She turned and smiled shakily at her husband.

Instinctively, he closed the distance between them and wrapped her in his arms. He dropped a kiss on the tracks of her tears. "Please don't cry, sugar."

She shook her head and leaned heavily against his strong, warm body.

A band tightened around his chest. "I have to go back to New York tomorrow, but you and the children could stay and visit with your father for a while."

Her head fell back on her shoulders. "Are you getting tired of me?" Her voice was thick, betraying emotions that she allowed no one but Heath to see.

He tapped her nose. "I won't dignify that with an answer, wife." Raising his eyes to the horizon, he could only imagine what she must be feeling. "I know how much this all means to you. If you want to stay home awhile, I'm a big enough man to understand."

She stepped back, too close to the edge for Heath's peace of mind. He grabbed her and pulled her against him again. They stood like that for a long time, embraced, rocking gently as the late afternoon breeze flowed over them.

"Heath," she said finally.

"Hmmm?"

"I love this land. I love my mother's people. I miss Pa and Jeff. But this isn't my home. Where you are is home."

A strangled sound came from deep inside his chest; a knot formed in his throat. Gazing down into ebony eyes filled with tears and love, he whispered roughly, "Do you have any idea how much I love you?"

"I think I do. And it fills my heart until I can barely catch my breath."

"Ah, sweetheart, let me help." He dropped his head and kissed her ravenously, thrillingly, stealing her life's breath and returning it to her, sweetly mingled with his own.

Afterword

Every part of this soil is sacred in the estimation of my people. Every hillside, every valley, every plain and grove has been hallowed by some sad or happy event in days long vanished.

The very dust upon which you now stand responds more lovingly to our footsteps than to yours, because it is rich with the blood of our ancestors and our bare feet are conscious of the sympathetic touch. Even the little children who live here and rejoice here for a brief season love these somber solitudes and at eventide they greet shadowy returning spirits.

And when the last redmen shall have perished and the memory of my tribe shall have become a myth among the white man, these shores will swarm with the invisible dead of my tribe and when your children's children think themselves alone in the field, the store, the shop, upon the highways or in the silence of the pathless woods, they will not be alone.

—Chief Seattle

Suvate

A Note From the Author

This book is set slightly earlier than the glory days of such colorful historical characters as John Chisum, Alexander McSween, J. H. Tunstall, Pat Garrett, and Billy the Kid. These larger-than-life men did live and wage their own private wars in New Mexico, however. I appreciate your indulgence in my manipulation of the timeline, for I couldn't resist using them in *Velvet Thunder.*

About the Author

Like her heroine, Teresa Howard boasts a proud Native American heritage, having both Cherokee and Creek Indian ancestors. She is also a descendant of Cynthia Ann Parker, the white mother of the last free Comanche war chief, Quannah Parker.

Teresa lives in north Georgia with her husband, George. Her hobbies include reading, watching old movies, adding to her hat collection, and spending time with her family in their cabin in the foothills of the Smoky Mountains.

In addition to *Velvet Thunder*, Teresa is the author of three previous Zebra Heartfire Historicals. *Cherokee Embrace*, January 1992, *Desire's Bride,* November 1992, and *Confederate Vixen,* October 1993.

She is hard at work on two upcoming Time Travel Romances to be released by Pinnacle Books under the pseudonym Teresa George. The first, tentatively entitled, *Yesterday's Promise,* a November 1994 release, is set during the American Civil War in Richmond, Virginia, the cradle of the Confederacy. The heroine, Serena Gray Brooks, is a 1990s woman swept back in time, inhabiting the body of her great-great-great-grandmother. A handsome ghost charms and bedevils Serena during her sojourn in the past. A Confederate surgeon steals her heart.

Teresa's second Time Travel, tentatively entitled, *The Times of Her Life,* will be released in 1995.

She enjoys hearing from her readers. If you wish to receive an autographed bookmark and updated newsletter, please send a legal-size SASE to Teresa Howard, c/o Zebra Books, 475 Park Avenue South, New York, NY 10016.